BOOKS BY EDMUND SCHIDDEL

Good Time Coming (1969)

A Bucks County Trilogy
  The Good and Bad Weather (1965)
  Scandal's Child (1963)
  The Devil in Bucks County (1959)

Love in a Hot Climate (1957)

Safari to Dishonor (1956)

The Girl with the Golden Yo-Yo (1955)

Break-Up (1954)

The Other Side of the Night (1954)

Scratch the Surface (1939)

GOOD TIME COMING

🌷 🌷 🌷 *a novel by*
EDMUND SCHIDDEL

Simon and Schuster   New York

Second printing

SBN 671-20221-9
Library of Congress Catalog Card Number: 73-79639
Designed by Irving Perkins
Manufactured in the United States of America
By American Book–Stratford Press, Inc.

TO PIERRE DE RAEBIGER AND ALDO BRUSCHI
Paris qui rit, Paris qui dort

i

Upper Air

❧   ❧   ❧   IT WAS one of those bright, sunny days that can happen only in New York in late May. The soft wind blew sweet, barrows of flowers halted briefly at street corners, and a four-man string band with a drum played somewhere a tune a little like Mozart gone wrong, but gone wrong happily. And from the East River to the Hudson, Harlem to the Battery, the sky stretched over the city like an infinite turquoise dome.

Above the streets, in the eyrie of the offices of Kastner and Kennerly, Publishers, could be heard the movement of air that hovers about tall buildings at all seasons, lightly buffeting the windows of Anson Parris' thirty-second-floor office.

Parris sat leaning back in his swivel chair, feet propped on his desk. The desk's top, kept almost scrupulously bare by Nina Gerson, his secretary, and by Parris himself—he disliked clutter—had on it only a small electric clock with a sweep second hand, a red morocco oblong framing the photograph of a boy of about five—his son, Todd—and the two classic telephones of an executive editor: the day phone, which went dead at five, when the K and K switchboard shut down, and the night-number phone, which would then be plugged in. Propped on Parris' lap was a large yellow scratch pad on which were numerous doodlings, notations of exact times of day and a string of dollar signs and large figures.

Anson Parris was not a night-phone man. Any normal Friday he would already have left for his apartment, a third-floor through in an old Park Avenue house cached behind the Union Club, reading, listening to music—or both—and hating it, facing the weekend as best he could, waiting for Monday. But this was not a normal Friday, as his closed office door and scratch pad told. As soon as the business hieroglyphed on the pad was completed—and it would be finalized today—he would shower and change clothes in his office before leaving for the Hudson pier where a spanking-new Greek passenger ship had docked that morning, and in which the big publication party for David Steen's new novel would be given. The party was scheduled for six, which would give those invited time to leave their offices early, have a few on their way to the pier, and be feeling no pain when they arrived. Parris' air of rigid relaxation in the face of stress seemed to have been achieved by an effort of will. He had placed a call to David Steen almost an hour ago, but Steen was still out to lunch. Parris was waiting for Steen to return the call.

Anson Parris was thirty-three. His hair was sand-colored and worn somewhat long—he had the kind of haircut that twenty years ago would have implied special sophistications and unemployability. Special sophistications were there, but his sharp, direct glance, arrogant nose and sensual, firm lips showed him to be a worker, the kind of young man trained by men in their forties and fifties who were now learning new publishing techniques from him. He wore eyeglasses with thick frames (he was myopic), and when he took them off, his bright blue eyes seemed larger than expected, like those of a growing child asking, "Well—what?" His clothes were nothing to judge him by, and they changed in style from one day to the next, Pierre Cardin or Alexander Shields, as he pleased. He had never worried about his virility. If, on the street, he seemed dandyish and in a hurry to get where he was going, in the office there was about him the calm that betrays purposeful determination to keep everybody up to the gold and win. He drank when he needed to. He smoked ten cigarettes a day, never more nor less, biting them from the rationed pack in his shirt pocket, rarely offering them lest he lose count of how many he had smoked. He had ruddy, unsunburned skin, strong spatulate hands, muscular fore-arms and a health-club body—three workouts a week instead of lunch hours. The Man in the Gray Flannel Suit had long since lost to him; *he* now was one of the late forties and fifties learning from Parris. Parris was a man to watch, and the trade watched him; already he had changed the shape and content of the American novel, and he would change it more. His present civil status bothered him deeply: one wife, Faye, from whom he was, momentarily, separated; his one son. The situation was complicated—Faye was Catholic, WASC, though, as she put it, she was a collapsed Catholic; Parris was one quarter Jewish, three quarters German, Irish and Dutch. As his Jewish grandfather complained, "You're not a Yid, you're not a goy, so what are you? You're *nothing!*" Parris knew what he was, but didn't like to talk about his upset marriage and rarely did. He had been in Vietnam—NC, because of his nearsightedness—and he had nothing whatever to say about those wasted years.

Parris looked at the clock. The minute hand jigged past 3:40, which meant David Steen was having one hell of a long lunch. Parris got up and walked to the window. A pristine copy of Steen's new novel, *Good Time Coming,* lay on the sill. He picked it up, raising and lowering it in his hand as though weighing it. What there was about *Good Time Coming* that was making it the hottest and most contended for book of its year (and, as reprint money went, any other

15

year), he did not know. The book, of course, met Parris' formula for a best seller: it dealt with a current topic, was factually and carefully written, contained several sections of salacious sexual description, and had an agreeable boy-girl ending. It had, too, a selling title: slightly suggestive for those who wanted to find it so, promising an ultimate optimism to others. But the books of a dozen other successful novelists contained these ingredients in varying proportion. David Steen clearly had some hard-to-define ability to seize readers' interest and hold it: a *soupçon* of shock, a *soupçon* of sentiment, a *goutte* of sadism—and they read to the end. Recent years had marked the emergence of this kind of novel, which had nothing to do with the struggling "prestige" novels of the past; Steen's books were expressions of this curious new phenomenon, which found its public with or without the approval of critics. "Selling" criticism abetted, but adverse criticism did not, necessarily, deter success; his books sold and were read and became major influences on millions who read them in twenty-four languages.

The book had a "title" dust jacket, nothing to suggest to a buyer what the story was about; word of mouth would do that, already had begun. When, a year from now, *Good Time Coming* came out in paperback, it would have tits all over the cover, even bleeding onto the spine, probably; but this hardback needed only the title and Steen's name. Ninety-two thousand readers had paid $6.95 for his last book in its K and K hardcover, and three and a half million had bought its Everest reprint at $1.25. David Steen was a pre-sold writer with a vast reading public and a long performance record of fat sums for fat sales in all categories—reprints, films, plays, musicals adapted from the plays, and films made from the musicals. Of this steady stream of revenue, K and K took percentages varying from the standard ten of film moneys to the considerably less standard twenty-five of paperback sales and resales when sales ran into millions of copies. In a

16

shrinking trade-book market, handling Steen's large octavo, 698-page novel was a little like holding a dignified jeweler's box in which nestled both the Kohinoor and the Star of India.

Today's particular series of feints and gambits surrounding the paperback deal that was keeping Parris glued to the phone had begun Monday morning, about the time the coffee wagon rattled through the outer office and Nina Gerson had come in and said, "Anson—Brown." Nina hadn't needed to say, "Jim Brown, of Everest Books, calling," because Parris knew all the paperback editors by first name and counted most of them as friends; shorthand sufficed. That was how it had started and Parris had closed his door, as he always did when an important title was being "shopped." The door had been closed most of every day since then, except for Nina's discreet entrances and exits. Everest, Quantum Books, Mc-Kay, Badger, all the big reprint houses had been bidding for Steen's novel vigorously. The smaller ones, hoping the book's indifferent critical beginnings just might result in its going for a small six figures, had been early contenders, but had dropped out Tuesday afternoon, at $180,000. During the week, *Good Time Coming* had begun to show unmistakable signs of making trade-book history: there had been seven bids for the film rights, which had gone, Wednesday, to Jules Frey, the independent producer, for $600,000 against a five per cent of the world gross, and that was when the paper bids began to rise in jumps of $10,000 or more. Almost all details already had been decided on, Steen's per copy take, the movie tie-in paper publication date, the channels through which payments would be made into Steen's Swiss banks over a period of five years. The rest was about to happen. Today, Reuben Block, acting for Quantum Books, had bid $940,000 (or nine hundred forty in clipped paperbackese, which can be both flip and angry).

"And that's absolutely our final figure, Anson," Block

said. "I've already cut off one ball for that Steen bastard, but I intend keeping the other for myself."

"Save it for next time," Anson suggested, then duly reported Block's bid to Everest. Jim Brown had upped Everest's offer to nine hundred fifty. Brown, too, indicated he would go no higher, and also reminded Parris that it had been Everest who had been responsible for David Steen's fantastic sales in the mass market, that Everest had held first option on *Good Time Coming* and felt that Kastner and Kennerly was overselling the book. Parris disagreed: no book was oversold if it brought big money; but he had detected the horizon of closure and his call to David Steen was to relay Everest's figure.

As he stood, occasionally checking the sweep of the desk clock's minute hand, Parris could not help smiling when he remembered the plaint, repeated at Wednesday conferences —the echo of the critical moan that fiction was dead—when David Steen, Irving Wallace, Harold Robbins, Uris, Burdick, even unknowns, were making more money on a single book (often from a three- or five-year license to rights of that book) than best-selling authors of twenty years ago could have expected to earn in a lifetime. By now everybody had heard of the movie figure for *Good Time,* and they would not soon forget, either, Steen's at-that-time record-breaking $640,000 for reprint rights to his last novel. It required an encyclopedic memory to handle a deal like this, remember which house owned what and who, controlling shareholders, recent exchanges of stock, subsidiaries, and Anson Parris had it; but not even he had been prepared for the near-million-dollar figures he was juggling now. Had it been entirely his decision, he would have closed with Everest and thanked the god all publishers offer sacrifices to: Paper. Other writers in his stable were kept in the dark until reprint deals had been concluded; all staff working on a particular book were given strict orders to make no calls to the author

18

during this period, lest he quail and, unfamiliar with the techniques of reprint deals, gum things up before the ultimate figure that could be squeezed by a pro like Parris. But David Steen was not other authors: he had a rider in his contract, and Parris, though he hated it, hewed to the line. *The Publisher, should negotiations reach $300,000 in any category, shall proceed thereafter only in consultation with the Author.* (The editorial staff had laughed themselves sick when Steen demanded and got this clause—he had been a $5,000-advance-against-royalties tyro then—as they had laughed when he insisted he would do publicity for major media only. Steen had made them swallow their laughter.)

"Shopping," with or without such clauses, required a laconic nervelessness and a seventh sense of when the ultimate figure had been reached and the squeeze was over. Anson Parris was far from nerveless; every nerve in his body was telling him that Everest's nine hundred fifty was probably top. Acting for—or even in consultation with—any author but Steen, he would have closed the deal, but Steen was a bind and the line was being kept open for his call. For a moment Parris toyed with going out to Nina's office and using her phone to tell Quantum of Everest's new figure, but instinct deterred him; in view of what Reuben Block had said, his anger, it was the better part of valor to let him alone, pro tem.

It was not always a requisite of these ruthless and chilling struggles for Parris to relay the new bid to the house that had made the bid before; often it was policy to let them fry, draw breath, let time pass. Equally often, while cogitating, or checking with David Steen, as he was doing now, news of the momentary bid leaked out, became known, somehow, to many parties, those in to the finish as well as those no longer in, and mere bystanders in publishing offices all over the city, who were curious. Publishing, Parris often thought, was a voyeuristic business: editors liked watching others do what they liked to do themselves or could not do, and the trade had its jokes about this, good and bad, clean and dirty. A celebrated one concerned an apocryphal bird that knew everything going on and flew magically from office to office telling what it knew. This bird was said to fly backward, tail feathers to the wind, and was called, no one quite knew why, the filly-loo bird. Just as there are many orders of birds, so there were several genera and species of filly-loos. (Parris remembered a species from his days at Andover. That bird flew backward, also—across Egypt—and, since it had a rectangular asshole, was said to have dropped the pyramids as souvenirs.) The Madison Avenue–Fifth Avenue filly-loo had no such specific anatomy, but was perhaps an unconscious admission on the part of publishers that some kind of sensitivity, not unlike ESP, bound them during these last tense hours of bidding.

Again Parris checked with the clock: 3:59. He could see Nina's shadow against the frosted glass of the door; she was waiting as anxiously as he, ready to monitor any call on her extension. It was so still in the office that he could hear his heart beating, and he felt a trickle of sweat run down his back, though the air conditioning was functioning perfectly. He unlooped his tie and unbuttoned the collar of his shirt. At that precise moment the phone rang. He waited for Nina to answer, then walked slowly to his desk and lifted his receiver.

"Anson, it's David."

"Yes."

"I hear you've been trying to reach me." David Steen's voice was relaxed and easy.

"I wanted to reach you, yes. Urgently."

"You sound kind of nervous, boy."

"Call it that."

"How's it going?"

"We've got Everest up to nine hundred fifty. While you were having one of your *langsam* lunches."

There was a whistle at Steen's end. "Then I see no reason

not to try for more. Seven figures—let's just call it One. One million lovely dollars."

"David," Parris said tensely, after a pause, "I advise you to let me accept Everest's nine hundred fifty—and run. Lock yourself in a closet and cry with joy."

"Quantum still in?"

"I haven't heard from them lately, so to speak. Contention's getting pretty shaky, David. It's slippery up here. I say, let's close before we slide down on our collective asses."

"I'd like us to try for the One," David said calmly.

"There's never been a paper sale in seven figures."

"Isn't there always a first time for everything? If Everest has gone that far, and if Quantum is still around—"

Parris interrupted, speaking in as controlled a voice as he could muster. "I crossed my balls when I refused Quantum's nine hundred *forty,* David. My crotch is raw from crossing them. To lay it on the line, Quantum has said they're through. Everest feels it's all right to chew the hand that's feeding you, eat up to the elbow, but don't bite the arm off, for God's sake!"

David Steen laughed. "I checked with Sales an hour ago. Fourteen thousand reorders since this morning. That tops anything we had on the last one." Steen didn't wait for the filly-loo bird, he always went behind the arras. "And so, let's chew a little higher. I'd like the kudos of the One—and wouldn't K and K? Think what it'll do to the press boys. And at the party tonight."

"I'm going to fall dead before that party starts if you don't close this, David."

"Anson, excuse me—call waiting on my other wire."

Parris could hear the ringing in the background. "Answer your other damn wire," he said angrily. He lowered the receiver of his phone into the cradle and it rang immediately. This time he didn't wait for Nina to pick up first. Jim Brown, he thought.

"It's Reuben, Anson." Block's voice, strained.

Parris could guess wrong.

"Where are we now on this thing?" Block asked. "Our information is that Everest's lost its head and gone to nine hundred fifty."

"Where'd your information come from?"

"The bird, natch. Why didn't you tell me?"

Parris stalled. He knew Block was aware that he was conducting an entirely private battle on the side, was fighting, dangerously near finalization, to keep Steen with Everest, where K and K wanted him. Silence had been the straw he had thrown onto the scales, to tip them in the direction he considered best for the going thing K and K had with Steen and Everest, without violating Steen's rider clause. He let Block sweat it out.

"So I was right," Block said, taking Parris' silence for assent.

"Yes, that's where it is," Parris conceded. "I assumed, after what you said, that you were bowing out," he added, covering himself for his silence.

Block seemed to have gotten stronger support, or interest, during the last hour and a half. "We've had second thoughts here at Quantum. We'd like to take your boy. What will it take? Don't say that nine hundred again, I'll vomit. Will seventy-five over that do it?"

"Is that a question or an offer?"

"A firm offer. Until, shall we say, Monday morning? At ten?"

"No Monday morning," Parris said.

"When then?"

"We intend to close today."

"You and who else? Who's lousing this up? Everest is crazy and we're even crazier. You're not going to get more than nine hundred seventy-five."

"Steen thinks we are."

"He couldn't be thinking higher than what I've just offered!"

Silence.

"Tell me what he has in mind," Reuben Block persisted in exasperation, a rasp in his voice.

"He has in mind One."

Block's answering silence was very long. Then, "One *million?*"

"That's it."

"He's *mishugeh!*" Block cried. "All right, we'll say the nine—it's killing me even to say it—the nine hundred eighty-five. Till five o'clock. Or you can take it now." Block's voice conveyed he was sure he'd nailed it for Quantum.

"You may still have contention," Parris said.

"Listen, Anson, this thing has got to end somewhere this side of madness. It's just a book. So nine hundred eighty-five. Firm. Okay?"

"I'll get back to you."

Parris sat back in his chair, staring at the two telephones. He had learned, long ago, that when you don't know what to do, you do nothing. He knew the filly-loo bird was flying now, butt to wind, and until it settled on its perch, nothing would be lost by waiting. He waited, watching the desk clock, doodling on his pad. 4:21. He felt the dampness at the back of his hair wetting his collar, then it joined the rivulet running down his spine.

At 4:24 the phone rang. Jim Brown.

"You don't want to talk to me," Parris told him.

"What are we waiting for?" Brown knew of the Steen contract rider, it was well known in the trade. "Let's fuck Steen and close."

"Fuck him. He's yours."

"Not my type. Has David no gratitude for what we've done for him? All that billboard advertising? Nobody else gets that."

"David has no gratitude."

"Well, then, keeping it in the family?"

"He doesn't care about that either."

23

"But he does know of our offer?"

"He knows."

"And? Don't *squeeze* me like this, Anson!"

"He refused it."

"He wants *more* than nine hundred fifty?"

"I told you you didn't want to talk to me. David's set his mind on seven round figures."

"Oh, come on, Anson!"

"That's what he wants. Who knows? He just may get it."

"Quantum!"

"Ah, the bird."

"Nine hundred *sixty?*"

"David says One."

"Nine hundred sixty-five?"

Parris said nothing.

"Seventy."

Silence.

"Seventy-five."

"One has seven digits, Jim."

"Eighty."

"I've got nine hundred eighty-five."

"Is Quantum the contention?"

"I thought you were talking to the bird."

"These seven round figures—"

"Just One, Jim," Parris purred. "On the nose."

"Will you close at that figure?"

"Yes, we'll close at that."

"But there's something in your voice, Anson. Don't tell me you've got a nine-hundred-ninety offer!"

"I well may have in a few minutes."

There was no sound at the other end of the line. The sweep hand of Parris' desk clock revolved several times. "I'll have to put this to the big daddy himself," Brown said then. "He took the three o'clock; he must be home by now. Give me fifteen minutes."

24

"Jim," Parris said, "now that I've told you we'll close for the One, you know, too, that I'll have to take it if it's offered before that."

"You could wait for me."

"Too risky." Parris knew he didn't have to explain to Brown what top heat was, how the track suddenly could become muddy and the race bog down.

"I know," Brown said. He'd figured out—or the bird had told him earlier—which way Parris preferred the sale to go, but he sensed that Parris had his limits of allegiance, and One was one million dollars. Cold. Astral. Infinity. He hung up.

It was 4:47. Parris bit a cigarette from his pack and lighted it and stared out the windows. The "666" sign atop 666 Fifth Avenue winked on—the building and sign he hated because they spoiled his view—and his heart raced now because neither he nor the bird could gauge which house would call back first. He was flying—even if he didn't get the One, both offers were firm; the sale would make publishing history. He knew he was still holding a pair of wild deuces: Everest's fear that Quantum would go all out to get Steen away from them, together with his back titles and the option on the next novel to come. On the other hand, there could, conceivably, be a balk; it had happened before, at figures that were puny in comparison, and then the whole business would begin all over again. When a balk happened, it usually meant that the final figure reached after bidding reopened would be much lower; the track would have cooled. Parris heard a little tattoo in his chest, his heart unloading a small cluster of systoles. Anxiety's peak. He began to make a series of doodles that were little tufted birds flying backward and felt a warming surge flood through him, as though he was about to have sex. He had always known that there was an explicitly sexual by-product of power struggles, and that when he felt this flush, he could be sure it was beginning to be over and he was winning. The sensation was brief, draining quickly away into the reality of the moment, the day fading, his heartbeat again on course. The knob of his door turned in the slow way Nina had when she was checking on his silence but didn't want to disturb him.

"Don't pussyfoot. Come in, pussycat."

"Anson," Nina said, looking at him with concern, "I'm worried about you. Isn't it ever going to be over?"

"Don't worry about me. Why don't you go home?"

"I can't until I know. Do you think we'll get it?"

Parris shrugged.

"Carl's waiting," Nina said. Carl was Carl Kastner, President of K and K. That would be history, too, Carl Kastner waiting.

Parris nodded. Nina went out. Her brief intrusion and the warmth of anticipation had made him forget the clock. The sweep hand pointed to forty seconds past 4:59.

Quickly, he reached for the nearer phone, dialed nine for an outside line, got it, then heard the line go dead as the minute hand swept past five. A seven-figure deal might be in the works, but the switchboard had closed on the prick of five. Before he could pick up the receiver of the night phone, it rang. He let it ring twice, then answered.

"Short and unfunny," Jim's voice said without preamble. "The daddy says we'll give the One. Done?"

"Done."

"Two things. He said to tell you he thinks David Steen is an utter, absolute shit, and you're a close second."

"I hate to be second. Besides, I'm not sure anyone who gets One can be a shit."

"The daddy loved it. He had a dominating father. He *has* to win."

"What's the other thing?"

"He wants to tell David about the One himself."

"Let him."

"Well, see you and Faye at the ship. Oh, I'm sorry, Anson. I forgot."

"She won't be there, but I will," Parris said.

He stood up. It was over. He wouldn't have to give the news to Block; the bird would take care of that. Nina came in, jubilant.

"Let me touch you, platinum boy!" She gave him the office kiss they exchanged before holidays, the briefest laying of cheek against cheek. "You're going to have to hurry to make the pier by six."

"Coming with me?"

"I've had it. I've a hair appointment anyway."

Parris waited until Nina had gone, then walked slowly down the hall to Carl Kastner's office. Kastner had waited long past his Friday leaving time, sitting in his small, book-lined room at the turning of the corridor, known as *la gare centrale* because he never closed his door and could keep an eye on everything. He looked up silently as Parris stopped in the doorway.

"We've tied the knot on *Good Time Coming*. With Everest. It was touch and go, but they came around."

"Seven figures, as the bird said?"

"One. On the nose."

Carl Kastner's eyes widened slightly and something happened behind them that made Parris think of a one-armed bandit flipping three bells in a row—he cared more for the kudos of the seven figures than K and K's take of it, though his computation of that had been immediate. Kastner never had to send down for contracts; he knew his percentages as well as his authors.

"Incredible," he said. "Congratulations—a somewhat inadequate word, I'm aware. I remember when David leaped like a trout to a fly at a five-hundred-dollar reading option."

"Things have changed."

"Are you telling me? I've been in the business since before the Depression."

"Do you know what's coming next?"

"Do I know what's coming next?" Kastner rarely replied to a question, even a direct one, except with a question.

"David's going to want eighty, maybe ninety, per cent of the paper now."

Kastner thought a moment. "We'll talk more specifically about this Steen thing next week, Anson—and the firm's gratefulness to you for the way you've handled it. Meanwhile"—he reached across his desk and picked up a sheet of paper—"I've been looking over the readers' reports on the new Galey Birnham. This is Nina's report. I quote: 'A switch on the Copenhagen boy-into-girl ploy. This time it's girl into boy-girl. A penis-envious lesbian is grafted with male genitalia—oversize, of course—and injected with massive doses of male hormones while retaining her mammillary characteristics, also oversize. She then avenges herself anally on heterosexual women who once spurned her.' "

"Nina's nothing if not concise." Anson laughed.

"Is that what it's about?"

"That's the gist of it."

"She adds that it's beautifully written."

"It is. Birnham has succeeded in doing a real lapidary job while keeping it kicky."

"Is that the same as kinky?"

"Kicky's beyond kinky. It's kinky, too, of course."

"I'm behind in my vernacular. Are we going to do it?"

"If we don't some other house will."

"Will it sell?"

"Thirty to forty thousand, depending on the presentation."

"What kind of presentation would it be?"

"We'd let it sleep. Let it come out cold. No fanfare."

"And no reviews."

"My guess is major critics will review it. If it were *verismo*

28

fiction, like Steen's, they might not. But it's written in epistolary style as fantasy and that'll enable them to cover themselves. They'll invoke Restif de la Bretonne, Burroughs,
Durrell, all the black boys."

"Birnham's sounds the blackest yet." Kastner shifted his
spare, angular figure in its vintage Hawes and Curtis tweeds
into another position. "As a man who turned down *Peyton
Place* and *Lolita*—I'd have turned down *Candy,* too, if it had
been offered to us—I think I'm going to leave the decision
on Birnham's new one up to you. And the lawyers. I rather
regretted *Lolita,* you know."

"There'll be no legal problems on this one. It won't even
need a disclaimer."

"There'll be the problem of seeing to it that I don't have to
know what my left hand is doing," Kastner said. "When I
think of the days we had to consider the mothers of Yorkville
when putting eff-dash into type!" Kastner got up and took his
old wide-brimmed Lock hat, which he wore summer and
winter, from the hook on the back of the door. "Publishing
used to be an occupation for gentlemen. After this Birnham,
I'm wondering what will come next."

"Maybe an Andy Warhol pop-up job with what every boy-
girl wants inside."

"When that day dawns, I'll take the advice of my doctor
and retire. No, not a doctor of medicine but a doctor of
philosophy. 'Is not life a hundred times too short for us to
bore ourselves?' That is Nietzsche, *Beyond Good and Evil.* I
suppose you're going to the Steen party?"

"I'm on my way."

"Well, give him my felicitations, if he cares about such
things."

"He does."

"And have a good weekend, Anson."

"You too, Carl."

🌿 🌿 🌿 CARL KASTNER hadn't asked about Faye, though how much he knew about the trouble up at Ditten's Ridge, which was what the rest of the K and K staff were calling it, Anson could only guess.

The complex of office cubicles was slowly emptying and falling silent. Parris' own was stillest of all, the phones reminders of one call that had been missing from his day— an extension of the Ditten's Ridge trouble. Faye used to call about this time if she knew he had been in the bind of a sale. *This is me,* she would announce, and Anson would ritually respond, *Hello, me. How are you?* She would ask how it had gone and for how much and when he would be home. He was hungry for her voice, and of all the people he wanted to know about the One, it was Faye. Impulsively he dialed his Ditten's Ridge number, heard her voice.

" 'Lo?"

"Were you in the garden?"

"Oh." Her voice dropped. "Yes, I was."

"Are you all right?"

"I'm the same, if you mean that."

"I mean are you and Todd all right?"

"Toddy and I are both fine."

"I thought you'd like to know. We closed the *Good Time Coming* sale a little while ago." He told her about the One.

"That should be enough even for our greedy David."

"You could say it's wonderful for me."

"It's wonderful. For you."

"It ties up the Steen package."

Silence. Then, "David's package or Jeannette's?"

30

"Can't you let up on Jeannette?"

"Can't you?"

Stalemate.

"It's money in our jeans, Faye—"

"Your jeans, lover boy." Her angry voice. " 'Jeans' isn't a word you should use with me!"

"All right, kill it for me."

"You said 'jeans.' I'm the wife who found them, remember?"

He remembered. "Jeans" had been inadvertent, an unhappy trick of his unconscious. Deflated, he said, "Listen, darling, I've got to show at the party for David's book—"

"A party," she said. "Lucky you."

"It'll run late and I couldn't get out tonight, but I'll come first thing tomorrow."

"Don't come at all, Anson. I've told you, it's no use."

"But I'm miserable!"

"So am I!"

"We could stop all this. You could forgive me. Forget."

"I can't forget." Then her businesslike voice. "Are you getting your mail? I've been forwarding it to the apartment."

"Yes, I'm getting it. Baby, have you any idea how long this month has been? I want you. Among other things, I'm horny as God!"

"Other things. Like Jeannette?"

"I haven't seen Jeannette. *Ask* God."

"I'm afraid to ask. He might tell me."

A click as Todd picked up an extension. "Hello, Daddy. When are you coming home, Daddy?"

"Soon, Toddy. See you tomorrow. Be a good boy and hang up."

"I don't want to continue this conversation," Faye said. "Not that he hasn't heard it all before."

"I'm coming out tomorrow whether you like it or not!"

"I like it, Daddy," Todd said.

"Anson, we'd only wrangle and quarrel. I can't stand any more."

"Stand any more, Daddy," Todd echoed.

The line went dead. Parris banged the receiver.

Anger helped him hurry. He laid out a fresh shirt and socks and the lighter of two suits he kept in the office; the evening was warm. Needle-showered, dressed, hair freshly water-combed, he was elevator borne and downstairs in minutes flat.

Fridays at this hour taxis were next to impossible to get. He left by the 50th Street doorway, hoping to flag one going west, but all fled by, occupied or darkly off duty. The hot asphalt summer that was to come already could be smelled in the air. He walked to Sixth, where chances were no better, continued on to Seventh. It would be easier to walk the block and a half farther, to the garage where he kept his Porsche; it might take minutes longer now, but he would be sure of getting to the party. And he'd have the car tomorrow. He waited impatiently in the garage until the Porsche came off the elevator, freshly washed and polished, like himself, got in and headed for the West Side Highway entrance. Everyone else seemed to have had this idea, too; it was jammed, but he saw a gap and raced through it, squeezing between a fat Cad and a truck. Both drivers cursed him as he cut into the downtown highway.

He concentrated on the coiling snakes of traffic, in, out, in again. Opposite, on the Jersey shore, the great neon signs winked against a sky no longer turquoise but a darkening sapphire. Faye's winning one more round bugged him. He hadn't seen Jeannette Steen, but would have to see her now. Fuck it, he thought grimly. All the rage and agony and tongue-lashings of the last month because of a couple of orgasms, no more, no less, as he'd tried to explain to Faye when she found out. Fuck it, over and out. He could see the ship ahead and slowed, nipping down the exit ramp and

32

across to the pier entrance, braking into a space as near the gangplank as he could get.

The ship's gigantic neon name flooded the pier, crowded with cars, swirling with taxis and people. Blazing from stem to stern, like a white dolphin, it rode the black, oily harbor water, seeming, with its lights, part of the lighted city beyond.

As Parris walked up the gangplank he saw the party was well under way; already it had reached a peak and a few early comers were leaving. "Everybody" was here—reviewers, columnists, flaks and PR people, actors and producers and their wives, brittle old girls from the fashion mags, the top of the rag trade, society women, writers not too jealous of Steen to attend, Hollywood people, agents, phonies. They were doing their scenes and bits, dedicated to convincing themselves that *Good Time Coming* was, if not a great book, already destined for best sellerdom, worth their time. At parties of this size almost anybody might turn up, from an astronaut to the most recent guru and his disciples. There probably would be no astronaut, but the guru was there (invited by PR, for flair), holding court on the deck. Just ahead was the seventeen-year-old "New Hollywood" actress who would play the heroine in *Good Time* when the picture was made, and, ahead of her, blocking the top of the gangplank, a group of passive beards and flower people, laconically disapproving; one wore a large lapel button: CHRIST WAS A DIKE. The jet set, both hard-ass and luxury-accommodation varieties, was there in force, behaving frenetically, the classic clutch of minor nobilities, vague princesses and *marquesas* and kept men.

That David Steen, who had written the book, and part of the K and K staff that had put the package together should be jammed shoulder to shoulder with these people was typical of promotional parties. Especially this kind, given on a boat just in from her maiden voyage. Because the ship was new it was news, as David Steen's book would be news. The party would rise to even higher crescendo and belief and lead to other, smaller, parties later. In turn, Fifth and Madison would bed down with Park and the Village, and the result would be double-page spreads on feature and society pages, photographs in magazines, TV and radio spots. The book would be talked about and gossiped about and sales resistance would crumble from Doubleday's in New York to Bullock's in Los Angeles; the requisite thousands of readers would buy *Good Time* and several million housewives would wait their turns in rental libraries and read it to shreds. A year later, an entirely different and much larger consumer group would buy Everest's reprint; uncounted millions would see the movie Jules Frey would produce. . . .

"Anson! Is it true? The million?"

Both of Parris' hands were being pumped in congratulation. He smiled, using Carl Kastner's technique. "What million?"

"Do we have to wait for the *Times?*"

"Why don't you ask David?" Parris countered.

"You can't get near him."

"We hear Quantum paid the seven figures. Is it true?"

Reuben Block was behind the group, leaving, and had heard. He smiled sourly at Parris. "If I were death, I'd kiss you. Hard."

Jim Brown and his wife came up.

"How do you feel, Anson boy?" Jim asked.

"Like a drink."

"I feel like if I took one I'd strangle—but I did the lovely with David. Not that the daddy hadn't given him the snow job already."

The Browns squeezed past and a surge pushed Parris ahead. Now he stood in the big lounge amidships where the center of the party was, seeing people he had seen so often he had to make an effort to see them again, all knocking themselves out to congratulate David Steen because he was making it bigger than ever. The music—the newest combo from England, all flopping hair and guitars and grinding pelvises —was deafening, an overall electronic blast from loudspeakers, defying anything but shouts between the mixed crowds at the bar and milling around the champagne tables. The tables were decorated with ice swans heaped with caviar. Photographers' flashbulbs were splitting the ship's soft lighting and a TV crew was making the tape that would be run in hour and half-hour versions all over the country. In the farthest corner he could see David Steen's sleek black head and Guard's mustache, Jeannette beside him in a glittering silver sheath.

The moment he dreaded, but it had to be got through. For nine or ten hours, the last of a long week of hours, he had been absorbed with *Good Time Coming* and the heady fascinations of big money and winning. His dealings with David had had Jeannette behind them; she was known to be the shrewd calculator of what the market would bear. For an instant the party blurred and lost contour for him. There was always this brief blank of time, in which he became another Anson Parris (one of many), unlike his business image, when he felt most deeply his essence—as though he suddenly caught sight of himself in a full-length mirror and rediscovered the body and mechanisms he had put by earlier, a *Doppelgänger* no one, not the Steens, not Carl Kastner, not even Faye, truly knew. Sometimes this little time, colorless and varying in length, happened while commuting from Ditten's Ridge, or in a taxi from the town apartment to his office—or at a party like this, where he felt split, half editor, half unpredictable self. His last encounter with Jeannette had had about it the vulgarity and immediacy of passion. In the station wagon quickly parked beside a roadside hedge, most suburban of symbols in the most suburban of places. A blow job with trimmings, meaningless to him, to her, too, perhaps.

35

Now he had to think of her, go to her, but not before the encounters he saw ahead. Vulnerable, he laced through the crush.

A rattlebones of a woman in a little-girl dress came toward him—Fleur Parry, fashion's oldest columnist, hanging on to gossip with the zest of Hopper and Parsons combined.

"Anson!"

"Hi, Fleur."

"Darling!" she croaked in her 1920 Mayfair English. "Adored David's book! His best—newer than new." She lowered her voice, camping on it, "And the dirtiest yet. Filthy!" She'd never crack the title page, but her next day's column would be full of the party and the book. "Is Faye here?"

"She's in the country."

Fleur Parry looked at him. "You don't fool me, Anson Parris. I know about you."

"What do you know, Fleur?"

"About you and Faye. That you're on those rocks. Oh, don't worry, I won't breathe it. I believe in the sanctity of marriage. Jeannette's over there." She kissed him fleetingly on his chin and passed on.

The warm hysteria, the people, the popping corks, came up to engulf him like a flood. He would try to forget Faye for tonight, and when the cold boredom and indifference to others filled him he would know he was succeeding. His glass was empty and he took another from a tray held high by a passing waiter and drained it. It helped a little. He was hard up. For warmth, even of this kind. For the smells of women. For tail. For somebody to sleep with after the tail. He reached for another drink, drank that, felt better and began to move toward the David Steens' corner.

Directly in his path was Galey Birnham, talking to a girl with a thatch of carroty hair and wearing something brightly green. Birnham had seen him and was leading the girl forward.

"Isn't Fleur the last camp?" he demanded to know, without greeting Anson. "The old girl does look good for her age, though, whatever that age may be. I'd like you to meet—"

Parris didn't hear the girl's name. The TV crew was moving in, making a wedge so they could train their cameras on David and Jeannette, and for a moment Birnham and the girl and Parris were separated.

"This 'do' is like the Capote party," Birnham said when they were again together. "Nobody missing but the Clutters. And people wonder what makes revolutions." His voice was deep and controlled. The girl laughed, smiling up at Parris over the rim of her glass. She had very large green eyes, which, unlike those of most other women in the room, were not made up. "If you'd only promote me like this, Anson," Birnham went on. He had a taut, exercised look beneath his nondescript dark suit, like a barbell boy dieted and grown thin.

"Well, if your books sold as well as David's, I would," Parris replied.

"Oh, to write as badly as David Steen!" Birnham was another part of the stable, his books farther out than far, implying that sex for everyone was a mélange of *soixante-neuf* and whippings. He was convinced that what he wrote would sell widely if given hard promotion. "I don't suppose you've any news for me about *my* new book? Surely you've read it by now, Anson?"

"Yes, Galey, I've read it," Anson said.

"And you mean, like, man, like you don't dig it, like?"

"Like, man, I mean, this is no place to discuss it, like," Parris handed it back. "Excuse me, I've got to get to David. So pleased to have met you," he added to the girl. Her green eyes blinked, once, and she lowered her glass to smile at him. She wore a bright lipstick that brought out the color of her eyes and no other make-up at all. He wormed his way into the group surrounding the Steens.

Jeannette saw him first. "You darling, you marvel!" she said, theatrically casual, grasping his arms. They exchanged the Madison-Fifth kiss, a dry brush of both cheeks ending with a peck on the lips. "This time you and David really have done it. David's delirious, of course."

"It was mostly David's holding out," said Parris. *Or you, Jeannette, you flinty, homemade bitch.*

"After this we're going on to La Grenouille. Where's Faye? You must join us. We can't celebrate without you."

"Faye's not here."

"But why not?"

He waited for a moment noisy enough to cover it. "Because she knows about that Sunday I drove you home."

Jeannette glanced quickly at her husband. He was thoroughly occupied. "But how could she know? It was only that once."

"How flattering. I counted twice."

"Is this why you haven't called us—except for business?"

"It's one reason."

Jeannette, a dazzling brunette, had an Oriental passivity of feature, but her eyes betrayed an agitated calm. "My God, Anson, if I thought about it—and I did—I supposed you didn't call because you were hiding behind the package. David's been *hors de combat*, as he always is at this phase. You should have *told* me Faye knew."

"What good would it have done?"

"I could have called her—"

"But you didn't call. And for God's sake, don't call now. I've told you so you won't. I'm staying at the apartment."

"Is it as bad as that?"

"She threw me out. Or I walked out. A little of both."

"Then I'll ring you." David had caught Anson's eye and Jeannette put back on her faithful-wife voice. "First minute I can, darling."

38

David did look deliriously satisfied with the sale and was in his glory. His eyes shone with success and its surfeit. His long cigarette holder was poised next to his left ear in a straight-up position that suggested the celebrated photograph of Virginia Woolf holding her pencil. "I love you in seven figures, Anson," he said.

"But don't let's count all seven ways," Parris quipped back. At least David seemed to know nothing.

"We must indulge ourselves a little. This time I buy *you* lunch."

"Can you afford it?"

"The Oak Room, Monday at twelve-thirty? Our usual time? I'll get Charles to save us a table on the side, with a telephone, so we can tie up the final knots." No matter how rich and successful, David Steen was still impressed by being seated in the first black leather armchair to the right of the doorway at the Plaza's famous restaurant, the result, Parris supposed, of his having been relegated to the center during his long journalism years. At least Jeannette would not be present, since the Oak Room was closed to women at lunch. But David would be seated when Parris arrived, cigarette holder in the Woolf position, telephone held to his right ear, projecting what he called his public image.

"You're joining us tonight, Anson, of course?"

"I've already told Jeannette that I can't." He'd had enough of Steens for one day. "But Monday, twelve-thirty, we'll celebrate."

As he turned away Parris realized that, out of the tail of his eye, he had been watching the girl Birnham introduced. It took him a moment to get to where she was, at the champagne tables, wolfing caviar from one of the ice swans.

"I was *starvy!*" she said when he reached her. "You know, I thought Galey's crack about the Clutters just the least bit hairy. I didn't know he went to that party. I thought he was in Morocco at the time."

"What's the difference?" Birnham called it Maroc, lived

39

there part of the year. Where the *kif* and hash were. Parris saw her more clearly now, her nothing of a dress, the top almost transparent, the skirt stopping an inch above almost nonexistent shorts. She looked like one of those openly rakish girls who have appeared in underground movies, always reported cast in professional films that never get made; he wondered if she'd hacked her hair off for some part that fell through and was now trying to make the best of it. It was genuine, carroty red, coarse and straight, brushed back from her forehead, all cowlicks.

"You're wondering about my hair. It used to be to *here*. I did a stint for Andy. Crack O'Dawn, I was billed. Forget it. But it led to a part in the Theatre-in-the-Buff. A bathtub scene, all ass and long hair. The critics couldn't see my face, so I cut my hair and lost the job. Now I'm stuck with being the poor man's Mia Farrow. I'm dying for a drink."

"Name it."

"Um—bourbon on the rocks. Stiffy."

"For me, too," Parris said to the barman.

"And a breath of air," she added, as though completing the order.

"Well, let's go out on deck," Parris had to say. He had to touch her, take firm hold of her arm and get them to the doorway.

They came out onto the port deck. Ahead of them the lights of Manhattan hung like a glittering scrim against the night sky. The black, oily harbor water lapped against the ship's white hull in shadow below. They walked along the deck, holding hands, the salt sea air blowing around them.

"I've had the bitches' stand-up," she said, in step beside him.

"What's a bitches' stand-up?"

"The brush from Galey. You know, like the bitches' curse? He found something in leather and clanking chains playing in the combo and's waiting to lug him home. He's

40

always doing that, dumping me for the padded jock and black rubber sheets."

Parris stopped with his glass halfway to his mouth. "Stop talking like a Birnham novel," he said, laughing. "Where did you learn that jive?"

"About the sado-maso boys? I don't *understand* all that. It's a sideline with Galey anyway."

"But you came with him."

"He dragged me along. He thinks I'm a dog. Don't you know about this town? *Real* men? Not enough to go around, so a girl's got to piece out with passing queers like Galey. He's presentable and I like him. He needed a girl to front for him and he knows I'm on the make and wanted like mad to come. I'm afraid I didn't say that very well."

"I think you said it very well. I didn't hear your name when we were introduced," Parris added. They came to a closed deck gate and stopped by the rail.

"No wonder," she said. "It's *really* Neile Eythe." She spelled it for him. "It's a drag. My parents wanted a boy, obviously."

"Why is it a drag? Better than Crack O'Dawn."

"Well, I hate it, the Neile, especially. But it's mine and I'm stuck with it." She smiled. "Ever see a pie chart? There's always one little hatched sliver of the pie so small they print the percentage outside the circle. That's me. I'm the other soap on the commercial with four bars instead of three. Bargain. I want to get *inside* the chart. *Whirl!* Be one of the real bars, not a bargain. Meantime, a drag ploy like this, the buff, anything—*to make it*. I need a millionaire. Are you one?"

He laughed, shook his head. "You're new to New York?"

"It's new to me. Don't you love it?" She looked up. "I was born in *Denver!* Not even Teenage, New Jersey. When I got on the plane I put a sleep shade over my eyes. Couldn't wait to see the last of *Denver!*"

"Maybe you were sorry to leave." He took a swallow of his drink. His drinks were getting to him at last. *Whirly!*

"I *hated* the fucking place. I'll never go back."

"But why?"

"Ever see a prairie dog? Awful trees, no rain. I mean nothing that *whirls*. The people! You see," she said, turning, leaning back on her elbows, "I always wanted one of *those*." She swung an arm, pointing upward. "That one. Whirly. The Whirl! Success!"

He watched her, fascinated. He saw she was jailbait, or almost. "What do you do, now you're no longer Crack O'Dawn? Model?"

"I'm not quite dog enough for that. I can tell my back from my front." As though to prove this, she threw back her head, closing her eyes, and he saw her smooth throat and shoulders, round young breasts riding beneath her dress. "I know what you do, you're a publisher. I don't mean that, I hate *that*. I mean, what *else* do you do?"

"Isn't being a publisher enough?"

She let her eyes travel over him. "I adore your suit."

"I don't like people who say 'I adore your suit.' "

"I only meant you don't look like a publisher. You know, those collars. Buttonholes. Cuffs and links."

"You still haven't told me what you're doing now."

"No millionaires in sight, not even boy producers who do buff. I told you, anything to make it. Right now, I'm writing a novel."

He knew the kind of book girls—*kids*—like this one would write. Heartbreaking probes into the childhood underground, or one of those imitations of the French, in which inanimate objects discuss people—the cigarette being moved from pack to lighter in three hundred pages. Or, maybe, since she knew Birnham, a phony Birnham.

"I've put you off," she said.

He finished his drink. "You're putting me up tight as hell."

She looked away. "You could say something, about what I said."

"What is there to say, except what's the book about?"

"It doesn't matter. It's just a book I hope will help me *get* there," she said, looking into her empty glass. "Nobody really knows what it's like to be me, to want it as badly as I want it. From the beginning I wanted it. Out west they thought I was crazy. That was when I decided that rather than live with the prairie dogs, I'd come here and try to make it. Big. In the buff. At the typewriter. Any way."

Her candor touched him and he understood that behind her story was another—as behind his was another—and that he had troubles enough without hearing it. Still, perversely, he wanted to hear it; perhaps it would make his own story recede. The lights of the city winked behind her. Her youthfulness leaped up in him, rekindled that surge of power and sex he had felt when the sale was finalized. He stared at her bright, thatchy hair, her face that was the face of an angel *manqué*. She was fascinated by the pushes and pulls, the many struggles that lay behind this party. She abruptly became exciting to him. He wanted her. He wondered if he should begin the make now or wait until they were in the car. He felt the familiar pattern beginning, the pretense of driving her home, a sudden grope, bed. He promised himself he only wanted her for tonight. To forget Faye. And Faye's knowing about Jeannette.

"You don't say anything," she said.

"Let's have another."

"Let's."

They walked back. The sounds inside the ship had changed. The corks had stopped popping, the combo was playing no longer, the party was ending. The ship's lounge was almost empty and already had a tawdry air; glasses were everywhere, with cigarettes that had been put out in them, swollen like fat worms. David and Jeannette had stayed to the end, but were leaving. David had put his long cigarette holder in his mouth and was smoking placidly. They had ceased being performers and now had an entourage of four, two critics, a woman who did a TV book show, and one of the photographers. Parris managed to cadge two last drinks. He walked with them to where the girl waited in a corner.

"Would you care to have dinner?"

"At some little bistro in the Village? No. I'm stuffed."

"Then let me drive you home."

"I live on Mott Street."

"You're Chinese," he kidded.

"It was the only place I could find a loft."

"Oh, a *loft* girl."

"I live a floor above Galey. Don't worry." She laughed. "His is soundproofed."

It wouldn't be her place.

"You're being resistive," he said.

"What's wrong with that?"

"It wastes time."

She frowned. "It ought to be possible to get to know someone like you without all this sparring."

"What do you mean, someone *like* me?"

"You know what I mean, it should be easy but isn't. You look so unhappy."

"That's my party expression."

"What's the matter?"

He shrugged. "I'm a happy man who looks unhappy. Why can't we go now?"

"Now that your friends have gone? I knew why you were waiting."

"All right, I was waiting. What do you want me to do, put you in a taxi for Mott Street and forget it?"

She smiled. "You're chicken."

"Not in the way you think."

It would be the apartment.

"Come on," he said.

She got up. They were the tail end of the party. It was after nine and a few people still stood on the pier, hailing taxis. The beards and flower people were walking toward West Street.

"It was a whammo," one of the TV boys who knew Parris shouted as they passed.

"Don't forget, we want a copy of the tape."

"Will remember," the TV boy said. He got into the field-unit truck and drove away.

Parris opened the door of the Porsche and the girl lifted her legs inside. The party had kept at bay the way he felt and when they were speeding uptown his desolation returned; now it was mixed with ambivalence about the girl beside him. He was so dispirited from his relationship with Faye that he wondered whether he could begin another, even one that would only last one night. However bitter and deep his anger with Faye, she had spoiled him for anything but top grade. He drove with increasing speed, cutting down the 72nd Street ramp and across town.

Between lights he studied the girl's face. She had a pout on her lips that promised humor, as if holding back laughter until it should be time for it. He sensed she was making this face for him, letting him know the chat at the party had meant nothing. At last she decided he had made judgment enough and turned away from him, staring out of the window.

They were on Park, heading uptown for his street. The last spring tulips planted in the center separating them from downtown traffic fled past. "Look," he said, "I want you to know the kind of box you're walking into. I'm married."

"Why should I care?"

"Do you want to change your mind?"

"Do *you* want me to?"

"No, I only told you because—"

"Because you don't want to get hung up."

"Yes."

"Don't worry about it," she said. "Neither do I. All I want is for it to be *whirly*."

"Okay," he said.

🌷 🌷 🌷 PARRIS BROUGHT the Porsche to a stop in front of his house and they got out. He locked it carefully and they went down into the small entrance hall. The self-service elevator was waiting.

"How did you find such a place?" she asked, impressed.

"Oh, we—I've had it for years. It's a place to stay in when I work late at the office and the last train's gone."

"Your little home away from home."

"Here we are," he said when the elevator stopped at his floor, and he unlocked the door and switched on the lights.

She looked around, like someone examining an advertised sublease, went from the living room into the hall and the bedroom at the rear. "You don't make your bed, or somebody doesn't."

"No. Not unless the maid comes."

"And there's nobody here?"

"Did you think there would be?"

"In this town you never know."

The living room had three windows overlooking the avenue. He quickly drew the curtains. She continued to look around, as though taking an inventory, at the two Dutch flower paintings Faye had inherited from an aunt, the wood-burning fireplace with a mirror above it, the two sofas flanking it and the coffee table between.

"So you're one of the Beautiful People."

He grimaced in distaste. "I'll fix us drinks," he said, going past her to the small kitchenette concealed by a lattice in the hall. She sat down on the farthest sofa. He could hear her flipping through a manuscript he had been reading. He filled two glasses with ice and poured bourbon over them until they floated, making his a little stronger than hers; he'd held off at the party because of the driving.

"I still can't figure out how you came to be there," he said, handing her one of the glasses.

"I told you, Galey brought me." She drank. "You don't think I sleep with him, do you? I don't. He's the King of the Gangbangs, though."

Parris frowned, sat down on the sofa opposite.

"Well, you asked," she said. "On the Saturday route up and down Madison, where you see everybody, that's what they call him."

"You've been reading that book."

She picked up the manuscript. "Is this what a book looks like when it's sent to you?"

"Some look like that, others look better or worse."

"Mine will look better than this," she told him, tossing the manuscript back. She hiked up one side of her skirt like a boy and brought out a pack of cigarettes. "I saw there weren't any, and you weren't smoking at the party. Don't you?"

"I do, but I'd already exceeded my quota for today."

"Those. I meant these." She struck a match and lighted up. He smelled the sweetish whiff as she exhaled. "Well, do you?" She leaned across the table, offering him the stick, mouth end toward him. He hesitated. "I mean haven't you ever?"

"Once. Long ago. It didn't do anything for me."

"One is silly," she said. "It's relaxing. You look as though you could use one."

"Did you learn this from Galey?"

"Darling, everybody smokes a little."

He wondered how she would be after she'd smoked it. She still held it toward him. He reached out and took it.

"Deeply," she said.

"I know." He inhaled, held it, blew out. He had said he didn't want to get hung up, and he didn't—the sooner he got her between the sheets the better. He'd never screwed on pot but had heard the stories. Just watching her made warmth run into his groin. He shifted because he was getting hard.

She saw. "You see?" She awarded him her smile. "But to come back to the party. I wanted to meet David Steen. I did. What a cube, and that campy cigarette holder. As his publisher—"

"I'm not his publisher at night."

She took a drag from the Mary-Jane and again handed it across to him. All right, one more puff, then the make would have to begin. He got up and walked to where she sat, looking down at her.

"I can't understand how people can read what he writes. It's shit." Her full, flowerlike mouth was distorted with the word.

"Don't use words like that."

"Don't you use them?"

"Sometimes. But we didn't come here to talk about that." He sat down close beside her.

"Ah," she said, looking at the rounded contour rising between his legs. "You're all boy."

"I didn't know girls were supposed to notice."

"They do," she assured him. "The eyes, the mouth, the thumbs—and that."

He leaned forward and kissed her. "You have a marvelous mouth." She tasted of the cigarette, wonderful.

"Are you a Jew?"

He drew back. "Not a Jewish Jew, but I'm partly Jewish. Why?"

48

"Those eyes and that nose."

"What *about* my eyes and nose?"

"Beautiful," she said, and then, explaining, "because out in Denver we never thought of Jews. Or they were those sweet people who had delicatessens."

He decided not to get angry. "Well, my grandfather didn't have a delicatessen, though he was entirely Jewish. Still is."

"And you're homogenized."

"I never think of it unless someone asks me."

"I'd love to be Jewish."

"Why?"

"Then I'd have a bone in the face, a real nose, instead of this Limerick button."

This time she kissed him and he didn't taste the smoke, but he could smell it again when they drew apart, drifting up from her left hand, where the stick, almost gone, burned. She took a last drag. Once it was tamped out, he thought, it would be the moment.

"Let's not wait," he said, his hand on her thigh, where her brief skirt met her stockings. He felt the pack on her leg.

"I'd like another, until we relax."

"I am relaxed."

"You don't know it, but you're not," she said. She moved a hand under his and brought out the pack. "Do you want your own this time or shall we share?"

"Share." He wanted to now. This time he lighted it for her. A last tremor from his censor warned him, but it disappeared when they kissed again, blowing the smoke into each other's mouth. When she drew away she seemed a long dream receding, a dream that had to be retrieved. The dream of her came forward easily, and without feeling himself move and walk, he made them fresh drinks and came back.

"Are you always like this?" she asked. "In such a hurry?"

"It's been a long time for me."

"How long?"

"Weeks."

"Too long. I'd go crazy." She settled herself against him. "Take off your glasses."

He took them off, saw her better, her green eyes half-lidded.

"Blue," she said of his. He felt fresh and smooth and lustrous, digging the things she said, loving it. Everything seemed very easy. He pressed her back onto the sofa. She seemed unlike anyone he had ever touched; he cared about nothing now but the hard, bursting muscle between his legs.

She made no resistance. "Well, if it's been that long, let's go. But slow."

"Here?"

"Here or there, wherever there is."

"The bedroom." It seemed planets away and not worth trying to reach. He realized he was high because of the way time seemed to have locked. He was staring into her eyes at the same time his hands, which miraculously seemed to have developed eyes, found the place where once he would have expected a garter clasp. There were no clasps on her, only the smooth, silken surface that was her stockings and extended upward to her waist, ending in a little roll. Then there was the time thing again—he had her dress off and was locked on her breasts, standing taut as temple mounds, the nipples ruddy and deliciously tough. She was flying, too, and let him hold her lightly by the shoulders as he unrolled the silken leotard over her ankles, bunching it and throwing it to the floor. For an instant he worried about his own clothes, but her fingers undid his tie and unbuttoned his shirt; he had no sensation of shedding them, or his trousers either, and since he never wore underwear, they were *there*. Then, trembling against her, he forced her beneath him. The pot had given him eyes everywhere, his hands, his penis, which seemed to see immediately where to go. She was all her nipples had promised, tight and taut and hard to enter, but when he made it she locked her legs around his hips and held him.

50

"Easy," she murmured, and let him begin, first slowly, then more steadily and deliberately, the ride he was afraid would be too quick for him, and for her. But time seemed to lock them on top of the peaks, then dropped them dizzily almost down. It was work, wonderful work, and a long job. He kept his eyes open, watching her face. Her eyes were closed tightly and her bright hair was like a small pillow beneath her head. Then she cried out, and he understood the timing had been hers as much as his. It was a time he wanted to remember forever, above all other times. And then nothing could have stopped him, not Faye coming in suddenly and finding them, and he came in a flood of breathful delight.

"I knew the minute I saw you," she said when it was over. "Did you know too?"

With the disgust that followed he loathed her for talking. He pushed her to the rear of the sofa, his breathing hard and painful in his lungs. He heard the small hall clock, of which he was never aware at night, tinkle. Five.

It couldn't be, but then she touched him and he knew it was true. They turned again to each other; she was now trembling as he had trembled at the beginning.

"You didn't answer me," she said, and kissed him.

He couldn't believe it, but her lips brought desire rushing back, though he knew that, for a time (what was time? now?), the pattern was as before. He pumped himself dry and they slept. An hour? No, more. He heard the clock strike again as he sat up, swinging his legs to the floor, seeing the glasses with the cubes melted in them, the sticks smoked and stamped out.

"What day is it?" he asked her, frowning.

"Does it matter?"

"Do you know?"

"Saturday."

He relaxed enough to feel his headache. Time to—something. He remembered something. "We—I didn't—and now it's too late."

She laughed at him, laying her head on his thigh, looking up. "You mean, did I take a fertility pill? Sorry to disappoint you, I take the other kind."

He sighed in relief.

"You're not a real Jew—they must have forgotten," she said, laying her hand between his legs. "But that's all right. Back in a minute."

He watched her run lightly to the bath. Her skin was a fabulous color, not skin, but the night turned apricot. Now time was jointed another way; it seemed an hour before she came back, and his bladder was bursting. He was chilly, too, and got up and staggered into the bedroom and found a robe. He passed the clock, saw its face, purplishly no time at all. The colors had been coming on with his sleep; now, with eyes open, he could see them. Hating her slowness, he lay down on the bed. She looked a running rainbow when she emerged, running back to the living room to dress. He locked himself in the bath and urinated gloriously and with pinpoint precision into the tub, thinking she might go—it would be like her to go—but when he came out he found her in the bedroom.

"I didn't see this last night," she said, going to the lowboy at the far wall, picking up a silver frame. "So this is what your wife is like."

He said nothing, wishing he had the gall to slap purple hell out of her and tell her to get out.

"Nothing to say." She got it. "Don't worry, did you really think I'd hang around? Oh, no." She turned, walked to the door, waiting for him to unlock it. He followed.

"Look," he said, producing words from another world, "have you taxi money?"

"Of course."

He'd have felt better if she'd said she hadn't, if he could have given her something. "Well," he said, letting her know by his grave, black silence that this was all.

She still waited for him to open the door. He unlocked it, saw her out to the elevator, saw her standing in a spotlight— her hair was fire and her mouth a sliced red fruit with white seeds. And he could see straight through her. He closed his eyes, opened them: it was true, she was transparent.

"So that was that." Her voice, too, was transparent. Glass.

"I suppose so."

"You said you didn't want to get hung up. But you were."

"So were you."

"Nothing to be done about it?"

"Nothing whatever," he said. The elevator doors pinched her from him, but he could still see her, glass in a glass cage, descending.

Then the magenta wind struck, lambent and caressing, a thick, heavy wind like a gelatine sea in a tank of himself that held him locked and suspended inside his own space. The wind *looked* at him. He moved unsteadily back into the apartment, carrying the thick, gelatine blast with him into the living room, to get away from himself. The flowers in the Dutch paintings stared at him too, all the colors in them brighter than any he had ever seen. He saw the butts in the tray, counted them, but refused to tell himself *howmany*— like *adoctorwithholdinghowmanybarbituratesittakes*. The cluster of orgasms he had had were the greatest of his life, and the memory of them made him think of Faye, not the girl. *The girl!* NEILE—her name flashed brightly. He had expected, if he had expected anything, to feel guilt when it was over, but all he felt was joy, holy and rewarding, and a slow fading of the eyes-everywhere sexuality and the excitement of being with her. The pot, his other world announced, had pervaded him since the second stick. He was locked in the vise of hallucination until it would wear off. He tingled and felt nauseated. The soft wind swept him back to the bath and he tried to vomit but the toilet and basin and tub were a howling trio of laughter. At last he felt tired and flung himself into bed, squeezing his eyes shut. But the colors were still there, forcing tears through his eyelids, delicious tears. He felt a transcendental fondness and love for Faye that he knew would go forever as he felt it and be forgotten. The magenta wind became a solid box enclosing him and he slept.

IN THE first pearly daylight, the house built into the soft slope of hillside resembled three transparent pyramids pushed together. The pyramids, mostly glass, were three gables beginning at ground level, extending triangularly upward to three ridged roofs meeting at the center. At their apex was a mobile of brightly colored spheres that twittered in the wind. It was the rare kind of modern country house that had remained loyal to its architect while revealing the year it had been built, 1960, as well as the money required to build it, a little over $140,000, which was a lot of money then, as it is now. It was a good house, perfect for its setting, and also rare in another way: it was paid for.

Before day came, lights had been turned on in one of the gables, where the bedrooms were, then turned off, as though someone inside was sleepless or getting up early and then deciding to go back to bed. Shortly after seven the glass rectangle that was the front door opened and a young, dark-haired woman held it as a large Doberman pinscher ran out. The dog loped down the white gravel driveway, past a blue mailbox lettered PARRIS, and across a narrow blacktop road into a stand of trees. The woman closed the door and while the dog was outside drew back long, white curtains in the front gable. Presently a child appeared, pressing his face against the glass, watching the Doberman, and a few minutes later the door was opened again.

"Netcher?" Faye Parris called to the dog. "Net—*cher!*"

Netcher leaped across the road and raced back into the house.

The house was almost midway between those of Faye's mother and Anson's parents; her mother, long a widow, lived in Greenwich, Anson's mother and father near Danbury. Inside, the house was spacious and sparsely but eclectically furnished. The living-room fireplace was flanked by the glass around and above it; it had a concealed chimney, a secret of the architect, and, though it looked impossible, drew perfectly. Anson's many books, rising high in shelves on one of the interior walls, were background for an oversized semi-circular sofa and a vast French armoire, into which his stereo equipment had been built, and, below, were his many cameras and slides and tapes, neatly filed. Next to a Saarinen table and set of chairs in the dining room (Faye had bought them at a Parke-Bernet auction) stood a Hepplewhite high-boy, another legacy from the aunt who had left her the Dutch paintings in the New York apartment.

Faye Parris moved about the house as though she was in a hurry, though there was no need; during the month Anson had been away she had learned that a wife with all the time in the world and everything possible to do could do almost nothing. Her days had been full enough: the incessant requirements of an only child nearing six; housekeeping; house cleaning with her cleaning woman on the two days a week she had help; the burgeoning garden; neighbors; *not* going into New York on Fridays, her usual day, because the pattern of driving back with Anson would be broken, make things even more broken than they were already. *Anson.* Anson at the end of a telephone, at first calling importunately, then less often.

It was as if their last, bitter quarrel had created an entirely different season through its virulence: the pink dogwoods had flowered more fully than in other years, tulips in the beds outside the windows were brighter and more erect; even the bed the moles usually invaded was more brilliant. The season so found was like a letter written to herself about other springtimes—Anson and herself the year when he had taken his vacation time early and they had stayed with Jeannette and David Steen at their house in the south of France, near Cannes; last year, when she and Anson and Todd had driven south to see the Charleston gardens. In this hollow month she had felt like someone beginning an illness, had noticed gaps in her days, when she couldn't remember what she had done or what day it was. Nothing hours, like a book bound with some pages missing and others out of order.

She was preparing to go to her mother's house in Greenwich this morning, and her schedule was bent to the end of being away from the house when Anson came. She had calculated: the Steen party would have run late, as he said; he would get up a little later than was his Saturday habit, tennish; an hour and a half, two hours, on the road, depending on weekend traffic—he couldn't arrive before noon. But she would be triply sure, be out and away by nine-thirty.

"Why are you going to Nana's if Daddy's coming?" Todd demanded to know. He stared at her from his chair at the kitchen table. He was a wide-eyed child given to questions, tall for his age, with his father's stockiness and persistence. Often bemused and quiet when at play, he was oververbal when eating, which was when the questions about Anson arose. Todd was playing a game with himself and her, Faye realized, a game becoming more difficult for either to win the longer his father was away. "Will Daddy be there to meet you at Nana's?"

"No. Finish your cereal. You know this is the day we go to the group. We have to hurry and dress."

"You aren't going to the group," Todd fought back with logic.

56

"Please, finish your cereal."

"I don't want it." He pushed the bowl away. He knew the group ended at twelve-thirty, that his mother wouldn't be back by then. "Everybody else will go home after lunch. What will *I* do?"

"Don't give that to Netcher!" Faye interrupted, snatching the bowl. "I've told you, we don't feed Netcher from the table." That *we* again, that she was not supposed to use.

Netcher licked her chops; then, seeing the cereal was withheld, lay down beneath the table. Both dog and child watched, aware of being imminently left behind.

"You're going to play after lunch with Roger Currie, until your naps," Faye patiently explained. "Then I'll pick you up on the way back from Nana's."

The Curries, an up-the-road couple with six children, were a godsend, especially Velma Currie. She had the Saturday morning group for neighborhood children of preschool age. Her views on child rearing almost exactly matched Faye's, or maybe Faye went along with Velma: not too permissive, not too concerned about the often frightening trials and errors involved in bringing up an only child. Velma Currie had been a psychological consultant before marriage and knew all about group identification. She assured Faye that Todd already was very adept at role-taking, but though markedly individualistic, had a tendency to disappear into the group. The Currie morning was therapy for Faye as well as Todd.

"I don't want to play with Roger Currie," Todd said. "Why can't I stay here with Netcher and let Daddy in if he comes?"

"If he comes, he can let himself in," Faye answered, realizing she was mixing a batter that might have to be baked later. The *ifs* would be remembered, would increase and multiply.

Somehow she got herself and Todd dressed and ready to leave without further rehashing of the conversation Todd had heard between herself and Anson the day before. She left a folded note for Anson on the front hall table, where he couldn't fail to see it. "Todd's at the group," it read. "I'll be back after six. Please don't you be here." Let him find an empty house, get whatever clothes he might need, again leave. Authority established for the day, Todd followed her out to the garage and climbed into the station wagon, sitting silently and obediently during the short drive to the Curries'.

Velma Currie gave Faye the smile of a diehard Freudian who knows more than she's telling. "Anson still away?" she asked, after Todd had joined the group in the house.

"Still away." Faye's neighborhood release on Anson was that he was in London on company business; it was not a whole lie, he had been, for one week of his absence, abroad on the Steen deal.

"London, wasn't it?" Velma was fishing with her past tense.

"Oh, he's back from there," Faye had to admit, "but he's staying in town for a few days."

"Oh," Velma said.

Faye backed the station wagon down the drive with relief. The wagon bumped along over the winding roads leading to the Interstate Highway. She knew the route to her mother's without having to think about it, so she could think of something else: *Anson.* She knew she was wavering in her insistence on being left alone; that was why she had been so determined to get out of the house. Being alone with herself now brought the whole bitterness of the quarrel back to her. If it hadn't been for Jeannette, or David's being in Hollywood the last week in April; if she hadn't decided to wash those jeans. . . .

Jeannette had telephoned from New York to ask if she and Anson would take pity and let her drive out for Sunday lunch. Anson had taken the call. She had been without David all week, she said, and was feeling lonely. As was often the case on weekends, Faye and Anson hadn't been doing anything.

58

"Unless you've got a houseful," Jeannette had said.

"No, just us," Anson told her. "We're taking it easy; we won't fix up for you. Potluck and all the gimlets you want." Jeannette was a gimlet fancier, the vodka kind and the driest. "Come on up."

Jeannette drove up in her Continental, arriving at noon. Everything had been easy and informal, Faye in gardening slacks, Anson in old white Levi's and tennis shoes, Jeannette wearing one of those perfect country dresses only great couturiers can make. She had seemed very relaxed at first, handling the drinks Anson carefully mixed for her with her usual competence. It had been such a warm, lovely day that Faye had broken her rule of not drinking before lunch and had joined Anson in martinis. They had talked about the time they had spent together in France, about Grasse and the hill towns on the road to Draguignan, and had eaten lunch piggy-fashion around the fireplace. Anson had played the new Bernstein Mahler he had just bought, and it was during the music that they both noticed that Jeannette was—in her analytic vocabulary—overreacting, to the spring, David's absence, her postlunch vodkas over the rocks, everything. She was a woman full of tensions and often took tranquilizers; Faye suspected she was on them and committing the great tranquilizer sin—pouring straight alcohol on top of them. By a quarter to five it was evident she would be unable to drive herself back, and Faye asked her to stay overnight; the guest room was torn up for repainting, but they could make do.

"No, no, I can't," Jeannette insisted. "I've my hour with *Il Dottore* at eight in the morning." *Il Dottore* was her analyst.

"We'll set the alarm for six, I'll get you there," Anson offered.

"No, I must be fresh from my own bed. And with David getting in on the noon plane. I simply *must* get back."

There was nothing but for Anson to drive her to town in

the wagon; he was planning to take Monday off and wanted to be home to work in the garden. Faye helped by generously saying that she would take the Continental in Friday, when she went to the city and always drove back with Anson. After the decision was made, Faye saw them off, put Todd to bed, and settled down to read *Good Time Coming,* first copies of which had just come off the press. After a few pages she had fallen asleep, and when she woke she shivered as she looked at the clock—almost eleven. She put on a sweater and returned to the book. But she began to worry that Anson and Jeannette might have had trouble on the road, or an accident. She had been about to call Jeannette's number in town when she heard the wagon turn into the drive.

"Darling, I was worried. What took you so long?" she asked when Anson came in.

"We had a flat. Luckily, it happened not far from a phone. Don't worry, I got Precious Bane safely home."

"Was she loaded when you left!"

"Was she ever!"

"And you'd had a few."

"I drove all right," Anson assured her. He always did. "I'd have been home two hours ago if it hadn't been for the flat." He looked at his watch. "I'm ready to fold if you are."

"We're all closed up," Faye answered. She meant the multiple checks of putting a country house to bed: the kitchen Frigidaire stove, off-off-off, Netcher let out and in, doors locked and bolted. Usually Anson did the night check and she opened up in the morning, while he bathed and shaved and got under way, but tonight she had done it; it had helped her nervousness.

"Remind me to get the spare fixed," Anson said.

"I wondered—wasn't it in the wagon?"

"I evidently forgot to get it fixed last time. It's been in the garage since." He looked, as he had said, ready to fold and went straight to bed.

"You didn't even brush your teeth," she reminded him.

"They won't fall out by morning." He was already over the rim of sleep.

It had been in the morning she had found the white Levi's. Anson had overslept a little and had gone outside right after his coffee to talk to the nurseryman who came to spray the plantings twice a year. She was doing her regular Monday morning pickup of last laundry. He had worn the jeans the day before and she automatically included them. When she was about to drop them into the washer, she stopped and something that was not quite a shiver, that was half shiver and half flush, ran through her. She had always accepted Anson's never wearing T-shirts or shorts; it had been one of the first things she had learned about him and no longer even thought about. He dressed like any teenager half his age when he was at home—Levi's, one of his old Alexander Shields pull-overs, socks and sneakers. She had always understood his pride in his body, his dressing to display it to show he could; she had her own figure vanities and forgave his, conceding that he was well enough built to pull on a pair of pants, zip them up and forget it. She had always washed his clothes and never ceased marveling how clean he kept everything, from his office shirts, which he wore only once, to the sweat socks he put on when working in the garden. But now the jeans told her something she couldn't ignore and she slowly put them to one side, then returned them to his bedroom chair, where he had flung them last night, unwashed.

He had stayed in the garden with the nurseryman all morning, discussing mulches, lopping dead branches, and came back into the house shortly before it was time for lunch. He quite often stayed home Mondays, reading manuscripts and dictating letters during the afternoon, and she couldn't remember the Monday he hadn't made love to her during the time Todd was having his nap. This was a different Monday.

"The holly at the north corner isn't getting enough sun," he said when he came in. He had worked hard and was sweating. "Think I'll have a shower and a drink before lunch."

"Why don't you?" she asked.

He had the shower and was sitting on the sofa, near the bookshelves, already turning the pages of a manuscript, when she joined him.

"You'd better make me one too," she said.

He looked up, surprised, then rose and went to the tray and mixed the kind of light martini she liked. "What's up?" he asked as he handed her the drink, seeing her face.

"It's down," she answered. "Me."

His eyes turned back to the manuscript. "That was a workout with Jeannette yesterday. I guess it was for you, too, since you're having a drink. I'll be glad when David gets back."

"Will you?"

"That's what she's like when he's out of her sight." He flipped through the manuscript, put it down. "Her whole universe falls apart. You saw how much she drank."

"Yes. I also saw how much you had."

"It took five so I could stand it. I thought we rather went over that when I came home last night. I told you, I drove well."

"Yes, I know."

He looked at her the way he did when he remembered it was her time, with concern, tenderly. "Well, then. I always could hold it and drive, if I have to. I've never had a ticket, you know that."

"I know that, too."

"Is your drink cold enough?"

"Like your blood."

He got up and went to her. She shrugged away. "I'd rather you didn't touch me."

62

"I'm sorry." He knew she was sometimes edgy, but this was more than that. "What is this?"

"What do you think it is?"

"Oh, no! You couldn't mean old Jeannette!"

"She *is* looking old," Faye said with relish. "A good forty-five if a day, though she insists it's thirty-nine." For a brief moment she wondered if she was wrong. "Anson," she said then, "I *can't* say this—"

"*What?*"

"Well, I do know you, all about you—"

"Don't flatter yourself. No one knows all about anyone."

"Not all, no. But you can't be married to someone and not know certain things about him. Little things."

"How little?"

"Well, how you—*invariably*—fold your necktie into the collar of your shirt *before* you put it on—"

"But that's not it."

"And never wear underclothes like other men—"

"How would you know what other men wear?"

"Well, it just happens I can see the Curries' laundry line from the kitchen. Other men *do* wear underclothes. Sam Currie does."

"Sam's blubber. He has to wear something to hold in that pot. And we're not going to discuss why I don't wear shorts and T-shirts. I'm warm-blooded, for one thing."

"He said, discussing it."

"Faye, break down. Tell me."

"Go upstairs and look at them. I didn't wash them. I put them right back where I found them, on the chair by your bed."

He frowned, uncomprehending.

"The jeans, Levi's, you wore yesterday."

Anson picked up his empty glass and made himself another. "I still don't get it," he said.

"You will when you look at them."

"Look, Faye—" he began.

"*Look!* That was my suggestion."

He got up and went into the bedroom. For several minutes she heard nothing, then the squeak of his tennis shoes on the floor as he returned.

"You're the new Modesty Blaise from outer space."

"I was right—unless you've taken up certain habits I don't think you have."

"Like what habits?"

"I'll have another." He took her glass. "What we're supposed to expect Toddy to begin doing, if he hasn't already begun, according to Velma Currie."

He waited until he'd made them another. Then he said, "No, I'm not giving myself hand jobs." He wasn't. The first night they ever got drunk together, he'd told her how he'd work out in the gym and take an ice-cold shower afterward, how he'd almost never given in.

"Only Jeannette jobs."

"Faye, darling—listen. Yes, I jumped her. She was in a terrible state, loaded, as you know, and when we were on the road she went all to pieces. No man on earth could have refused her, the way she was carrying on."

"Her oldest ploy. Lovely Jeannette, the unslept-with wonder."

"She's not so bad, whatever she is, forty-something. And it wasn't anything but what it was, orgasm, plain and simple."

"You made love to me yesterday morning."

"Well, I didn't make love to her."

"Merely jumped her."

"I've already made the distinction. I was surprised I had it in me, after our time, and working afterward in the garden. And the drinks and her going to pieces like that. She was in one of her fugue states, she said."

"But you had it in you. What in hell's a fugue state?"

"I didn't know," Anson said, "so I asked her. It seems to be what she goes into when reality's too much for her."

64

"So you went into her."

"My God, Faye, when a woman hangs herself around your neck and begs for it, what can you do?"

"I could say No, and often have. I can get along without albatrosses."

"Forgive me."

"I've forgiven before. It seems to make no difference. You go on, jumping, as you say, every woman who wants to get into your pants. *Jeans!"*

"Wait a minute," Anson answered angrily. "I'm not that old god with a seven-pronged prick. I've only got one, and you know it's for you."

"And Jeannette! God knows who else. There've been others, I know it."

"Not many. I can count them on the fingers of one hand. Well, one hand and one finger of the other. Jeannette was the sixth."

"And last, as far as I'm concerned."

"You forgave me the others. Why can't you understand about her?"

"Because I can't forgive her. I know her so well. I'd have to go on being wives and girls together, pretending I didn't know. And talk to David, wondering if he knew. Anson, it's not always easy being with David. Keeping your husband's biggest lion at bay."

"Has David ever put the make on you?"

Faye laughed. "You must be blind. Yes, I've been tapped —sampled, you might say."

"That son of a bitch!"

"David's our yearly K and K bonus, don't forget. Don't worry, there's never been more than being sampled. But he has wanted me."

"I don't forget. If he got as potted as I was last night, I might understand his laying hands on you."

"And that big, strong tongue. But David doesn't fool me."

"How do you mean, he doesn't fool you?"

"He has what Velma would call repressed hatred and denial of dependence on his mother. He denies his narcissistic defeat. Isn't that what's wrong with Jeannette? Partly at least."

"How would you know all that?"

"I can tell. Who's read every word he's ever written? I have. He acts out in his books a fantasy version of his mother and himself in his childhood. He *has* had writer's block, you know."

"You and Velma! Mesdames Freud and Adler."

"David's a little like Sainte-Beuve—his life's in his work. He's a pathological voyeur, as Sainte-Beuve was. You see, you can't forgive *me* even pretending with David that he's a Rubirosa. But you expect me to forget you and Jeannette. And wash pecker tracks from your jeans to boot!"

"Throw the damned things away!"

"They're your favorite outer skin. I know why you wear them, just as I know you dress right instead of left. And that it makes you walk a certain way."

"I don't walk in any *way!*"

"Every man has his own walk."

"Well, if you're so crazy about my walk—"

"And I am, I am," she led him on.

"—let's knock one off this afternoon, as usual."

She set her glass down, waited. "Prime situation for *you*—quarrel, more drinks, sandwiches, bed. Not for me, Anson."

"We've done it before."

"We won't today."

He lifted his shoulders and dropped them. "Okay."

"Though you did shower and wash her off you."

"Can't we stop this?"

"You started it."

"Yes. And it was nothing. It ended when it ended."

"Except for me, Anson."

"Have it your own way." He got up. "How about let's eat, then?"

"I don't feel like lunch."

"We could go out. Ask Velma to keep Todd until we get back."

"She's away today."

"Well, martinis have calories. I'm going to have another. How about you?"

"What can I lose?"

He made them killers. "Faye, I love you," he pleaded. "No, I won't touch you again. I love you, you know that. You're a big girl. You know a cock has only so much conscience. This isn't dear, old turn of the century, not even the age after some war. It's all war now, and I love you."

"I love you, too. That's what this is all about, no matter what age we're in. I love you, but I hate you."

"So hate me!"

"I wish you'd go, go stay at the apartment. I think I want to be by myself for a while."

"But you need me. In this house of glass—what if there should be trouble and you needed help?"

"I'd get it somehow."

"I'd worry myself sick."

"I'll bet!"

"Come on," he said. "I'll make us the sandwiches. We'll eat and tomorrow we'll forget this."

"You'll forget."

"Faye, I'm about to begin putting the Steen package together—it's going to be open hell this week, with David back from the coast—and I simply can't go through this."

"I said, go stay at the apartment."

"If it's going to be like this, I fucking well will!"

"And fuck."

"You overestimate my capacities. And interest. I've only one prong, I told you."

"I daresay you'll use it, and well."

"A compliment?"

"But not on me, Anson." She sat very still, staring at the floor. "Something about this time threw me."

"Don't tell me again why. I'll have David in my hair for the next month."

"Maybe Jeannette, too."

"One Steen's all I can take at a time. No, now David's back, she'll settle into the deal. She always does."

"Go. Go to your Steen deal. But don't come back here."

"I live here!"

"You've stayed at the apartment before."

"When you were with me. Or when you were having Todd. I don't like it there by myself."

"Don't be by yourself, then. Go on the town. Raise hell! Plug up your old Steen bag!"

"This isn't like you."

"It's exactly like me. This time it's done something to me and I want to be by myself. I want you to go."

"Now?"

"Why not? Then you'll not be here in the morning. I won't have to decide whether or not to wash your swinging, caked old jeans!"

She had cried bitterly, and nothing he had said or tried to do had made her feel differently. "Go," she had kept saying, "just *go!*" He had packed an overnight bag, slammed out the door, and taken the Porsche.

That had been it, except for a few severing links. He evidently had taken the hated white Levi's with him, for they had disappeared from the chair; Jeannette had sent a driver to pick up her Continental, perhaps betraying an unconscious fear that Faye guessed what had happened: odd, in view of Faye's offer to drive it to town. And Faye had discovered that Anson hadn't lied to her about having had the flat. The spare tire for the wagon was in the garage, as he had said, deflated from an earlier puncture. She had it repaired at once, realizing that there was something symbolic about her hurry to have it done, but of what it was symbolic she didn't know. Perhaps of time, of time's forgetting, and forgetting time. . . . Time and memory had telescoped her onto the familiar, remote, high-crowned road, left over from the days before turnpikes, that led to her mother's house. There it was, the Georgian double cube of her childhood, with many smaller cubes within it, as relentlessly unchanged interiorly as her mother's mind was unchanged. Faye drew up and parked beneath the portico.

🌼 🌼 🌼 JEANNETTE AND David had packed themselves, critics, TV interviewer, and photographer into their bright orange Lamborghini. David was superstitiously fond of orange, considering it to be lucky for him, his color. They had not taken the highway back uptown; David liked driving through cities and traffic did not bother him. They hadn't gone to La Grenouille after all because Jeannette worried about parking on 52nd Street and feared that their Lamborghini, which was new, would get banged or scratched. David never worried. He drove in an abstract way, with the trust in other drivers born of long years of freeways and autobahns. If some car tailgated him, or the driver of a car parked beside him opened a door and threatened the bright paint, he simply behaved as though it wouldn't happen. It was amazing how often it didn't; his optimism was an operational factor in everything he did. When Jeannette remembered what the Italian car had cost, even in Turin, where David had had it custom-built, her anxieties had gotten the upper hand. So they had gone to the Plaza instead, where the Lamborghini could be double-parked in full view of the doormen and they could keep watchful eyes on it. Besides, she got tired of not reading menus in French restaurants and then breaking down and reading them and losing her will power and eating rich food that would spoil her figure. She would have been content to eat broiled Dover sole or *filet mignon bouquetière* and a salad day in and day out. But not David; he had a passion for fine food and indulged it, though sparingly, and usually limited himself to wine.

The dinner had begun a little anticlimactically after the excitement of the boat party, but after fresh drinks had been ordered it soon became merry. Like many disturbed people, Jeannette either drank or drank not at all; tonight she drank nothing because she wanted to be at her best, and was. David had sewed up the TV interviewer with no trouble at all. The two critics, though not top drawer and careful to promise nothing, probably would allot *Good Time* space and attention. Only the photographer gave trouble. At the topless club they went on to afterward, he insisted on photographing the girls; the manager had asked for his camera, and when it was returned, the film had been removed.

It was after three when they all said goodby and David drove the short distance from the club to their small penthouse on East 73rd Street and turned over the keys of the Lamborghini to the doorman. Jeannette walked ahead into the elevator and they were silent until they were inside the apartment.

"Well, that's that," she said then. After the tensions of the long day and evening she felt genuine relief at being alone with David. Their moment of relaxation and pleasure, savoring the tying of the package with a seven-figure bow, had taken place before they left for the ship. "I don't know how you do it. I'm dead." Her eyes drooped with fatigue.

David showed little sign of the wear and tear of the day;

already she could detect in his expression that air of preoccupation she knew so well: he had achieved more than either had believed possible and was beginning to set his sights on further goals. He slipped her Balenciaga cape from her shoulders and they went through the living room, turning out lights David's secretary had left on for them, into the bedroom. He gathered up a sheaf of messages from the telephone table as he went.

"I listened as you sat and answered all those perfectly stupid questions," Jeannette said. "I felt sorry for you."

"Did you? You should be used to the eunuchs of literature by now." It was his favorite name for critics and reviewers, something he'd heard Hemingway once said.

"Asking how you worked."

"Well, they always ask that. I gave them the usual; they always seem to buy it. 'My own private shorthand nobody else can read, tape, then three separate and slowly improving versions on papers of different colors. Pink to blue to white. *Et voilà!*' "

"You know you never work that way, or use tape."

"Course not. But never tell them the truth. They hate that."

"And that impertinence about did you or did you not have a certain film actress in mind for the character of Julie."

David said nothing to this and began to undress. He hadn't minded any of it, even when the older and more important of the two critics had suggested that, with his fabulous storytelling abilities, he should next time do something really marvelous. Then he said, "I wish Anson had been with us, it was his baby as well as mine."

Jeannette waited. A chilling, familiar sickness filled her, for to remember Anson was also to remember herself a month ago, when David had been away. She listened for an overtone that would betray David's knowing about the Sunday, now a cold month dead; but she heard none, only his words; he knew nothing. "You know how Anson is, he doesn't believe in buttering up critics."

"I don't like them without butter myself." He returned from the bath after brushing his teeth. "I noticed you were hitting it off with the photographer."

"Well, young flesh. You know. I saw you gobbling it up, too, at the club."

The younger of the critics had been a poet, and Jeannette had expertly taken him off David's hands along with the photographer. Photographers always went for her. But she had followed all threads of conversations, as was her habit. "He wants to photograph me for *Bazaar*," she said.

"Well, why not?"

"That's what I thought, why not. But I don't know why we had to see all those girls naked to the waist." She found topless waitresses, who invariably talked about their husbands and children if asked, disturbing, and was puzzled as to why so many wives tolerated them. "I can do almost as well myself, and no pasties." Standing in front of her dressing-table mirror, she unbuttoned her silver sheath and slipped it down to her hips. One of her rings caught in the fabric and she stopped. "Damn!"

David went behind her and extricated the thread of fabric, then unhooked her brassière and lifted it from her. They smiled at each other in the mirror. Jeannette's breasts stood out above the silver folds of fabric like those of a Cretan snake goddess and her black hair and luminous dark eyes, elaborately made up, confirmed the resemblance. The concave, dark ovals that were her nipples rose to his touch. Despite her many problems, she had a dynamic femininity, which never failed to make him aware of his dependence on her. She had always been his catalyst, the substance facilitating his creativity, changing him but remaining herself unchanged. He was prepared to make humble love to this hieratic priestess of his success, concede to her, as always, the power over all his decisions, pay whatever tribute she might demand. Her magnificent breasts would be erect and firm long after he would have wilted.

"Nettie," he said softly, calling her by the name he used only when they were alone, "let's make love, celebrate. I feel like it, don't you?"

She was silent but seemed, in the bright light of the mirror, to tense. She turned, taking him by his sleek black hair, and drew his face to hers, kissing him lightly and making a face. "Duvidl," she said, "my Duvidl." Then she drew away and, with a quick movement, as though protecting herself, reached for her nightgown and held it before her. They continued to look into the mirror, but he saw from her eyes that the moment had passed.

"It's terribly late," she said, "or early. I have to face *Il Dottore* at eight."

"But you don't go to him Saturdays."

"This week I do. I've been having a hard time, David, whether you know it or not. *Dottore* thinks I need an extra day. You have no idea how terrified I am sometimes." Her eyes beseeched him.

He sighed, remembering how often *Il Dottore* had stood between them. He had almost stopped asking what her terrors were; whatever they were, they were another side of her night he could not evaluate. At moments like this he resented her analyst, hated him, as only the unmet and unknown can be hated, thinking how much *Il Dottore* must know about him, while he had no knowledge of those fifty-minute sessions, was left holding the empty bag of speculation. But tonight he asked.

"What are you terrified of?"

"I'm no longer young flesh, David. It's all going. I'm a running-down clock."

"So is everyone."

"Do you think that changes anything?"

"I don't think much about it."

"You do. I saw the way you looked at those bunnies."

"Abstract appreciation. I much prefer you. You looked at them too."

"There's not much else to look at when they're around."

She fell silent. It was to her silences he listened, when they came. He often suspected she provoked these discussions as a way of reaching another that would be more meaningful for her, grist for her session with *Il Dottore*.

He went to his bedside table and read the messages his secretary had left. All could wait. Then he picked up a writing block and pencil, jotting down a reminder to himself of the hour he would tape the interview with the TV reviewer, and made a note of a *graffito* he had seen during the evening—WHERE ARE YOU LEE HARVEY OSWALD WHEN YOUR COUNTRY HAS NEED OF YOU? He thought a moment, then added the legend on the lapel button worn by one of the bearded flower people at the party.

He made notes of everything; anywhere he was there were bits of paper. He collated and filed many of the *graffiti* he came upon, scrawled on walls or sidewalks, anywhere, cherishing them for the protest they represented against finely screened, news-skewed America. Since the sexual revolution there were fewer obscenities; anonymous political wits were now having their day. These scratchings, these ana, aside from their interest as uncensored opinion and protest commentary, had more than once furnished him with clues for his writing, even a ready-made title. *Good Time Coming* originated in a *graffito* chalked across a headstone in an English churchyard; he had been surprised, when having decided to use it and his secretary made the usual checks, to discover that it was, also, part of the first line of a poem by Charles Mackay. Thread passing neatly through a two-eyed needle.

"Darling, what on earth are you writing at his hour?" Jeannette asked as he got into his bed.

74

He told her about the Oswald *graffito*. "Would you like to hear what was written beneath it?"

"No. Go to sleep. You need your sleep and I need mine." She wound the little blue enamel Fabergé clock he had given her at Christmas, setting it for seven.

"My God, you use *every*thing!" she said. "I wouldn't be surprised if someday you'll use me."

"It's an idea."

Presently the sounds of the pencil stopped. Jeannette fell asleep doing her exercise of delivering to her unconscious the day just passed, so she would be ready to begin her hour with *Il Dottore*.

❦ ❦ ❦ VERA WILLIAMS, Faye Parris' mother, was one of the rich Greenwich Democrats. When JFK was in the White House, she had fantasied herself a kind of papal princess, safely settled on a great manor, not far from the Curia. *The Assassination* had been the severest trauma of her life, more harrowing, even, than the loss of her husband in the Battle of the Coral Sea. She regarded JFK as a sacrificial figure, whose murder had the divine purpose of bringing America to its senses, Oswald as the end product of the American process of corruption. In the years since, her trauma had become somewhat sentimentalized, and the adoration she had had for Kennedy transferred to his widow. Jacqueline, or Jackie, as she fondly called her, was her obsession and delight; she followed television and press coverage about her with frantic zeal.

Vera Williams had never remarried. Now she was a diehard, as once she had been a married maiden. People who sometimes got lost on the maze of roads leading to her house felt that they had blundered onto some small, perfect local shrine on a day when it was closed to the public, often remarking that they had not known there still were houses kept up like that, even in Greenwich. The lawns were like English lawns, the flowers so well tended they looked as though they had been grown in a greenhouse and set out in pots, and they had been. A perfect curve led to and from the large Corinthian doorway, perfectly balanced between two finely proportioned wings. Vera was lucky; she had protective property on all sides. The lost drivers, if they got as far as the chain across the driveway, quickly backed and drove away. Vera found these visitors irritating, her view being that if they *had* to get off the Interstate Highway, they could at least stay on Putnam Avenue and not wear out private roads and gawk at private houses. Had they caught a glimpse of Vera, they would have been disappointed. She was small and plain, wore suits of neutral tints, tweed in cold seasons, cotton in hot, and a freshly ironed silk blouse. She was a firm believer in a little touch of white next to the face, a stitch in time, never touching principal (she called it prin), and hot water in the morning until you do. Trespassers, of course, never saw her, and when friends did, it was as she wished them to see her. Adelaide, her seventy-four-year-old Irish housekeeper, answered the door and showed them into the thirty-foot-square living room, where Vera would be sitting in one corner of a Chippendale sofa, beneath Savely Sorine's pencil portrait of her as a young girl. She had about her the neat, pat air of a woman who keeps occupied in a world of women. Even Faye rang when she came to visit.

"That you, Faye-dearest?" Vera called.

"I'm a little early." Faye conducted her usual affectionate exchange with Adelaide, who had been her nurse as a child, then met her mother halfway in the living room. They kissed, Vera carefully holding herself so that her hair should not be disarranged.

76

"I hope you don't drive fast in that horrible traffic."

"No, I'm early because I came as soon as I'd taken Toddy to his group."

"Oh. I was hoping you'd bring him."

"I wanted to come alone today, Mother."

"Well, all right, dearest. Would you like a sherry? Lunch will be a while. We're running late today, what with getting ready to leave and everything."

"No, dear, nothing. I see you're already packed," Faye answered. She had seen the two large Vuitton trunks, without which her mother never traveled, with their red-white-and-blue French Line tags, standing in the hall.

"Traveling these days!" Vera returned to her accustomed seat on the sofa and Faye sat at the other end. "If you sail, and with those dock strikes happening all the time, it's best to send luggage well ahead."

"If you'd fly there'd be nothing to it."

"Why should I fly? I've all the time in the world. Besides, Adelaide regards planes as instruments of the Devil."

Faye had never known her mother to vary her yearly departure for Europe by more than a few days, and those days were conditioned by the French Line's schedules. She and Adelaide sailed on the *France* in late May and returned the week after Labor Day. Adelaide disembarked at Southampton and went on to Ireland, to County Wicklow, to visit her people; Vera followed an unvarying itinerary—London for a month of the season, Paris for July, Rome and Venice in August, then the Simplon back to Paris, and directly to the *France* for the return from Le Havre, with Adelaide rejoining her at Southampton. The arrangement suited both: it enabled Vera to visit her favorite churches and shrines, and it bound Adelaide gratefully to her for life. Though the two women had lived under the same roof since Faye's childhood and were close, mistress and maid relationship was carefully observed.

The opening conversation took into account Adelaide's lingering in the hall to open one of the trunks and put something into it. "You look well, Mother," Faye said.

"I'm always well," Vera brushed this aside. "Catherine was here last week." Catherine, a remote, elderly cousin, often spent Friday to Monday. They had watched a new TV talk show—Vera couldn't remember its name but liked the MC—and played a little game.

"How can you do both?" Faye asked.

"Catherine and I have bets. I give her a quarter for every-one that comes on who's not Jewish. And Catherine pays me the same for everyone that's not colored."

"Mother, really!"

"It passes the time."

"How are you doing?" Faye asked ironically.

"Neither of us very well, I'm afraid. Everybody's either a Jew or a Negro these days, it seems."

"What do you pay each other if it's Sammy Davis? He's both Jewish and colored."

Vera looked confused. Then she said, "We hadn't thought of that. Catherine says it's all part of a conspiracy. Jews touch their noses—some secret sign about Israel—and the coloreds always sing some song that has hidden meanings about a black uprising. She says the networks *have* to have them."

"Show business has always been Jewish, Mother."

"I meant the coloreds. Oh, I know there are black saints. Father Callahan told me."

"Saint Mary of Egypt was black."

"Was she? If I thought about it, I imagined she was just dark, from being so long in the desert."

Faye remembered discussing Saint Mary of Egypt with Madame Doheny, the principal of the Sacred Heart convent school she had attended, until she decided her faith had deserted her. Her lapsing had left her without the inner torment Madame Doheny had assumed.

"Well, just the same," Vera said.

"Just the same what?"

"Just the same."

It was no use, Faye knew. She was used to the Greenwich anti-Jewish virus; once it had been confined to keeping out the Baruchs, but now had multiplied into many strains. Adelaide, evidently, had enjoyed the conversation; she relocked the trunk and went out giggling.

"Anson still in the city?" Vera asked when Adelaide had gone.

"Yes. He was in London for the time I told you about, but he's back."

"There's no point in being evasive with me, Faye-dearest. You said enough on the phone for me to know something's very wrong. Not that I mightn't have guessed anyway."

"How could you have guessed?"

"Anson." Most of Vera's references to her son-in-law were, like this one, brief; she always had disliked him and reacted with relish to any unevenness in Faye's marriage, of which she had strongly disapproved to begin with.

Faye lighted a cigarette, then, too late, as she returned her lighter to her purse, remembered. "Mother, I'm sorry. I'll put it out."

"Why don't we go out to the terrace? It's such fine weather, and we're going to have lunch there." Vera stood up; she had a thing about anyone smoking in the house because the smell got into the upholstery. "You're not looking yourself," she continued, as they walked outside. They resumed places at opposite ends of a glider. "You haven't—"

"No, Mother, I haven't missed my period."

"Then what is it? Of course, if you don't want to talk about it—"

"I do, but I don't know how to begin. Anson's been away a month. I haven't seen him."

"But why?"

"We had a quarrel. A terrible one."

79

"You've always quarreled."

"This was worse than any. I can't get over it."

"The usual?"

"The usual, yes. And me. The way I feel about it."

"You mean the other woman."

"And everything else."

"Do you know who it is?"

"Jeannette Steen."

"The wife of the man who writes those horrible books?"

"They're not horrible, Mother. You don't read—"

Vera closed her eyes. "I read one of *his,* or tried to. Why, it was worse than *Peyton Place!*" Vera's house contained only two books, spectacularly bound copies of *The Foxhound of the Twentieth Century* and *Stag Hunting on Exmoor,* displayed on a table behind the Chippendale sofa. She had read *Peyton Place* years before, knowing well it was on the Index, and it was her single criterion for judging fiction. "Is this Steen like his books?"

"David's sweet and Jeannette's very nice. I'm fond of both of them. That's what makes it so hard."

"Well, I saw the first time I met Anson how it would be. His background."

"Mother, don't get off on background again."

"Background tells every time, like blood, and the older people get the more it tells."

Faye laughed. "Like our background, Mother? You know grandfather was lace-curtain Irish. Now we're white-brocade Irish, though you like to pretend it's English."

"I've never pretended anything."

"You never go to Ireland. Adelaide goes, but you go to London."

"Yes, and Paris and Rome—"

"Places."

"I go to see friends first, places second. Don't let's get off, as you say. If you'd married a man of our faith, things would have been different."

"It's no longer my faith, Mother."

Her mother again closed her eyes. The subject always came up, often led to others Faye wanted not to discuss: her refusal to have Todd baptized, her practice of birth control, Anson's family.

"Daddy was of the faith," Faye said, "and I know there were times when he was no different from Anson."

"You were not quite four when your father died."

"But I wasn't four when the Navy returned his effects, after the war, and you found those letters."

Vera looked away. "Your father did have his ways, like Anson. I didn't know at the time it was going on, or I wouldn't have put up with it. After talking it over with Father Callahan I forgave it."

"Post facto. I've often wondered if you'd have forgiven Daddy if you'd really loved him."

"Faye," Vera said, bridling, "my feelings for your father were sacred, and that was long ago."

"I wish what *I* feel was long ago, over," Faye said miserably. "If only I didn't love him so!"

"You've been through this before."

"I know, I sometimes wonder if I'm to blame. He always says it hasn't anything to do with the way he feels about me."

"Men always say that."

"And, from his viewpoint, maybe it's true. He doesn't love Jeannette. He couldn't. She's very unstable; she's been in deep analysis for years, and I know she's as much in love with David as I am with Anson."

"But Anson wants you to go on as though nothing happened, is that it?"

"More or less. This time I blew up. I told him to go."

"And he went."

"I told you, he's staying at the apartment."

"And seeing this Jeannette there?"

"He insists not. He telephoned yesterday to say he's coming out today. He's probably there now. That's why I came over, because I can't stand to go through it again."

"I thought you'd come to say goodby. I am going to be gone three months, you know."

"I did. That too. But it was a little wanting to get away from the house."

"You sound as if you'd made up your mind."

"If only I could!"

"Faye-dearest, you don't suppose it could be—I mean to say, I know husbands often want their wives to do things—"

"Mother, I know what you're trying to say. Do I refuse to do what he wants in bed. No. People in love do anything they please in bed—"

"But don't talk about it!"

"Anson and I talk about it."

"Don't talk about it to me!"

"The thing is, Anson does love me. I feel it. He says it. I know it's true. I do sometimes sense that there's something he *has* to have that I don't know how to give to him. Not entirely physical."

"Some kind of intellectual thing? You know, how Frenchmen keep mistresses because they understand them better than their wives? And the wives have lovers because they have to have the love their husbands no longer give them?"

"I understand Anson. And it's nothing intellectual. We're fairly well matched that way. Sometimes I think he's two people, not one. Of course, his work puts lots of women in his way; maybe he simply can't say No."

Vera sighed. "I suppose it's no use asking, but I do wish you'd go and have a talk with Father Callahan."

"What could he do? He knows nothing about sex and marriage."

"Don't say that. Father has helped me through some terrible times. The time when you lost your faith and wouldn't go back to the school. I still pray for you, so does Father."

"Prayer never worked for me. And people don't go to priests any more, at least I don't. If they go anywhere, it's to doctors or to analysts."

"Yes, and look at them! That Jeannette! If she had faith, she wouldn't have to go to an analyst."

"Jeannette and David are apostates."

"Terrible word. Really, dearest, Father Callahan might tell you something about yourself and Anson you don't know. You see, when you lose your faith—" She broke off. "And when I think of Toddy. I can't *bear* to think of his not having been baptized! It's like the time you were in the hospital having him and we despaired of your life and I sat by you, praying for an act of contrition, and none came!"

"It never will come, Mother. Let's get off this. It hasn't anything to do with my faith or lack of it. Nobody else can help the way I feel, not you, not Father Callahan—only Anson."

"Well, take him back or don't take him back," Vera said irritably. "Decide. It's not as though you'd been married in the Church—"

"You're saying again I'm not married. Look at me! Do I look married or not?"

"You're not wedded in the sight of God. Perhaps it's as well. Maybe it's time to get a separation."

"I am separated, that's the trouble."

"I mean a legal separation."

"Can't you see that's no solution?"

"Faye-dearest, it's an idea—it might lead to a solution. Everything's on your side. You'd get custody of Todd. And support."

"But I wouldn't have Anson."

"You don't have him now. You want him, you can't stand anything, you can't decide."

"I know. Oh, everything was so wonderful in the beginning!"

"Nothing stays the same. You should have learned that."

"I don't want a separation. This past month is what it would be like. I'd be like you, rattling around in an empty house. I wouldn't even have an Adelaide."

"I happen to think I have a lovely life."

"With other women."

"Women can be better company than men at times. At least you don't have to wonder where some man is spending the evening when he's supposed to be working overtime."

"You sound as though you know about that."

Vera pressed Faye's hand. "All women know about that, sooner or later. Well. Adelaide."

Adelaide had come out of the house to lay the table for lunch. Vera got up. "Come," she said, "I want to show you what Wilbur has done with the box *allée*." They walked along the terrace, past the small greenhouse, to a path leading to the sundial and the pool. "You remember these," she said, indicating rows of boxwood that had been freshly transplanted on either side of the path. "Never plant box close together; before you realize it, they're crowding each other and have to be moved, like these."

"I know. Anson's always moving ours."

"Anson again."

"Yes." Faye stood looking at the pool and sundial. "Mother, have you any idea what's happening out there?"

"Out where, Faye-dearest?"

"Beyond here, this house. All this safety."

"Well, I watch the news on television, all of it. In fact, I was saying to Catherine, I think we look at it entirely too much."

"And do you remember what you said about it?"

Vera frowned. "Oh. That little game Catherine and I play?"

"Yes. How can you say such things?"

"It was a joke."

"That's what makes it so horrible."

84

"A joke about the way things are. I consider myself lucky. I still have the best of the last century in this one."

"But Mother, it was the worst time in history!"

"Isn't that a matter of opinion? You *are* upset."

Faye stood, looking at the lawns, the road beyond.

"Well," Vera said lightly, "as for the world out there, I intend to stay in my world as long as I can. Until they drop that thing. Catherine says it's not going to be the Russians at all but those horrible Chinese."

Faye again saw it was no use. They returned to the shelter of the terrace and Adelaide announced lunch. Despite being about to be closed for the summer, the household was running with its customary smoothness. The blue Rockingham plates were hot and Adelaide set them down on snowy linen mats that matched the napkins. She handed the soufflé, encased in a napkin folded into points. The field salad was served from a chilled crystal bowl.

"Mm, wonderful, Adelaide," Faye complimented, tasting the soufflé. "Dry, the way I like it."

"I should know the way you like it by now," Adelaide said.

"Dr. Adams says I'm only supposed to eat three eggs a week," said Vera. "I always save them for soufflé Saturday."

"I'm afraid I've spoiled your day, Mother."

"I've been thinking, Faye-dearest. Why couldn't you come with Adelaide and me to Europe? You could think things over. Let Anson stew in his own juice. I have my usual suite on the boat, and with another bed put in there'd be room for Todd, too. He can play in the ship's nursery and you'd have a real rest. Is your passport in order?"

"Yes, I got a new one when Anson and I visited the Steens. But if I went, nothing would be changed when I got back."

"Seriously. We could settle down for a month or two in Menton. I remember you always loved Menton."

"I'd have to come back to Anson just the same. No,

Mother, it's wonderful and generous of you to offer, but it wouldn't solve anything."

"Never say I didn't try."

"You always tried, Mother." Suddenly, Faye wanted to be away. It wasn't anything her mother had said, but now she wanted to get home. It was only midafternoon. If she drove even slowly she could be there in time to see Anson. "I've got to be on my way," she said as soon as they had finished their coffee. "Mother, you were a darling to put up with me."

"I *am* your mother."

They embraced. "Have a good voyage," Faye said. "And write."

"I'll do both," Vera assured her. "One always has a good voyage on the *France,* and I answer letters the day I receive them."

"*Au revoir.*"

"*Au revoir,* Faye-dearest. I'll pray things will be better."

Faye could not repress a twinge of envy as she drove away. She could never be like her mother, nor had she ever wanted to be; almost half her life had been a running away so she would not be like her. But today she was jealous of the safe, closed, mollusk world she had just left, as she was impatient of its viruses and limitations; stupid and rich as it was, it worked better than her own, which she and Anson tried to keep virus-free. Even before she reached Velma Currie's, she sensed something had happened, and when Velma met her at the door she was sure. Todd was standing beside Velma, tearful and flushed, and Faye saw at once that he was not wearing the clothes in which she had brought him but a shirt and pair of shorts much too big for him, obviously hastily pressed into service.

"But what has happened?" Faye demanded to know.

"There was a—an accident," Velma Currie said. "I think, Faye, it will be best if we don't discuss it in front of him."

Faye nodded and took Todd's hand and let him out to the wagon, making sure that he was well settled into the seat and

86

the door firmly closed. As she walked around the back of the car, Velma met her.

"What on earth has happened to that child?" Velma asked.

"But that's what I asked you." Faye stared at her, comprehending that not only did Velma know about Anson, but also that she was relating it directly to whatever Todd had done. "You must tell me."

"We'll talk later about it," Velma said, and went into the house.

The note Faye had left for Anson was still folded on the table; he had not been there. It was all she could do to cope with Todd, try to get him to eat his supper and get him into bed.

🌷　🌷　🌷　A SILVERY ringing jangled through Anson's sleep. The hundreds of springs that were his rest-softened body tautened and he reached for the telephone as he sat up.

"I have a call from London for Mr. Anson Parris. Is that Mr. Parris?"

"Speaking."

"It's Mr. Colin Vaughan calling. One moment."

The susurrus of afternoon London washed across the conduit and was presently pierced by Vaughan's voice. "Anson?"

"Hi, Colin, what's up?"

"Well you may ask. I've got Ethan Fleming here."

"Are you both on?" Anson asked.

"Fleming, here, Parris. I'm simply out of my skull about the new Birnham book. Still untitled, I take it?"

"We'll have a title this week."

"I'd like to buy film rights," Fleming said.

"But can you film it?"

"In black comedy, yes," Fleming assured him. "Unless rights for it are already sold."

"Offers only, so far," Anson said automatically. "Of course, Birnham wants script approval."

"No problem."

"Very well," Vaughan came in, "get Birnham into your office tomorrow afternoon and we'll have a round robin and settle. Okay?"

"Okay."

"You'll call us?"

"I'll call you."

London rang off and Anson fell back in the bed. *Tomorrow afternoon?* He took stock: it had now to be morning. The light fell limpid and existent in the well of brick and mortar onto which the bedroom gave. Beyond was a faraway kind of light, into which solitary risers got up and reassured themselves. Morning was easy, which day was the puzzle. It had been a long night and he could not find the day it should be.

He had never before been where he had been with the redhead—NEILE; the neon still glowed with magenta edges. Perhaps a racial memory, bones gone to dust that lived on in his bones. He studied the ceiling, brilliantly sky blue, with familiar cracking at one corner that could be the rivers of Brazil or the palm of his left—no, his right—hand. In the heightened, lingering overcolors he recognized that some fuller dimension had widened his senses, a diapason had clutched him into a wholly new world of sorrow and joy. In panic he felt himself, recognized himself, limp but *there,* breathed free. And got up.

As he made his coffee in the small kitchen, he imagined how he might be today if his conversation with Faye had ended differently, if he had, despite it, driven late to the

Ridge and gotten home. He did a cleanup job on the apartment any butler could envy, airing the rooms, depositing the paper sack into which he emptied the Mary-Janes in the hallway incinerator. One, Egyptianly fatter than the others, had been the bomber, he supposed. When dressed he examined himself: no wife could guess his interval, his eyes assured him. *I am Anson Warren Parris, and I am returning a distance in miles fully familiar to me, to my wife and to my marriage, which I shall restore to its former state. Moreover, I am in love with my wife and I shall live with her the life we had and will again have, which, despite its interruption, is the life I want.* This instruction given to himself, he locked up with care, and remembered to carry the suitcase with which he had left, believability for Todd. He found the Porsche, already hot with the day locked within it, and drove to his newsstand on Lexington, buying the day with its headlines. *Sunday:* he had slept, but his lost, lightless Saturday lived in him happily, an extension of his long night.

As he drove homeward, the London business and the business of Faye and home filed themselves. He would not alert Birnham until later in the day. And Faye . . . It struck him, like a retreating zephyr of the magenta wind, that a skein, arachnoid and delicate as a cat's cradle laced between fingers, had come into play between Neile, Birnham and himself. A deal as surprising as Vaughan's transatlantic call. At Stamford he stopped for two smaller deals, flowers for Faye (coals to Newcastle) and a child's gardening kit for Todd (matériel bought ahead for diluting the questioning he knew would come). He eased the Porsche into the drive under sun-warmed and rain-washed trees.

Netcher's yelps of recognition and the scratch of her paws against the panes announced his arrival. The sinking feeling that precedes reconciliations filled him; then, gifts and suitcase beneath his arms, he saw Todd's face and Faye, standing unsmiling, in the doorway. His eyes found hers, blue into darker blue. Their lips met, half in passion, half in the agony of being together again.

"Faye."

"Oh, Anson!"

"You knew I'd come back."

"I didn't know. Yesterday I didn't want you to. I went over to Mother's for the time I thought you'd be here. When I got back I missed you."

"Did you?"

"Did I!"

Reconciliation at least formally effected, they played it out for Todd. "Did you get the London call?"

"Yes."

"Who was it, on a Sunday?"

"I'll fill you in at lunch." With momentarily easy effort he accepted the pretense that Jeannette, the last month, Neile, could be wiped out. "There was no yesterday," he came back to it. "Shall we agree on that?"

She pressed her cheek to his in affirmation, the tears in her eyes absolving him. Todd peered, wide-eyed and waiting, knowing all, knowing nothing. Anson lifted him up and kissed him.

"You've been a good boy."

"No, Daddy, I've been bad!"

Faye could and would wait for the moment when moods would be established, but not Todd, though the gardening kit was diversionary. "I thought I'd do some work in the garden and limber up," Anson said, as a bridge. "I saw as I came in that the holly needs trimming out."

"Can I work in the garden too?" Todd crossed the bridge willingly, following Anson and the suitcase into the bedroom. Anson changed into work clothes and the questioning began.

"Where were you all this time, Daddy? Where did you go?"

"To London."

"Where is Lon-don."

"England. You remember. Across the sea."

Todd nodded, remembered, but was unsatisfied. "Didn't you go anywhere else?"

"Well, to a party."

"Who gave a party?"

"People you don't know." Easier.

It was easier in the garden, too, Todd following at first with his new little spade and bucket. Anson rhythmically increased the game of sending and fetching and by late noon-time Todd had lunched and was tired enough to be put to nap without protest.

Anson cleaned and put away the garden tools. He was having a reaction—the garden had not solved anything. Already he had remembered Neile's *Nothing to be done about it?* and his *Nothing whatever.* In half a weekend he had come to possess the heady magic of a night world, the burning-rope smell, the bomber summoning up a self he never knew, deadly nightshade that annihilated forgetting. He saw Faye waiting for him, without impatience, curled up on the semicircular sofa, reading the papers. Presently he must face her and the prospect brought him down. As they settled into pre-lunch drinks (desperately needed, as desperately unquestioned), he knew from long experience that only one of two things would paste them back together—either a post-mortem or bed. He dropped waiting ice cubes into the pitcher, poured gin, passed the Noilly ceremoniously over, stirred and handed.

"How was the party?" Faye asked.

"Banal. Did the trick. You were missed."

She let this go. "The million must have helped."

"It did. Kastner's rewarding me for sticking in my thumb and being What a Good Boy Am I."

"How?"

"A block of stock, I hope."

"Wonderful." He had always to remember that to Faye blocks of stock were commonplaces. "What was the London call?"

"Vaughan."

"I guessed that."

"And Fleming—the producer who made *Dimple*."

"Oh, yes."

"He wants to buy film rights to Galey's new one."

"Is it out? You haven't brought it home."

"Still in manuscript. Not for you anyway."

"What's it about?"

He told her.

She laughed and he was grateful. "But it's—I mean, boy-into-girl, yes; isn't girl-into-boy surgically impossible?"

"Nina's making a check, not that it matters; the book's wild, beyond way out. It might be best if that part's fantasy."

They sipped for a moment in silence. "How was Vera?" Anson asked.

"My God, Anson, you know how she is. Capitalism's third act. Sailing the end of the week. Full Vuitton, the down pillows, her own linen sheets, the works."

"Did she ask about me?"

"It was all about you—us. I couldn't help telling her. I've been so alone I had to tell somebody."

"And?"

"Well—" Faye set down her glass, lighted a cigarette, passed it to Anson, lighted another for herself. "Do you want the long or the short version?"

The cigarette tasted tasteless, bothered him. "Short."

"She thinks I should decide whether to stay with you or not."

"Not again!"

"You asked."

It was to be post-mortem, after all. "All right, I asked. What did you decide?"

"I'm here."

He moved over beside her, resting an arm on the sofa's back. "And I'm here. Let's kill the yesterday bits. I thought we'd agreed on that when I came in."

Unsmiling, Faye said, "Kill the you and me bit, if you like. But there's another you don't know about. When Todd was at the group yesterday there was, well, what Velma called an accident."

Anson's face clouded. "What kind of accident? Why didn't you tell me when I came in? Why didn't you phone me at the apartment?"

"One question at a time, but not in any particular order. We're supposed not to discuss it in front of Toddy—"

"Well, what *was* it?"

"I only know from what I got when I picked Todd up and a short phone talk with Velma, but it seems Todd went for one of the Draper girls—Kathy, she's just seven—and scratched her cheeks."

"But kid stuff."

"He drew blood. Wait, that's not all. When Velma entered the situation, Todd turned on her, screaming, and was very resistive—"

" 'Entered the situation!' That's very Velma. You mean to say she grabbed our darling and whacked him one?"

"Am I telling this or are you?"

"Sorry. Go ahead."

Faye punished him for his interruption with a silence and a delaying detail. "Velma doesn't ever touch a child, and you know we don't touch Todd either, unless there's a meaning, a reason for touching him."

Anson did not interrupt this time. He waited, frowning.

"What it all comes down to," Faye said, "—and I got some of this direct from Todd himself, after I got him home—was that he lost control of his bowels. There was a terrible mess afterward."

93

"Is that the story?"

"What I know of it."

"He's a little old to shit his britches, but kids do, sometimes, don't they?"

"Anson, don't call it that. Todd's toilet training was so terribly difficult, if you remember. Velma thinks it's—"

"Hostility, of course."

"Well? Todd, when Velma tried to take him into the bathroom to clean him up, fought every step of the way. Tooth *and* nail. She had the most terrible time getting him bathed and into fresh clothes. I didn't have too easy a time of it when I got home either."

"What happened then?"

"He cried. Not loudly, just sobs. He ate almost nothing and it took forever to get him to sleep. It's not that it happened—Velma thinks it might have been partly involuntary—but what it shows."

"About him, yes. Suburbia's Anna Freud must know all about that. Didn't she have her explanation ready?"

"She said children know if there's a situation of tension between parents, if they're *only* children, especially, and that what happened was Todd's anger and insecurity about us coming out. Translated. I called Rose Draper and apologized as nicely as I could. She was very understanding, very."

"Meaning Rose and Sherm Draper know about us too?"

"Well, this *is* the Ridge. It gets around fast. Rose could have been nasty about it. Todd did a real job of scratching on Kathy."

Anson sat silent, looking into his empty glass.

Faye got up. "I'll make us this round. I knew we were going to need a few to get through this."

"You sound as if you're going to slug me for the real denouement."

"No, that was all. Or just about."

"Tell me the rest."

94

Faye's hand was less steady than Anson's and she spilled a little of his drink as she handed it to him. "You asked why I didn't call you at the apartment to tell you. I did, and there was no answer."

"The party ran late, as I told you it would. And I was in and out."

"Mm-hm. How's Jeannette?"

"She seems all right again. I mean, no longer in that fugue state she talked about. I told her you know about that Sunday night."

"I'm glad she knows I know. The bitch! I hope you told David, too, or that she did."

"She wouldn't tell him."

"What if *I* did?"

"*What?*"

"I may."

"Why would you?"

"As a gas. The results might be interesting. I get a little tired of being out of things. Like the party, having to read about it in the papers. Have you seen the papers?"

"No."

Faye unfolded and folded the stack of newspapers until she found the page. It was a large spread, with Jeannette and David featured, but there were other photographs, one of Anson as he turned to leave the Steen group. "It's good of you," she said.

Anson studied his face, sober and intent; he had no memory of the picture being taken. In the background, beside the ice swans and caviar, was Neile. "Not bad."

Nothing to be done about it? Nothing whatever.

"Who's that?" Faye asked, pointing to Neile.

"Some redhead who's writing a book."

"A redhead."

"Birnham's girl."

"So it's girls now?"

"He brought her." It was truth, but dangerously close to his Saturday, which, he realized, could best be compressed into a lie. But he played with truth around the edges. "Jeannette and David wanted me to go on with them, but I begged off."

"What did you do yesterday?"

"Reread the Birnham." He realized the fiction of what he was saying but went on anyway. "Then I had a nap."

Faye was studying the picture of Neile. "She looks like something for Ivory Liquid on TV."

"All *right!*"

After this, both knew that the reconciliation was a conditioned one, and that bed, if there was to be bed, would not be now. After lunch, Anson's Saturday nap came true, no less refreshing for being a day late. Before their dinner, *à trois,* with Todd behaving perfectly, he did the checkbooks (the blue, Faye's, for household bills, and the yellow, their joint special account) and for the first time a sense of return and contentment crept over him. Faye felt this too, and after a short stint of TV, they called it a day.

The day had become night, with the earth singing outside the windows. Wordlessly, they turned to each other and made love. For Faye it was possession, utter and complete. For Anson it was an experience totally different from the night with Neile, that transcended, went beyond, the love he had for Faye and the sexual hunger he had felt for her the past month. In the beginning sounds of summer in the garden outside, he heard a chord, slightly dissonant, changed from the diapason of morning, as though Mahler had reached for a resolution and, after innumerable rising explorations, had found it in a long, slow breath of expiring gratitude. They slept.

🌷 🌷 🌷 FAYE INVARIABLY woke and got up first, except on Saturdays and Sundays, and this morning, as usual, Anson did not cut off the alarm but let it run through. Turning over, opening his eyes, he saw Faye already stretching and drawing on her robe, saw with a familiar, sharp happiness her cascade of bright black hair, her eyes blue and awake as though she had been up for hours. The heightening of colors, though fading, was still with him.

She sat across from him in the kitchen and their morning conversation resumed as though never interrupted.

"More coffee?"

"Mm. I think I'm running late."

"You're *just* all right," she assured him, checking with the clock. "I forgot to tell you, Velma and Sam would like us for dinner this Thursday."

"Uh. All right."

"I thought we could clear up whatever it is we should do about Todd."

"Let me think about that later." She was already losing him to the office; he was, intently, building his day, dovetailing it into segments of varying length.

"I'll tell them we'll come, then, and get a sitter. You'd better hurry now, only twelve minutes to make the station. Darling, if you have a minute during the day, please think about our spring party. We've got to give it soon, if we're going to."

"Let's discuss it tonight." He gulped the last of his second coffee, got up and kissed her a longer goodby than the twelve minutes permitted, and ran out the door to the Porsche, dragging on his coat.

The Ditten's Ridge station, a scaly and bedraggled Gothic-and-Richardsonian relic of the days of leisurely commuting, already was surrounded by the hundred-odd cars parked around it on weekdays; others, with wives who had driven husbands and had run inside to snatch a newspaper, were driving away. Anson drew up on the fringe and got out. The Ridge "Bug," a long, diesel-powered coach, was jammed with regulars for the brief, swaying ride to the main line. Anson had just time enough to fling a dime in the cigar box, grab his own *Times* and clamber aboard. People he knew from the Ridge and other small villages using the Ditten's connection greeted him with Monday-morning joviality; he quickly got it that he had been thought to be in London the entire time he was away. Presently, the Stanford–New York express achieved, he settled down in his usual seat, in a nonsmoker behind the restaurant car, and hid himself behind his newspaper.

He turned first to the book pages, seeing the scheduled half-page ad for *Good Time Coming* crowding to the left a review of a new biography of Isabella of Spain, which he could skip and did, reading instead, with satisfaction, a quarter-column coverage of the book's phenomenal seven-figure sale. After a cursory rundown of "New Books," he scanned, in quick order, the front-page news, the feature story beginning the second section, and the stock-market reports. But the numbers and fractions in small print told him more clearly than anything else that his mind was not doing what he wanted it to do this morning.

Nothing to be done about it?

Nothing whatever.

In a day or two, he hoped, he would be able to banish the transparent ghost of Neile Eythe, before she fitted herself into personal history, never to be dislodged. Or did he hope this? Had he meant the orders he had given himself before shutting up the apartment? He was sure of only one thing: that he had not yet manufactured the stamina even to face what had happened with her. He reminded himself that the reconciliation with Faye had been deep, and deeply needed. Reconciliations, the refusion of things broken, no matter how boiled in the milk of pretense so the cracks will be invisible, are like mended teacups and must be handled with care. Twice within a short, springtime month, he had gone off the deep end. The night with Jeannette in the wagon, crass and meaningless—and Neile. Neile was a story of another kind, possibly prophesying fresh denials of the thesis he had presented to himself almost daily since his marriage: that he was wholly capable of, and dedicated to, monogamy and the marriage bed. Having fought this repetitious battle, which had been firmly joined with contrary evidences after Todd's birth, he had tried to make clear distinction between himself faithful and wife-adoring, and himself wife-adoring but girl-prone, voyeuring every tock of buttocks, every bulge of breasts, every twink of ankles proffered. No one was more aware of the unreality—and unworkability—of his behavior code than he. But this made it no easier to distinguish between his protective love for Faye and Todd, and the fresh hunger, which had begun to gnaw at him Friday night, almost as desperate as a hunger for air. Not the air of his paced Ridge-to-New York, New York-to-Ridge life, but a heavier air, magenta-winded, that carried him to a cloud above himself, observing as though he were an automaton coldly and carefully checked by a computer. And that chord, that diapason. Try as he would to forget it, for all sane reasons reject it, he could not. He recognized it as clearly as a number on an unopened door in a corridor of doors: a blatant invitation to fly away and discover another part of himself. Rashly, he had already opened one door; it was that which had brought the chord, the dissonance. He yielded, at last, to a kind of stubborn acceptance of the fact that two people, who seemed to have nothing whatever in common, could be harnessed together by a chance encounter and be hung up, shackled.

The train was slowing for Grand Central. He saw Carl Kastner come out of the restaurant car and waved. Kastner returned his greeting, then looked away, guaranteeing both himself and Anson their inviolable commuter privacy. No surprise showed in his eyes, but by the time Anson reached the office—Kastner taking his usual taxi, Anson walking as was his habit—he could sense that a subtle exchange of private informations had taken place. Nina, whether or not this intramural intelligence had reached her, betrayed in her eyes her awareness that he had arrived from the country instead of the apartment.

"Good morning, Anson!"

"Morning, Nina."

"Summer suit."

"Fine weather. Remember to get out the list of the party Faye and I gave at the Ridge last year, will you?"

"Right away. How *is* Faye?"

"Blooming." Nina had a particular smile she gave when asking about Faye; he felt everyone who had known about the trouble at the Ridge was now prepared to be a Chinese monkey.

"When are you planning to have the party?"

"We're going to set it up tonight."

"You've seen the *Times?*"

"Yes."

"And the Birnham. Anson, they *can't* film that!"

"They think they can, which is the same thing."

"The Vaughan and Fleming confirming cables are on your desk."

Anson went into his office, hung up his coat and rolled up his sleeves. On his desk in neat piles were the morning correspondence, cables, a stack of new manuscripts with agents' covering letters, and, centermost, the pages of Birnham's book, to which had been clipped an interoffice memo from Claxon Kennerly, the firm's younger partner. Kennerly had read it over the weekend, evidently. "Disgusting!" his memo read. "But since Carl says we're going to do it, full speed ahead."

"David's secretary called to remind you that you're lunching with him at twelve-thirty, Oak Room," Nina said, following. "The Philadelphia Booksellers Association wants you to speak at a dinner June fourteenth. Joanna Summers wonders if we'll let her have a further advance so she can go to Denmark. She wants to come in and talk to you before she goes."

Anson listened, nodding, locking the day's puzzle into its design. His lunch with David would necessitate canceling his noon hour and a half at the health club. He told Nina to move his appointment up to four-thirty; he needed his regular Monday workout, the relaxation on a rubdown table afterward.

"Will you do the Booksellers?" Nina asked. "The fourteenth is a Friday."

"I never speak on Bastille Day, especially in Philadelphia."

"This would be *June* fourteenth."

"I guess I'm stuck with it. Whatever woke them up?"

"Even Philadelphia wakes up for seven figures. I'll call them back and say you accept with pleasure. What about Joanna Summers?"

"Put her off till the end of the week. Friday." Friday was the day he reserved for his lame ducks, of whom Joanna Summers was one. "I was unable to reach Birnham yesterday. Try him now, will you?"

"I knew you'd be wanting him. I've been trying. No answer."

"Keep on trying. Get him in here as soon after lunch as possible. Three."

Nina returned to her desk and Anson went through his mail, placing letters Nina would answer for him in one pile, those he would dictate himself in another. Turning his chair so his back was against the light, he collected the typewritten foolscap pages of Galey Birnham's book, shook them so the edges were level, and began to reread them.

He was a rapid reader but a careful one and made notes of stylistic points as he went along, realizing, as he always did, that first readings are never sufficiently detailed. The turning of pages evoked their author, as any book does. Anson liked Birnham in a friendly, editorial way, having coaxed him from a smaller publishing firm and sponsored him within the house, making sure that his books were well produced and launched with the publicity they deserved. Though the story was fantasy, Birnham was revealing himself, as he had in his previous books; but nothing that had gone before prepared for this one. Birnham was known to be either homosexual or ambisexual; the reports varied. And Anson had heard the stories about him, paying little attention because Birnham's behavior to him was always impeccable, almost square; he did not wear his heart on his sleeve. His neat but nondescript dark clothes made him seem a professor from some Midwestern college in New York on vacation; only his rather dated camp talk gave any clues. Anson had known from the time he was young that he made homosexuals' mouths water and would have recognized the usual overtures, but there had been none. He had put Birnham down as a pantheist with special tastes and let it go at that. Birnham worked out at the same health club he belonged to, and Anson had been surprised, on first meeting him there, to see that he had a hard, boxer's body, as lean and well cared for as his own. Whatever Birnham's vices, they had left no physical evidences; or perhaps he kept up his body the better to enjoy them. Who could say? In any case, he always observed the detached pruderies of shower room and gym. Anson had at once understood Birnham to be a writer to whom talk about uncompleted work would be disastrous, just as he knew that for David Steen discussion of work in progress was necessity.

Birnham's neatly mortised story was, like all good pornography, convincing without being believable, making full use of the audacious permissiveness of the sixties. Omniscience alternated with passages written in historical present; the characters moved against settings kaleidoscopically sketched and laconic as pop art. It was a nightmare world in which Birnham's own libidinous desires and neuroses ran riot, hilarious as well as disturbing, as satire should be. Popes disguised as hustlers cruised choirboys; not-yet-nubile daughters fellated their fathers between dressing dolls and making mud pies; unlikely people met cute and, without so much as a handshake, copulated and parted, to search for fresh, equally depersonalized partners. Birnham achieved his effects by having his personae pretend to tenets of Victorian innocence while performing the most taboo practices without preamble. Where once under-the-counter novels were fleshed out with descriptions of scenery, now lists of moralities and romanticisms were inserted as comic relief.

The central theme concerned the dilemma of Little Marka, a petite and beautiful lesbian. As a child Marka had been violated regularly by her father and older brother, who practiced on her all the vices of the purple Caesars. She enjoyed these experiences (indeed, her childhood had been one long series of tumbles and *partouze* in all possible combinations) but enough was enough. These adventures resulted in severe trauma—a longing for a penis of her very own—while totally destroying her desire for men and fixating her on women, not women who preferred other women, but women passionately fond of men. Little Marka is obsessed by the knowledge that she cannot truly conquer with-

103

out a complete male member with which to satisfy—and punish as she has been punished—the kind of woman she craves. An early chapter depicted her almost total recall of her incestuous experiences, another her fantasies of having a penis that would resemble her father's and brother's as closely as possible. Since it is imperative that her sexual health be no further impaired by this lack, she enters a famous Copenhagen clinic, where she undergoes an ovariotomy and a scrotal and penis graft. The longest chapter devoted itself to her difficulty in making a choice from the clinic's penis bank, richly stocked with all varieties discarded by men who have had themselves altered into women. After much indecision, she chooses the largest and most perfect (happily reminiscent of her brother's) and the graft is successfully effected. The plot hinged on Little Marka's contriving to withstand the necessary hormonal injections without growing a beard, and retaining female characteristics essential to lesbianly attracting unlesbian women, for only by violating normally directed women sadistically in a wholly masculine way can she take revenge and reach fulfillment. The switch came at the end when, wholly healed and ravishingly androgenic, Marka falls for a fabulously lovely woman who hates women even more than Marka hates men: the challenge long awaited. After incredible resistances, Marka captures the citadel (symbolically during the blackest of nights on the battlements of Elsinore), only to discover, with the coming of dawn, that her toothsome quarry herself (or himself) also has had the Copenhagen surgery, but the reverse kind, and is really boy-become-girl. In a tempestuous scene it is revealed that it was her (his) penis which Little Marka had, by instinct, chosen for herself. " 'S truth!" she cries ecstatically. "It's *Brother!*" Their many mutual memories deepen their love and all ends happily.

It was a short book and did not take long to get through. Despite its specific situations, impossible to take seriously, the story exuded an overall, androgynous sexuality, and while reading, Anson found himself skipping the blocks of connective material and substituting and imposing his own, quite different, fantasies. Neile Eythe's last words kept burning through his attention and he found himself wondering about her world, somewhat close, he was sure, to Birnham's. Had she not said she lived above him? Yes, she had; she had added something else, too, but he could not remember what it was. But how did she live, and had she thought about him as much as he had thought about her? Where had she gone after she left the apartment Saturday morning, and were the colors lingering for her as they were for him? Had she slept long? Had she . . . What *was* she, in her Mott Street loft, writing whatever it was? Yes, a novel. Was she hidden, like Birnham, behind hazes of speculation and an unlisted phone? From simple curiosity to finding out involved only putting down the manuscript and reaching for the telephone directory. She was listed, and Parris made a note on his pad of the unfamiliar downtown exchange and number with the unthinking automatism with which he added the exact address: a researched fact.

"Anson?" Nina's voice.

He turned, feeling guilty for having looked up the number and address, then tore it from the pad and stuffed it into a pocket. "Did you get through to Galey Birnham?"

"He's coming in at three. You're not going to make David and the Plaza if you don't go now."

Anson rolled down his sleeves and went for his coat.

🌷 🌷 🌷 "Buon giorno, *Dottore!*"

"Good morning," Dr. Cimino replied. Though Jeannette persisted in calling him *Dottore,* he never addressed her either by her first or last names, using only "you." He stood behind his desk and waited until she had settled herself on the low couch that faced away from him; like most Freudians, Dr. Cimino avoided eye contact during the analytic hour.

The couch had two foam mattresses, for extra comfort, and was covered with a brightly colored Chimayo blanket, a souvenir of one of his trips to Mexico. Dr. Cimino could tell at once, from the way Jeannette lay down, that she was tired, sometimes the best state, for then the dream material of night still lingered and could be recaptured before day whitened it out. It was typical of this phase of the treatment that Jeannette waited for Dr. Cimino to speak first.

Dr. Cimino, a swarthy Calabrese, sank into his Art Nouveau Thonet rocker, beyond which was a footstool on which to rest his legs if he chose. He suffered from a chronic ailment of psychoanalysts, low-back syndrome, and, sometimes, when his analysand was settled and could not see him, face forward (for faces tired him almost as much as his last three vertebrae), he quietly stood up and conducted the session on his feet, while doing his internal exercises to lengthen and strengthen his thorax.

Jeannette's assumption that he would begin mildly annoyed him, rather in the way her insistence on calling him *Dottore* annoyed him; he had explained to her, often, that the reason she did this was because she could not accept him for what he was, but had to pretend he was someone more "interesting" than a first generation Italian-American, but this had done no good. At the beginning, he had been enthralled by her; up to that time he had never had a patient so honest, so responsive, so insightful. But after the third year of her analysis, he had begun to like her less, and now, in the end of her sixth treatment year, interrupted only by his own vacations and Jeannette's absences abroad with her husband, he was simply bored by her. Moreover, he long since had ceased to be very interested in going on with her case, had wearied of her extended dreams and painful recall of a life long dead—which only confirmed the theory he had formulated about her after two months of listening: that she was not able to be helped beyond a certain point and could only be compensated. Now he often talked as much as she; the sessions had become a kind of breakfast for them both, as if they were old lovers no longer sleeping together but blowing reminiscence into fond times past. Dr. Cimino's fee was one of the stiffest in the business, and his morning hour of eight was prime, expensive time, for which David, who paid for the sessions with a weekly check—fully deductible, of course—had, over the years, developed resentment. This had transferred itself to Jeannette; she several times had told him she had figured up what her thousands of hours had cost and could have bought a Modigliani or all the Fabergé Easter eggs and gold-and-enamel cigarette cases she wanted with the money.

Particularly during the last month she had become resentful and repetitious. The resentment was all right, even healthy, perhaps; after all, Dr. Cimino existed to be abused and stormed at, but he was not prepared to listen to repetitive material—he could get that from his wife at home. He was supposed to prod and move the long saga of Jeannette's identity loss to its end, try to prevent her descent into her fugue states and help her crawl out of them.

"Begin," Dr. Cimino said.

"I had a dream. A terrible one."

"Tell it."

"Well . . . It was all so clear when I woke up, but now it's going. Even as I start to tell it. There were these elephants, and someone—I think it might have been me—"

"You are always the protagonist of your own dreams," Dr. Cimino reminded her.

"Yes. I was sitting in the howdah of one of the elephants —I think it's called a howdah, that canopy thing you sit in—but the howdah was really a large penis, a phallic object, anyway, about to ejaculate. But it wasn't like penises really are, because on the end of it was a kind of big opening surrounded by fur. That's all I remember. It goes away as I tell it."

"Yes," Dr. Cimino said. He made a brief note on his pad. "Let us come back to that another time. I see that you seem a little tired this morning."

"No, but last night was the party for David's new book."

"Ah. And how did you do with the drinking?"

"I took two of the blue pills you gave me and managed not to drink anything."

"Excellent, excellent."

"No, but we stayed up very late celebrating. The paper rights of the book were sold for a million, you know."

"A million," Dr. Cimino repeated, the burr of his voice soft with envy.

"Of course, that's only a figure. We get only our percentage of that, not the whole thing."

"You've told me about that percentage."

"And of course there are the taxes. *Taxes!*"

Dr. Cimino did not want to waste time on tax complaints. Once he had gone so far as to tell her that the best way was to pay up and shut up, as others did. But once or twice a week taxes cropped up and had to be put down by silence.

Jeannette felt she either got her money's worth or was cheated by the ratio of times she could elicit a suggestion from *Il Dottore*. But sometimes he would hear her out on a particularly disturbing dream or happening and then say nothing, as though she contained the interpretation or answer in herself. Which she understood was true, of course; *Dottore* was only a gentle guide through the undergrowth of her unconscious. His suggestions and comments, when they did come, seemed earned—ten-dollar lollipops (the hour costing what it did, his words being few as they were) for having been "good."

The office smelled of the coffee Dr. Cimino had drunk before she arrived. She sniffed it absently and stared at a large Jasper Johns painting which hung at the foot of the couch. *Il Dottore* could afford to invest in good contemporary painters, as she could afford to indulge her passion for Fabergé objects. The canvas, a bold bull's-eye target of circular colors, was intended to aid in recall, Dr. Cimino had explained when it appeared on the wall two years ago. There was a chip of paint missing from one of the corners. Since then, Jeannette had stared at it, often wishing she could paste the chip back on, if it could be found.

"I notice that you said the million was 'only a figure,'" said Dr. Cimino. "I wonder if you could be trying to say something else."

"About figures? I hate *my* figure, as you know."

"But you have constant compliments and assurances from people about it, you have told me that."

"*I* know it's not what it was. I think that's why I tend to watch beautiful people, you know, follow them with my eyes."

"Beautiful."

"Well, men can be beautiful. To me."

"Of course. There is nothing unusual about that."

"But I feel so guilty about it."

"Why?"

"No. No matter whom I see, I keep remembering that night—"

"One moment. You are still beginning affirmative sentences with 'No.' "

"No, I'm not."

"That is one of many instances."

"Yes, I see now. Well, I keep remembering that night a month ago."

"In the station wagon." Dr. Cimino leafed back in his notes. "At that time you said it meant nothing."

"Then I did. But now I keep coming back to it. Last night, David wanted to make love, and I couldn't. Or wouldn't."

"Did you begin?"

"No. He was standing behind me and looking at us both in the mirror, but all I could think of was that night. And Anson."

"Anson Parris. David's publisher." They had been over this time and again. "Possibly you need to explore it further."

"It's just that I can't forget it. Him. He's not like anyone else I ever had sex with."

"Oh?" Dr. Cimino's voice lifted in interest. "In what way was he different?"

"Something about the back of his head. The way his head fits into his shoulders." She sighed.

"Shall we recapitulate?"

"I've told you all there was."

"Except what you have not told me, which perhaps is why you speak of it again. I suggest you have more to tell me and want to."

Jeannette liked this best, when he challenged her. "What didn t I tell you about it?"

Silence greeted this; she knew better than that. "I suppose what you're going back to is that I didn't experience orgasm with Anson." Her voice wilted. "I very rarely do, you remember, even with David."

"Yes." The silence lengthened. "There is some question you are waiting for me to ask you," Dr. Cimino said with grave playfulness. "Am I not right?"

"I suppose I know. Yes, *he* did. Twice. Twice, I *think*."

"But one knows that."

"One I was sure of, the second not."

Dr. Cimino waited. Jeannette stared at the Jasper Johns bull's-eye, concentrating, then closed her eyes. "The first time I knew about because I sucked him off. The second he—we did it the usual way."

Surely now there would be a lollipop, but none was forthcoming; *Il Dottore* withheld everything but his silence. "I never get used to saying that."

"But you do it. You have done it with your husband."

"Doesn't everybody do that?"

"No. Many people have no oral wishes whatever."

"It happens rarely with David. He hates it. He says it makes him think of Algiers during the war. The whores always preferred that because it was supposed to excite the men and be quicker. The men liked it too because then they didn't have to worry about prophylaxis."

Dr. Cimino made a sound of impatience. "That is nonsense. One may contract diseases quite easily by the mouth. In fact, the mouth is far from being the cleanest orifice of the body." He stopped. "That is irrelevant here. I suggest that sometimes you prefer the oral way."

"Well, David had been away. I was terrified I might become pregnant. I'm not that old; I still could become pregnant."

"I am not questioning that." Jeannette could almost hear *Il Dottore's* mind ticking now, like a Hollerith tabulator sorting cards. "You are not pregnant, are you?"

"No, I'm sure now I'm not."

"So now it seems you have found yet another reason for not sleeping with your husband. Could it be that you do not wish to resume relations with him at all?"

"No. I love David. It's only that—I look different, to *myself*. I know I'm not so very changed, really; men still whistle at me in the street. Truck drivers, especially."

"Why do you mention them?"

"Oh, because. No, I mean. *You* know."

"No, I do *not* know. That's why I'm asking."

"If I'm wearing a new dress or coat, anything new, I can tell if it's good on me by whether or not I get whistled at."

"By truck drivers." He held her to it.

"They watch women more than other men."

"I doubt that. Maybe they only whistle more because sitting in the cabs of their trucks they are safe."

"Well, they whistle. When they do, I feel wonderful."

Dr. Cimino leafed back in his notebook. "I would like to go back a little, to Anson Parris. When did you decide to have relations with him?"

Jeannette opened her eyes and brought her attention back to the painting. "He's always been attractive to me."

"And you to him?"

"No, I don't think so."

"Then it was you who—you made the preliminary approaches?"

"I was drunk, drunker than I've ever been, I think. Those blue pills—"

"But I have expressly *warned* you not to drink when on that medication."

"I know, but I did. David had been in Hollywood—still was—"

"I know that."

"Well, when Anson and I were in the station wagon, my leg happened to touch his."

"Did you not do it intentionally?"

"I suppose yes. But—and this I haven't told you—what really excited me and made me know I would touch him was, well, the back of his head, as I have said."

"Go on."

"Then I touched him, you know, there. I mean—I mean I knew I would go through with it. He had an erection."

"But erections have nothing to do with the back of men's heads."

"Uh—no."

"Sorry I interrupted."

It took Jeannette a moment to regain her pace. "What I did was—well, he was driving and I unzipped his fly and did it to him while he was driving. It was very quick. He said it was a first for him."

"Mmmnh."

"But do you know what really excited *me?* That he didn't have anything on underneath. I've done it to David—not in a car—but David wears knitted shorts and it's—"

"It's what?"

"The whole blowing bit is so much trouble."

This time Dr. Cimino sighed. He waited. The hour was running through. He could see how excited Jeannette was, trembling, her voice showed great agitation. "I get the picture," he said, since she seemed badly to need reassurance that what she had told him had not shocked him.

"No, you *don't!*" she cried. "Why should I have been so excited by that, the nothing underneath?"

"Perhaps you are trying to tell yourself that underneath such relationships, such actions, there is nothing."

"But that's what I remember, what I felt on finding out he was wearing nothing, that it—his penis—was just *there,* that something might happen to it, his fly might come unzipped—" She stopped.

Full block. "Fetishism," Dr. Cimino said, pronouncing it as though the word was a caress. "Fetishism of the purest kind."

"If only you'd tell me what to do! I mean, this is almost the seventh year, and I'm still having the problems and troubles I came to you with. I try. Oh, how I try! I knock myself out to be a good wife to David, I stay with him on his deals, I give him courage and support when he needs it—and it's no good."

"You change the subject very suddenly," Dr. Cimino observed. "But all right. Does David lack courage?"

"Not really. I meant that sometimes he would close deals before it's time, if I didn't urge him to hold out. Like yesterday—he was ready to give in long before the million."

"All that money. What are you going to do with it? It, and what already you have told me is in the Swiss banks."

"David says one more book and off we'll go."

"To where?"

"Klosters—where the movie people live who've managed to get it out."

There would not be time to explore *get it out:* Dr. Cimino's small watch, which had a tiny striking mechanism, sounded; though the sound was almost inaudible, Jeannette heard it and got up from the couch. It had been quite a session, and before turning to *Il Dottore* she took her compact from her purse and dabbed at her face. Then she found the check for the week's hours and placed it, silently, on the desk.

Dr. Cimino made a point of not looking at the check. "You ask me to tell you what to do," he said. "To begin with, your fugue states are increasing in frequency. Secondly, you invariably do things during these states that you regret or are ashamed of. Before, it has been swimming instructors, golf professionals—no, you have not forgotten them, you only pretend to have forgotten. And, further, you invariably draw a red herring across the situation—like your pretending to fetishism today. You still imagine that your very much impaired ego structure is somehow connected with your husband, which it is not."

"But I did feel that about the nothing underneath."

"Very well. Yes. You will come Monday, as usual."

It always seemed strange to Jeannette that *Il Dottore's* making a mark in his book should make her feel so much better. He stood up and smiled and she smiled back. She took a last look at the bull's-eye and went out. For a few moments, going down in the elevator, she felt euphoric, marvelous; but by the time she reached the street all the old uselessness gripped her like a cramp.

"Taxi!" she called, and as one drew up, got in. At least there would be David waiting, sweet, ununderstanding but patient David. She cried all the way up Madison Avenue, she was so grateful for him, so appallingly ashamed of herself.

"Lady, are you all right?" the taxi driver asked.

"Yes, I'm all right." She noticed that he had thick wrists, on one of which he wore a curious bracelet that seemed to be made of strips of red flannel braided together. She could not help asking about it.

"Oh, it's just a thing," the taxi driver said. "Something my grandmother taught me to wear. She's Russian. It helps you to work out your devils."

"We all have them," Jeannette said, fascinated.

"Want it? Here, take it." The driver slipped the red bracelet from his wrist and handed it to her through the little window in the partition. "It'll bring you good luck."

"But what about you?" Jeannette asked, taking it.

"Oh, I'll get another one." He looked back at her, smiling. "You didn't have to give me the address. I know."

"Didn't I give it?"

"I've driven you before."

"Have you?"

"Three times. You always go from your house to the place where I picked you up. The fourth house from the stand, off Madison, is yours. Right?"

"Yes, that's right."

"You see, you don't need to tell me the other address, either. You look mighty sleepy in the mornings."

"Often I am."

"You're married to that big writer, What's-his-name."

"I see there are no secrets."

"In this town? None."

By the time she reached her house she felt far better than *Il Dottore* had made her feel. Because the taxi driver was so nice and had given her the bracelet, she gave him a five-dollar tip—just in case he should ever drive her again.

🌸 🌸 🌸 ANSON HURRIED up the steps of the Plaza. The revolving doors at once swept him into the lobby's faded Belle Époque atmosphere. The masses of fresh flowers, the ladies in the Palm Court, and the luggage piled near the elevators denied the almost weekly rumor that the hotel, like so many others, was about to be torn down.

David waited at his usual table, left hand on a telephone, his long cigarette holder in his right. The holder was as long as FDR's, and nobody else, not Michael Arlen, not Maugham, could have gotten away with it; but David got away with it, and it was known (as though it were a fact of importance) that he did not inhale, did not, actually, like cigarettes, that the holder served to keep people at a distance. He looked the successful man he was; there was an aura surrounding him not unlike that of a banker. Despite his big sales, most people who looked at him and knew who he was had never read a word he had written; but they had heard so much about him that they felt as though they had.

David lowered the phone to the floor. "I've just found out that the *Times* is reviewing *Good Time* this Saturday. The Saturday's bad enough, but they're doing it in 'End Papers.' "

"Well, better than nothing," Anson said. David's rootings

behind the journalistic arras often produced information in advance even of K and K's. "What's the lead review, did you find that out?"

"A first novel by someone called Shirley Jane Fenn."

"Last Saturday they had a first novel too."

"And today Isabella of Spain. She's so safe."

"What do you care? You don't read reviews anyway."

"No, I don't," David admitted, "but it makes me feel like that old Pennsylvania Quaker who writes about Israel—they do him in 'End Papers.' " He always pretended ignorance of the names of other novelists who did as well as he.

"Well, at least you liked the ad."

"Yes, I liked it, if only because it shoved Isabella onto her big Spanish ass. What'll you drink?"

"Nothing, I think," Anson said.

"You can't drink nothing. This is a celebration. I suggest a martini, it's the only thing that doesn't spoil the tongue for the wine. Château La Louvière, Léognan—they have two bottles on chill."

"All right," Anson told the hovering wine waiter. "Make mine dry as dust, and please very cold." He turned to David. "I talked with Sales this morning. 'End Papers' or not, you've nothing to worry about."

"I know, I checked too."

David Steen would never have been a great writer, but once he could have developed into a good one. At first it was the critics who stood between him and his public; now it was the public that stood between the critics and his work. The relatively few "name" personalities controlling the world of criticism required cultivation, and though David did his knitting, mended fences, cemented friendships, his heart was not in these rituals. He was by nature a solitary and shy man, and the question of reviews had become an interest in the space they occupied rather than what they said. Critics had made him into what he had never intended to be. They praised his first book and then he began to write what he thought the critics would like, only to discover they liked it no more. He had believed them when they said he was good, and when they decided he was rotten he had believed that too—once. Then he stopped reading anything written about him and wrote as he pleased. What he wrote now was sometimes good and other times not, but it was better than when he was believing what the critics said. Now the critics were after him tooth and nail for having found a formula within which he could write and—what irritated them most—sell, no matter what they said about him. Anson sometimes reflected that though the critics had ruined David Steen as a writer, they also had put The American Dream into Swiss banks.

"How's the family?" David asked.

"Both fine. Faye and I are getting ready to give our spring party. I hope you and Jeannette won't take off before we set the date."

"We're not leaving until the middle of June."

By this Anson guessed how long David gave *Good Time Coming* to hit the top of the best-seller list. David liked to savor the take-off, watch the book rise, and then let go of it forever. "I think Faye has in mind the second weekend in June. The eighth."

"Mm-hm."

The martinis arrived.

David slowly stroked his Guard's mustache. "Did you and Faye see anything of Jeannette while I was away?"

"She was out to the house for lunch the Sunday before you got back. Didn't she tell you?"

"No. How was she?"

"All right."

"I wondered, because I was paying the garage bill this morning and I noticed there'd been a pickup of the Continental at the Ridge."

"I drove her into town that night," Anson said, trying to get rid of it.

"Was she tired or what?"

"I think she was tired."

"Mm-hm. The drinks are getting cold."

Anson raised his glass. "We used to drink to seven figures, but I can't for the life of me think of what to drink to now. Except, don't ever leave us, David."

"I've no intention of leaving you," David said. "I'd only leave K and K if you went to another house."

"That's not likely to happen. Absent friends?"

"I never drink that one. 'My friend, I have no friends,' " David quoted. "I guess we'll have to drink to lust."

"Lust for money?"

"Plain, simple lust."

"Okay."

They drank.

"I know about the other offers you've had," Anson said then. "The bird kept me posted from day to day on Triana's heavy-handed efforts to pry you loose from us."

"They were seven-figure efforts, heavy-handed or not."

Anson had worried at the time about Triana's campaign to take David from him, but friendship had diluted his worry; in the end, it was friendships and trust that determined whether publishing agreements worked or failed. He had counted, also, on the fact that K and K's promotion and advertising were superior to Triana's.

"Would you like to know why I froze on Triana? I never had any intention of going with them, was just letting them talk themselves out. One always learns something, you know." David smiled. "That was long before we got the seven figures from Everest, of course, and they wanted to give me the seven figures for *both* the hard and soft."

"You see how right you were to refuse."

"I do. But this is how it went. There'd been a short story of mine in a collection Triana did years ago, long before I hit it big. It wasn't an important story, but I liked it. I was pleased to be in a collection with Mary McCarthy and Faulkner and H. E. Bates, though I was at the bottom."

" 'A Hot Line to Heaven.' Was that the story?"

"That was the one. Well, the collection went the way of all short-story collections, they remaindered it. But then, when they began to buy up reprint houses, somebody at Triana had the bright idea of reissuing the collection in soft covers. They dropped my story."

"Peanuts, David. Forget it."

"Peanuts, yes; but novelists are like elephants, they never forget. During my talks with Triana I asked them why they had cut the story. They replied that at the time I was not a very well-known author. It gave me the chill, that 'at the time.' I told them I'd never sign with them, if only because of that."

This detail of the Triana negotiations had been reported to Anson by the bird, but he had disbelieved it. Now he knew it was true. Authors' egos were fragile, and the wear and tear of life—of success, particularly—often destroyed them; authors were capable, too, of hanging on to the most trivial mistakes on the part of others in the past.

"Perhaps we should have another," David suggested, pleased with his story.

"I've a conference with Galey Birnham at three."

"In that case, another is mandatory." David signaled to the waiter. "I hope you're not in too much of a hurry because there's something I want to ask you about."

"Ask away."

"It's about Jeannette. I've been worried about her for a long time, but now I'm more than worried. I think she's about to have the change. None of the usual symptoms, headaches, hot flashes. With her it's all that Parke-Bernet life she leads, dragging home all that old Czarist rubbish. She thinks, too, that young boys are after her. It's all a total blank to me, and that *Dottore* of hers doesn't seem to be helping her any more."

"She believes in him, though," Anson said.

"I don't. I've always thought Freud and his obsessive quest for sexual symbols the really sick bit of our times. Nineteenth century, fusty as Freud's own office—have you ever seen pictures of that? God! Maybe that's why Jeannette buys all that Fabergé, to offset the medieval shabbiness and thinking."

"Faye and I urged her to stay overnight when she was with us, but she insisted she had an analytic hour and had to get back to town."

"You drove her. Why?"

"Frankly, David, it was the only thing to do, since she insisted on getting back."

"How drunk was she?"

"Five of her gimlets before lunch, several drinks after."

"And Freud only knows how many blue pills, not to mention pink ones. What did she do, pass out on you?"

"No. We had a flat going in, and that was a drag."

"But did she say or do anything unusual?"

"She was—herself," replied Anson carefully. "She'd told us she was in a fugue state."

"Which covers many things."

The pause following this was awkward, so Anson said, "I'd had a few drinks myself. I don't remember too well what we talked about. I got her back to your place all right."

The Château La Louvière and lunch arrived, and while the wine was uncorked and presented and the plates set down, Anson tried to evaluate David's questioning. He had the feeling of standing in the center of a wide net. David sniffed, tasted, nodded approval. The waiters left them.

"I never had any trouble with my first wife," David said. "I married Jeannette two years after Sarah died, you know. My boy was nine, then, I wanted him to have a mother."

"How is Jim?"

"At school in Gstaad. Making all the protests of seventeen. Hair. Ashamed of my vulgar success. Got a girl he's serious about. He's joining us in June at Cannes. But to come back to Jeannette. It was after I married her I really started to write, unblock, make it the way I wanted to. Up to then I was killing myself doing Sunday mag articles, the *Esquire* and *Post* bits. I've always wondered about that. My first wife was an ideal writer's help. She could type, take dictation, she saved money in an old sugar bowl—but I couldn't write books."

"What do you think it is about Jeannette?"

David considered. "Well, inspiration—so to call it—doesn't come directly from experience, what happens to you. I find it develops from stories told through another voice. Jeannette's my voice. Proust picking Montesquiou's brains, so to speak."

"Montesquiou was a birdbrain," Anson said.

"Yes. But what Proust took from him was wonderful." David looked across the room and for a moment said nothing. "Scott Fitzgerald and Zelda, too, I've often guessed. As a matter of fact, my next book is about a wife in deep analysis and what her analysis does to the husband. You see, I can only use material when it's gone from me, and Jeannette's gone."

Anson was silent.

"I can't help myself. It's the only way I can hold on to her—to use her. I know what she does sexually. I shouldn't be jealous, but I am. Aren't you jealous of Faye?"

"Yes."

"And I've tired of the marriage bed myself. Haven't you?"

"Well, yes."

"Often?"

"Number of times."

"Does Faye know?"

"She knows."

"And?"

"It's hell. Don't *you* know?"

"We're both ganders, and that old crap about what's sauce for one being sauce for the other is nonsense. I'm never more jealous of Jeannette than when I'm having it with someone else. But I can't bear for *her* to have it with someone else. You know, I'm a novelist and it's hard not to know. Novelists know things they don't even want to know."

"I don't know what to say," Anson said, which was true.

"You don't have to say anything to me. I know what my problem on the new book will be. I'll need a wife—in quotes—because of course, though the story is about a wife in analysis, I must draw from another woman. Jeannette's already mixed the palette."

"You mean someone else's wife."

"Isn't every woman someone else's wife?" David took a sip of his wine. "With certain exceptions. Young exceptions. I'll bet your redhead is not a wife."

"I thought I'd kept her out of your way," Anson said, remembering how he and Neile Eythe had waited for Jeannette and David to leave the party first.

"I have twenty-twenty vision. She's a friend of Birnham's?"

"You don't miss much, David, do you?"

"I have an inborn sense of observation. Are the stories I hear about Birnham true?"

"How would I know?"

"There's something Huysmans about him. *Là-Bas.*"

"He could do the both of us in singlehanded. He has a black belt."

"Karate?"

"Chop for you, rabbit punch for me, and that would be it."

"Birnham has bad hands," David said; "they don't seem to go with the rest of him."

"I've never noticed."

"What's his new one like?"

"Hairy as they come. I'd rather not spoil it for you by telling you about it. But I'll send you a fax if you'd like."

They went on talking, Anson uncomfortably conscious that he was himself a digest of what was in David's mind. The net was tugged lightly, then released. He did not underestimate David's precision of indirectness; it was a little like observing the detonating of a bomb through protective dark glass—and not hearing the thunder that should follow. The room was thinning out. Covertly, he looked at his watch—already ten minutes of three.

"I'm afraid I've got to go, David. It was a wonderful lunch."

"And rather instructive, I thought. I'm going to finish my coffee, if you don't mind."

"My best to Jeannette."

"And mine to Faye."

❦ ❦ ❦ MORE THAN ever when he was out in the street Anson felt he had walked into a net, though he had, for the moment, stepped out of it. The lunch had put him out of joint. He was not a wine man and felt heavy and full of food. The weather, which had been so bright and dry, was now turning humid. He was experiencing, too, that vague unease that follows on hearing the troubles of others. He felt like doing a fade; if it hadn't been for his promise to Colin Vaughan and Ethan Fleming to set up the round-robin telephone call with Birnham, he would have canceled the rest of the afternoon and taken the first train out to the Ridge.

He found Birnham waiting in his office, leafing through the readers' reports on his book, which Nina had placed on the desk that morning and he had forgotten to put into a drawer. As always, Birnham had brought his private world with him. It was strictly against K and K rules for writers to see these reports; most, if they even chanced to hear about what staff readers thought of what they had written, became upset.

Not Galey Birnham; he had no rules except those he made himself. "Hi, Anson," he said, waving one of the reports. "They really did hate it, didn't they?"

"You're not supposed to read things on people's desks."

"I always do. Do these reports mean you're not going to publish the book?"

"Of course not." Anson quickly scooped up the reports and put them into his desk. "We've scheduled it for November." He sat down in his desk chair, indicating that Galey should take the one opposite, pushing one of the phones toward him. The desk clock pointed to 3:22; it was now evening in London, and Vaughan and Fleming would be waiting.

"This will be cart before horse, Galey," Anson told him. "Later I want to talk to you about the book, but just now there's this." He handed him the confirming cables that had come that morning and, when Galey had read them, recapped the Sunday morning phone conversation.

"Sunday morning? They must be interested."

"They seem very interested."

Vaughan, with whom K and K had an arrangement, had placed Birnham's earlier books in England and he and Galey were friends, which made that easy; and that the producer of *Dimple*, the brightest of the new, young English film men, was interested in doing his book impressed him. One question was, since Birnham had never had a film sale, Did he want K and K to represent him, or did he want an agent brought in?

"I've no use for agents," Galey said. "The one I had when I was doing film treatments on the Coast only slowed the checks up five days, took ten per cent, and I did all the work."

"We'll handle negotiations, then, if this matures. I mentioned script approval to Fleming. There's the possibility he might want you to do the screenplay."

"I'd rather die than do another screenplay, and I don't care about script approval. The book's over, gone from me. Besides, I'm leaving for Maroc next month. I'll take their money and run."

"You may be wise," Anson said. "All right, they want a four-way conversation and they're waiting. I'll tell Nina to put the call through."

The call went through quickly and the four had a seven-minute conversation, of which two were devoted to pleasantries and one to the weather in London, which was chilly. What it came down to was that Fleming wanted to confer with Birnham. He was flying to New York later in the week. Would Birnham confer? Of course.

"Serious interest," said Anson when they had hung up. "Now, a further bit of advice. Try to put this from your mind. Keep eyes open and mouth shut."

"Will do. What about the book?"

Anson looked at the clock. It was minutes before his appointment at the health club. "I'm due at '53' at four-thirty. Why don't you come along? We can have a sauna and massage and talk about the book there."

"Tuesday's usually my day. All right. After my weekend, I could use a sauna."

"After mine, so can I," Anson said. "Let's go." He remembered in time to get from Nina the list of last year's party for Faye.

"53" was one of the smaller health clubs, only a few years old and in its way unique. Membership was limited and there was always a waiting list; those who joined were subject to investigation and had to be able to afford the membership fee, $625 a year; individually supervised exercise routines and massages were extra. The place had none of the usual gymnasium smells and was hygienically clean. Fowler, the owner and manager, made clear that he was not operating a fat factory but an informal club, where men could stay in shape and the pressures of the city could be kicked in an atmosphere of pleasant informality. Members signed in and signed out. Telephones were available, as were drinks and sandwiches, served at the small café-bar around the pool, carefully supervised by Mrs. Fowler, who had a flair for chic. It was always possible to find a quiet spot at "53."

There was no one in the sauna room and Anson and Galey were able to talk freely. They sat on opposite sides of the small cubicle. Galey had wound his towel around his head; Anson had spread his across his knees.

"You know, Anson," Galey said, "at the party Friday you were so mum about the book I thought you were getting ready to give me the old K and K one-two. Then you call me in, cold, and put me onto a movie sale. I don't get it. I saw those reports."

"Let's talk about those, since you read them. I won't pretend to you that there was any unanimity of opinion. The reports were so restrained they meant almost nothing, flabbergasted, straight-faced condensations, which always means the readers don't know what to say. Carl Kastner doesn't read books, but was shocked just by reading one of the reports. He took my word that the book is exceptional and that we should do it. That was before the London interest. Kennerly thought it disgusting. He did read it."

"And you? What do you think about it?"

"I have reservations about it, of course, but I think on the whole you've done a very funny and kicky job. You've fixed

Lawrence's 'dirty little secret' forever. It's all shock, no smirk. Straight pornography with a Voltairian twist."

"It's supposed to be Juvenalian. I patterned it after the sixteen *Satires*. Surely, you saw that."

"Any reading of Juvenal I did was long ago. I think we should settle on a title. You sent it in without one. Why?"

"I didn't know what to call it."

"It doesn't much matter what a book like this is called," Anson said. "But I thought *Little Marka.*"

"I thought of *Little Marka,* of course; but then I wondered if something out of Juvenal might be better."

"Don't spoil your chances. I doubt whether one reader in a thousand has heard of Juvenal. Keep it simple and specific, stress the girl aspect; that'll be safer and insure you a wider public."

"*Little Marka* is jake with me," agreed Galey. "What were your reservations?"

"Well . . ."

"It's not the worst book ever written."

"In a way it's too well written. But the sex will carry it. I reread it today. It's a 'jack-off' book—masturbatory fantasy. That's what it'll do for most readers, give them a hard on they'll want to do something about."

"That tells me I've succeeded. What about women who read it?"

"Women are odd when it comes to pornography," Anson said; "they resist it, though they don't mind reading about sex written from a woman's angle. It can be kinky if it has that angle, as witness the success of lesbian novels, most of which are bought and read by married women. If women read your *Little Marka,* they'll either laugh or be upset; they won't have a sexual reaction to it. The book has problems."

"Meaning you want changes? Christ, Anson, after *Last Exit to Brooklyn, The Soft Machine* and *The Ticket That Exploded* and *Numbers,* why should there be problems?"

"Little Marka is a far different book from any of those, far more dangerous. Even last year it couldn't have been published."

"I suppose not. But it has to be faced, Anson. All freedoms are go now."

" 'Freedom is the recognition of necessity.' "

"I don't get you."

"You may know your Juvenal, but not your Marx. All true necessities are dangerous—that's me, speaking as your publisher. The necessity of your book involves determining whether we can do it with or without cuts."

"But it's happened, Anson," Galey argued. "Now writers can say what they please. There've been all those other books; it's not as though I'm breaking ground."

"No, but you've dug awfully deep. I found myself getting stiff as I read it, and I can tell you Little Marka's not at all my cup, in any of her his-her guises. I've never had a homosexual experience and don't want one, but I got a hard on reading about Marka."

"Haven't you ever, Anson? Really?"

"No. Not in prep school or college. Not in the Army, either."

"I always thought asshole buddies made out."

"I never had an asshole buddy. I was behind the lines, NC, so maybe I wouldn't know. Besides, there were plenty of girls, nice ones. Galey, to put it bluntly, there's nothing like cunt."

"If you've never tried anything else, how would you know? But seriously. All sphincters have been exposed—politely, as I think the *Times* put it in a review of one of those books. Everybody knows about queerdom now, sixty-nine, blow jobs, dildos. David Steen's last book had a dildo in it."

"But a dildo *heterosexually* used," Anson qualified. "Steen's an innocent, really; he put it in thinking it would send his readers. It sent them—flying to their dictionaries, his readers being what they are. But when people read those other books, they feel they're reading about someone else, not themselves. Though you've used high camp, epistolary form, mixed tenses, *Little Marka* implies that everyone has these kicky desires, indulges in backasswards sex."

"People do, of course."

"Some do; others don't. They may have their fantasies, but not all act them out. You've been out to the Ridge, met the people Faye and I, for want of a better name for them, call 'The Assortment'—couples who live up and down our road whom we know well. All ages. Squares, cubes, oblongs, even a few trapezoids. They constitute a fairly representative longitudinal sampling of suburbanite husbands and wives. They screw, of course. Some husbands keep those Japanese books about positions near the bed. Me-Jane blows Tarzan, but they don't talk about it. Junior's got to be bubbled and changed, his formula heated. The wives worry about the pill giving them cancer, or getting pregnant, natural childbirth, having their tubes tied; the husbands sweat over taxes, the mortgage, insurance, retirement plans, and getting their jollies—in about that order. They're lucky to have it off a couple of times a week without interruption from the nursery. A good many of that group will buy and read *Marka,* of course."

"Why do you think they'll buy it?"

"Because almost all of them are curious about homosexuality, even though they may regard it as a disease or a sin. It fascinates them. America's hung up on diseases and sin. It's a puritan country still. That's why the dirty book is 'in,' so people can complain to one another how dirty it is and how shocked they were by it. Housewives really dig death and the female-tit kind of books, but they'll read yours too."

"*Death Valley of the Female Tits.*"

"They're half your public."

"And the other half?"

"Queers. You don't have to worry about them; they'll read anything dirty, even if it's about her-sex, especially if they can identify and somehow conceive of themselves in an active or passive male role. You've done a superb job of celebrating cock while camping up the vaginas, fake and otherwise. Still, it's 'Assortment' readers you've got to cut for."

"What do you want me to cut?"

"The chapter on hair. It's too much."

"There's nothing in it Juvenal wouldn't have written about. Do you know his 'Ninth Satire'? On homosexuality and what hard work it is? I quote: '. . . this job of cramming my cock up into your guts until I'm stopped by last night's supper.' That's exact. You're worried about *hair?*"

"Juvenal worked that one out with his publisher, I'm sure," said Anson. "Besides, he's a classic. What I mean about your chapter on hair is, you can write about chest hair, face hair, head hair, leg hair, underarm hair, but you cannot—I repeat, *cannot*—write about pubic hair. Not yet. It's the last bastion of comstockery, the last defiance against censorship."

"But pubic hair is exciting."

"Yes, but people avoid admitting it—in print. It's got to be funny and off-camera, like the pubic shave in movies. In visual reality it's dynamite—that's why strippers shave down to their G's, why you can buy pubic wigs in Yokohama. It's the last twentieth-century baddie. Pubic hair is more disturbing to people than sexual parts. Some women can't stand body hair at all. One of the wives in our 'Assortment' forced her husband to take wax baths before she would consummate their marriage. She's even nervous now if he rolls up his sleeves. I'm not demanding that you delete certain of your references to it, only suggesting that it might be safer."

"Do we still have censors? I'd like to think we don't."

"Readers are censors."

Galey's sweating face became stubborn. "I don't believe in playing it safe. I'd like to have you print the book as I wrote it."

Anson's policy was never to overstress a suggestion. "It's your name that will be on the book," he said.

"Of course. Author takes ultimate responsibility. Who would sue? Everybody's got pubic hair, whether they admit it or not."

"Well, then, that's it."

They sat for a time without speaking. Anson saw less well without his eyeglasses. He looked through the steam at Galey, his head turbaned with the towel, face and body streaming and lighted by the gleaming sauna fire; he seemed a figure out of a Pompeian fresco, an athlete resting after a decathlon. But his hands, as Steen had observed, did not seem to go with the rest of him; they were square and brutal, contrasting oddly with his almost classic torso and legs.

"How'd you make out with Neile?" Galey asked.

Anson wondered how much Birnham knew. Neile had told him about the leather-jacketed boy from the combo, with whom Galey had left the party; possibly she had said something about himself. "Why ask me?"

"Well, I gather you had it off together."

"Did she tell you that?"

"I guessed. She lives in the loft above me."

"I know," Anson said.

"It's an old house, the stairs are dark. The light was out on her landing when she came home. She did something she's never done before—knocked on my door. She was absolutely bombed."

Anson mopped his face, but said nothing.

"Neile and I have a deal—we phone, never drop in, just as

though we didn't live so close. Neile was way up there. I got it without her saying anything that she'd been up there with you."

"We made it," Anson admitted. "I hope that can be our secret."

Galey shrugged. "If it's a secret it's safe with me. Who would I tell it to—who would care?"

"How much did she say?"

"I told you, I got it without her saying anything, actually. A fix of grass. So what? Surprised me a little about you, though, Anson."

"Why should it?"

"Oh, because you're what you are. Establishment playing it safe. Wife, kid, that house. Grass didn't seem in the picture for you."

"It isn't."

"You don't dig pot?"

"Well, the other night I did."

"First time?"

"First time I had enough to know what it's like."

"How was it?"

"Incredible."

"The colors?"

"The colors, yes." Anson hesitated. He had recognized that a cat's cradle had been woven between the three of them, but could not help feeling uncomfortable about the turn the conversation was taking.

"Don't make bones with me, man," Galey said, laughing. "I know. It was the orgasm. That's why anybody lights up."

"Yes, it was the greatest," Anson admitted. "It seemed to go on for an hour. I'm still hung up on it. I can't forget it."

"Often it's like that the first time."

"What's it like the second?"

"I've had it be the same twice in a row," said Galey;

"other times it's all right, it's good, but you don't get there. And I've had it no good—worse than nothing—and then the next day it comes on like a delayed punch. Fast and easy and beautiful. And long."

"I guess I had it both ways," Anson said, thinking of last night with Faye. "The colors are beginning to go now."

"You sound as though you have the perfect sensitivity for it. You kept the colors all this time?"

"And the sound."

"I don't know about the sound." Galey was fascinated. "What kind of sound?"

Again Anson hesitated, this time because he was disappointed that there seemed no confirmation in Galey's experience of the deep, wide diapason that had flooded him. "Impossible to describe," he said.

"Lots of what goes on over on the other side is impossible to describe."

"By 'the other side' you mean what happens when you're under—whatever the drug is?"

"What seems to happen. It doesn't matter what the medical term for pot is. Nothing to remember. Its colloquial names are interesting. Mary-Jane, locoweed, grass, all are efforts to throw the name away, because for something to have no name is magical. The first time's the one you can't believe; subsequent ones you look forward to."

"It will be the first and last for me," Anson said.

"You're trying to tell yourself that."

"I mean it."

"*That* indicates conflict, that you're already having trouble making yourself believe it was the first and last time. You intend it. There's nothing new about any of this, Anson. All religious experiences, true ones, are associated with drugs of some kind. There's that tree in Judea people eat from to this day. I can see you have guilt about your long orgasm."

134

"Yes, I do."

"But why?"

"I wish I knew."

"Maybe because it was so long you were afraid it might be one of your last."

"Possibly."

"Why don't you kick it, your guilt? I had guilt once, but no more. Physiologically, the orgasm is not extended, the duration is an illusion. I learned that if you want to get over onto the other side, find the illusion, you take chances."

"I can't afford to take chances."

"For a good look at the other side? Haven't you ever wanted to reach, man? There's another world over there. It's worth taking chances. I've taken them. Once or twice it was paradise."

"What about the other times?"

"You've read Dante, seen those Doré illustrations. Nothing can convey what a crawl-down is like. Sometimes in paintings you see what others have been able to bring back after they'd hit the wrong track and wound up in what they called hell. There's one canvas in the Correr Museum in Venice that tells it. Bosch *must* have known. Nobody paints men on all fours with funnels in their assholes with birds flying out of them unless they've known. Temptation as comedy, or the other way around. But it's only a pinhole in the big scrim that hangs between where you and I are now and where you were the other night—and where I've contrived to be more than once."

Anson said nothing.

"And there are the other selves, the selves of yourself you meet."

"Well, now you've gone this far," said Anson, "level with me. I suspected two or three of the sections of *Little Marka* —not the pornographic ones—must have been written while you were under something."

"I know the ones. No, not while under. *Over*. But it's the grace of the gods if you bring anything back. Nothing works as a way of seizing or capturing anything, not tape, not friends to whom you talk or have had the experience with, who write it down. It comes afterward. Sometimes a residue seeps into the unconscious and comes forward of its own accord. Not in words. There are no words. It's another language, in the cells, the blood, the orgasm itself—if it can be deciphered. Then it's yours and you tell it or write it down. I did, a little."

"What if you go over and never get back?"

"You get back, believe me."

"Yes, I guess I'm back now. But some of what I remember I'd like to forget. There was this wind—not actually wind, more like a sea of jelly carrying me along—that became a box. I'll never forget that box. It'll terrify me to the end of my life."

"Everybody who takes the chances has truly private experiences, I think," Galey said. "Your wind, the jelly becoming a box, was yours. I've had terrifying ones, too, but not at all like yours. I can tell you, you'll forget it. What you experienced is probably only a hundredth of what you'd have experienced on peyote—mescal, mescaline, the small cactus of the Indians. The first time I took that was in the Southwest. I was with a motorcycle guy who held me down, took care of me, or God knows if I'd have come back, ever. That time I got into a dimension I've never recaptured, though I can remember it was the greatest. I've tried to bring back that trip, go back to that magical country, but I never got there again."

"You've tried?"

"Several times. It's something to do with light, at least it is with me. You know, you get curious when you think of Goethe's last words, *'Mehr Licht!'* Did he see more light, or was he seeing darkness and begging for light?"

"We'll never know that," Anson said. "There are other last words—'*Che cosa terribile!* A darker speculation.'"

"Whose words are those?"

"The painter Tchelitchew's."

"Yes. His *Phenomena's* the monstrous outside world, his *Hide-and-Seek* the membranous world within. I remember, he was engaged on a work to be called *Paradise* when he died. I've tried getting inside my own paradise. Once even with belladonna. Never touch that one."

"I don't intend to touch that or anything else."

"Don't be too sure. The redhead got under your skin, didn't she?"

"It was what it was."

"You got under hers, too," Galey said. "She's a nice kid. Don't hurt her."

"Are you reading me a lesson? *She* was the one who had the sticks."

"I know. She wants to go over like all the others. But you should have heard her when she was climbing down."

"You told me she said nothing."

"Nothing about you, but since I'd pieced together that you'd taken her somewhere, I knew you must have been with her on her flight, given her the big, flowering orgasm. That was what she talked about, this great flower thing, opening and closing and opening again. That was before the horrors hit her."

"What horrors?"

"Plain pot horrors. Watching her was almost as horrible for me as what she was saying going through them."

"Christ!"

"She was bombed, I told you. It hit her the wrong way coming down."

"What else did she say?" Anson insisted.

"Isn't it enough—about the great orgasm? The flower

137

orgasm you gave her? With that cock you really can deliver, evidently."

"Who cares? I was born with it."

"No, seriously, Anson, I like Neile."

"I liked her myself."

"What was it you liked?"

"Her youth. Knowing the minute I saw her we'd make it big. She knew too."

"She has few inhibitions."

"How do you know? She told me first thing that she didn't sleep with you."

"She doesn't, yet. Maybe one day we'll make it. There's one thing you so-called normal people seem never to think of. Though some of you are aware of your own occasional homosexual conflicts, it probably never occurs to you that homosexuals have their hetero conflicts too. I have mine. I don't fuck women at the moment. I like to be my own man. I can't stand being possessed; I have to do the possessing. My hangup is callow, straight butch boys. I've never pretended, Anson."

"But you've not said it."

"Does it disturb you?"

"Why should it?"

"You're secure enough so it wouldn't."

Anson looked at Galey quizzically. "Ever think of giving in to your hetero conflict, as you call it? Trying something different?"

"Why don't you give in to your homo one? Try something different yourself."

The door of the sauna room opened. It was Fowler, the manager, carrying two terry-cloth robes with "53" embroidered on their backs. "Are you boys trying to cook yourselves to death?" he asked, looking at his watch. "You'll just have time for a dip in the pool, and then the masseur will be

138

ready for you, Mr. Parris. I know you don't want to miss your train. Mr. Birnham, you'll be next."

Anson stood up and slipped into the robe Fowler held for him. He could feel Galey's bright, chiaroscuro eyes watching him, could feel them following him through the closed door, drilling through his robe as he walked down the corridor to the pool.

ii

❧   ❧   ❧

The Ridge

❧ ❧ ❧ "THE ASSORTMENT," the Parrises' private household term for the people they knew in the Ridge, had been coined by chance. During their first year there, they had been invited to a large Christmas party given by a youngish middle-aged couple, Martha and Stig Lavrorsen. The party, an annual Ridge tradition, was much talked about and everybody who was anybody was asked and went. The Lavrorsens, who lived in a fine old salt-box with a modern wing, did things well; drinks were the best and the collation afterward was beyond anything usually served at big parties in the area; Martha was an Eastern Shore girl and her board literally groaned with Smithfield hams, smoked turkeys, a glazed suckling pig, beaten biscuits with damson preserves, miraculously light spoon breads and other Southern delights. Faye had been in her eighth month of pregnancy and Anson had been for regretting the party, but Faye would not hear of it; though she had enjoyed excellent health in her first months, the later ones had been difficult, and her doctor had advised her to be careful. But it was a policy with her never to decline invitations unless there was serious illness or a family problem, an attitude she got from her mother.

The Parrises had had a fair time at the Lavrorsens', though they had not cared for many people they met there. It had reminded her, Faye said afterward, when they returned home, of the big holiday "do's" of her girlhood around Greenwich; she would have preferred a smaller party, with a few *tête-à-têtes* that could be remembered, instead of the rather stiff and formal crush it had been; the Parrises preferred, as Faye shortened it, *la tête*. Because of her pregnancy she had drunk nothing (though Anson had) and had eaten sparingly, even passing up the baked Alaska at the end, which she liked. When she got back to the house, a laggard, irrational hunger struck her in her sweet tooth. Her eye lighted on a box of chocolates beneath their Christmas tree, one of those samplers of fruit centers, opera creams and nougats someone at K and K had sent them. She opened the box, choosing a square of chocolate encased in waxed paper; but after biting into it, she returned it to the box and took another; that one, a nougat, was hard, also not to her taste.

"Why not throw them away after you've bitten into them, if you don't like them?" Anson, watching her biting and discarding, asked. Faye's gynecologist had been explicit about their avoiding any sexual excitement, since the baby was imminent, and he was resenting his enforced bachelorhood; he was a little tight from the Lavrorsen champagne, too.

"You don't have to eat all of what's in an assortment," Faye answered. "I may want to come back to those and eat them tomorrow."

"That was quite an assortment we were mixed up with tonight," Anson observed, minting the term. It was to stick.

"And thank God we'll not have to finish some of *them,*" Faye said. "What a bunch of squares—ninety-eight per cent, anyway."

"Squares, cubes, oblongs and a few trapezoids."

"I like Stig Lavrorsen." Faye licked her fingers. "Even if

144

he is square. He seems hipped on who people are, or were, asked me my maiden name. Said he knew lots of Williamses, but none from Greenwich. He has a nose for money."

"Why shouldn't he? He's a customers' man. And you don't look entirely poverty-stricken, you know." Though Faye had worn her black Kasha "fool them" maternity dress, bought for shopping trips to New York and nights at the theater, she had felt it looked plain and not enough. Before going, she had added her single-strand pearls—genuine—and the marquise diamond ring she had inherited from her Aunt Susan. They had helped, made her feel less ungainly in her black tent.

"I should have dressed up more, I guess," said Anson. He had gone in a dark gray tweed suit. Many of the other men had worn conventional dark blue, and a few of them—latecomers obviously going on afterward—had been in black tie.

"Yes, Stig Lavrorsen got the jools. He's *très* snob. He liked me better after I said Round Hill, too, even if I do look ready to drop a Mack truck. He knows all the officers at The Putnam Trust."

"You looked superb, you always do," Anson assured her, kissing her, then drawing back, because they were having trouble keeping out of the sack, no matter what the doctor said. "Did you meet those Drapers?"

"Both of them. She asked me to call her Rose. *Rose d'Ishpanhands*, I thought. No 'jasmines of Mosul' on her breath." Faye turned a sharp pun.

Anson laughed. "Shame. *'Les Roses d'Ispahan'*—Leconte de Lisle. *'Les baisers ont fui de ta lèvre si douce.'* But not bad."

" *'Tous les baisers,'* " she corrected him, often did. And was right.

"What does Draper do?"

145

"Nothing at the moment, I think. I've heard they're having a hard time of it. *They* have *seven*."

"Who wouldn't be hard up, with seven? Or limp. Wait until we're on our seventh."

"That, Anson Warren Parris, will be the day. It's going to be two for us and the vasectomy for you."

"And that, Mrs. Faye Williams Parris, will be a day that never dawns. I cherish my *vas deferens*."

"I may have hurt Rose Draper's feelings. She asked if we were members of The English-Speaking Union. Imagine! I wondered why she thought we would be. 'Well,' she answered, 'my husband—Sherm—and I find it a little constricting out here, culturally. We belong as a way of brahnching out.' "

"*I* had a character named Boyle? Doyle?"

"Doyle," Faye supplied; she never forgot names. "He's a failed writer, as you probably found out, and his wife's that tall horse who sells insurance."

Anson, cued, remembered. "Doyle, yes. He did get right on to his writing, so I asked what he wrote. When I said I was with K and K he came all over nervous and couldn't wait to tell me how he'd finished his first novel two years ago, and that just when he was putting it in final draft the barn where he wrote burned down."

"Notes and all, leaving only ashes. His wife told me the same story. Name's Alma."

"But wait," Anson said. "They come funnier than the Doyles."

"That'd have to be screamy. Maybe he's a barn burner."

"How about that Nowells pair?"

"I met them. He has some kind of rare gout. Not the rosy kind."

"She reads *Time, Life, Newsweek* and the *Reader's Digest*."

"Yes; she'd read in the *Digest* there was a new thing for

this kind of gout her husband has, supposed to get rid of ten times the uric acid whatever he's taking now gets rid of."

"Maybe he shouldn't drink."

"He doesn't, she says."

"I had an uncle who had gout. Every time he smelled a cork, his big toe blew up to the size of a football. He used a gout stool."

"Apparently Nowells can't eat, either. Food's his nemesis. No beans, meats, cheeses. He's fair as long as he sticks to carbohydrates and fats, but that runs up his cholesterol."

"Fascinating! How old did you think them?"

"She's fiftyish. He married his daughter, clearly."

It was a crystalline night, cold with Christmas and pine smells. The snowdrifts fluffed over the tall, pointed gables of the house, and there was a sixteen-foot icicle hanging outside the glass wall above the trick fireplace; it looked like a white jade chimney. Anson poked up the fire they had left to go to the party and they settled down on the sofa in front of it, continuing their evaluations.

"Well," Faye picked it up, "they were old, yes, but some there were younger than we are, so I think we should be kind. Did you meet the couple called Burgess?"

"Chester Burgess. He's a famous ear-and-throat man in New York. An F.A.C.P. Yes, I met him. His wife is named Grace."

"She used to be his office nurse."

"Who told you that?"

"Velma." Most of the early information Faye garnered about Ridge neighbors had come through Velma Currie. "Chet Burgess does the Curries' youngest boy's sinuses."

"I liked the Burgesses."

"I *just* met him, at the end. He said with my high cheekbones he could have a ball."

"Those cheekbones are mine, girl-wife with my child."

"Not the insides. If I needed him professionally. He probably meant I have a natural opening—for whatever it is they put up there when you have trouble with your sinuses. He said most people do."

"I don't want him around any of your openings."

She kissed him in gratitude for his jealousy. The fire popped and crackled. They went on comparing notes, sorting, eliminating.

"Lavrorsens, Drapers, Doyles, Nowellses, Burgesses."

"That was about it."

"There were those boys in the matching jersey suits," Faye said.

"I didn't see any boys."

"They saw you, dear. Closet queens, Velma says they are."

"You girls have quite a vocabulary between you. Do you mean those two hanging around those old thirties dikes? I thought they were somebody's older sons being nice to unattached women."

"Listen to Egeria, my sweet. Those men play it straight, but they're lethal." Faye filled him in as Velma had filled her. "They live with those women, on that big abandoned-kind-of-thing farm down in the valley. Rent a cottage from them. The women are called the Misses Taylor and Grumbacher; I don't know which is which yet."

"We don't buy them," Anson decided.

"The dikes, as you call them, do needlepoint and read."

"Natch. What would you call them?"

"Maiden ladies, *I* was always taught to call them. Anson, you can't be as sure about women deviates as you can be about male queers."

"They hide behind the skirt, I know. But men can tell the very minute they talk to a woman if she likes men. I couldn't sleep with either of those women even if we were on a desert island."

"Maybe you'd prefer the closet queens. They'd take you.

148

Both asked me if I was the wife of that good-looking, sandy-haired man in the dark tweed suit."

"Christ, Faye! Sometimes I wonder what we've moved ourselves into. Have you ever thought of it?"

"I've thought of it."

"Maybe this is what happens when you buy a house because it speaks to you from across a valley."

"You adored it, even before we got inside," Faye remembered. "You said Philip Johnson could learn from it."

"I said that. But it's where it is."

"Our Ridge. Are you trying to say we should have bought that other house in Darien?"

"No. But you saw our assortment tonight."

"Put it in quotes."

"Quote Assortment unquote." Anson moved closer to her, put his head gently in her lap. "I thought, 'That was very pretty, and that will do.' "

"It would have been the same in Darien. Or Westport. And we simply couldn't have stayed on in the apartment."

"No, no. No place for children." They'd been over this before.

"Even in New York we'd have been stuck with the problem of finding that one pivotal couple enough like us so we could stand it. There would have been all your family's New York friends, Mother's too."

"This house is perfect for us," he said, thrusting from them all qualification. It was a prayer.

Faye ran her fingers through his hair. "I did meet someone there tonight I'll treasure forever, if she'll come to us."

"Who?"

"The wife of the man who handed drinks. She was over there by those dishes with steam under them, carving the pig and dishing the spoon bread. She and her husband cater for the Lavrorsens every Christmas. She said catering's rather thin out here after the holidays. She's looking for work several days a week. I told her *please* to come look us over, see if we could work something out. She's calling right after New Year's."

"Praise God!" said Anson, who had been known to polish a floor. "What's her name?"

"Give me my purse." She fished in it and found a business card that read: C. F. AND R. J. HAINES, PARTIES CATERED FOR. "I like catered *for*. Mrs. Haines, anyway. She lives only eight miles from us and has her own transportation. I practically hired her for life on the spot. She'll be perfect when I get back from the hospital." Todd was to be born in New York, at Doctors.

The Parrises had been settled in the house for the better part of a year without the kind of help the place required, and in that time both had learned that owning any house is an intense and intimate matter, not unlike love. Though Anson had found a man to cut the lawn on a yearly contract, had made arrangements with the nurseryman for care of shrubs and twice-a-year spraying of trees, interior problems had been solved less easily. Faye had tried breaking in a succession of day women from the area, but without success. They came, they saw the expanses of glass to be washed, the wide oak flooring, broken by scatter rugs, to be polished, the thousands of books to be dusted—and none was conquered. For a time, Faye made do with a professional cleaning service, staffed by college boys, which she found not too satisfactory since she literally had to flee the house while they were there and kill time with Velma or one of "The Assortment" wives. Mrs. Haines, however, had called, had worked out, and had been the house's twice-a-week godsend since then. She came oftener, if needed, without complaint, and when there was a party, her husband catered and did everything, supplying the extra help needed, even arranging the flowers.

That Christmas holiday night, Faye and Anson had sorted

out the people they met at the party, evaluated them, filed them for their Ridge future.

"The Lavrorsens will do," Faye decided. "Definitely."

"Straight squares, especially him," Anson defined them.

"Drapers?"

"Squares in round holes."

"What about those Doyles?"

"Mm—oblongs. In square holes."

"Nowellses?"

"Cubes."

"The Burgesses?"

"Squares in square holes, perfectly fitted."

"The Misses Taylor and Grumbacher?"

"No recognizable shapes. Or trapezoids. The boys in the matching jersey suits too."

That left Sam and Velma Currie, for whom they were grateful. The Curries were not, strictly speaking, "Assortment," were old shoes, real friends in fair weather or foul, though Anson was openly skeptical of Velma's Freudian distillations. They became grateful for "The Assortment" couples too, in time, even for those trapezoid women (one soft, one hard), who, on a number of occasions, when the Parrises were in a baby-sitter bind, willingly sat. They would sit all evening in front of the fire, Miss Taylor doing needlepoint, Miss Grumbacher reading, staying until Faye and Anson got home. They didn't have to have the fireplace explained to them, or anything else. Anson called them "Gertrude" and "Alice." They were not unlike those formidable ladies of the Rue de Fleurus, and Miss Grumbacher had a literary bent. There was no question of offering them money, and they did not drink, so cocktails were no good either. Faye solved it by picking up the yarns Miss Taylor needed when she was in New York, and giving Miss Grumbacher presents of books from the British Book Center. They very rarely saw the boys, though they heard a good deal of gossip about them. Local rumor had it that they took discreet, paying weekend guests, other boys like themselves, needing a country change and a place to screw; it was said, too, that doors had viewing holes, so the screwing could be watched. "Watch queens," Velma finally classified them. The shutters of their rented cottage were closed Fridays to Mondays, and the boys cooked and baked up a storm. Anson occasionally saw these "horizontal customers" on the Monday morning "Bug" connection. More than once, when feeling the constriction of the house and the Ridge, Faye had dropped in on "Gertrude" and "Alice" for tea, yes, real tea, not a drink, but plain, perfectly brewed Hu-Kwa, made in a pot and served in warmed cups, with scones, perfection. Over the years, they got to know "The Assortment" couples well enough to wear them smooth, to learn what they were like beneath their suburban surfaces, to like them or dislike them, often to do both.

Martha and Stig Lavrorsen, who entertained so beautifully in their perfect house, were the Parrises' first Ridge disillusion. After Todd's birth, they began exchanging dinners. Martha was almost *cordon bleu,* having studied for a time with Dione Lucas, and took time to prepare all kinds of wonderful dishes: *Boeuf Wellington, Homard Archiduc, Suprême of Pike à la Dijonnaise, Truffes de Chambéry, Pommes Crainquebille, Coq Vent Vert, Schenkels.* She made her own bread, which spoiled you forever for Pepperidge Farm's. Faye was glad for the services of Mrs. Haines when having Martha and Stig back, though of course she couldn't compete. The Lavrorsens served very white martinis in glasses chilled with frost, and the kind of hors d'oeuvres permitting guests to have as many drinks before dinner as they liked. These drinks inevitably led to confidences. One awful night, Martha got unmanageable and said the reason she and Stig had no children was because he was sterile, she was sure of it. Besides, she said, he was built so large that sex with him

152

was a nightmare. "I can wink at it, and that's about all there is. Not that he cares—Stig's really in love with him*self!*" She screamed and cried; nothing Stig could say or do quieted her. At last, since dinner seemed somewhat academic anyway (Martha had been boozing all afternoon), Faye and Anson decided to go home. "You might as well," Stig told them clinically; "when she gets like this I just slap her to sleep. She's always over it by the time I get home next evening." This scene was never mentioned afterward by either couple, and their relationship went on quite placidly, really. Martha always took on the Red Cross campaign and the headaches dreamed up at zoning-board meetings, and almost always went to New York with Faye on Fridays. Recently, Martha had bought herself a beagle for company and had gotten rather fat.

The Drapers were, Faye and Anson considered, a little on the sad side, though kind and well-meaning. They had less money than other couples of "The Assortment," though they lived in a large, rambling house of Tudor pretension, vintage 1910, with wonderful grounds and an orchard. Rose did all her own work. Sherman, who looked solid as oak, had always had trouble keeping jobs. He one day would inherit money, when his mother died. Their seven children ranged in age from four months to twelve years. Rose had had her tubes tied; they were not going to have any more. She sometimes popped in on Faye mornings, to beef about her life, which was one long nightmare of laundry, shopping, car pools, cooking, picking up after everybody, and stretching dollars until the eagles screamed. Half the kids were at the stage where they smashed everything, and Sherm had moved their good furniture into box rooms so it would not be ruined. Often mornings, when other husbands were in the city, Sherm could be seen mowing their vast lawns, or raking their rutty drive, which needed gravel, or spraying the wormy trees in the orchard. This meant he was "between jobs." It was Rose who stretched what dollars there were, supervised building of a rental unit in one wing, decided to sell four acres of land during a crisis, a shame, since they had bought the place to have *Lebensraum.* "If only the old bitch would die!" the Drapers said openly of Sherman's mother, who took long trips around the world, hoping for a new husband, to whom Rose feared the money might go in the end. But the old bitch lived on, and Sherm would take nothing from her while she lived. The eagles could be heard screaming all over the Ridge.

Alma and Ray Doyle were a much older Ridge story. Like community needlework, the story had been worked on by everybody, and there were many versions. One version, the shortest, went something like this. Alma and Ray had married because each thought the other had money. Soon afterward, it was discovered that neither did. Ray had been an idea man for some TV serial, but had given that up to write. He yearned, as root vegetables yearn to be pulled up, for fame. He began writing in their barn, and Alma started selling insurance to make ends meet. The barn burned down and with it—as everyone had heard a thousand times—Ray's novel and all of his notes. Faye had been right in wondering if Ray was a barn burner: most in the Ridge thought he might be one. "So terribly anal, *such* a mess," Velma Currie said. "Don't you see, he *had* to burn it?" Martha Lavrorsen said the barn's going up in flames had been the perfect solution for Ray; she had heard a part of the novel—he was the kind of writer who reads his work aloud—and it was, she asked everyone to believe, beyond any belief of which they were capable. The novel had been his last as well as his first, evidently. Now he drove his three daughters to school in the mornings and fetched them in the afternoons and, in between, did the housework and shopping. He had even been seen wearing Alma's aprons. Alma's business was flourishing, and there was an interior story about that: she got her

154

tail from her clients, it was thought, since Ray wouldn't (or couldn't) give her any. Ray, when drunk, often got rather moony about the nearest husband in sight, but seemed unaware of his problem on a conscious level. His vocabulary was straight out of an Ed Sullivan broadcast ("tremendously exciting," "handled herself very well") and his verbal delivery was almost identical with Sullivan's. Of course, he did imitations; he was mimetic, and Sullivan was his best *shtick*. People being told this long story grew impatient and always said, "But whether or not there was money could have been cleared up by a simple question early on, *before* things became such a mess." "Ah, yes," Faye would reply—she had investigated all versions of the story, boiled them down— "but then, don't you see, there wouldn't have been any Doris Day movie." And Anson would add that, with a little rewriting, it would be a perfect script for Doris, as soon as she got old enough to play the Alma part; and everybody could just see her stamping her feet, acting with her tongue, switching her outdated bob from side to side because things weren't going her way.

And there were the Nowellses. Both Amy and Herb had been married before, unhappily, and now, though childless, seemed content. In addition to his gout, Herb had some kind of bladder trouble that often made him appear uneasy, as though he wasn't sure he could make the can in time. Amy was always talking about building with a view to the time when a one-floor house would be necessary for Herb. She was, also, an authority on deodorants for men. "Come to me in the dark of the moon," she would tell young men about to marry. "I can tell you a lot. My first husband *stank!*" She it was who demanded and succeeded in getting Herb to have the wax baths for his hirsuteness. Bets were made at Ridge parties as to whether or not Amy would let Herb roll up his sleeves because only in that way could it be known whether he still had the wax baths and, presumably, sex. Who would want to sleep with Amy was a question no one debated. She was, said Anson, so fucking dainty. In the last year or so, she'd gotten to behave like Herb's nurse, which, in a way, she was. Ray Doyle, who got off a good one now and then, said he was sure Amy Nowells made Herb put a plastic sheet between them when they had sex so she wouldn't be touched by his hair growing back; it did grow back, as all were aware, though none so aware as Amy.

The Parrises' alternate pair of old shoes, though not as informal and easy as the Curries, were Grace and Chet Burgess. They presented an unvarying picture of placid domesticity. Their one son was at Choate. Grace had studied at the Art Students League in New York, but had never gotten anywhere with her painting. As an otolaryngologist, Chet occupied a special niche in the little community of the Ridge. Neighbors who were having a little trouble with their sinuses (and few did not, Ridge winters being what they were) sometimes tried to consult him at parties. Chet was adamant about not giving information, always saying that, if the questioner cared to consult him professionally, his secretary would be glad to set up an appointment. His office was on Park Avenue. Rose Draper had gone to him years ago, and had had the bilateral Caldwell-Luc procedure for tumors in her maxillary sinuses. It was a tale, to hear her tell it—and she told it often—of medieval torture: four hours under a local, and her face had never looked the same since. Chet's fee had been one thousand dollars, and the Drapers still owed him most of it. Amy Nowells wondered if Chet couldn't do something about her chin; he was, also, a plastic surgeon, renowned for his nose jobs. Chet said he could do her chin over, so it wouldn't sag, but asked if she'd looked at herself in a three-way mirror lately. "You should stand up straight," he advised—one of his rare free consultations. "You'd be surprised what would happen to your chin if you'd work on your posture." Amy had thought him rude and said so. "Assortment" gatherings not infrequently broke up in such small enmities, unimportant; group members made up easily, aware of their dependence on and need for each other.

"Leaving us Velma and Sam," Faye would say when "The Assortment" had proved too much, though both she and Anson forgot and forgave, as did the others. "Lovely Curries. Not squares, not cubes. *People!*" Separate and apart in the Parris affections. But even Velma and Sam had their imperfect aspects, times that were hard to gloss over, friends hard to take. One of the Curries' oldest shoes, a Viennese named Huldah, who had been analyzed by an analysand of Freud's, was, Anson thought and said, the absolute, utter end. Huldah was Velma's friend, really, not Sam's; through her Velma kept up on the newest psychological wrinkles. For several years, Huldah had come out for weekends, when Velma discussed with her problems of the children in the group. Sam would try to ease things for Velma, give her more time with Huldah, by cooking the Saturday night dinner. It irritated him, though, that whenever he announced the meal was ready, Huldah made a beeline for the downstairs w.c., often spending some time there, making it necessary to hold the food, even warm it over. Velma said the reason she did this was because she had been in a concentration camp during the war and something had gone wrong with her kidneys. "Kidneys, schmidneys," Sam disagreed. "She's like that dachshund we had. We trained her to go outside by showing her her food. Food—toidy. She's anally oriented, obviously," he imitated Huldah. "She is *not!*" Velma cried. "Do you realize who her analyst *was?*" "I don't give a fuck, I've made the dinner, and by God, she's going to eat it!" "You're so hostile to her, Sam. Why?" "When Freudians don't get their way, everybody's hostile." Huldah's immolations while Sam held back the dinners continued. At last, after one of her longer sessions in the can, while he watched a soufflé fall, he demanded to know her reasons for making him wait dinner. Huldah was furious and went all to pieces. "But there is no connection whatever in my— Sam, it is your hostility toward me you are showing. Oh, yes, that's *very clear!*" "Shit!" Sam said to this. "You see?" Huldah asked, turning to Velma. "Am I not right? He connects the eating and excretory functions." Later, she asked Velma how she endured Sam's hostilities, how she rationalized letting him make the dinner. He was overweight, of course, she added, as though that was an answer to her question. Sam had gotten so browned off with Huldah that, one Saturday, he drank up the cooking sherry, and after calling out that eats were on, quickly secreted himself in the can, not bolting the door. Huldah, true to form, marched straight inside and secured the inside latch. Turning, she discovered Sam urinating. "This is monstrous!" she screamed. "This is absolutely intentional on your part!" Sam made no denial, casually zipping up his fly. Huldah trembled so she could hardly unlock the door. Sam made horns with his fingers and held them to his temples, wiggling and grinning like a devil. Huldah finally got the door open and fled. She never came for weekends after that.

There were other Ridge couples, people who came and went, but it was "The Assortment" and the Curries Faye and Anson saw most, made their life with. There were, of course, the people they had known before their marriage, bachelors and bachelor-girl friends, now married themselves and gone away, growing fewer and fewer in number with each year. And there were their Kastner and Kennerly friends, an assortment of quite a different kind. But they were another story.

🌷 🌷 🌷 THE RIDGE had no good dry cleaner and Faye had solved the ever-present problem of clothes and slip-cover upkeep by using a Stamford firm that picked up Tuesdays and returned on Fridays. These were, also, the days Mrs. Haines came to iron and clean, and between the two days, Faye brought the house and its routines back from weekend indolence and prepared it for the next. Anson was particular about his clothes, and before sending them, she always carefully turned the pockets inside out and brushed lint, noted any repairs that needed to be made, and pinned penciled instructions to each garment: *No creases in sleeves, roll lapels, soft finish*—though the cleaner had learned that long ago. The summer suit Anson had worn on Monday had been a leftover, cleaned a year ago and now in need of pressing, and as Mrs. Haines ironed the shirts Faye had washed and sprinkled on Monday, Faye got the week's stack for the cleaner ready. Anson usually left things in his pockets —odd silver and bills, every wife's perquisites; charge slips from restaurants where he did not use his credit cards, to be saved for tax deduction; match folders and mashed packs of cigarettes. Early in her marriage she had discovered that it was possible to trace, in a general way, his movements on any day simply by emptying the pockets of the suit he had worn. The Plaza match folder told her what she already knew, that he had lunched with David, and a curious series of indentations along the edge of the folder, made with thumb and forefinger nails, possibly indicated a certain nervousness during the lunch. Matches, stale cigarettes, and other odds and ends she discarded, but she was careful to save whatever notes or slips she found that might have importance to him. Thus, when, in a trousers pocket, she came across Neile Eythe's telephone number, scribbled across a desk memo pad with FROM THE OFFICE OF ANSON PARRIS embossed across the top of the sheet, she knew it probably had been written down at his desk, since on warm days he worked without his coat. She preserved this carefully, slipping it beneath a glass ashtray on a chest of drawers. She once had studied shorthand at Katharine Gibbs and, though never expert, could often decipher the odd squiggles and squirls Anson used as shortcuts. What she saw and read was N E, a Mott Street address and a downtown telephone exchange with a number following. The slip had been crumpled, she noticed, not folded, and this small detail made her wonder whose number it was. She began going through the list of their New York friends—but no, he would hardly have noted the number of a friend, would already, probably, know it, or have it in his book. The crumpled notation bothered her and she kept coming back to it in her mind as she worked and conducted the routine Tuesday gossip with Mrs. Haines.

"The young Carlsons are expecting, I hear."

"Who are they?"

"I thought you knew them—they've taken the apartment above the Drapers' garage."

"No, I haven't met them." But she hadn't met anyone this past month of Anson's being away, had seen little of "The Assortment."

"It's their second. Her first looks young enough still to be nursing—if she nursed. Did you?"

"Yes, I nursed Todd from the beginning."

"*I* always nursed mine. That slip cover on Mr. Parris' chair by the bookcases needs cleaning."

"Yes, I'll send it. It's time for summer covers anyway."

N. E. No, no periods. Just N E. Already she half knew the

number. Faye again went back to the ashtray and studied the slip, holding it in her hand tightly, as a medium clutches some keepsake of a loved one that is supposed to convey vibrations of a life on which curtains have been drawn. She sensed still another alien object on which Anson was focusing the attention and affection she once supposed would be exclusively hers. She sighed, remembering that it had been during her pregnancy that she became aware that Anson was sleeping with someone else. With old, tired, rose-petaled sadness, she again realized how almost incapable of betraying him in return she was, cursing the years of girlhood communion and confessions and Madame Doheny which had formed her and made her so, however resolutely she now rejected them. Never in her marriage had she been more dependent on Anson and needful of him than now. Their rapturous recoupling the night of his return at first awakened, and now confirmed, that between them lay not only the ghosts of other, past women, but a new one, thin and crumpled as a shadow broken by a wall.

Something about the crumpled slip reminded her that she was about to become thirty. Thirty to Anson's thirty-three, or, in his exact way, *in my thirty-fourth year.* I am, already, in my thirtieth year, she thought, as she remembered her meeting with Anson, when she was at the peak of her torments with her mother and Father Callahan, was protecting her freedoms at Katy Gibbs—for want of a better excuse for getting away from Greenwich and living in New York. She had been one of the unenthusiastic Radcliffeites, with more than the credits needed to graduate but no interest in graduating, though she had her sheepskin, still rolled up in its tube on the back of a closet shelf; whenever she cleaned and came across it she wondered why she kept it. At the beginning of her senior year, when she was most vulnerable, she had fallen deeply, irrationally in love with a geneticist at Harvard, a gaunt, ramlike Jew named Baumgartner, whose father had been a tailor. He was a grind, fast rising in the world of Klinefelter's syndrome, and would establish, with the aid of foundation and government grants, a minuscule certainty about abnormal chromosome patterns. She cared nothing for his shop talk, only for him. There had been a quietness about him that matched her own, a sympathy with her resolute casting out of saints' bones and plaster madonnas, for he, too, was in flight, from matzoh balls, the prayer shawl and the Torah. Together they found excitement in breaking dietary laws, eating rare roast beef on Ember days, crustaceans and pork whenever they pleased. His face was Assyrianly ugly, but his body that of a primitive Greek, hard and segmented. She had still been almost girlishly soft and roseate, nymphlike, fresh from the experimental squalors of the quick, alcoholic grab and messes in parked cars or urine-smelling dorms. He was the first man with whom she experienced orgasm easily and without effort. He tolerated no hangovers of Catholic restraints, and she learned with ritualistic submission the posturally uncomfortable delights of sixty-nine, and, most enthralling of all to her (because it seemed annihilation of her guilts about Madame Doheny and Father Callahan), patient blowing. Baumgartner had a long, upcurving penis, surrounded by a bush of violet-black hair that exactly matched the hair of his head, which she hallowed with its softer term, phallus, a little tormented, always, by her first confrontation with this Dionysian image, *phallus impudicus,* in a biology book illustrating gasteromycetous fungi. He celebrated, too, that part of her that had been blushingly euphemized as *my place down there,* and she learned to speak of things by their more worldly names. As she held him in her mouth the strains of "Panis Angelicus" would flood her brain, and she enjoyed her great guilt over having left the Church and her mother and the Greenwich double cube: Baumgartner was for all that college year her Host, her Eucharist. And, like the faith that had deserted her,

162

he went with the summer vacation. He had received a fellow-ship to work in New Mexico, and that was that. Though there had never been any question of marriage, she would have married him, adjusted. *"Shiksa, shiksa, iksa diksa."* He had laughed when, once, she brought the subject down. "I could never stand that double cube in Greenwich, and she would loathe me."

"We wouldn't have to see my mother," Faye replied seriously. She had painted the holy-picture canvas of her mother and the house itself, so he knew it as one knows the castoff stories of others' castoff lives. Two years later, he married a Jewish girl and moved to Israel.

She suffered as uncontrollably as an Ibsen heroine, loving Baumgartner but hating him for his rejection of her; yet she was grateful for him, too, for he had brought about in her a long falling within herself which she needed; he had taught her what she was: passive, possessively jealous, ardent, hungry for love. Then she met Anson, ruddy, the reverse of Baumgartner's dark coin, unbelievably handsome, fleeing from his own cultural-hybrid cage but with easy determination. She had almost made up her mind to give in to her mother's tireless logic and crawl back into the double-cube fold, rich and warm, with all problems settled, and to become (perhaps through lip service that would return her to faith) virginal. Somewhat to her surprise, she let Anson take her the first night of their meeting, and was later glad she had, because, even then, she divined his was a sexual tempera-ment that waited on no woman's whims. His Andover-Harvard ways, his bravura clothes and assurance made him seem like a rich boy, and he behaved like one. He was the son of easygoing parents, who early had given him his rein, who were modestly well off but unpretentious, who laughed about what they called their sheeny blood and let the world take it or leave it. Anson was afraid of nothing, tried every-thing, and if he failed, laughed and tried again. After her relationship with Baumgartner, which had almost turned her sour, Faye found the belief she needed in Anson's unswerving assumption that whatever he wanted would be his, was his to get and keep. To her he was Marvell's golden lamps in a green night: he discovered what she was and loved her for it. She accepted with unguilty relief his strapping, bulging white muscles, his fiery fall of wiry red-gold hair that began at his collarbones and descended in the pattern of a cross: not the true cross she had lost, but a *crux ansata*. He was uncircumcised, for her, after Baumgartner, more complete; unmaimed perfection; he was imperfect only when she crossed him on some small matter he considered fell within masculine prerogative—and when she died the harrowing deaths of the times she knew him to be unfaithful. There was no helplessness in the passion he returned to her, and she perversely liked and respected that; and he made no secret of the fact that sleeping with other women—when she had ferreted it out—made him desire her the more. Her early passion for him was laced with relief—he was someone she could present to her mother. Vera Williams might carp—and did—that he was not a Catholic; but even her shrewd, Celtic nostrils had not at first been able to sniff the seasoning of Semitic blood.

"Well," she had said, from the corner of her white-brocaded sofa, no longer hopeful of a controllable son-in-law, grandchildren to whom she could apportion her overflow of faith, "you say he is a paragon? In what way is he a paragon?"

"I love him."

"What's his name?"

"Anson Warren Parris."

Her mother's brain silently shuffled and calculated. "The Warren's all right, and I suppose the Anson is Texas. What's the Parris? It sounds Jewish."

"His grandfather is Jewish. That's his name, and I'm going

to marry him." *I am going to marry him tonight, lest you spoil this for me, as you've spoiled so much else,* she was saying to herself as she talked.

Vera Williams' inner ear had picked this up and she capitulated—she had known about Baumgartner, and later gave thanks with Father Callahan that matters were no worse. Somewhat with the air of conspicuously leaving behind a pistol for one certainly doomed, she asked no questions about when the wedding was to be. Faye and Anson understood, and were married within a week by a J.P. Afterward, a meeting of the families took place in the Greenwich house (Father Callahan not present) in an atmosphere of forbearance and good will. Anson's grandfather had reservations at least as deep as Vera's. Anson's parents were unimpressed by the Georgian grandeur, though factually accepted it. His grandfather, not as rich as Faye's mother, insisted on giving them the honeymoon, two months of flying travel, which they began in London and ended in Israel, to please him, for he was an ardent Zionist. Vera, not to be outdone, was insistent that the young couple should start life together with a paid-for house to move into when Anson's apartment became too small. It was, she said, only fair, since one of Faye's father's insurance policies had been accumulating compound interest in The Putnam Trust since his death.

"Never, never, pay interest on anything—no mortgages," was Vera's advice, and Anson's grandfather agreed.

Anson, during this discussion, frowned.

Faye, seeing his expression, said, "But I told you I was one of *those* Williamses."

"You're Parris now."

"If we can take the honeymoon, why not the house?"

Anson conceded, but added, "House, yes. In Faye's name. But everything else I buy and pay for. I like to sit on my own chairs."

That had been the arrangement, and it had not changed.

Since they had begun to live in the Ridge house, he had bought two contiguous parcels of nearby land, one with a stream, for protection. "Gramont to Rothschild—in reverse," Anson joked about it.

❦ ❦ ❦ IT WAS through Kastner and Kennerly that the first, slightly conditioning withdrawal from "The Assortment" came about. In a way, it was a relief, in the way that a holiday spent away from loved ones is; they missed them, then rewelcomed them freshly on returning. Todd had just become three when David and Jeannette seeped into the Parrises' lives. They had been there all along, of course, background figures, surmised but not known well, suddenly moving forward with David's second big novel for K and K and becoming friends. Faye had liked David's book, even had predicted its great success before master proofs had gone to the printer. After the domestic intensity of "The Assortment" couples, the Steens had seemed exotic, perhaps that pivotal, double friendship of which Faye and Anson often had spoken, and for which they hoped.

Faye saw much more of "The Assortment" than Anson, possibly had begun to tire a little earlier of the tit-for-tat entertaining, the spur-of-the-moment cocktail gatherings that turned into potluck and pickup dinners, as well as the times when they entertained each other more formally and planfully. And it was curious, the way she and Anson tended to think of "The Assortment" in order, as though they constituted a list: Lavrorsens, Drapers, Doyles, Nowellses, Burgesses, "Gertrude" and "Alice" and, last because *not* least, the Curries.

166

Martha and Stig were, for the most part, Saturday and Sunday night entertainers: Rose and Sherm were considerably more casual—when a clutch wound up at their place, often a bottle or two had to be sent for, the others, knowing their difficulties, chipping in; Alma and Ray became a little tacky after a while, Ray's inevitable leg of lamb *en daube,* with peas, mashed potatoes, gravy and a *coupe* (Dolly Madison vanilla, marrons and rum), was always the same, and no one invited to their house in advance ate lamb for a week beforehand; Amy and Herb were much better at cocktails with elaborate hors d'oeuvres than at dinners, and besides they ate out a good deal and played bridge with several couples even squarer than they, not at all fun or young; the most back and forth of all were Grace and Chet, and anyone they entertained could be sure the invitation had been as carefully considered as one on a list for a Presidential dinner; "Gertrude" and "Alice," since they were antialcohol, anticigarettes, antieverything, almost, except tea and reading and needlework—and tolerance—were friendly with everyone, but early faded from the forefront of the original group; and, though the Curries often were invited with "The Assortment," they seemed never to enjoy themselves, because Velma was always evaluating group behavior and reactions, and Sam was trying to get away from her and flirt with other women, to cut the grease (as he said) of the Fried Freud she dished up afterward. Though familiarity had not bred contempt, exactly, it had brought knowledge that was not always expected or welcomed, and clay toes were beginning to show. The Lavrorsens, for example, were quarreling more openly, Stig punishing Martha for private behavior the others were supposed not to know about, and Martha was growing more sardonic about everything and everybody, except her beagle. "You don't suppose . . ." Ray Doyle once suggested, when in his cups, only to be shushed by Alma. "You didn't let me finish," Ray protested. "You filthy-minded little man!" Alma snapped. "*I* know what you were going to say. You don't have to finish, you never finish anything anyway." Surmounting another financial crisis, evidently a major one, had left both Drapers haggard, looking more resigned than ever. The Doyles were proving more interesting in their odd way than any Doris Day script; perhaps it wasn't true, as Grace Burgess said, that Loretta Young had sold all her secrets to Doris for a cold million; anyway, things were very nervous *chez* Doyle. Alma was reputed to be having an affair with a black who played bass fiddle at a weekend dancing place outside Stamford, and Ray was taking it out on a new electric typewriter, which he had set up in a renovated corncrib that had escaped being burned with the barn— "Working *toward* a next novel," he explained, covering himself in advance for any lateness of execution, or for there being no novel at all, maybe. Anson showed patient interest, saying K and K would like first whack; you never could tell, the oddest people did produce novels sometimes; he might just pull it off. "The crib bit is too perfect," Martha Lavrorsen said of Ray's fresh effort. "Ray cribs everything from best sellers, but Alma a crib hath not in which to lay her blackamoor—I hear they do it in the basement of the dancing place. If Ray'd write what *he* thinks of that lovely black, phallic idol, but he won't." Amy and Herb were shuttling back and forth between the Ridge and the Mayo Clinic; Herb was having some new kind of bladder treatment. When not away, the building of their new, one-floor house absorbed them; Amy was a riot describing how she had gotten the toilet and bidet bowl levels just right by having Herb squat while the plumbers measured. "You'll see," she promised, "wee-wee will be a creature comfort at last." "Who's the bidet for?" Anson asked. "Really!" Amy answered. Then, "No, really, Americans simply are not *clean*. Europeans always wash—that's why there's never any bumf in their ladies' rooms." "And what's 'bumf'?" "Toilet paper," said Herb; "she read about that in Lady Diana Cooper's autobiography." "You know, Anson, your house is so perfect in many ways, I'm surprised you don't put in a bidet." "Anson and I are two-baths-a-day people, we don't need one," Faye punished Amy for this criticism, adding that when she and Anson were in Europe, they kept ice in the bidets, for cooling the champagne. Grace and Chet were holding up, but Faye and Anson both felt they didn't want to go on seeing quite so much of them; they were rather *sec,* both conversationally and at their playroom bar, where the next one everybody thirsted for often was not offered. Chet said alcohol dilated the capillaries; all right, flush the arteries with one or two, but he could tell just by looking up a septum how many the patient had drunk the day before. The Curries were—Velma and Sam. Special. "But we can't make a meal out of them every night," complained Anson, "even if Velma is the authority on Todd and his potty." Todd's toilet training, for some reason, had proved very difficult. (At ten months he had been cranky, and at eighteen matters had been little better. He was a refuser. It had been an issue which Velma, in her patient way, helped Faye to resolve. "His age group eats what it does. Fill him full of meat and fruit and he'll go," she counseled. And Todd did; they won, literally, by letting him be; but he was, still, a watchful and suspicious child.) That year, "Gertrude" and "Alice" had gone to Ireland for the summer, leaving the jersey-suit boys as caretakers. Very shortly afterward, the Friday night "Bug" was loaded with additional customers, soon to become horizontal.

It was no wonder the Steens seemed a relief and exotic, with Jeannette's porcelainlike perfections of clothes and grooming, and David's bright sheen of success. "Success sure do smell different, do it not?" Faye asked when the Steens had become friends. "Honey, it sure as hell do," agreed Anson. "You should smell some of my poets and lame ducks. It's not called a stable for nothing."

A raid by a rival publishing firm on Kastner and Kennerly's editorial department the previous January had resulted in the defection of the two older editors and Anson's being moved into the head editorship and a second vice-presidency. The departing editors took sizable blocks of their individual stables with them, but Steen was one of the authors who had remained loyal; he slipped easily into Anson's shed, which, until then, had comprised mainly the firm's difficult writers, those whom K and K published for prestige purposes and lost money on, and the lame ducks, who, because he was the youngest editor, always had been his. He was still the youngest, the two replacement editors, Hanson and Stein, being in their early and late forties, respectively.

David and Jeannette were considerably older than the Parrises, but that was all right, Faye said. "Then there won't be that inevitable moment for both of us, when we sit and look at each other and wonder *if*."

The winter that David's second big K and K novel was being put to bed, Faye and Anson were happy to be thrown together so often and so casually. To the occasional cocktails and dinners Friday nights, when Faye had been in New York for the day and was meeting Anson at the apartment, had been added weekends in town, with and without Todd; Mrs. Haines adored him and many times stayed over until Mondays, after the Fridays she baby-sat with him anyway while doing the housework. The Park Avenue hideaway was a perfect place for meeting Jeannette and David; they had not yet bought their small cooperative penthouse in East 73rd. While Jeannette and Faye talked clothes and furniture, or ran up easy on-the-lap dinners in the slatted kitchenette, Anson and David would discuss books and the unpredictability of critics, the mercurially shifting picture of trade book publishing, the grave stupidities of the Johnson Administration, television's degradation, anything and everything from Saltykov-Shchedrin, the Russian novelist they mutually admired, to the paranoia of De Gaulle. David was an author

170

who was not very like his books; he read French and German easily, preferring Flaubert and Proust to Stendhal and Zola, Grillparzer and Hesse to Mann and Sudermann; he enjoyed English criticism, almost never read American fiction, especially that resembling his own; but especially he was appalled by the gulf separating America's bright promises from its sordid realities.

"It could, all of it, come crashing around our heads any minute," David said, one of the times they had met to have dinner and go on to the theater afterward. "Your head, mine, those of our worse halves, everybody's, into the ghettos."

"Yes, America's all ghettos, always has been," Anson answered. "That's why your Swiss banks, of course."

"One reason. And my absolute, almost total inability to endure and watch one more Administration come and go. And take and take. I can't *bear* them to take it from me, Anson. I was once poor, you know, not like you and Faye."

"I was never rich, my parents were merely comfortable. I used to spend some of my summers on Nantucket, painting houses, to help out with my tuition. Faye's mother's got money, and Faye has a trust her father set up for her before the war. But *we're* not rich."

"But you never had to do articles on spec and then, after weeks, sometimes months, of work, have them turned down by some shit of an editor who'd meanwhile changed his mind."

"No, never that. I'm only an editor myself, David. I can't really write anything, except memos, and a fairly concise letter."

"You do the accepting or rejecting."

"And try not to be shitty. It's not an easy job sometimes."

"You're good with me. I know you're *there*."

"I understand your motivation. Money. Numbered accounts in Zurich, savings accounts, bonds, blue chips too—right?"

"Wrong. The Zurich accounts, yes. I have no American savings accounts or stocks."

"Are you kidding? You don't let hard cash lie around, surely?"

"What's wrong with hard cash? It's always quickly available. My real fantasy is a box I'd keep under the bed, the way the French keep the gold louis in an old stocking beneath the mattress. A box with real gold in it."

"There's a law against hoarding gold."

"It can be arranged," David said; "gold's what it always comes down to when the pound falls and the dollar skids. Every time Washington messes up world change, I make a little something."

"I'll bet you do."

"It's nervous work, more nervous than writing novels."

Jeannette came in from the kitchen. "And that's why my Duvidl is so fond of orange; it's even richer than gold, which is only yellow."

"I like 'only yellow'—make a fair title," David said.

Faye followed, bearing drinks. "And Jeannette loves her Fabergé. So do I. I wish I could afford a few examples."

"Gold is better," said David. "But you could afford it, I hear."

"Who told you that?"

"Anson says you have a trust."

"And won't let me touch it. No, I can't afford Fabergé. When my mother goes, we may be glad of that money in my trust. We're saving it for Todd."

"We'd like for Todd to be able to tell the world to go screw, if that's what he wants," said Anson. "Faye's mother lives as she lives, but you know what happens after death. In come the state and the federal tax people—and then there's the auction at Parke-Bernet."

"Where the Fabergé always winds up, eventually," David said.

"Anyway," Anson went on, "I don't want Todd to have to flatten his ass on an office chair like his old man."

"What are you, Anson?" Jeannette asked. "Early thirties?"

Anson was then thirty-one.

"And your ass isn't flat," said Jeannette. "David's is. Flabby."

"Thanks." David laughed. "Flabby from applying the seat of the pants so you can buy all those Czarist Easter eggs."

"I don't only buy Fabergé's eggs," Jeannette defended herself. "He did many other things, cigarette boxes, etuis, dressing sets—those divine enamel cuff links I gave you on our last anniversary."

"You buy mostly eggs," David said laconically. "The eggs you never laid yourself, I suppose."

"Yes," Jeannette answered, "that's what *Il Dottore* tells me too."

"Who's *Il Dottore?*" asked Faye.

"My analyst."

"Oh."

"When I married David he said we were too old to have kids. He said that if we did, by the time they were teenagers, we'd be —"

"Don't say it, Jeannette, don't say it."

"I won't tell."

"One kid was enough for me," David said.

"We're going to have another," confided Faye.

"Are you preggers?"

"No. But we plan to have two. And stop."

"What are you waiting for?"

Faye looked at Anson. "What are we waiting for, Anse?"

"*I'm* waiting for the moon to be in Virgo," Anson said mysteriously. "I still have places to go, visit, see."

"What places?"

"We've been almost everywhere," Faye answered; "at least, Anson has. Except South America and darkest Africa.

173

We can do those when we're old. Ninety-nine-day cruises. Safaris."

"I don't mean places *qua* places," Anson tried to explain. "I meant, of course, extensions of living, experiences that can best be had before you start living in the nursery and schoolroom entirely."

A small shadow passed across Faye's face, less a shadow, really, than a draining of expression; it conveyed the introduction of a subject never discussed at home, vague and disturbing, unsuitable in company. There was an awkward silence.

"Well, no hurry for either of you," Jeannette broke it. "You're both still babies yourselves."

"I'm an old bag in her late twenties," Faye said.

"I'd still like to know what you meant, Anson," said David.

"I meant— It's extremely difficult to put. Another part of the forest, might be one way. Some farther landscape, a sea without tides, a moon without orbit. There must be something beyond."

"Beyond what?" asked Jeannette.

"Here. Now. Us."

"Why, Anson, you sound as though you have depths." David laughed.

A second silence fell, heavier than the first.

"Let's get off it," Anson said tersely.

"Yes, let's," Faye agreed. "If we're going to make Voisin and the play, we'd better be going." They had learned that by dining at the famous restaurant, it was possible to avail themselves of a limousine that took them across town to Broadway. That night, they saw Zero Mostel as Tevye. It was a wonderful evening, in tone and quality quite unlike "Assortment" evenings when, occasionally, two or three couples braved the complications of Manhattan theatergoing and the harassing returns to the Ridge following, harassing because of the transport involved.

❧ ❧ ❧ DEEP MARITAL friendships which remain friendships are few, and that of the Steens and Parrises was a bet hedged from the beginning. It was during its burgeoning second year, when the four-way relationship was at its happiest, that Anson and Faye went to stay with David and Jeannette on the Côte d'Azur, Anson taking his five weeks of annual vacation in a lump, though, usually, he liked to break it in two: three weeks in summer, and two (stretched between weekends before and after) in deep winter, when Faye said she went stir-crazy in the country, needing a baking in the sun before spring grudgingly came to the Ridge.

Jeannette had found the house, a seventeenth-century bishop's palace perched on a hillside overlooking the Gulf of La Napoule. She had rented it for the season from a widow whose late husband had been someone important in the Théâtre de France. The house, a curved melon slice embracing the sea view, two-storied with a loggia, came staffed with servants who seemed figures out of the century the house had been built; they murmured, as they moved softly through the rooms in their dark clothes, *"Madame, je monte"* and *"Monsieur, je descends"*—attentive, fascinated, never inquisitive. The spacious white rooms, walls plastered in semblance of *boiseries* with motifs of shells, fish and festoons of flowers, were crowded with superb examples of eighteenth-century furniture. The walls were hung with Chagalls and late Picassos; there were Chagalls even in the kitchen. Over the lighthearted, Fortuny-curtained salons, subaqueously luminous with jalousied light, lingered a hangover of Film Festival activity and an ambiance of the Riviera's better days, La Casati, George de Cuevas, Madame Volterra, the young

Signoret. The air was resonant with gossip, anecdote, re-countings of other times.

From the magical, blue-misted moment of their first aerial view of the Côte and the Iles de Lérins, Faye and Anson had the illusion of descending into a bright dream, stopped within itself, a kaleidoscopic *optique* defying time's change and toll. The house, in which they had an entire wing to themselves, was a luxurious base from which to explore. New to them were the great hotels, the dazzling candy confection of the Carlton, the yellowish Martinez, favorite of Argentines, the pompous and sober Majestic, the villas of royal mistresses building protective walls of treillage higher and higher, only to be overlooked (like Buckingham Palace by the London Hilton) by American drip-dry secretaries arriving one day and leaving the next. They loved the *sablé* beaches, the pineapple palms lining the Croisette; the fleet, seemingly always in, sundered the air with the roar of jets leaving and returning to aircraft carriers. And there were the winding roads leading to the dry, wide valley of the Var, into which they penetrated ever more deeply—Vence, St.-André-les-Alpes, Seillans, Draguignan, Digne; the dusty, wind-washed pines; the thrilling tingle after bathing in the cold waters of the Baie des Anges. At Le Cannet they drank a light, pink wine, cusply ripe, which fell apart as they sipped. The place, pleasingly, had no sense of community; its high excitement was fed by constant activity. There were only the beautiful young—themselves—and the hideous old—others, groping through rich reminiscence for the tail of yesterday.

Though David was revising early chapters of *Good Time Coming,* he worked only mornings and had boundless energy, a high appetite for the next thing and enterprise in setting it up. Cars appeared and were whisked away from the *porte-cochère,* all glass and curvaceous twining green metal, like an Art Nouveau Métro station, by dark, respectful boys he had purchased with lavish tips. Clothes worn once disappeared and were returned, hours later, sea-washed and sun-dried. David was prestigious; bell captains, hall porters and *téléphonistes* snapped to attention on seeing him; if a difficulty arose, John, the Carlton's English concierge, overcame it. After late coffee and *croissants* on the loggia, telephones began to ring. Toothsome Israeli film actresses commanded, Americans of a stamp they never saw in America dropped in, parties grew on chance acquaintance, flowered through midnights, died with daybreak. Jeannette seemed to know everybody, and everybody wanted to know David.

The people the Steens had acquired during their foreign residences were varied, if rather strange. Fleur Parry came for overnight, with a young Balkan prince in tow. There were a Chilean millionaire art collector, Sanchez, a nonentity preoccupied with himself and tracing early Matisses; two blond, bronze statues of men, who seemed to do nothing but oil themselves and wrestle at Professor Muller's beach, the sea their mistress; a drunken, mismated couple, she an early exponent of Milhaud and Satie, he a *maquereau* who had been a friend of Cocteau's in the old *Boeuf sur le Toit* days; a stray from The Country Club of Virginia (*"Suh!"*) named, of all things, Hoopie Gooch, a table-hop and cadger of drinks, dubbed by Jeannette "The Souse of France"; a former orchestra leader seven times married, "Always," quipped David, "to himself." This menagerie was at first amusing, but second encounters betrayed desperate and pathetic pretensions. "They make me feel solid and stable," Jeannette explained; she was approaching the *phase aiguë* of her illness and sorely missing *Il Dottore*.

Todd had been left with Faye's mother, who had provided a nurse, but they worried about him nevertheless, telephoning Greenwich each week they were away. The calls, slow to come through, were shadowy and dim, though Vera Williams' disapprovals burned through her assurances as clearly as though they were calling from the Ridge. Faye's convent

French was more idiomatic, less flat than Jeannette's; but Jeannette knew the shops, which *bottier* would make golden sandals overnight, why one spent the long, blue hour heralding sunset on the Carlton terrace, but took the before-lunch *apéritif* at the Majestic. "The Carlton waiters are not chosen for their looks; the Majestic has only fauns—best seen in sunlight." Faye laughed along with this and other odd comments of Jeannette's, but began to wonder about her. Together they shopped, Jeannette with the aggressive prodigality of a once poor woman who needs nothing, Faye with the sparing care of one who buys only bargains, expensive, but bargains nevertheless, because needed. Often, when days ended, after the surges of other people, they were glad to be simply two American couples together; nights, sandwiched between the days, Faye and Anson were supremely happy by themselves.

In these starlit nights, with the pungent sea air drifting through the windows, Faye and Anson would lie together, thinking, but not often speaking, of their other, their true life, far away. Both felt it crucial that they should enjoy this holiday, for though both still were lingeringly burnished with first youth, responsibilities and problems already tugged at them, beckoned them back. Anson would hold her gently to him in the great, paper-scrolled bed, a Provençal fugitive descended to the littoral, still with its *aide-posture,* like that attached to Josephine's couch at Malmaison—memorial to countless couplings of past lovers, his hands tracing the delicate curves of her back and legs. They held these silent moments carefully, lest they shatter, precipitate them back to American tensions and the Ridge. Faye in these nights wore nightgowns bought in Cannes, spider-thin wisps showing the darkness of the declivity between her breasts, her nipples flushed, *mons Veneris* plump with excitement, black hair a lustrous fragrance about her face.

One night, after a long day's sight-seeing, sea and sun and

wind and a particularly heady wine had delivered them into a glowing, nacreous fatigue. Anson's hold strengthened and he seized her freshly, as he had during their courtship, finding her familiar flesh cool as an abalone shell to his touch. His heavy eyeglasses stashed in the bedside table drawer, his sandy head moved downward, traversing the gown that separated them, and his hands pushed it upward until she lay free, the spider web a phantom moonlight halter about her throat. His lips salivating, matching the shivers of her undulations, his tongue found and parted her, discovering her newly fresh and deliciously tart. He submerged himself in the world through which he had entered into this world, her fingers caressing his ear lobes, pulling them sharply, painfully, as she came in a writhing of rosy delight. Then her hands drew him upward, and raging with the delay within himself, he plunged deeply into the froth until, all senses winning at once, he ejaculated in flood, a flood higher, even, than the rushings of their honeymoon weeks six years before.

He gasped, falling upon her, flattening her breasts with his own, annihilating them in momentary anguish that it was over. "God! Where did that one come from? We've got something back."

"You're always wonderful. Everything."

"But that one I'll remember always."

"Hush," she said, fingers across his mouth.

But he demanded to be listened to, if only in grunting whispers. "Purest, most celestial of cunts—yours. None of the Helens, Grecian or otherwise, could have been like you. Now."

"You're my Paris."

"The only one like that, ever." He had to tell her. Too late, he heard the echo of his own confession.

"I'm sure you know." She turned her head away.

"It was flatteringly intended, believe me."

"But it reminds me I'm not the only one."

179

"You are, you are!"

She pushed him from her. "I'm not going to think about *them* now."

"Don't," he pleaded. "There've not been many."

She laughed unexpectedly. "We must sleep now and be fresh. Tomorrow we go to Grasse."

He returned her laughter in recognition of her banality. "I'd like to be put out in your pasture forever," he bettered it.

"It's there. Always yours."

"Never anyone else's—since we've been together?"

"Never."

"You never want other men?"

"I'm not like that. Maybe there's something wrong with me. All I ever wanted was you."

"After the ones who were before me, of course."

"Naturally."

"That Baumgartner."

"Don't say his name. After them—him—only you."

"I want you again."

"No," she said, punishing him. "I told you, we must be fresh tomorrow. It's quite a pace they've set, we can't lag behind."

"I can lag behind. Try me."

Sleepy laughter. They laughed together before they slept, as they laughed through the pale azure days hung on the white horizons of Africa, sensed if not seen, against the Esterels, forever mammillary, to the west.

They did not go together to Grasse the next day, though, as it turned out, Faye and David did. Jeannette had broken a tooth, and since the only dentist who would take her that day was in Nice, Anson offered to drive her. They left shortly after ten. Faye washed her hair and was drying it in a breezy corner of the loggia when David joined her.

"I suppose they'll lunch in Nice," he said. "Depending on the tooth."

"Which tooth was it? When did it happen?"

"A front incisor. She has a cap on it and it came off while she was brushing. We could drive to our bouillabaisse place for lunch."

"All right."

They took the low sea road to Antibes. Finding their restaurant closed, David suggested the Colombe d'Or at St.-Paul. They shared a bottle of Château d'Yquem in lieu of dessert while the diminished, inland wind rattled the summer leaves and flared the edges of the tablecloth. A slight hint of weather to come hung in the air.

"It's only two-thirty," David said. "We'd have time to go on to Grasse, even beyond."

"Shouldn't we save Grasse for a day when the others can be with us?"

"We can just drive through it and explore beyond. Did you know you have truly cerulean eyes?"

"I know they're blue."

"More than that—they're the color of the sea, when it's blue."

"When isn't the sea blue?"

"When it's wine-colored, as in Homer."

"I never believed that."

"I've seen it so, in the Aegean."

Two hours later, Grasse and the Musée Fragonard behind them—it was uncivilized to pass it up, David said; he had seen it a dozen times, each time more happily—Faye thought, So I have cerulean eyes, do I? Well, well. She asked, knowing he liked talking about his work, about the novel.

"It comes first, as you see from my mornings."

"Before Jeannette?"

"Jeannette *is* the novel. Of course, a whipping girl sometimes helps."

"Surely, David, not you!"

"Figure of speech, merely. I sometimes like a dangerous

situation, but whips, no. I'm gentle, girl-loving, haven't you guessed?"

"I'm not good at guessing," she said.

"Try."

"What to you is a dangerous situation?"

"This."

"It isn't a situation."

"Any proximity of woman and man is."

"I'm not one of your heroines, David."

"You could be. In a way, you already rather are."

"Oh, no."

"The danger's better if there are wives and husbands."

She sat beside him in the deep seat, aware that the challenge of the day excited him. He would see himself as an observer would see him in a situation, which perhaps was why he was a novelist. In the way of many novelists, he had both a feminine and a masculine side, and was narcissistic enough for it to show. He would see himself and he would see the woman he conveyed into danger, just as he would also see the man he was deceiving—and the woman beyond that man.

He read her thoughts. "A triad, a quartet, even, gives me both an orgasmic and a creative charge when working. A plus in the game. You and I'd be perfect, at least you'd be perfect for me."

"I don't feel like becoming a chapter in a book."

"Why not?"

"I've never been unfaithful to Anson." But no woman truly dislikes being told how desirable she is. She let him tell her how marvelous he knew they would be together, heard him out to the end as they stopped for a *citron pressé* in Peyminade.

It had turned into a hot, dusty day, and the wind that had blown at St.-Paul had risen, there was the promise of mistral in it.

"But he's not been faithful to you," David said when they were again in the car.

She considered whether to admit this. If she admitted it, she might learn something she did not know. It might be painful knowledge, but she plunged in. "Yes, I know Anson's had other women. He's discreet, but I hated it, suffered terribly when I was pregnant. I always knew, even if I couldn't guess who the woman was, even if we didn't sleep together during those last months. A woman knows. Don't men?"

"I do."

"You've known about Jeannette?"

"Of course. Surely, you've sensed her conflict?"

"Beginning to. What is it?"

"Well—to stay off analytic jargon—there's what she's always been told she is, and there's what she really wants to be. Those are the twin horns of her dilemma."

"What's the first horn?"

"She's lovely, feminine, yielding, loving, faithful to me, herself, to what we both are together in our marriage. The second horn's very unpretty. She wants, really, to be a whore. Sometimes is. Anything—from the pimpliest Gristede delivery boy to a tattooed man in a French circus."

"What do you do about it?"

"Suffer. Hate her. Quarrel."

"And it passes?"

"I don't think any infidelity is ever truly forgiven, if you mean that. It's never the same, exactly, after the suffering and the hatred and quarreling."

Faye stared straight ahead as they drove along the tortu- ous, hairpin turns, wondering where they would have stopped to dally had she said—*if* she said—Yes. "I agree with you it's never the same. Whenever I find out Anson's been with someone else, I could scratch his eyes out. Once I think I could have killed him."

183

"But if, as you say, he's discreet, how can you be sure?"

"David, don't be stupid. I told you, a woman knows."

"Not always for sure?"

"Always," Faye said, sure of this. "The residue of another woman always lingers. I know that after I'd had Todd Anson started doing things in bed we'd never done before."

"Subtleties?"

"So to speak. You must know about what lingers on from another man," she challenged him. "This talk is so foolish, David," she said, before he could answer.

Perhaps he had not intended to reply. He was odd about Jeannette, curiously loyal to her and the problems that made her the way she was. "Well, I've wanted you from the minute we met," he said then. "Remember when that was?"

Faye did not exactly remember, but it must have been one of the first spring parties at the Ridge house. David still had been on the rise then, not where he was now, had been less smooth and sure. She was silent.

"You don't say anything."

"I've said it: I've never been unfaithful to Anson."

"That's no answer."

"It is if you understand that I mean it."

They were on the rim of one of the wooded gorges, where the road was being repaired. The CHANTIER signs loomed ahead and David slowed to let one of the roadmen flag him on. They approached a deserted old villa at one of the oblique turns, rotting into the hillside, and again David slowed.

"*If* you mean it," he said. "If we don't talk about it any more, there'll be no problem. We can stop here."

"Please don't, David."

Ignoring her, he cut sharply left into the villa's deserted courtyard, bringing the car to a stop. There was a great doorway, with gates sinking on their hinges, half open.

"We could go in there," he said. "Anson and Jeannette

184

need never know." His eyes challenged her. He rested his arm on the back of the seat and touched her hair.

"David, I asked you nicely."

"Why make it hard?"

"I'm not. And I'm not going to say again why not."

"You're afraid Anson will somehow find out."

"It's not that. I simply don't want to."

"And that's that?"

"As that as that can be. David, we've had such a wonderful time here with you and Jeannette. Don't spoil it."

"What would be spoiled?"

"Everything—for me."

"You know, Faye, I think you'd like to fuck—or do you prefer calling it making love?"

"I'm ready to call it fucking when it's that, but I like the other better."

"Wouldn't you like to? Confess."

"I hate 'confess.' You should know that. I'm a lapsed Catholic."

"*Malgré elle,* evidently. I'm a bad Jew. What's that to do with it?"

"I couldn't tell you in a million years." She drew as far away from him as the seat permitted. "I don't want to talk about it. Let's go back, please."

His direct approach had been wrong with her, he understood, and he tried another. "It's an interesting old house. In ruins, but the floors and roofs are still sound."

"I hate old abandoned houses."

"Maybe you don't trust yourself."

"Maybe."

He took her folded hands in his, held them. She made no resistance. His long, spatulate fingers laced themselves through hers. For a moment she was reminded of Baumgartner. She realized she was seeing things about David she had never consciously noticed before. The skin of his forearm was fine, shadowed with its design of thick black hair, slightly sweaty where his wrist watch broke its progress from elbow to digits. She already knew, from beach observation, his deep barrel chest, the bird of hair spread nipple to nipple, rising to his throat.

"Please," she said again, "let's not begin this."

He leaned toward her, kissing her lightly on the lips. She stiffened against him. He forced her lips apart, his tongue exploring hers. "You're wonderful," he said. "You taste of sun."

Suddenly she turned her face away and went limp, and knew she would not give in. He tired of her passivity, drawing away. It had become farce.

"I believe you really mean No."

"Let's go on." She could see she had knifed him deeply in his ego. "They always give in to you, don't they?" she asked.

He started the motor, backed out into the road. "If you mean I've had few refusals, that's true. I rarely start something unless I'm sure I can finish it."

"What made you sure this time?"

"Yes, I was wrong, evidently," he answered, not answering exactly. "I thought you liked me."

"That one. I like you very much. Anson and I both do. You and Jeannette. Let's forget this. I intend to."

"I won't forget it," he assured her.

"Perhaps that's the way to be remembered," she said lightly, putting on fresh lipstick, taking a comb from her bag and running it through her hair. She felt anticlimactic, deflated, almost half sorry she had refused him. They were approaching the sharp turn right for Cannes. "Supposing we had," she said.

"Are you changing your mind?"

"No. Only wondering how I'd have felt when we see Jeannette and Anson—if we had."

"It wouldn't have made a difference."

She felt hot and flushed, inexplicably tired. He had roused her. For the first time in her marriage she knew herself to be vulnerable—as vulnerable as Anson, probably. It was a distinct horizon and she closed her mind to it.

Jeannette and Anson had been back for hours and were sitting in the sun.

"Well," Jeannette asked, "where did the two of you go?"

"To Saint-Paul for lunch," Faye answered, as though it had been her idea, "and then we went to the Fragonard Museum at Grasse."

"Kind of a trade," Jeannette said, laughing. She showed her recapped incisor. "Anson and I had lunch at the most wonderful place, just off the Place Masséna. The Bloody Marys were marvelous."

Anson looked at Faye with the merest spark of speculation. She scotched it by going to him and kissing his cheek.

"There's something in the weather," said Jeannette. "Why don't we do something special tonight?" Her eyes, as well as Anson's, showed the Bloodys they had drunk; both seemed euphoric. "Let's all have a rest and dress up and really lay it on. Faye and I both have new dresses we're dying to wear. What about Château Madrid, David?"

"All right," David agreed, "if we can get in." He telephoned. It was to be a gala night; Princess Grace and Prince Rainier were expected, and Monsieur Steen had reserved only in time, the restaurant would be crowded.

When Faye and Anson had gone up to their rooms, Anson asked, "How far did you go with David?"

"Well, from Saint-Paul—I don't know the roads. We went past that cemetery, and we stopped at a really crazy shop with marmosets in cages and a tiny dachshund whose name was Monsieur."

"And?"

"Then Grasse and back here. There are so many little hill towns."

"How was the museum?"

"Worth it. David said we'd all go back together."

He went to her and returned the kiss she had given him minutes before. She wore a bright blue sailcloth dress buttoned at each shoulder. He unbuttoned her, letting his lips linger on her breasts as the dress slipped to the floor.

"Un peu d'amour?"

She corrected his *peu* with schoolbook lips, her kiss lingering. "Love to."

"Not laid today so far, *hein?*"

"Hein! Of course not!" She had determined not to tell him, not to spoil anything. "You want to look-see for yourself?"

"I do."

A small, dark cloud of question floated between them.

"And I'll look-see for *my*self," she said.

"Look as closely as you like."

She felt him. "You're hard as a rock."

"Prime of life. Undo my pants, I love that."

She unbuttoned him and he wriggled neatly, stepping free. Her hands clasped him and her eyes became complacent. "Mine," she said.

"All yours."

He walked her backward to the bed. She smelled of sun and sand, and the glare of the Corniche fell across the lavender-fragrant sheets, already turned down for the night. He covered her, licking her eyelids, fingering her soft down, moist from the long day in the sun. He spread her thighs wide and entered her, the first, untensing resistance, then the hot depth beyond. She opened her eyes wide, as she always did at this moment, then closed them.

"How could you think I did?" she blew into his ear.

"How could you think *I* did?"

"Let's forget."

"I'm forgetting."

He surmised a beginning crescendo in her, more rapidly

mounting than usual, and as his pulse rose and raced, he forced her eyelids open, staring into her eyes so closely their lashes tangled. Then, suddenly, she arched beneath him, reached and found her climax before him.

"Anson! Oh, Anson!"

"Down easy," he said. "This happens." He hurried a little, then, his buttocks tight, his hard belly slapping hers. Softly she lay in the descending shadow of his delight, her eyes squeezed shut. "My God, you were quick!" he said, panting.

"I'm sorry."

"Don't ever be sorry about that. It was perfect."

She lay beneath him, very still. "Yes. Me too. I love you. Do you know that?"

"I know that," he whispered beyond her cheek, obliterating their earlier question. "I love you. You're lovely. It must be the sea—we've not missed a day. Some days twice."

"Darling, move now. I'm so hot."

He unstraddled her, rolled to one side.

"You asked me a question," she said. "Did this answer it?"

"A thousand times."

"I'd never have asked you if you hadn't asked me first."

"Give us a cigarette."

She reached. "Gaulois or Camel, we seem to have both."

"You decide."

She brought the strong, acrid butt to his mouth.

He drew, exhaled. "Christ in-Hades! Is Jeannette a kook! I like her, but she's got more loose with her than screws."

"Screws. The unconscious speaks."

"Not so unconscious with her. Do you know what she did at the restaurant, during lunch?"

"No, what?"

"She groped the waiter. Openly. You should have seen his face."

"As long as she didn't grope you."

"She did. Has. The *patron* obviously saw it, so I called him over and explained that Madame was sometimes not herself. It was an expensive lunch, with the tip I had to give him."

"How many days before we leave?"

"Are you counting? We fly back next Thursday. Why? Has something happened?"

"Just thinking of Todd, getting home."

"I think of him, too," he said, giving her his promise kiss that promised others.

"We must dress. I'll go first."

"Fair enough. You came first."

"Fool."

He was grateful for the extra minutes of rest; he had hurried and was half tired, half wanting her again. Both felt privately happy during the long, rich, ceremonial dinner. *Leurs Altesses Sérénissimes le Prince et la Princesse de Monaco* were anticlimax, after the way they had felt.

"Why does she always walk ahead?"

"Because he's shorter."

"She's a pot of honey."

"You men and blondes!" Jeannette said.

"Nevertheless, they are different," David stated.

"Shall we blonde ourselves up tomorrow, Faye?"

"Don't you dare," said Anson.

They drove back to Cannes through the beginnings of a vicious mistral. Inside the house the lofty, white rooms seemed to flutter and move with the gale, and there was a hollow blowing in the fireplaces that made sleep impossible and became a steady roar by morning. Outside, the palms bent and swerved, the sea writhed, and petals fled from the stems of the flowers. Ominous thunderheads glowered over the bay and the Esterels turned to a line of gray mist—the unmentioned sorrow of the Midi. The mistral lasted three days, during which time they were immurred in the house, with little to do except drink to keep up their spirits. When

David and Jeannette drove Faye and Anson to the airport at Nice, the curtains of rain abruptly parted and paradise resumed.

"Goodby, you darlings," they said. "It's been perfect."

"Never say goodby," said Jeannette.

"We love you," David said.

"We love you, too," the Parrises cried through the glass as the great Caravelle taxied down the runway.

🌷　🌷　🌷　NESTLING IN its greening hillside, three transparent pyramids shining in last evening sun, the Ridge house wore its conventional late-springtime look. Mrs. Haines's car was just leaving: Tuesday. The mobile of brightly twittering spheres on the roof's crest undulated in the breeze. The whole gave Anson a feeling of warmth and gladness after the heat of the city and the "Bug."

Already the routines, lost for the month of his absence, were reasserting themselves, welcoming him. The lawn was freshly mowed; a fragrance of hay drifted from the farmer's fields beyond the house. The big holly had been moved to a spot in full sun, bordering on the field. Netcher, having chosen a last patch of sun on the terrace from which to watch for his arrival, leaped forward, followed by Todd, waving his butterfly net. Anson drew into the garage, bringing the Porsche into its place beside the wagon. But though Netcher's reflexes had snapped back, Todd's were slower to resume. He waited, watching the routines of rolling up windows, dropping keys into pockets, and assembling a stack of manuscripts brought home for reading, with a quietness bordering on awe. The informations stenciled on his young memory during the past month seemed to have resulted in a slow re-evaluation of probabilities, and in his childlike, withholding silence Anson could feel a conditioning to the reunion of days ago.

"How's my boy?"

"You took the early train," Todd answered, as though that were wrong.

"Because I wanted to get home. To see you." He was glad for the quick, comforting contact of lifting Todd up, the kiss of arrival, standard assurance at day's end that day had gone well, the carrying of his warm, young body indoors.

"See my butterfly?" Todd half opened one hand, revealing small, folded blue wings. "Do you like him, Daddy?"

"It's a beautiful butterfly," Anson agreed. "Let it go now—it should be free to fly away."

"But I want to keep it."

"It'll die if you do."

"Die?" Todd slowly uncurled his fingers. The blue butterfly struggled, then, through the door Anson held open, flew out of sight.

"Where will he go now? Back into his coon?"

"Cocoon. No, he'll never go back there, it's too small."

"But it's night. Where will he go?"

"To a flower the color of himself, maybe," Anson answered.

"Why, Daddy?"

"Toddy?" Faye's voice from the kitchen.

"Yoo hoo," Anson called. The manipulation of child, doorway and butterfly net had dislodged the manuscripts tucked beneath his arm and they fell, scattering, to the floor.

"I'll pick them up," Todd offered, with frowning care assembling them and carrying them to the fireplace table. The house shone from Mrs. Haines's ministrations. Magazines were neatly laid out, title above title; ashtrays were pristine. A pile of shirts, freshly ironed, lay in a basket in the

192

hallway, ready to be put into drawers. But there was a metallic reservation in the twilight, as though a stranger had come and gone, and in Faye's voice, again calling, Anson could sense that first optimisms of the rapprochement had dimmed. Todd followed him into the kitchen.

Faye was preparing Todd's supper. "How was your day?" she asked, as Todd obediently took his place at the table.

"Routine." She raised her eyes to his, unsmiling, and he kissed her. "Yours?"

"Harassing. Mrs. Haines has just gone. They moved the big holly. They brought some kind of a tractor with a shovel on it. I supervised, made them go around the drive, so they wouldn't spoil the gravel. It took four to do it. The man came and did the lawn."

"I saw."

"*And* Mother telephoned twice—she's decided to cancel her trip."

"But why?"

"Oh, there's that dock strike, and the men who were to take her trunks didn't come, and Adelaide said it was a sign there's going to be trouble this summer."

"Trouble here," said Anson. "Daddy De Gaulle is safer."

"She even called Morgan, in Paris, to ask how things are there."

"What did Morgan tell her?"

"I don't know, but she said she's heard the French are refusing to cash dollars. You've seen the papers yourself."

"An unforeseen interruption in Mother-dear's career of conspicuous waste. What else?"

"I marketed. My day." Faye was doing two things at once, dishing Todd's plate and placing it on the table, adding pinches of herbs to a casserole she and Anson would eat later. She was, on occasion, an ambitious cook, but on days Mrs. Haines came they ate simply, one main dish and a salad. She placed the casserole in the smaller of the two ovens and set the timer. "Amy and Herb wanted us to come over for drinks tonight."

"Back from Rochester again?"

"Yes. Herb's more comfortable, Amy says, but the Mayo doctors as much as told her he's going to wind up in a wheelchair. He's using a walker now."

"What in hell's a walker?"

"A thing they lean on and move along as they walk. I saw a woman at Saks using one once."

"I don't want to see anyone using a walker tonight."

"I told them no," Faye said. She still wasn't looking at him, was watching Todd as he ate. "We've got the party to settle. I thought we could do it over drinks. Why don't you shower?" The rest of her message was wordless, her eyes conveying that, so far, Todd's supper was proceeding without refusals, and that when it was finished and he was in bed, she would join him.

With this equivocal silence in his ears, he went past her to the bedroom. He stripped and stepped into the tub, pulled the glass doors closed and turned the shower head to needle. He had told Faye that his day had been routine, but in fact it had been anything else. He had given what outwardly seemed undivided attention to the office, but felt his grip on *nothing to be done* about Neile Eythe slipping and becoming less sure. He waited hourly to forget her. That he had looked up her number and address told him what he knew already: that he was hung up, the very thing he wanted not to be. He knew, too, that she was equally hung up. Remembering address and phone had become resistance to calling her; he had mislaid the slip on which he had noted these—equal chances, he hoped, that losing it had been intentional, that his better self wanted *not* to call her. He had spent his lunch hour alone, in his office, with the door closed, eating a sandwich and dragging the problem into the open so he could look at it. He faced it squarely: crowding on his return to Faye, it was a double split in his integrity, double jeopardy. A man may wear two masks, rarely three. This isolation resulted only in introspection, which, by temperament, he resisted to a marked degree. It was not only the physical memory of Neile; it was that the door had been opened on a world about which he had once only speculated, but the sampling of which now openly fascinated him. His conversation with Birnham in the sauna had been the exact equivalent of placing a foot in that door, so it would not close. He had handed himself all the weapons he needed for dismissal of the whole business, but by midafternoon he was doing so badly with the problem (he had looked up the address and number again, this time memorizing them) that he knocked off work and went home early. That many more miles of safety between himself and the *nothing to be done.*

Here, with the shower enclosing him, its needle noise obliterating the day, he tried on the oldest of his masks: that the weekend of magenta fantasy had nothing to do with Faye and his real life. But the mask at once washed away: anticipation of return to town next day, to where Neile was, thundered in him, deafening him to all the sense and caution Faye and Todd and the house represented. He rubbed down, taking stock of himself in the fogged mirror—how could he feel and be so different, when he looked the same? Finding fresh, easy clothes, he tried to see ahead, beyond the evening, to tomorrow, to the struggle that would repeat itself. If only, he thought, it were possible to live life in the sequence of one's choosing, to delete guilt's censor. Neile should have happened to him long ago. But life was not amenable to rearrangement; hours and days followed on one another in order, fell into inexorable pattern, to be lived one by one in order. He looked out at the diminishing day, already marine with evening, the holly newly transplanted, moths fluttering over the fragrant lawn. The thing had happened, was what it was, and he was the way he was. Defeated by this admission, the ambivalence of his day fled: he knew now what he was going to do, and payment and punishment could follow later, at some time he wouldn't think about. He would get through with this thing, kill it forever, and it would be over. As he told himself this, he heard Faye setting out the ice bucket and swirling cubes around in glasses to chill them: tinkle of reassuring reality returned. He accepted it with the complacence reserved for the continuance of interrupted life, forgetting, because it was easier, his day and its conflict.

"Here," Faye said, handing him his drink, "the way you like it, dry as dust, but you'll have to twist your own lemon peel." No matter how often she had tried, she had never quite mastered to Anson's satisfaction the squeeze that sprayed a film of the oil of the rind over the martini's surface.

Anson, ritually, did it for them both. They sipped, then set their glasses down on the table between them. The moment had about it a conferential quality, the table round, obviating any sense of head or foot importance. Faye opened with a peripheral query.

"What did you tell him about the butterfly? I heard his question but not your answer."

"I think I said it would go to a flower of the same color. I don't know where butterflies spend their evenings, do you?"

"I never thought. He asks harder ones than that."

"How much harder?"

"Well, you know how they are, his age; they look into and under everything. He found a salamander under a stone and brought it in, all red and wiggling. I hate things like that and showed it."

"What did he ask about that?"

"If he could keep it—to feed to the snail he keeps in that glass jar on the terrace."

"Did he put it in the jar with the snail?"

"I think he did. Of course, there's the garter snake down

by the stream, or snakes; he kills those, though I told him they're harmless."

"I wonder which one of us is the salamander?" Anson asked.

"You, I think."

"Or maybe you."

Faye said nothing.

"Perhaps we should ask Velma."

"Don't forget, we're dining with them Thursday."

"I wrote it down. I hope you like where they put the holly."

"Yes, I like it; it'll give us more protection on the north side."

"Is Vera really not going to Europe?"

"Evidently not. She's scared. The market dropped today, too."

"She'd have made such a wonderful Republican," Anson observed. "Do you remember the night she told us about how they'd finally put in central heating at Versailles? She even worked on the committee for it or something."

"She's an *Amie de Versailles,* or whatever that ribbon she wears means. Anson, don't beat her. She's my mother and I can't help the way she is." She rummaged on the table, found the list Anson had brought home and another sheet on which she had made notations. "I think this is pretty much everybody. Last year's people and this year's."

"Good."

"I've talked to the Haineses about a good date. They can do it the eighth of June. That's a week from Saturday. Long enough notice, don't you think?"

"Plenty."

"And I thought we'd do the same as other years, it's worked so well before. Late cocktails and the buffet setup and let people eat when they like. Mrs. Haines will do different dishes from last year's, of course."

"Have you thought about the music?" Anson asked.

"I'll get onto that. I thought of asking Alma if her bass fiddler might know someone who does parties. An accordionist. Should we have a singer too, do you think?"

"An accordionist would be perfect. No singers. I remember that false Joan Baez we had two years ago, and not with pleasure."

Faye made a note—*Accordionist, Alma*—and held up her list, reading from it. "Well, all the K and K people, Kastners, Kennerlys, Hansons, Steins . . ." Anson nodded as she read. "Are there any new people?"

"There's a new girl in PR, and a boy in the art department."

"What're their names?"

"PR girl's is Cahill. I think the boy's is Watson."

Faye wrote these names down. "You'll ask all of them tomorrow."

"First thing. Or Nina will."

"And I'll telephone 'The Assortment' in the morning." She counted with her pencil, saying over their names in the order they always used, beads on a string. "That still gives us only forty-four, even with Velma and Sam."

"We need more than that, in case some don't make it."

"I know. Bodies." Faye concentrated. "What about Galey Birnham?"

"If he'll come."

"Why on earth wouldn't he? He came once—the second year."

"And was bored because there was nothing he could pick up. He hates what he calls normies."

"If he knew what I think of queeries, he'd faint. Forget him then."

"He's leaving for Morocco some time in June, but I'm going to ask him anyway, in case. David will be head lion, but it won't hurt to have a cub as well."

"We could ask the jersey-suit boys, to balance Birnham,"

suggested Faye. "If they don't have a houseful, that is; I won't have their customers."

"Make it clear you want only them—use Birnham as bait, queers know him. They can all stand off in a corner and dish us."

"Or talk about chocolate cake mixes. That's what 'Gertrude' and 'Alice' say they talk about."

"That'll not be what Galey'll talk about."

"When are you going to bring me his new book?"

"Nina had the manuscript faxed today. I brought you a copy. It's over there with that stack of others. Take a deep breath before you begin."

"I'll start reading it tonight. We still need bodies," Faye said, making marks on her list. "How about a few of your lame ducks, to fill out?"

"Joanna Summers will come. I'm seeing her Friday."

"She can balance 'Gertrude' and 'Alice.' "

"I don't think Joanna's lesbian, do you?"

"She's always with that lady-wolf who is. Aroon Rigo."

"She's supposed to be the American Colette."

"Well?"

"And I'll get Nina to smell out what poets K and K has left." Kastner was tired of losing money, he said, and was slowly sloughing off both poets and writers of juvenile books.

"And, oh, yes," said Faye, remembering. "The young Carlsons."

"Who are they?"

"Just moved into the Draper apartment. I met her today in the market. Nice. Vassar. In her late twenties. Don't know about him, but they'll be bodies."

"We must be beyond fifty by now," Anson guessed.

"I always think invite sixty and hope thirty-five will show up."

"Maybe some of 'The Assortment' will have overnight guests."

"Maybe. But no overnights for us, agreed?"

"Jeannette and David stayed over last time."

"I'm not sure I could stand having her stay over now," Faye said.

"Come on, I thought we'd buried that."

"She keeps coming back, like undigested cabbage."

"Don't be bitchy."

"She does, though. If they stayed, I'd keep wondering where *you* were. If you read me."

"Give me your glass," said Anson impatiently. "Look, Faye, Jeannette was a *discrete* incident." He spelled it for her.

"I went to Radcliffe."

"Then you should know. It means 'not a series.' "

"It means nothing of the sort. It means 'separate, detached from others.' We looked it up only a few months ago. I'll get the dictionary if you don't believe me."

"Don't. You're right, I remember now. But you know what I meant."

"Say what you mean. Or mean what you say." An almost forgotten axiom of Madame Doheny's, at the convent.

"Do we have to quarrel about it?"

"I'm not quarreling."

"Or forgetting."

"I have gray matter, like everyone else. Memory's a garden that's hard to weed out."

"The weeds go to seed—and begin all over. Let's talk about something else."

"All right. We've settled the party. What was David like at lunch? You didn't tell me."

"Himself—in one way. In another way I don't entirely understand he was rather odd. He said some strange things."

"David *is* a strange man. Let's not say what Jeannette is."

Anson stared at the surface of his martini; the citrus oil atop it seemed floating in the design of a net. He wished he'd never started this.

"Well, what did David *say?*"

"I probably imagined it. We loved them once."

"Yes. It seems a long time ago. I wonder why you thought him odd."

"I said I didn't know why."

"My irony eludes you," she said.

"Well, he's watching *Good Time* climb—we think it'll be number two on the *Times* list this week, fantastic for a book just out. And he's on the early drafts of his new one. Involved in Jeannette's problems, of course."

"Dear Jeannette."

"I think you don't quite understand what's happening to her."

"I remember her the last time she was here. That Sunday."

"She's in terrible shape, from what David says."

"He told me all about it long ago," said Faye, "when we were with them in Cannes."

"He did?"

"The day you drove Jeannette to the dentist. It was quite a session. He laid on hands. He has the gift of the tongue, too."

"Say what you mean," he threw back at her.

"I'm saying it. I didn't tell you about it then."

"Why not?"

"Do you tell *me* things? Did you?"

"I told you about Jeannette at the restaurant in Nice. I'll never forget that waiter's face as long as I live."

"Though David didn't need to tell me. I was getting it from her whenever we went anywhere together. Those fauns of hers at the Majestic, the *téléphoniste* at the Carlton she was mad about. Even Arabs working on the roads. She's man-mad. She liked the shape of your ahss straight off, remember?"

"No."

"She told you. In front of me."

"No," he said again. "When?"

"When we first were seeing them a lot. It was at the apartment, that night we went to see *Fiddler on the Roof.*"

Anson said nothing. It was not that his memory was poor, but the desire to batten on the past was almost nonexistent in him. He looked at her. "You're spoiling for it tonight. What's wrong?"

"I'm not spoiling, only discussing—*trying* to discuss—our onetime darlings, David and Jeannette. She's like a drink of loaded milk—you believe it until the poison starts creeping through your veins."

"They're still our friends, if no longer so darling. Friendships change. I still think you're spoiling."

"All right. Who's N E?"

"NE means northeast to me."

She recited to him the address and phone number written on the slip she had found in his pocket.

"Oh, that. She's a girl writing a book."

"You should have added that to the slip."

"I must have written it down at the Steen party."

"Oh, no, it was in the suit you wore yesterday."

"Well, whichever day I wrote it."

"She's the redhead."

"How did you guess that?"

"You told me when we looked at the party pictures in Sunday's papers."

"What a memory."

"I left the slip on your bureau."

"Not that I need it now, now that you've memorized what was on it. Did you call her up, too?"

"You underestimate me. Darling."

The buzz of the stove timer interrupted. Faye put down her glass and stood up. "It's going to be on the lap tonight, I haven't set up the table."

"Okay. Shall I do the salad?"

"It's done. I'll bring both plates." She went out. "Well,

what kind of book is N E writing in Mott Street?" she continued when she had brought their dinners.

"How should I know?"

"I thought you just might."

"Why would you care if I did?"

"I wouldn't, particularly, but I was curious about her name. It wasn't in the papers."

"It wouldn't be. She's not anybody."

"You must know it."

"It's Eythe."

"Mm. Irish. Did you see her after the party?"

"The party was the whole evening," Anson said.

"An evasion if ever I heard one. Why not ask her to our party—with Birnham? She was his girl, you said."

"Yes, I said. And I remember what you said. 'So it's girls now?' "

"She'd be another body."

Anson finished and carefully set his plate on the table, placed his napkin beside it. "I'm tired of this," he said. "I think I'll read." He went to the stack of manuscripts and chose one, carrying it to his chair by the bookshelves.

"Are you really not going to answer my question?"

"Which one? There seem so many. I've got to chew my way through at least two of these scripts tonight. Tomorrow's Wednesday conference."

"All I asked was did you see her after the party?"

"I offered to drive her home. She's just a kid and Birnham had ditched her and you know what Hudson piers are at night."

"Did you take her home?"

"No."

"You went on to dinner."

"No."

"I'd like an answer."

"I said I'm going to read."

"So read. You're impossible when you're like this," she told him. "I sometimes feel a stranger—like those times when we're out somewhere and you get that look and talk about places you want to go to. You never talk about them when we're alone together. Remember the night we saw Tevye and you went on about 'extensions of living, a sea without tides, a moon without orbit'? You see, I remember, if you don't."

"I remember that night and what I said. And if I could transmigrate myself to Borobudur right now, I'd like nothing better."

"Wherever Borobudur is."

"You went to Radcliffe. If you don't know, look it up."

Faye slowly rose and gathered up the plates. Anson's eyes were fixed on the page. "I think, since you're going to read, I'll go over and see Velma. It's Sam's bowling night. I'll see you later."

"If I'm up."

"Let me know if you go to Borobudur," she said.

Anson decided to read in bed. He checked the house, leaving hall and porch lights on for Faye. Last of all, he very quietly opened the door of Todd's room, but quiet as he was, Todd stirred in his sleep and turned over. The light filtering through the door crack showed Anson his face, startlingly like himself as a child, his tousled hair golden in the beam, eyelids like the petals of white poppies, ringed by sandy lashes. His cheeks were brushed with the pulsing health of childhood. Anson had an impulse to go to his side, press his lips to the downy, pink cheeks, but caution restrained him. Todd, once wakened, at whatever hour, was difficult to put back to sleep. Leaving the door ajar, he tiptoed to his own bed and read until he fell asleep, the manuscript a *circonflexe* atop his chest.

Faye found him like that and carefully lifted up the manuscript and put it aside, marking the place. She had found Velma alone and they had had a long talk—about which she wanted to think no more tonight. When she had come in, she had gone to the bookshelves. The house had a rather better-than-average clutch of reference books, and after some trial and error (because unsure of the spelling of Borobudur), she found what she wanted:

BOROBUDUR bō'rō-bŏŏ-dōōr', Buddhist temple in Java thought to have housed a relic of the Buddha. After the Mohammedan conquest of 1475–79, swallowed up, like Angkor-Wat, by heavy jungle growth. Explored and excavated in 1814 by Sir Stamford Raffles (*q.v.*), lieutenant governor of Java. The temple consists of a terraced pyramid rising on a base 600 feet square. Galleries extend along each terrace and are covered with fine bas-reliefs. The walls support 436 niches containing life-sized Buddhas seated on lotus cushions. . . .

This told her something about Borobudur, but very little about Anson, except to remind her again of his curious words of the Tevye night, years ago. His words, cached in memory, came forward like messages on a revolving sign: *Some farther landscape.* . . . Borobudur, she understood, symbolized the "extension of living" he craved, some place he wanted to go to, but alone, without her. She looked over at his face, blank with dreams, stared for a moment fixedly, then picked up the manuscript of Galey's book and read herself to sleep.

❀ ❀ ❀ WEDNESDAY CONFERENCES at Kastner and Kennerly were serious, and staff attending invariably appeared preoccupied both before they began and after they ended; beneath the surface of relaxation in which they were conducted lay the awareness that decisions made there were final and affected many people. The K and K imprint was prestigious, and Carl Kastner's critical acumen both acute and flexible; he had, also, an extremely practiced ability in balancing literary and commercial values. When he emerged from his *gare centrale* and walked slowly to the conference, all others already were assembled.

The conference room was white and square and high, with a broad, glass-topped table at its center. Easy chairs, upholstered in white leather, were grouped around it, and on the glass surface were thermos carafes and drinking glasses, ashtrays, pads and pencils, staplers and paper clips. Synopses and sample chapters of nonfiction books, commissioned in advance, lay before Claxon Kennerly's chair; he was known in the trade for his almost uncanny ability to feel the market two years ahead and to marry the right author to the right idea. Great blowups of K and K successes were framed around the walls; newest of these was the just-hung enlargement of the *Good Time Coming* dust jacket, to which Carl Kastner, as he came in and took his chair, paid homage with a wave of the hand.

"There, ladies and gentlemen," he said, "is the subsidizer of at least half the books on our projected Fall List which we can count on to make losses." His way of putting the group at ease.

There were, also, at either end of the room, oil portraits in Barbizon frames of Carl Kastner's father and uncle, who had founded the firm in the 1920's, beginning on lower Fourth Avenue in a modest two-room office. Kastner presided at the opposite end of the table from Kennerly; between were seated Anson and his associate editors, Hanson and Stein, PR, advertising, promotion, foreign rights, the art designer, and, anywhere in between, the salesmen. Kastner's secretary, a lovely Haitian girl, sat a little behind him, near the one telephone; the phone had no bell, a small light showing on it when, very rarely, an urgent call was put through. Nina Gerson sat at Anson's left. All listened with great attention while Anson, with laconic modesty, recounted the hour-to-hour progress of the *Good Time* paper sale to Everest, and the salesmen read out the book's extraordinary reorder figures. Anson told what he knew about David Steen's next book, which was not much, though its delivery date had been set. Birnham's book and the film interest in it were discussed. The fates of two first novelists were summarily settled: one, a young black writer, would be second on the Fall List; the other, a Yale dropout, would spend his next six months rewriting what was expected to be the fiction success of the next spring. The question of Joanna Summers' further advance rose and was questioned by Kennerly.

"What does she do with six years?" he asked Anson. "Isn't that how long we've been nursing her?"

"About six," Anson confirmed. "I think she'll come through."

"If she'd stop writing criticism and being a judge of the novels of others on all those panels, she might finish her memoirs," Kennerly said.

"She judges others, herself she cannot budge," Kastner capped it. He left to Anson the decision on the further advance she wanted.

Anson took advantage of having most of the staff together to invite them to the party Faye and he would give June eighth, Nina ticking names off a list as he made the rounds of the table during the coffee break.

It was a lengthy conference. Disciplined, Anson pigeonholed his decision of the night before. He had felt embarrassed at having to relate the progress of the One sale, ashamed at seeming to have the key to expertise when it had been the market and the book itself that had done the work; he had only guided it. The voices of the others at the table reached him remotely, as though emerging from tape. He listened intently, sucking the stem of his eyeglasses between his teeth. Though capable of following conference procedures and thinking of personal matters at the same time, he could concentrate on his private life only in segments. His love for Faye, for Todd. . . . The crumbling friendship with Jeannette and David. . . . Neile and the magenta wind. He thought of last night's nagging, undiluted by morning-after making up: Faye had stayed in bed, let him get himself off for work. This whole day had crystallized for him, determination reached during his shower banishing all compromise. His mind froze at the thought of Neile. Here, at the core of his life that made the periphery of his life possible, he felt he was closing his eyes like a roller-coaster rider about to plunge downward. He feared seeking out Neile, despaired of his inability to reject the world he was hurling himself into. But he was strengthened by the quarrel with Faye—how difficult it might have been to do had they once more kissed and started over! He was operating from the point of her rejection, a point from which he had operated before.

Conference concluded, its decisions and duties allocated, he returned to his office and dialed Neile's number. He waited for six rings, feared he had misdialed, dialed again, this time hearing the intermittences of silence dully, as though having made the decision not to call her at all. This depressed him.

"Are we all squared away on the spring party?" he asked Nina.

"I made notes of those who can't come—only two—and I'll work on the car pool this afternoon," Nina said.

"Don't forget the stockroom boys."

"I'm going to invite them now, before they go to lunch."

"And I think we should ask Jim Brown and his wife, as well as the Reuben Blocks."

"Got it."

"Do I have a lunch today?"

"No, nothing. Shall I order you something sent up?"

"I'll get a bite downstairs," Anson decided, leaving just before the noon exodus lest he be inveigled into eating with Hanson and Stein.

The streets were warm with heavy-moted sunshine. He walked uptown and at 53rd paused, hearing the deeply buried roar of the subway far below. It seemed a sign. Neile might not be at home, but he could at least see where she lived. Perhaps she would have returned by the time he reached her house. Descending the many levels of stairways, stairs glassed in, stairs hedged with bookstores, stairs flanked by long, sealed display windows housing summer clothes that already looked tawdry, he came to the escalators and tunneling clatter, asking of the token seller the stop for Mott Street. It seemed less furtive than taking a cab: underground darkness ending in sunlight in a part of town he had not seen in years. The stop and its street were question marks, vaguely remembered from college days, when he and a now forgotten roommate had gone searching for the Chinese theater and, not finding it, wound up at a restaurant on Pell Street. The food, better remembered than the place, had been sweet and sour, the mustard very hot.

He climbed up out of the subway. The wind from the Hudson blew through the streets, carrying on it smells of sea and docks. Among the chipped cement and asphalt, in this anonymous neighborhood, it seemed easier to feel what he did: curiosity, desire, rut.

The house on Mott was a brownstone with pedimented windows boarded up on the street floor in a row that anywhere else would have been torn down to make way for progress. It had only barely escaped; next to it but one, a demolition squad had cast onto the sidewalks a tumble of old doors and plankings; their work stop for lunch had plunged the street into quiet, except for an occasional window flung up or slammed shut. A huge gold wrecking ball, limned with

209

brick dust, hung still against the sky, attached to the jib of a bright yellow crane.

Anson went into the small entrance hall and studied the mailboxes. With characteristic Manhattan uniformity there were four, proceeding left to right, street floor to top. The names above the bells, like pencil erasers, were a mishmash: Epstein, Ah Ching Moy, Birnham, Eythe-Peckham. He rang Eythe-Peckham and waited. No buzzer sounded, but the door stood ajar and he went inside. At once he was in a dark corridor with blank doors at each end. Soup was cooking somewhere, a smell like armpits. The halls were as dark as Birnham had described them; in the gloom he could see the dust-hung walls and caked paint that had been old at the century's turn; the banisters were rickety and the floors creaked. A smudge of gray light, filtering from above, enabled him to find his way to the top floor. That, also, had two doors, one, at the rear, with a peephole. Wavering a last moment, he listened, hearing a dry rattling and tinkling, a typewriter run by hunt and peck. He knocked. The rattling stopped and the peephole opened, became an eye, closed again. After a noisy sliding of bolts the door swung wide.

She looked smaller standing in daylight, flooding the stairwell gloom. "You," she said.

"Do you mind my arriving like this?"

"A surprise," she said. He saw again her bright thatch of red, her green eyes; her forehead, freckled as he remembered, was lightly luminous with the day's heat. "I remember your last words."

"So do I."

"I was working, but come in for a minute." She waited until he stepped inside, then shot the bolts of the door, walking past him through many small rooms into a long, gray-walled one with a skylight. It had a canvas curtain drawn across it, torn and stained, through which sun filtered. There were low, truncated windows, below eye level, giving onto a garden in which grew a heaven tree, thin and skimpy from its climb out of sour soil, but fully branched where it had found the light.

"I tried to telephone you before coming," he said.

"That's no good." She turned to the table where she had been working, covering the typewriter. She pointed to an overnight bag on a chair, from which protruded a telephone cord. "I keep it there so I won't hear it ring. Besides, think how much more you find out by just knocking on the door."

"You're really writing that book."

"Yes, I am. Does that surprise you?"

"A little," he admitted. "I'm sorry if I broke anything up."

"Don't be." She wore a yellow halter and faded dungarees, shortened above the knees and roughly fringed, and was barefoot. He remembered her feet. "Did you make a point of coming down here, or did you just happen to be in the neighborhood?"

"I made a point. It's not a neighborhood I'm usually in."

"I suppose not. Beautiful Person."

"I remember not liking that the first time you said it."

"It's a handle. Clichés are good for clichés."

It was hot in the room.

"Why did you come?" she asked, facing him.

"Because we were good together."

"Oh, yes," she said, as though remembering with difficulty. "We made it really big, I know. I was bombed out, thought I'd never make it back here. I felt pissing awful, if you want to know."

"I shouldn't have let you go."

"What was there to stay for? You were bombed yourself. You must have slept."

"I did. It seemed like days."

"Didn't you feel awful?"

"No, all right. I kept thinking of you."

There was a crazy upright piano with candleholders beside

the music rack, and its sides were covered in faded pink plush. She perched on the stool in front of it. "A little something the previous tenant left behind," she explained.

"Was she Peckham?" he asked.

"No."

"Then she's a roommate?"

"He."

"Oh."

"Did you think there was nobody?"

"I didn't think about that."

"He's in and out," she said. "Why don't you sit down? Like a drink?"

"No, thanks."

The only other place was a bed, low, with no headboard, a spring and mattress on stump legs. He perched awkwardly on the edge. She looked at him, her green eyes smiling.

The afternoon hung around them, a dusty clamor from the demolition that had started up again. The wrecking ball could be heard crashing into walls, which sank in thunder. There was always a silence before it struck again, filled with shouts. The silences were moth down—his stupefaction and delight at being within touch of her. He said, "I thought about you all weekend. I wish you'd come over here and sit with me."

"It wouldn't be any good."

"I'll make it good. Come on."

She got up from her stool and crossed to him, her green eyes looking soberly down at him. Taking her hand, he drew her down. "I want you," he said. "Let's undress."

"Can't have today," she said.

"Why not?"

"Because—you know."

"I hate 'you know.' Why should there be 'you know' between us?"

"I can't because—my glimpse of the moon, you fool!"

"I'm sorry," he said again, comprehending.

She shrugged, her thatch of hair against his shoulder. "I hate it, but there it is."

"Shall I go?"

"No. Move a little. There. Unless you must."

He lay beside her now, stretched out on the bed. The wrecking was going full blast, and with each swing of the ball, the house trembled. They lay, staring up at the rusty canvas curtain of the skylight, saying nothing. Then, raising herself on one elbow, she put her small hand, short-fingered, to his throat, loosening his tie.

"Thanks," he said, and drew her face down to his, kissing her, but lightly. Outside, in the sunshine, the ball pounded. She unbuttoned and folded his shirt back with the care of a cutter laying out a pattern.

"I remembered how red you are," she said. "Like me." Her fingers plowed through the cross of hair on his chest, plucking at his nipples until they became hard.

He closed his eyes against the bright, hot curtain. "Oh, do that," he said, holding her, his mouth again finding hers. He could feel her hand moving downward. Her fingers traversed the electric path of his zipper, found the tab flattened beneath his belt, and slid it slowly down. He shifted and raised up so she could draw his trousers away, her fingers a warm rake, nails lightly scratching the corrugations of his scrotum, rising and tightening.

"You witch, you bitch!" he said. "I've got to have you, moon or not."

She shook her head as she kissed him. "Lie still." She grasped the shaft of his penis, hotly tumescent, teasing from its base upward, squeezing hard as she took the pulsing head in her warm palm and held it. "You like that?"

"It's bliss—but don't stop kissing me!"

She imprisoned his lips in hers. The blatant wrecking sounds rose like a wall around them, but there were smaller, nearer, sounds on the landing outside the door. Footsteps rose from the creaking stairs and paused. A door opened somewhere.

Anson broke his lips away. "My God! I thought you bolted that door!"

"I did. That's only Galey," she reassured him. "Going up to the roof for his sun bath. You heard him opening the roof door."

He fell back, sweating. The fear of discovery had cut him back. But she returned him slowly and rhythmically to where he had been and held him there. *Stop!* She knew when to rebegin. There were changes in the demolition sounds. Invisibly, a section of wall fell with a flat thump and dust rose in the air, spattering finely on the skylight. Then a steady, mechanical stitching of great tappets in a motor being slowed. The motor chugged to a stop and all was quiet. They could hear the voices of workmen, leaving for the day, followed by the sigh of the heaven tree as the dust settled on its leaves. His heart rose in rhythm, pounded, and his mouth hungrily opened, begging again for hers. Her clenched fist drew him forward, back, forward. *Don't stop now!* He grunted as his flanks leaped, leaped again, fell back. She held him resolutely until it was over. He shuddered into limpness, her lips now beside his ear, waiting for his breath to level.

He said, "You're a stout one. I came and went before I came."

"Juicy boy. You swung. Next time I'll be all right."

"You were fabulous," he assured her. "And next time, I'll fuck you proper."

He rested. She rose and went into the next room and closed a door. He heard a tap running. She came back, casually tossing him a towel.

"That was a near thing," he said, "when Galey went by. Are you sure that's who it was?"

"Positive."

"Not Peckham?"

"No, it was Galey. I know his timing."

"Baby, you know all about timing!"

"He goes up to get the last sun. Says it makes the best tan."

Still it bothered him. "You're *sure* it was no one else? Not Peckham?"

"Forget Peckham," she said impatiently. "I told you it was Galey. Epstein on the first floor is an old woman who can't climb stairs—"

"I smelled her soup."

"She cooks lungs, I think. Anyway, Ah Ching is a spice man, you know, a wholesaler for dried ducks or something—we call him the dried Chinaman. Galey's on the third floor. And me."

That satisfied him. He nodded, lying with hands behind his head, towel bunched on his chest, his belly silvery with tracks of dried gism. (Let the K and K stylists, resolutely unembarrassed, insist on *jissom* when editing for house style; to him it would always be the more terse term of boyhood, cryptic, secret.) Tardily blushing, he spread the towel over himself. For a thin, rust-colored stretch of minutes he must have slept, dreamy and relaxed and far away, then fully waking. He asked her the time.

"Quarter past four."

"It can't be!"

She laughed. "These things take time."

"I must call the office," he said. "Should have called earlier."

She unlocked the overnight bag near the desk, took out the phone, brought it to him. He dialed the K and K number, reached Nina.

"Why didn't you tell me you'd be lunching late?" she asked.

"Uh—I didn't lunch." At once hunger pangs struck him. "I got involved. I won't be back today."

"Somebody nice, I hope."

"Girl-type novelist."

"No kidding! Did you forget you had a three-thirty with Carl?"

"Clean forgot. Give him a snow job."

"Already covered for you."

"Thanks. See you in the morning, then," Anson said.

"Anson—are you okay?"

"Of course. Why?"

"Tomorrow's Memorial Day. No office."

"God, so it is! Well then, see you day after."

"And you've got Joanna Summers first thing in the morning. Ten-thirty. Don't forget."

"Happy Memorial."

"You too." He hung up.

Train. Ridge. Taxi—or subway, faster at this hour. He got up and she showed him where to wash. It was a fantastic place, long and narrow, with a blue porcelain urinal at one end, a whooshing old toilet with elevated oaken water box and chain, a tiny basin set very low. Remembering the jeans that had begun his jeopardy, he found a box of Kleenex, providentially full, wrapped himself as carefully as any ballet dancer, and made do. Once more in the skylighted room, he found his tie, tied it, flung his jacket over his shoulder.

She watched him wryly. "I suppose I can call you Anson now."

"Why not?" He went to her, kissed her. "Neile."

"Did you tell your wife about Friday night?"

"No, and won't tell her about today." Blackmail beginning—she wasn't as indifferent a swinger as he'd hoped.

"Maybe she'll guess."

He said nothing.

"Because *I* could guess you've been with someone else since Friday. Your wife?"

"Why would I tell you?" he asked roughly.

"Next time I won't ask—when I'm fucked."

"Trying to turn me on again?" He kissed her, remembering her hidden lips below, secret in fiery down, hard to the parting, grasping when entered. "What *about* next time?"

"Up to you."

"I'll phone—if that thing's not in the suitcase."

"Want to fly a little? I've still got five bombers Galey gave me."

"But you told me you felt pissing awful."

"It was worth it, to go where we did."

"No."

She let him go to the door, pull the bolts, let himself out. On the stairs he threw on his jacket, shivering, but not from cold, groping his way down, grasping the banisters at each landing. The street was where he had left it, tawdry in last, oblique sunlight. His stomach was growling now, he was starving from no lunch and sex. He made his train, seconds to spare, just contriving to grab a hot dog with mustard in the station, sleeping the hour to Stamford opposite Ray Doyle, who had been in town for the day. He looked sweaty and tired.

"A day away from the novel?" Anson asked as they walked toward the "Bug." "Thanks for waking me, by the way. I was bushed."

"I'm kind of bushed myself," Ray said. "There isn't going to be any novel, Anson. I'm probably going to go back to writing 'Love Me Today.' Where I was years ago. But to vomit!"

Anson nodded, vaguely remembering the first time he had seen Ray's name on the parabola of credits, the TV agonies of heartbroken mother, betrayed wife, the classic sexpot hidden away on the classic American back street. "Maybe you can work on the book weekends."

"Nope. 'Love Me Today' has spoiled me for anything but soap dialogue. Probably where I belong. Anyway, better than wearing the apron and pushing the vacuum."

They parted in the "Bug's" parking lot.

"You've got mustard on your chin," Faye told Anson when he got home.

"Mustard?"

"Look in the mirror."

"I ate a hot dog before getting on the train. Light lunch. Saw Ray." He told her Ray's news.

"Poor Ray," Faye said. "Or poor Alma—I've never been able to decide which I'm sorrier for."

"Bring me my first drink in the shower, will you?"

"Coming up," Faye said.

iii

❦   ❦   ❦

The Road
to Borobudur

🌷 🌷 🌷 JEANNETTE TURNED in her sleep. "Oh, God! God, why?" she cried out in her rich, deep voice. "Why, God, *why?*"

It was an anguished, chilling question, piercing to the heart. Almost at once her blue enamel clock sounded its alarm. David already had been awake for some time. He lay very still, head covered by his sheet, as he listened to his wife get up and pace through her pre-*Dottore* routine. Coffee. Her first cigarette, smelling far sweeter than his own first ever tasted. The tap of her brushes and comb picked up and put down on her dressing table as she did her hair. The slide of zippers. Her closing of the apartment door. The hum of the elevator as she fled downward to her analytic hour.

David waited until he heard this hum, then got up and went at once to his writing room. Even before he had had his coffee he was beginning to work. He knew as little as anyone else about the mysterious business of writing and the ways in which it poured from his unconscious into reality. He understood only that if he could come straight from his night into his day, without speaking or being spoken to, the miracle would happen: the gates of night would break open and become day, the flow would begin. Jeannette and he had long observed a pact of silence in the mornings, she because she wanted to be fresh for her hour, he because he wanted no voice to disturb the miracle's happening. His writing was less an act of creation than of discerning what was already there to be written down; the *donnée,* in all senses a true gift, awaited him. The pouring from him of what was there was connected closely with the assurance of sexual potency, which he took for granted. Finding the exact voice in which any day's work would express itself (and there was only one possible, immediately recognizable and pursued) was not unlike the variation of sexual approach to different women: always the same, yet always varied. His coffee consumed, twelve freshly sharpened pencils to hand, cigarette burning (mostly in the tray, forgotten), he then entered into a state of happiness that was unlike any other part of his life. It was beyond sensuality, beyond narcissism, and in this condition of grace, he became his true self: sentences flew from his pencils' tips, grew into paragraphs, paragraphs flowed together and became the reality of the veiled, unconscious vision he had had of them in sleep. Curtains dropped, mirages became horizons to which he traveled in sure knowledge that there were no others so ordered or exact for the story. And when, after fifty minutes, an hour (rarely more), he threw down his blunted pencils, he experienced a delicious exhaustion, totally without anxiety; everything that was going to happen to the book that day had happened, a good hour before his secretary appeared; the rest, though necessary, would be anticlimax. During that hour he shaved, bathed and dressed, and then his marital world and its disorder returned and he prepared, again, to take his place in that disorder. There would be Jeannette: disorder incarnate. But while he had been alone with his pencils, he had lived the short segment of a secret life that would enable him to endure the hours of the day to come.

222

Now it was slightly past noon; his secretary had gone to lunch and David was sitting in the living room, reading over typed first drafts of work he had done the day before. He heard the hum of the elevator rising, then Jeannette's key in the lock. She came in, looking radiant.

"I've been shopping." She placed a long, white florist's box on the hall table and drew off her gloves. "I went straight from my hour. I found the most beautiful larkspur and stock for my new urn." The urn, a bright blue Sèvres one, stood on the coffee table, its orange lot number still glued to the base, her purchase from Parke-Bernet's last French sale of the spring. She undid the box, held up the flowers. "Aren't they simply perfect?"

"Perfect," he agreed.

"I must get them into water." She held the larkspur and stock in one arm and came to get the urn, cradling it in the other. She went out to the kitchen. David watched her speculatively, then returned to his typescript.

There were clues to the relentless force with which he worked. He understood some of them; others he resisted analyzing or thinking about. One he understood went so far back in his life that remembering it was difficult. He had had an illness in very early childhood that had resulted in his left leg being slightly shorter than his right. This had dealt a severe blow to his early image of himself; he had limped his first day in kindergarten, a day he had never forgotten. The psychological reverberations of this outweighed by far its importance; the limp was slight always, no longer noticeable because of a small corrective pad he wore in one shoe; but the rich fantasy life he had led as a child was related to it, was responsible for his strivings to overcome the leg's shortness. He had been rejected for football and basketball, but had excelled in track, not breaking records, but holding his own. Early in his writing career he had undergone a complicated struggle. He would have signed any pact, either with

223

God or the Devil, in return for fame; but neither had seemed interested, and the final agreement had had to be made with himself. It was a very real pact, in its way as binding as any of the papers he kept in his bank boxes. This was a secret he kept from everyone, including Jeannette. When he thought about it, and he often did, he realized it had much to do with the death of his younger brother in childhood—that, and the death of his first wife, after which his first great spurt of narrative writing had gushed from him, washing away his grief, eroding all banks of his former self in its flood. How he had loved Jeannette! Loved her still, though she had taught him that love does not, of necessity, have to do with happiness.

Her flowers, arranged in the urn, took precedence over his reading. She carried them in, placing them before him, like an offering.

"Our Mediterranean colors," he said.

She sighed. "I wish we were there."

"We soon will be. Le Grand Charles permitting."

"I was thinking this morning, if only we could go now, tomorrow, instead of next month. Couldn't we?"

"There are things to be done before we go. I have to get this part of my next in shape. I have broadcasts and telecasts, so that *Good Time* will hit top."

"It'll hit it anyway."

"And there's Faye and Anson's party June eighth."

Jeannette sat down and lighted a cigarette. "I rather dread that. All those suburban wives and husbands."

"You were a suburban wife once, don't forget. Remember? That dreary bungalow on Halldale Avenue, before the great dressmakers and Cartier and Parke-Bernet? Sèvres urns? What did you pay for it?"

"I'd rather not tell you. It's of the period."

"All right, but don't tell me about suburban wives and husbands."

"David, of course I remember—but who wants to go back?"

He still wore the green eyeshade he used at his desk, pushed back on his head. "The people we know in Europe aren't so very different from those we meet at Faye and Anson's."

"They're European."

"And there's something wrong with everybody."

She laughed. "Of course!"

"I promised Anson we'd come."

"Then I suppose we'll go."

"What happened between the four of us, I wonder?" David asked.

"Friendships fade."

"Mine hasn't faded for either of them."

"Well, I suppose mine hasn't either. But things are different."

"You saw them when I was on the Coast."

"Yes. Did I tell you?"

"Anson. I'd have known anyway, when I paid the garage —you had the Continental picked up at the Ridge."

"The Sunday before you got back. I—I wasn't at my best. I was missing you."

"You got stoned."

"Is that a guess or an accusation?"

"Neither. But not hard to figure out, from what Anson said."

"What did Anson say?"

"Was he supposed to say anything?"

"David, you're trapping me!"

"No, only interested in what you do."

She closed her eyes, holding her cigarette before her. "Ah, yes, what I do. David, I told you the other night, I've been having a hard time."

"What does *Dottore* say about it—if I may ask?"

"He doesn't *say* anything, at least not very much."

"Do you really tell him everything?"

"Almost everything."

"What do you withhold?"

"Things I can't tell anybody, you *or* him."

"Do you ever ask him questions?"

"Sometimes. When they come up naturally."

"How much does he question you?"

"Very little. Only enough to keep me on track."

David considered this. "I wonder if you told him about that curious thing you've taken to wearing around your wrist."

"I've just noticed—I'm not wearing it."

"You left it on your dressing table. What is it?"

"Oh, sort of a talisman. For good luck."

"Rather shabby, your watch and bracelets considered. Where did you get it?"

"One of the taximen at the corner stand gave it to me. David—it's not what you think."

"How do you know what I think?"

"I know how you look. He's a driver who's driven me to *Dottore's* a number of times. I didn't even recognize him until he told me he knew my address."

"He gave you that thing?"

"Yes. For luck."

"Did he drive you this morning?"

"As a matter of fact, yes, he did."

David said nothing, waiting.

"I wore it one day to *Il Dottore's* and he asked about it. He said I'm very primitive, that the bracelet means something magical to me."

"So you leave it behind on your dressing table."

"I forget things in the mornings. I'm tired."

They sat looking at each other across the flowers.

"When did you sleep with Anson?" David asked.

Jeannette's eyes narrowed. "I knew he'd told you!"

"He didn't tell me."

"But you couldn't have known! It wasn't what you think—"

"I've told you, you have no idea what I think. It must have been the Sunday he drove you home. He did tell me he'd driven you."

"Did he tell you why?"

"I knew you must have been drunk."

"That's why it happened. I was missing you."

"Yes, so much that you've refused to let me make love to you ever since I came back from the Coast."

"I've told you and *told* you what a hard time I'm having!"

"About what? You know, Nettie, some day you're going to have to stop being in analysis and start living again. Talk to me as though I exist. I am your husband."

"Not that *you* haven't had your bits on the side!"

"If I have—"

"And you have—"

"—it's been because of you. You strayed first, Nettie."

"I'm not so sure of that."

"I am. I remember when it was and who it was. You see, I was capable of fidelity, once. I was faithful to Sarah, and Sarah was faithful to me."

"You know I've never liked to talk about her. First wives!"

"But there it is," David said. "And I'd have been faithful to you."

"Of course it would be my fault!"

"It wasn't mine, at least in the beginning. Certainly Anson's no fault of mine. Was it the first time, or have you been sleeping with him all the time we've known them?"

"We've been abroad half the time."

"Answer me. When Faye and Anson were with us in Cannes. Then?"

"No. And that's the God's truth. Believe that. I wondered about you and Faye, that day you went off together."

"The day you and Anson went to Nice. To be honest, Nettie, I was so sure you'd put the make on him that I tried to make Faye."

"And—did you?"

"She can't be made, at least not by me."

"You've tried since, I've no doubt."

"A few efforts in the pantry. But no dice."

"Good for her!"

"Why? Nettie, I *need* sex."

"You get it."

"But not with you. You'll screw anybody but me, evidently."

"David, I— Sometimes I can't help myself. It just seems to *happen* to me."

"I know how lovely you are."

"Not any more I'm not."

"But to me. I adore you. The other night, after the big party—why did you turn me away?"

"I had my hour to go to."

"Shit. You simply didn't want to."

"No, I didn't."

"Why? It was the top of my life, getting those seven figures. They were your idea, really—you're the one who held out, helped me to hold out till we got them. It would have meant everything for me if we could have been together. The way we used to be."

She laughed silently. "Forgetting the ones in between? Yours *and* mine?"

"When I'm roused and passionate I forget both. Everything. Have you had that taximan who gave you the bracelet?"

"No."

"But sex is in the situation."

"Yes. He waits for me to come out of *Dottore's* office. He waited today."

"Ah! And did he drive you shopping?"

"He was there, as I said, so I took his cab. I had him wait while I went looking for the stock and larkspur."

"On the expensive side. Difficult, too, with no double-parking."

"He drove around and around until I was through."

"I saw your face when you came in. I knew there was something. I suppose he's what you call young flesh."

"He has nice wrists."

"Where that crazy bracelet came from," David guessed.

"Well, yes."

"I give up. But then, I'm not *Il Dottore.*"

"I sometimes think he's given up on me too, or would like to."

"Not at fifty bucks an hour, five or six times a week. He won't give up."

"Even he doesn't understand some things."

"I suppose not. But like what?"

Jeannette hesitated, taking another cigarette from her case, lighting it from the stub of the one just finished. "If I tell you—now you know about Anson and me—you won't hold it against me, make fun of me because of it? Promise?"

"Promise."

"Because, in an odd way, I think it might help to tell *you.*"

"I'll try to be *Il Dottore.*"

"Don't. Just be my Duvidl. When *Dottore* asked what it was about Anson, I told him the back of his neck—the way his head sits on his shoulders. I can't see *Dottore's* face, you know, but his voice sounded as though he thought I was crazy. Would *you* understand it?"

David looked blank.

"As a novelist, surely you see?"

"Well, I'm fairly straight, though not entirely. Nobody who can write about women and men is a hundred per cent straight. I think I'm about eighty-five of one, fifteen of the other. Let me think. If I were doing Anson as a character. I see the shoulders. Erect posture. That?"

"You're straighter than you think. No, not that." She laughed. "No, I can't expect you to see what I meant."

"Perhaps I do. I'm getting quite slumped from sitting at that desk in there. Maybe you mean that."

"You relate to yourself."

"As does everybody."

"I do, too. But there's something else about Anson *Dottore* did seem to understand. He doesn't wear anything under his clothes. *Il Dottore* thinks I have a fetish about that. David, if we're going to go on talking like this, I've simply *got* to have a drink. Or a pill. Or something."

"Have you taken pills today?"

"Not yet."

"Have the drink."

"One for you? No, I know you hate gimlets; you'd only let it sit and get warm."

"Today I'll try one. I'm learning." While she went to make the drinks, David took off his eyeshade and carried the typescript into his writing room. When he came back, Jeannette had moved over to the seat beside his.

"You nipped in the kitchen."

"A little," she admitted. "Drink up."

They drank, Jeannette quickly, David only sipping. Taking his hand, lacing her fingers through his, she said, "You know I love you, through everything."

"Everything."

"You know what I mean. When I've been—" She broke off.

"Bad," he supplied it.

"Yes, I guess that's what it is. Daddy's girl, being bad."

"Is that straight from *Il Dottore?*"

"He's never that banal."

"Maybe he should let you analyze yourself. It wasn't only the—what did you say of Anson? The way his head fits on his shoulders?"

"I think I said 'sits.' No, it's fetishes, everything."

"What other fetishes?"

"I can't tell you the ultimate one. I've never even told *that* one to *Dottore*."

"Tell me."

"Never."

"Come on, Nettie."

"Anson's not—like you. I mean, he's not a Jew."

"But he is, partly. He's told me so."

"No, no. If you don't get it, let's forget it."

"I'd like to forget it. And you to forget it, too. *Them*."

"I try, David, really I do." She mashed out the end of her cigarette. "It's not only *la poursuite*. Once when *Il Dottore* answered some emergency phone call and turned in his chair, I contrived to see what was written across my file card. 'Manic-depressive, paranoid pattern.'"

" 'Apt to crack under stress.' I know that shit lingo."

"You play rough."

"No rougher than you. You couldn't even leave my editor alone."

"No, I couldn't. I've often wondered what we'd have been like if I'd been—your phrase—capable of fidelity."

"It's a little late to wonder about that."

"Yes. If we'd traded—you know, that time in Cannes, after Anson had driven me to the dentist in Nice, I made a joke about it. Or if we'd settled what we probably all felt during that terrible mistral with one big *partouze* to get it over with."

"I don't like *partouze*. If there are three, the one not *en face* gets left out. If it's four, it's not truly a *partouze* but two couples."

"And five?"

"I don't know about five."

"How do you know about three and four?"

"Long ago, before I married you. Before I even met Sarah."

"You never told me that."

"No, it was so boring. Taped fucking. Nettie, there's us. Now. Let's stop this talking and go to bed."

She hesitated, then to his surprise said, "All right—it's been a long time—long enough for me to get pregnant by somebody else."

"If you did that I'd kill you."

"Don't worry. Are you sure you want to? I may be a big mess, cry."

"Go ahead and cry."

"Oh, David—Duvidl! I *am* crying!" She found a handkerchief, dried her eyes. "But first let me bathe off my hour and *Il Dottore*. Wait for me."

"That would be the idea."

He followed her into the bedroom, leaving behind his drink, hardly touched, though she had carried hers with her. He closed and locked the door, undressed and lay down on the bed. His writing block was on the table beside him, stripped of last night's notes, innocent and bare. Jeannette was taking her time and presently he reached for the pad and made a note: *She was a scrabble of reflexes and automatisms. Her persona was the willing, and entirely passive, victim of the causes and effects operating outside it: and so neither the truest of freedoms, to love, nor responsibility for or toward others with whom she coupled (to say nothing of the transcendence that is possible through love, or the binding of the self to another) was possible for her. When Nettie delved and David span, who was then the victim?* Then he carefully folded the page over the back of the block, exposing a fresh page, as she came floating from the bath, an unconfident galleon, her breasts with their dark alveolae pendulous and sweet with scent.

232

David still did not believe she was going to go through with it; it had been so long. But she dropped down beside him, pressing her lips to his, letting him cup her breasts in his hands. It had always been her breasts that excited him and he took their dark oval tips ritually into his mouth until they were firm and hard. She felt him rise against her, anxiously ardent, impatient to begin.

"My Duvidl," she murmured. "What would you like?"

"Don't talk like a whore."

"I am a whore."

"Lie beside me. Be *with* me."

Obediently she stretched out beside him and he turned his body to hers, his left arm encircling.

"I know," she said, "the left for holding, the right free for exploration."

He closed her mouth with his own, his fingers finding her massive bush, black and straight as a fell of dark curtain, parted it to pluck her lips, still damp from the bath. "Bathsheba," he whispered to her, "ebony and white, a psalm, mine." Parting then her round white thighs, he brushed aside her slight wince, her first, ambivalent resistance, which excited him, found her familiar deepness. Lest the perfection of the moment pass, he tightly closed his eyes. The many clamors of a Manhattan noontime blew upon them—sirens, whistles, a vibrant, faraway blast from some liner preparing to sail. She lay supine, whitely helpless against him, as he sought to bring her into pace with his own hurried ecstasy. She lagged. He slowed, sensing her listlessness, began again, trusting she had merely waited, would meet him in the way she once had long ago, joining her time with his in a way that was her own. His desperation to bring her to the brink undid him. In her familiar warmth he faltered, once again quickly found himself, ejaculated, held her. He fell into her listlessness, softened, felt her black, enclosing curtain brush him excruciatingly as he withdrew. He shuddered.

"You didn't come," he said.

"You know I never do. Almost never did."

"Is it only with me?"

"No," she said, "it's always the same for me. Almost, not quite."

"Then why do you go with others?"

She raised up, speculative, fumbled for cigarettes; she was remembering, too, he knew, her glass, empty in the bath, thirsting for another. *"Dottore* thinks it's because I hope I may somehow come. Easily, without struggle."

He turned onto his back, away from her, watching the play of light on the ceiling. Through the bedroom door they could hear the turn of a key in the door of the hall, his secretary returning.

"Easily, without struggle," he repeated after her, as though it were a lesson.

"It's not your fault, it never was. Do others come with you?"

He waited until there was an interval of stillness, rarest of Manhattan moments. "Yes," he said then, "they do, or most have. Maybe I'm not big enough for you."

"It's nothing to do with that," she said.

"Did Anson make you come?"

"No."

"But you hoped he would."

"Yes, I hoped."

"That way his head sits on his shoulders gave you hope."

"Well—he *looks* infallible. And I thought he would be, even though he was as drunk as I was. He hurt me. I ached for days."

"Why you liked it, perhaps."

"And he is very picnic."

"Picnic? What's *that?*"

She sought, found a phrase. "Pectorally high."

David sat up. "Give me my pad."

"Get your pad yourself," she said, and got up from the bed.

"Picnic. Pectorally high."

"I suppose from that film, *Picnic,* with William Holden." She laughed. "He took it off in that one."

"Took what off?"

"The shirt, of course."

David continued to scribble.

"And Holden was hairless. Plump, like a chicken. Hence, picnic."

"Did you tell that to *Dottore?*"

"Probably."

"What did he say?"

"He used his silence on me, his disapproving one. David, that's part of it, analysis, telling."

David returned the pad to its table, feeling put by, rejected.

"Do you want a drink?" she asked.

"No, I do not want a drink. At least, not the kind you're going to make yourself."

"Well, I do. Then we'll go out to lunch. All right?"

"All right. I'm amazed you're hungry."

"Always eat."

"I suppose it's a solution," he said.

"For what?"

"Getting you to the next drink, getting rid of this time, so much like our other times. I'm not good for you."

"I've loved you. I love you. I always will love you."

"The terrible thing is I believe it."

She drew breath sharply as she found a robe, unlocked the bedroom door, paused. "Is anybody good for anybody?"

"I'm tired of this. And hungry."

"I'll have her call the Carlyle. We can easily walk there." She went into the living room and he heard her talking to the secretary. She called to him. "Two o'clock, David?"

"Any o'clock for any solution," he called back, lumbering from the bed to the bath.

When he came out, Jeannette had dressed and was sitting beside her dressing table, a fresh drink carefully set on a coaster so not to ring the surface. With the mannered quietness that invariably resumed between them she said, "So now you know what I'm like."

"I've known a long time."

"I'm—I'm the way I am. I can't promise you anything."

"I no longer ask for promises, anything. I love you. I'm a victim."

"Whose victim?"

"Yours. Who else's?" He put on his coat. "Let's go."

"And you forgive me? You'll always forgive me?"

"Good victims always forgive."

"And I forgive you. There'll always be us, Duvidl. Bad as we are together, it's not like with our others."

"No, not like them."

"Say you love me."

"I've just said I'm a victim."

"But again."

"You know I do."

She sighed, finished her drink. "I can go on."

"Don't go too far."

"And don't *you*," she said.

🌷 🌷 🌷 GALEY BIRNHAM stood for a moment in the street, opposite his house, then crossed over and went inside. The windows of his third floor, unlike those of the house's first, were not boarded up, but might as well have been—opaque, long-unwashed panes, against which the jalousies had been closed for years and no lights ever showed. His pause had been a ritualistic assurance; whenever he looked up at those dark third-floor rectangles, he experienced the satisfaction of security: they revealed nothing about him. He liked to think of the space he occupied as being nowhere, street rooms dark, leading to those at the rear, where the heaven tree filtered the daylight. This nowhere, this obscure address, was the key to his freedom, as his small house in Tangier, light-flooded, was freedom of another kind. Like Neile Eythe's, his doorbell was out of order, and he opened his landing door only when he was sure who would be outside it. Few knew of his unlisted telephone; it rang infrequently, and the ten digits on the dial face had been replaced by a blank—this added to the safeties of his nowhere. Galey owned no clock, only an old dollar Ingersoll, got up and went to bed when he chose, wrote any time he pleased. His chief anxiety was that someone intruding might waste an hour or minutes of his day or night, divert him from his anonymous life, which permitted him to live exactly as he liked.

Birnham was a man without emotional allegiances: he had no one, and that was the way he preferred it. He was incapable of friendship and also of being a lover, in the senses in which most people think of those words. Even Neile, whom he quite often spent time with, was less a companion than a random integer in his depersonalized world. In the span of his thirty-five years, he had contrived to have more of what he wanted than most men of his kind. He had known many bodies, both purchased and freely given (and, sometimes, only their parts, which for him often was preferable), finding, never to his surprise, that possession meant an almost immediate destruction of interest in the body or body part just possessed. He liked bodies once only, after which they reverted to the strangers they had been before he possessed them. Later, if he encountered them in the street or in a bar, he did not speak, saving himself for the stranger who would be next.

Galey lived simply for the orgasm and his power over it.

In first youth he had been wasteful of himself, but no longer. There was an unknown number of orgasms to be snatched from life, and he was dedicated to experience them all, and entirely on his own terms. He made few errors now, had even been known to pass up a trick, no matter how promising, if the orgasmic outcome was uncertain. He had days when abstinence, because of selectivity, gave him vertigo, when his whole being tingled with voluptuous denial. Sensuality to him was a symbol of the body's and the spirit's freedoms, as is the ability to wander and traverse distances, hence his white house in Morocco, the precise address of which in the Rue de Vigne as few knew as knew of his floor-through on Mott Street.

In the sauna he had confided to Anson a preference for callow, butch youth, and that was true; but it was not his first preference, which, as first preferences often are, was virtually an impossibility to indulge, and quite different. What he desired were Johns, truly heterosexual males who either had never experienced homosexuality, or, if they had, rejected and resisted it. His dream was one of these "impossible" males, whom he could net, indoctrinate and persuade for an hour, an afternoon. Then his passionate handicap (the true passion of his life) would come into play, thrusts and feints and parries, tierce requiring as nimble an expertise as in swordplay, to bring the quarry down, so that he could dominate and possess him, compel the John, if possible, to assume a passive role. Galey's successes in this unlikely game had been few, but they were the achievements of his life that he valued above all others. True quarry was as rare as it was unpredictable, and until he found it, he occupied himself with second best—abstract admirations of the pectorals and deltoids of barbell boys, or as *maître* of gangbangs, at which, often as not, his participation was also abstract, as voyeur. He sometimes went to parties, like the one given for *Good Time Coming,* searching for the square victim who could be

238

rounded to his tastes—the unlikely Johns came from back-grounds of the everyday; truest perversion lay nearest normality. He had early seen at that party that the hunt would be conditioned, had settled for the combo boy, who turned out to be disappointing, a low-class, cockney Englishman, concerned and anxious about his future in America, his black leather and chains the fakest of male drags. Galey was contemptuous of drag in any form, feeling that it connoted that *he* was the impossible quarry, as unlikely to be ensnared as the quarry he sought for himself. Had his conquests been books, had he kept notes or documentation, his library would have been small and eclectic. But Galey was no saver or documentarian (he tore out the page as he read) and his belongings were few: bed, tables, nondescript chairs, ancient typewriter, exercising equipment. The money he made from his books went far; he paid little rent, wore cheap clothes, traveled tourist, ate in scrounge lounges. *Kif,* hash, pot, peyote, mescaline, even proscribed vials of Sandoz LSD-25, did not come high if connections were right, and Galey's were. But, had they not been, he would not have stinted, for drugs were his release from the bourgeois strangulation, often persuasion for reluctant quarry, his own open sesame to the *notis variorum* of the orgasm. Galey Birnham was a limited but not unhappy man; every sunset was his last, every day a fresh beginning.

Until the day of the sauna, it had not occurred to him that Anson might be concealed quarry, coated over with square-dom's laconic assumptions. Anson's moment of hesitation in the sauna, before going out to the pool, had given Galey the clue. All Johns proclaimed innocence of homosexual experience, protested they wanted none. In Anson's case that could be true: most tantalizing of handicaps. His full-fleshed Anglo-Saxon whiteness, his buttocks round as snow apples, owned by women and accessible only to them, provided a further urge to break him down. Anson had taken a first, mild flight with Neile, had admitted to liking it, despite the wind and the sea of jelly. And the sounds. His announced resolutions (*It will be the first and last for me. I don't intend to touch that or anything else.*) had been the betrayal: deepest urges are those most strongly resisted. In Anson, Galey was now certain, persona wrestled with imago. Not only was he genuinely curious about the other side, going over, the forbidden city; his steps were already hopefully turned toward paradise.

The day was hot. Galey climbed the flights leading to his apartment, a jungle enclosed in the new Chinatown tongs, the youth gangs (Flying Dragons, White Eagles, Black Eagles, the knifings in doorways, the sudden machete attacks); survival in it required wit as well as anonymity, and Galey had ways of ridding himself of occasional complications that arose. As a fox with fleas takes a piece of wood in his mouth and sinks himself, tail first, into a stream (the fleas driven forward along his fur until only the wood on the water's surface is a refuge, which the fox then sets adrift), so Galey from time to time disappeared, retreating to his *milieu alternatif,* Tangier. He had just changed from his dark suit, cheap white shirt and black tie—his John disguise—into the jeans he wore at home, when his telephone rang. Lifting the receiver noiselessly, he listened, characteristically waiting for the caller to speak first.

"It's Neile."

"Hi, Baby." He pronounced it *Bey-béh,* a fusion of countless jukebox hearings. He preferred that to using her name, sometimes reflecting that it was perhaps the one word that had transcended generations, still used by squares as well as hippies, with varying shades of attitude. It was as close to a term of affection as he ever got.

"I heard your door close," she said. "Gale, I need to see you."

"Come on down."

Galey padded in bare feet from chair to back of door,

hung up his clothes, pulled on a T-shirt in deference to her coming. Presently Neile knocked their double signal: *shave-and-a-haircut-six-bits,* plus the *dot-dot-da-daa* of the opening bars of Beethoven's Fifth. He let her in, afterward chaining the door, a house rule, double security against the jungle of the street outside.

"May Day," she said.

"You've been flying? In trouble?"

"Distress call."

"You still down?"

"Not still. I came up. It's *again.*"

"The magnum opus?" She often read to him her seemingly endless novel in the form of a diary, in which hours were long as days, days months, the sentences invariably bleeding into one another.

"Oh, no; I did my thing, my stint for the day. It's the hangup I told you about Saturday."

"Parris."

She nodded.

"If you limited it to once with anybody, you wouldn't have hangups," he said. "My rule, and it works."

"I'm not you." She turned and went to one of two chairs in the room, Salvation Army buys of long ago, painted red, and straddled it, facing him. "A week ago I'd never heard of Anson Parris, was trying to shake out Peckham. Now I can't breathe without thinking of Anson."

"What *about* Peckham?" Galey asked. He'd known the listless twenty-one-year-old hip who had been in and out of the house for months, using Neile as a mail drop, spending most of his time at a crash pad near Mulberry and Bayard, where twenty or thirty others like himself nightly created a nether world for themselves.

"Finished," she said. "He found himself an heiress from Scarsdale. He was shooting the main line, tried to give me the needle too."

"Baby, you didn't!"

"No."

"Never," Galey said softly, "never that. Speed, yes, a little now and then, but no horse. *Never!*"

"Pot's as far as I've gone. Never touched H."

"And don't," he said, even more softly. He sat down opposite her, also straddling.

She felt the warmth toward him she always did when what he said to her seemed like counsel, involvement. But she understood now, as she had not at first, that the warmth was in herself only. Early in their curious relationship she had turned this warmth of herself, which was hungrily sexual, toward him, but he always blew back cool. His canceled maleness, which was the way she thought of it, infused her like a drugging sting; no matter what he confided to her about himself, he was still male to her, a principle. What she felt with him now was a leaning, a need to tell him what she felt about Anson, as though he were not Galey but a quasi-brother or the youngest of surrogate fathers, freshly met. At the beginning, his dark, Pompeian quietness, his lack of sentimentality, had bothered her; but now they were friendly strangers with few allegiances, mostly hers, exactly spaced in an equilibrium that had stabilized.

"Oh, I don't, *won't,*" she said, giving a promise he had not, really, asked for.

"Anson's been down here, hasn't he?"

"Yes, but how did you know?"

"The other afternoon, when I went to the roof for my sun, I was sure I heard the sound of hands as I passed your door."

"We heard you go up. He was worried. Galey, you're uncanny."

"There are ears that see. Anson and I had a sauna together, you know. He's hung on you too."

"Did he tell you that?"

"In many ways."

She sat, eyes moving from his eyes to the closed jalousies of the windows beyond. "I don't think his hangup's only me. We were fabulous that first night, as I told you. Yes. But I have the feeling about him that he's trapped, or thinks he is. Trapped in himself, and any girl would do."

"And does."

"To spring him, for just a little time, from his trap."

"You're right about his being trapped," Galey agreed, "and wanting all the things he probably passed up so that he could be trapped. He's got all the cube trimmings, wife, a kid—a boy—five or six years old."

"What's his wife like?"

"A beauty. Out of that box of beautiful girls of her year. They live in this glass house some famous architect built."

"In a trap called Ditten's Ridge."

"That's its name."

"He's the big noise at K and K, your publishers. I found that out right away. Square, glinty on the edges, and all of him's tearing to get out."

"Yes, he is tearing. A nice square. Squares want to play what we play sometimes. Anson's searching for the structure of illusions he's living within. But he doesn't know how to begin."

"He began with me," she said. "It was like love."

Galey laughed softly. "Call it that if you like. Deadly opiate. It depends on the particular kick you want. You want the bits and pieces?"

"Oh, I've already got *those,*" she said with an edge.

"Easy things in any hangup, like yours on him, happen first," he told her. "I've plotted the course of love affairs— that thing you have with Anson. They're disastrous. It's all posturing anyway. My advice is have him, really ride it, but get out first."

"Yes, you've warned me," she said. "And there I went. It's a whole new bag; I can't fight it."

243

"Great for inflating the ego, but beware. Keeping it skin to skin, membrane to membrane's best."

"I'm more than skin and membrane," she said. "I know, you've told me about the body, the nonlanguage, how to keep it separate."

"And—did you make more flower orgasms?"

"He made it. I was wearing the rag. Off now."

Galey laughed mirthlessly. "So I *did* hear the sound of hands!"

"But he hasn't phoned me."

"He will."

There was the silence of midafternoon in the room, shattered suddenly by a barrel organ playing "Chinatown, My Chinatown." It stopped, moved down the street, resumed. In the interval it was again quiet, so still the ticking of Galey's Ingersoll on a table was audible.

She laughed a little. "I wonder they have the nerve to play that. But how do you know Anson will call, come back?"

"I told you, he's as hung up as you are."

She smiled with her green eyes, then said, "I suggested to him that when he came back, we should fly a little. We were *way* over, that night of the ship party, on the sticks you gave me. But his answer was a flat No."

"That was a *fun* No. Anson needs struggle, he's made that way, but he wants to go over all the way, just as you do."

"Yes," she said.

"Want me to put you over together?"

"On acid?"

"Not the acid they sell at the sheds; it would be the legit Sandoz if it were going to be that, but it wouldn't be. Just as I've told you no horse, you should remember that LSD is a *private* trip, not what you want with Anson. '25' makes no orgasms, flower or otherwise."

"Peyote?"

"Peyotl. Mescal. Mescaline."

"I remember, from the Indians in the Southwest."

"Mescaline's best for you."

"I wonder if Anson would, or if he'd be afraid?"

"Anson's less afraid than anyone I know. He's simply conditioned by all those suburbanites around him, living on sixth-hand vicarious experience. He'll take it like a baby." This time Galey stretched it, *baay*-bay. "I'll be Head Cactus, sit on the world's thorns, take care of you both while you're over and away."

"And watch?"

"Don't kid. Participate."

"But I want Anson to myself."

"You just think you do. Anyway, that's the deal."

"I knew you were Gangbang King, didn't know you went for couples."

"I don't, usually, unless I have to, to get the John. I don't mind being in competition with a girl. When she's warmed him up and he's all set to go, then I can get jealous and envious, have him too. Both jealousy and envy are aphrodisiac, and mesc is a kind of third in the bed anyway."

"Like Lucky Pierre?" She liked showing her knowledge of queer camp.

"Or Fortunate Ambrose, maybe. One between two couples. Baby, don't go constitutional on me; you've been in gangbangs before."

She said nothing.

"You don't buy?"

"You've always said you're not interested in girls. You could stay out of it, do it for me, let me have the whole scene with Anson."

"*L'acte gratuite?*" He laughed his mirthless laugh. "A gratuitous act is a fallacy. I'm no more capable of an act without motive than you or anyone else. I know, it's supposed to be freedom's symbol, the id bursting through, but it doesn't work as well as a setup. *En groupe* or nothing. Which means a psychodrama: whoever there is can be in on it. You'll have your trip with Anson, and I and the rest will be ballast."

"I told you, this thing I have for Anson's more than skin."

"Maybe it is, maybe not. Don't look too closely at the rest until you're over, assuming you get over. It'll be more than skin then, and then look carefully, come back with some of it. Use it afterward."

"Like—psychedelically?"

"That's the meaningless word, a little Art Nouveau camped up on posters, flowers painted on cars, shit. Psychodelic, if you must, which, in the strictest sense, means personality change for the better."

"I'm downer than ever," she said.

"Let's have a couple of sticks. Okay?"

"Okay. It'll make me feel better. At least I'll sleep."

Galey went into the next room, was gone for a time, and returned, lighting the kind of bomber he had given Neile the night she met Anson. He inhaled, handed it to her: politesse of the stick. The empty room felt cubed with heat. She dragged deeply, returned it.

"Better?" he asked.

"Will be. The mescal—the cactus. Tell me about it."

"Were I a wooden werewolf, I'd mock it up for you, tell you how it's done by the Indians, who shave off the top, dry it, grind it into powder. I had it first that way, in double-O capsules. Hard to get down. You'll have the medical dose, the purest. You can start slow, go on as you like, go as far over as the nausea will let you. You'll first be sick, but that quickly passes."

"You've been over often?"

"Yes, and had good and bad trips. And can't tell you a thing about what *you'll* experience. Except for the divinity of the experience, not describable in words. But you'll lose this street."

"Find the nonlanguage?"

"There'll be a breaking down of time barriers—everything will seem to be going on at once, as well as seem to be lasting forever. It'll liquidate your defenses."

"I'd like that."

"Baby, I've got to be with you. First rule is, trippers must never be left alone."

"All right," she said. "The deal. Gale, how *do* you get the stuff, the mesc, the rest of it?"

"I know the right intern at the right hospital. I'm his type, of course, but it's the crisp new bills that really matter. Who's the old boy said 'Only connect'? I connect."

She was rising in mood now, finishing the stick, not bothering to share it. "Why do you play your games? Do you know?"

"It's all to do with my desire to be sexually assaulted by my father. Freud couldn't fix it; society—so called—doesn't help. Call it a battle between mucosa and erectile tissue. I don't ask questions of myself about it."

"I ask questions of *myself*," she said.

"The wrong ones." His voice became kidding. "Crack O'Dawn."

"I hated that."

"Only because it didn't move you up. Baby, you've never fooled me. I know your pattern. Fail at the buff, think sentences will do it. You can't even punctuate, much less write. You're wasting your time."

"But I'm trying to write it like I live it."

"And don't. Look, you've got that body, and that's what you're going to make it with, if you do. Flesh. Young flesh. Not quite dry behind the ears, a little skinny past the elbows. There's a market for that. If you can find it. Kiddie, you're jailbait, the hardest commodity in the world to come by."

"If anybody wants it."

"It's in demand. Find your market."

"I wish I could. I want my whirl! But I'm hung up."

"Mixed up."

"Right now, I'd like to call Anson."

"Don't."

"Easy for you to say."

"Listen, Baby, stop fooling yourself. You'd screw Frankenstein if you thought it'd get you that whirl you want. Anson could have his dong out and half in you, and if you saw the ghost of Louis B. Mayer you'd get right up and try to screw him. You'd forget your hangup."

"Yes, I'd forget anything for the whirl."

"And let me tell you, if it comes—and it's a vibration you can feel like you stuck your wet finger in a light socket— move into it. Don't wait."

"You're right," she said. "Gale, I'm hungry."

"So am I. Let's go to Fishy's. Or do you prefer the Pagoda?" Both were places nearby, where they sometimes ate.

"Either one, doesn't matter. It'll get me away from the phone. The hangup."

"You're getting the idea," he said.

❦   ❦   ❦   A SHARP needle of sunshine broke through the half-drawn curtains of the bedroom. Faye slowly opened her eyes. She had had no dreams she could remember. She oriented to the hour, seven, and the date, Memorial Day; Anson would probably sleep late. Satisfying herself by an automatic inner listening, a scrutiny of morning sounds, eliminating bird calls, the drone of aircraft, until she could hear Todd's breathing in the next room, she conducted that part of her thinking that was most private. Borobudur still hung in her thoughts, that terraced pyramid around which the growth of the not-quite-quarrel between herself and Anson was growing, unresolved, perhaps not possible to resolve. Instead of receding, it seemed to move closer, become more vivid with each hour. Anson's breathing was slow and deep, and her thoughts returned to her visit with Velma, two nights before. Sam was bowling; the customarily noisy house had been quiet. Faye had walked across the field with a flashlight and found Velma in her kitchen, finishing the washing up.

"Oh, how nice to have company!" Velma exclaimed when she came to the screen door and unhooked it to let Faye in. "As you see, woman's work is never done."

"You're telling me."

"Don't *you* complain, you with your Mrs. Haines."

"Well, twice a week."

"My two oldest were supposed to do this," Velma said, "but they've gone to the movies."

"Dates?"

"Yes. I guess the boys they're going with are all right. They all seem to have so much hair. If I thought about it, worried, I'd be incapable of doing even so pedestrian a thing as scrubbing out a sink."

"But I imagined you thought about everything, Velma."

"Mm—not always. Sometimes I find I simply have to go on and not think. My grandmother's way. Troubled dishwater, she called it."

"I left my dishes in the sink," Faye confessed. "Sloppy, I know. But I just *had* to get off the lot. I've been practically nowhere else, lately."

"Yes, I know. Day after tomorrow's Memorial Day."

"America's *Jour des Morts.*"

"Don't say that. That's the night you and Anson are coming for dinner."

"We haven't forgotten." Faye perched on a stool at the end of the sink. "When I was a kid, we always called it Decoration Day."

Velma wrung out a cloth and hung it up to dry. "In my family, we always went out to decorate the graves. My father was killed in one of the raids over Peenemünde, you know."

"I lost my father too," Faye said.

"We're war's children. Iwo, wasn't it?"

"The Coral Sea. He has no grave. They never found his body."

"You've told me. Terrible. And we're doing the very same thing in this generation, only worse. Vietnam. Have you seen tonight's papers, heard the TV reports?"

"I'm sick of listening to TV *and* reading about Vietnam," Faye answered. "If we talked about that, we'd never talk of anything else."

Velma looked at her sharply. "Sounds as though you've got something on your mind."

"Yes, I do."

"Well, let's go out to the side porch. It's cool there, and Sam's fixed the screens, so we'll be away from the bugs."

Faye was grateful for the darkness on the porch. They sat down in the swing at the porch's far end, which made her remember her talk with her mother in Greenwich. "I seem always to be sitting at the end of sofas or gliders, telling my troubles."

"What's wrong?" Velma asked gently. "Do you want to tell me?" She waited. "I know there's the Todd worry, but I thought we'd discuss that when Anson's with us."

"I guess I do need to tell somebody," Faye said hesitatingly, unsure how to begin.

"How *is* Toddy?"

"All right. I mean the same. He seems to have forgotten what happened at the group Saturday."

"Seems to is right. He hasn't, of course. And Anson?"

250

"He's home, reading manuscripts."

"I haven't seen him since he came back from London."

"He was in London only part of the month he was away," Faye said. "He was at the apartment the rest of the time."

"But why didn't he come back here? At least weekends?"

"You must have guessed there was something. We'd had a quarrel, a really bad one. We've had others, but that was the worst yet."

"I wondered, naturally," Velma said. "Seeing you so much alone."

"I hated that, being alone."

"Because of what's in the papers? Even suburbias, such as our Ridge, aren't as safe as they were."

"Velma, I'm the best locker-up there is. Sometimes I think I'm nothing but bolts and switches and keys."

"Which conceals what?"

"I'm upset. Not only tonight, Velma. It's my daily state."

"But surely, now Anson's back. Sam and I did notice, of course, we can see your house so well from here. Isn't the quarrel over?"

"In a way it is, in another way not. He asks me to forget and forgive. I try—tried. There must be something wrong with me. I'm not like other wives I know. I can't stop remembering, especially when the whole thing starts to repeat itself."

"Why don't you come out from behind those defenses?" Velma asked. "Tell me what it is."

"Women—partly."

"Other women, yes. I *knew* that. The first time I saw Anson, I guessed that about him. Didn't you, when you married him?"

"No, I honestly thought I'd be the only one," Faye said.

"And you haven't been."

"No. Sometimes I know who they are, have been—when it's over—and sometimes I don't know. The big-quarrel one, Jeannette Steen, I did know. It's killed me."

"Jeannette Steen's a very sad case," Velma pronounced.

"I know she is. *Now* I know, and so does Anson, but at first we had no idea. She's all right sometimes; she's chic and rich, and, I don't know, there's something exotic about her, so lacquered. But I had no idea she'd come between Anson and me."

"Evidently she has. Your voice is very tense, Faye."

"Anson says it happened only once, and that it meant nothing, has nothing to do with him *or* me."

"All men will try that one."

"You know about these things—*could* that be true?"

"Supposing it were. What's the difference? You're the one who's suffering. I had it with Sam a couple of times."

"Sam's been unfaithful to you?"

"He'd *like* to have been. You know how he goes on at parties, as though he hasn't had bed for months. Oddly enough, I think Sam has been faithful to me, physically. *Faute de mieux.* He's beached now, or is mostly. We still sleep in the same bed, of course."

"You mean sex is over for you?"

"It's a relief, in a way, not to have to go through all that romantic bit, get greased up, worry about getting pregnant. Our generation didn't have the pill. There are times, but it's not the same as it was."

Faye swung forward and backward in the darkness. "I shouldn't have asked you that, Velma. I'm sorry."

"You needn't be. I couldn't care less. When you're my age, you won't care either. Go on about you."

"Well, I tried the forgiving and forgetting, for Todd's sake. But I think my inability to do either must have to do with my Sacred Heart years. You remember—my long fight against old powdered bones and deathwatch beetles."

"Forgiveness, if it's to be of any use, should be complete. There's the way you must feel about Jeannette Steen, if you see her again, too."

"Oh, I'll have to see her—at the spring party we're giving

Saturday week. You and Sam will come, I hope. We'll need you. I'll see Jeannette. I'm rather looking forward to it in a grisly way. It'll never be the same between us, and I'm going to let her know it."

"Nothing is ever the same. Accept that."

"You know," Faye said, "there's a really desultory thing about our friendship with the Steens. Remember when we visited them in Cannes? Well, David propositioned me then. He still looks at me as if he's wondering if I'm going to change my mind."

"When was the thing with Anson and Jeannette?"

"Five or six weeks ago."

"You see, you *are* forgetting—five *or* six weeks. I assume you didn't take David up on his proposition."

"Oh, no."

"Do you think you would have, if you'd known what would happen with Jeannette and Anson?"

"I don't honestly know. David's attractive, very Mediterranean-looking, dark. The opposite of Anson. Often I find myself wishing I *had* slept with David. I might have learned something about myself that would make it easier for me to understand Anson."

"I hope you don't," said Velma, "because of Todd, if for no other reason. Children know. Todd knows all kinds of things you'd never guess."

"Yes, he seems to. If you were with him every day, when Anson's away or at the office, you'd realize how much he must be aware of. And takes out in the strangest ways."

"How strange?"

"Those animals he keeps in his glass jar, his water snakes, the salamander, a snail, caterpillars. Usually he kills the snakes."

"Children kill things. That's all right."

"But he *saves* them, dead."

"All forms of collecting and saving, even in children, are a

253

form of anxiety. That's what he's playing out, or trying to play out—his anxiety about you both."

"I hope you'll try to explain that to Anson."

"If he asks, I'll try," Velma said. "You see, I'm a little fonder of Anson than he is of me—"

Faye protested. "He's devoted to you."

"These things are never equal. And one knows."

"Anson's as puzzled by the emotions lavished on that glass jar as I am."

"But there's something besides Jeannette Steen and the Todd thing, isn't there?"

"Yes."

"Is it still Jeannette, do you think?"

"I think Anson's honest about some things. He said it was only once with her, and I believe him." Faye sighed.

"Each sigh a drop of blood."

"There are things, a something—that bewilders me far more than Jeannette or Todd's glass jar."

"Not another woman?" asked Velma.

"Well, yes, probably, and in a funny way I understand that, though I hate it, *her*. The other thing I don't understand. I can't isolate what it is Anson wants that apparently he can't get from me. And *don't*, please, tell me, as my mother has done, that it's something about bed I can't or won't do. It's not that."

"Yes, your mother would think it was that." Velma had met Vera Williams. "She's the best-preserved Greenwich fossil I ever met. The only thing that surprised me about her was that she's a Democrat."

"I know," said Faye. "If only Eisenhower had been a Catholic."

"But I'm not about to tell you anything, Faye. Unless, maybe, to suggest there may be something about Anson's work."

"I'm sure it's not that. He loves his job, is wonderful at it."

254

"Yes, I read about the million-dollar sale in the *Times*. Well, with any couple as good-looking as the two of you are, there are bound to be competitors on both sides. I daresay David Steen's not been your only proposition."

"Yes, there've been others," Faye admitted. "Ours is what I call a 'kitchen' culture. You know, at any party for couples, if you go into the kitchen, someone else's husband follows. But not only kitchens. Stig Lavrorsen—" She did not finish.

"What about Stig?" Velma prodded.

"Well, Martha's martinis are real killers and her dinners, however wonderful, often are delayed—"

"I used to know those ten o'clock dinners of hers."

"Well, I try not to eat all those things she has beforehand and I often get hungry. And tighter than I intended. One night Stig followed me into their upstairs bathroom. I had the most terrible time getting away from him and back downstairs, so Martha wouldn't know."

"Oh, Martha knows about Stig." Velma laughed. "He's lousy in the sack, arrested at masturbatory level."

"I don't think I know what that means."

"He's a phallic narcissist. His exhibitionism, his very evident pride in his equipment, as he calls it, is a dead giveaway. One trouble with their sex life is that he plays with Martha, as though she were just part of him, an extension of that big penis, of which he's so proud. He exposed himself to you in the bathroom that night, didn't he?"

"How *could* you know that, Velma?"

"Guesswork, merely. You see, he's exhibited it to me, too. Asked me, point-blank, to grab hold of it and tell him if it wasn't the biggest and best cock I'd ever seen."

"And did you?"

"I simply looked at it and laughed. He needed cutting down. I told him that Sam's is much bigger, which was true at the time. Sam's no longer as big as he was, though."

"When on earth was this, with Stig Lavrorsen?"

"Oh, long before you and Anson came here to live. You

see, Faye, Sam and I've been through this community like a dose of salts. That's one reason, though not the only one, that we've pretty much settled for our kids' and our own company. *And* yours and Anson's. God knows how we'd feel if we didn't have you, or if we should fall out and quarrel."

"I can't imagine that happening, Velma."

"Well, friendship sometimes fades before the flower that bore it, or whatever that American writer living in Paris said."

"Before the Flowers of Friendship Faded Friendship Faded," supplied Faye; she knew her Gertrude Stein.

"Nothing would surprise Sam and me," Velma said. "You know, we were very close with Grace and Chet Burgess once. You know those things she calls her 'Assemblies,' her collages, bits of old window screens, odds and ends of plexiglass? Well, when she would show them, I was never quite able to conceal I thought them proof of how really sick in the *Kopf* she is. So that friendship went."

"But you've never told us any of this. You've met them at the parties we give for the——" Faye caught herself just in time.

Velma said it for her. "Your 'Assortment.' It's known, what you call them."

"Is it? Well, yes, we do call them that. We don't mean anything derogatory by it."

"Don't protest too much. Yes, Sam and I meet them at your parties."

"And you speak, and talk——"

"Yes, just like real guests, real people," Velma said, an edge of bitterness in her voice. "We enjoy them as a menagerie. But we're all through. Like I said, a dose of salts."

"Dear God, no wonder you look the way you do when we ask you to come with 'The Assortment'!"

"I suppose it shows, though I try not to let it. You see, Faye, when you've heard Martha Lavrorsen out on what Stig's like when they try to make love——"

"And I have, Velma. It's awful!"

"Yes, straight out of *The Psychiatric Quarterly. And,* when you realize what the private arrangements of the Doyles must be like! I hear it's a bass fiddler this time."

"A black one."

"Alma's always insisted she likes primitives—and black. Black as a telephone, she used to say. The bass-fiddle part's the only twist—this one's a gimmick."

"What do you mean, gimmick?"

"Probably doesn't exist, except in fantasy. Remember Dickens' Mrs. Gamp's Mrs. Harris? There was no Mrs. Harris, though she's one of Dickens' best characters. Mrs. Gamp used her for excuses. I think, in a different way, Alma hides behind these probably nonexistent lovers, into whom—or which—she pours her illusions about herself. It assuages her in some way, comforts her id. This bass-fiddle man, however she has managed to create him for herself and us, never was. I'm sure of it."

"Poor Alma!" Faye said. "Though I've never liked her."

"And Ray Doyle's supposed to be writing a book isn't anything new, either. He's as jealous as he can be of Alma's primitives, of course."

"I knew he had a homosexual side, but he doesn't do anything about it." Both had stopped swinging and now sat very still. "My God!" Faye said after a long minute, "it's all so awful. Maybe I should be grateful for Anson."

"Maybe you should. But since I've begun on this about Ray Doyle— No, I'm sure he doesn't do anything active. Perhaps his pyromania is enough—for the moment. But Alma's told me how he's always put his cigarette ashes into wastebaskets; they've had several near-fires in the *house.* He may burn up that corncrib he's writing in now, as he burned the barn."

"I think I'd like a cigarette," Faye said. She found one in her pocket and lighted it, seeing in the flare of the match Velma's composed, complacent face. "Well," she said, again beginning to swing, "do tell me more about our 'Assortment.' "

"If you like. You must know about Amy Nowells, all her fussing about Herb's body hair?"

"Alas, yes; I know about it."

"She gives him the wax baths herself, now, and he lets her do it. He may even enjoy them. Wax baths don't permanently remove hair, and as Herb's grows back, Amy becomes more and more anxious. She begins her washing ritual."

"Washing ritual?"

"Her hands. Wash, wash, wash, over and over. In fact, it's possible to guess the growth of Herb's bush by the number of times she goes to the bath."

"She does go to the bath a lot," Faye remembered.

"And makes a nest of toilet paper on the seat whenever she has to sit down. Everybody and everything's dirty, too dirty for dainty Amy."

"Did you used to know *them* well, too?"

"We knew Amy when she was still married to her first husband. *He* wouldn't put up with her terror of the male. It took her some time to find Herb. He was hirsute enough, you see, to invite her dominance. And his general physical collapse, though it's related to his years, is related to those wax baths."

Faye, as she listened, had unconsciously been rearranging "The Assortment" couples in the order in which she and Anson spoke of them, and she came up missing the Drapers and "Gertrude" and "Alice." "What about Miss Taylor and Miss Grumbacher?"

"Your 'Gertrude,' and 'Alice'? Funny, Sam and I thought of that, too. What is there to say? They're terribly nice women, and truly devoted. I sometimes suspect them of looking at the rest of us, who are supposed to be normally oriented, and having a good laugh about us in private. Of course, they *could* be like the real Gertrude and Alice, sado and maso—the way Hemingway described them in that memoir of Paris. I don't buy anything Hemingway says, never did. All his shadowboxing, fake bullfighting, lion hunting never fooled me. He tried Catholicism, did you know that? Didn't work for him either. Huldah, if you remember her, well, she predicted Papa's suicide almost to the month. Violent life, violent end; even his myth is violent. But I got off. Hemingway's problems are over. Let's get back to yours."

"Not until you tell me about the Drapers."

"You might as well have it all," Velma said. "Sherm Draper's what used to be called, in social-work parlance, a constitutional psychopathic inferior. The constant money crises he and Rose have could be avoided, but he keeps thinking of the money he's supposed to inherit, meanwhile pretending to all that faded gentility thing. His idea, not Rose's. Rose would really love to get rid of all that fake, termite Tudor and set up in a split-level, with one acre instead of forty. But Sherm won't hear of it. It would really be awful, if there weren't money in the end."

"Libby Draper's sitting for us day after tomorrow night," Faye said.

"I'm surprised Rose would let her, after the scratching job Todd did on little Kathy."

"So was I, but I was desperate. Mrs. Haines sometimes can baby-sit, but this week she can't. So I took advantage of Rose, in a way; I know what the few dollars will mean to Libby."

"Libby's a lovely girl," said Velma; "luckily, there are children who can't be ruined by anything, and she's one."

This positive kindness reminded Faye how sordid the evening's gossip had been, making her a little sorry she'd come. "It must be very late," she said. "I must go."

"You haven't told me what you came to say."

"You must want to go to bed."

"No, tell me, and take your time. Sam won't be home for

hours. He and the bowling buddies have to get stupefied before they count the evening away from wives a success."

Faye hesitated. "I wonder if I can convey it."

"Try."

"It goes deeper than women, other women. Or me. Anson seems to want—well, sometimes, when we're out on a party, with others, he gets a look in his eyes and talks about— You see how hard it is for me."

"Yes." Velma patiently waited.

"In his own words, and I remember them quite separately and apart from other talk, he says things like 'There must be a farther landscape. A sea without tides. A moon without orbit.' "

"It sounds like the sixth martini."

"Anson's limit is five. He's never really drunk; he never loses identity, misses a syllable. He *means* these things."

"Drinking brings them out?"

"I guess it does. I sense what he means, his hunger for something new. Who doesn't have that? But this world, our Ridge, is all there is, to me. If there is 'something beyond'— another of his phrases—I don't care about it."

"He's struggling toward a fuller realization of himself," Velma interpreted. "He wants total identity. Selfhood."

"Yes, yes; I know. That is, I know as far as I can understand in *myself*. But *my* sense of identity, who I am, springs from reality, from what happens. Anson seems to me to be trying to destroy that identity."

"Don't be so sure. If you start out with a fixed belief like that, you'll only prevent yourself from understanding him."

"He's so—so sexually greedy," Faye said; it slipped out before she could stop it.

"Sexual greed is activated by fear and hatred, has nothing to do with love or selfhood, Faye. Yes, you're trying to hold on to your reality, and Anson's trying to fly from it. His straying, his aggression, is his way of projecting his repressed destructive impulses on you."

Faye felt tears sting her eyes. "I've always been so satisfied with him, with what we have together. I've never wanted to be other than what I am."

"But, inevitably, you're being affected by this farther reality, so to call it, that Anson wants."

"The curious thing is, he never talks of this when we're alone together. At least he didn't until tonight."

"Why do you think he did it tonight?"

Faye was weeping now. "I don't know, unless it was that I was badgering him about a telephone number and address I found in one of his pockets. I saw he was tired, tired of what I was trying to find out, but I couldn't stop. Finally, he said if he could transmigrate himself to—to Borabarur, some such place, he would. Though I never heard of Boro-whatever-it-is, I got his message. Have *you* ever heard of such a place? What is it?"

"Never heard of it. It's a symbolic reference, in any case."

"I knew that. But then I just *had* to get out of the house. And came here."

For a long time Velma did not say anything. Then she said, "I've always thought Anson hard to figure out, most interesting people are. There's a restlessness about him, a true love of risk for its own sake. But I see no reason for you to get upset. All husbands, as well as wives—ourselves—get tired of the marital coil, pulling along the cart with square wheels. You do, I do. Marriage, somebody said, is a disappointing salad. It's the art of the impossible. But I've made it possible for myself, and so have you. I think most husbands get itchy, and not only in the crotch, in the feet, too. Years ago, Sam got it in his head he couldn't stand America any more, wanted to pull up stakes and move to Brittany, of all the sunless, rainy places. He would harp on it whenever there was a problem, when we were low at the bank, or if his work wasn't going the way he thought it should. I argued with him about it at first, but after I understood it was just a steam valve for him, for dashed hopes, I no longer bothered. He's over it now. But it was his idea about his own private road to China. Wait. I think that place Anson mentioned—what was it?"

Faye repeated her phonetic version of Borobudur.

"I think it's something to do with China—the Orient, anyway. Shall we look in the *Britannica?*"

"No, no," Faye said, drying her eyes. "I really must go now. I'm just one of those wives, I guess. I can *smell* that there's somebody else in the picture and I'm upset."

"Maybe she'll pass out of the picture. Maybe she'll take off for Borobaro."

"Not the same time as Anson, I hope. She's a redhead."

"They often are. Or blondes. I wish I could say something to make her go away. I know how you're feeling. I've had those feelings myself."

"And what did *you* do?"

"Oh, dogged it out. Repressed it. Tried to do nothing about it. There's not much use in trying to keep them out of nets if they want to get themselves tangled."

It had begun to rain lightly as they talked. "You must let me drive you over," Velma offered as Faye rose to go. "It may come on hard and you'll get soaked."

"No, I'll walk, Velma, thanks. As I walked over, with my flashlight—looking for truth, I suppose. My journey to Borobar—I'm beginning to get it right. I'm going to look it up when I get home."

And, before settling into bed with the manuscript of the new Galey Birnham book, she had gone through the trial and error of getting the spelling right. Not that looking it up had done any good. Velma's talk, so corrosive, did contain kernels of insight. What Velma might say of Anson and herself, when they were not within hearing, she didn't care to speculate about. Soon, Little Marka was having her panties pulled down by her father and brother, and Birnham's story had taken over. Now, in the light of morning, Velma's counsel

262

seemed less helpful than upsetting. Sibyllike, she had spoken out, presenting the depressing details of "Assortment" lives as though, in some way, the answer to Anson and herself was to be found among them. They, too, were "Assortment."

The cold nose of Netcher, who had been waiting in the doorway and was becoming impatient, nuzzled Faye's cheek. She reached a hand out, caressing the Doberman's soft, warm ears, and got out of bed. The dog's quivering poise and patience, her routine spring through the door, her lope into the woods and her bounding return indicated comprehension of a morning bent to silence, so that Todd would not wake too soon and Anson could sleep. Netcher beside her, Faye returned to bed and Little Marka's progress down the incestuous path.

❦ ❦ ❦ ANSON WAS still lightly sleeping. His dreams had been of pagodas, rising through low-lying mists, with roses ringing like bells, of a shapeless continent, far beyond the confines of the real world. Those dreams slipped into forgetfulness, another coming forward to obliterate them. This dream, which came just before waking, he remembered. It was disturbing. He dreamed that he had an ejaculation, the experience of it entirely visual, with sperm pluming from his penis. The plume became a flood, continued. At its beginning, he had anticipated the exciting kind of dream he had in adolescence, with full sensation accompanying the sexual act. Strangely, he had been alone, there had been no partner. The sperm continued to flow from him in unending spurts. Between the spurts he had the sensation of urinating, almost through, but still with the last drops to

263

squeeze out. Half asleep, half awake, he recognized that the dream, in part, was one of typical morning urgency. He was sure he got up and went into the bath. But it was not urine that came out, but more sperm, without pleasurable sensation or relief. This perplexed him and he realized he had not gotten up and was still half in the dream. Urgency prevailed, and he stumbled out of bed and went barefoot into the bathroom. He washed his face and combed his hair, but he couldn't lose the dream. It was not like other dreams, washing quickly away with daylight, but clung to him like a soft, humming barnacle. *If only,* he thought, *I could go back into it, dream it thoroughly out, maybe I could forget it.* But he knew that returning to dreams after a waking interval was impossible.

He tried to interpret. It related, of course, to his time with Neile Eythe, which had been a pure spilling of seed; faced squarely, perhaps symbolizing a loss of power over himself, a slipping. When Todd asked him the question about the butterfly, he had felt, though he did not know why, ineffective as a father, as though part of the function of manhood was knowing the destination of diurnal Lepidoptera. He had said exactly what he meant to Faye after the discussion about the party, had been honest, too honest. If the dream symbolized an inner threat, he wanted to forget it. At the top of his bleaching interpretation was his memory of his descent into the Mott Street jungle: no Cathay that. The attrition had begun there, leading, through who knew what subterranean mazes, to this moment. There should be some strength in him to fortify himself against the repetition of behavior he was beginning; he should find the courage and honesty to block out the already magical number of the house on Mott Street, and what lay beyond its dark windows. Lay. He silently laughed, laid it out cold, etherized: he must be in the grip of multiple panics to have had such a dream, split multiple ways, like himself, Kastner and Kennerly editor and vice-president, lover of all love, paterfamilias. The daylight drove the dream from him, and he shed it with relief, for it was a dream he could never tell. He came out of the bath to hear Faye's fresh morning voice, Todd's questioning replies.

"Isn't Memorial Day when everybody plants a tree?"

"No, dear; that's Arbor Day. That's past for this year."

"But I'd like to plant a tree—with Daddy," Todd insisted.

"We can plant one if you like," Anson said as he came to the table for breakfast. "We can all go out and buy one. We can all do anything today we'd like."

"Anything *you* like," Faye qualified. "Holiday or no holiday, Mrs. Haines and I are going to finish the spring-cleaning. We begin with closets." She was wearing housedress and apron and her head was bound up in a turban, ready for work. "I wish you'd take Todd off my hands for a few hours," she said when Todd was brushing his teeth.

The yearly spring-cleaning, scrupulously approached, as though it equated examining one's soul or salving conscience, was something Anson dreaded being around. He was only too glad to agree.

"Libby Draper's baby-sitting tonight while we'll be at Velma and Sam's," Fay briefed him.

"I am not a *baby!*" Todd shouted, overhearing. "And I hate old *Libby Draper!*"

"How I wish there were a tranquilizer for kids!"

"I'll be his tranquilizer today," promised Anson, going to find Todd before he went to his glass jar. "We'll plant a tree, as you wanted to do," he told him. "We'll drive out to the nursery and pick out something like a small holly for the north hedge. Okay?"

"Can we go in the Porsche?" Though already under way, Todd tried to impose a condition.

"No. We'll have to take the wagon so we can bring the tree back," Anson said. Todd nodded. It was incredible, the way he accepted direction from Anson, Faye's expression said; she had been over this question of which of the two cars it would be, always, somehow, coming off loser, no matter how she handled it.

"Take his red sweater," she said, her head already buried in the hall coat closet as Todd and Anson went out.

Mindful of the weeks he had been away, Anson did a rather better-than-usual job of his paterfamilias role. They were gone not only all morning, but most of the afternoon as well. They stopped at several nurseries, in the last finding the suitable holly, and had a late lunch at a Howard Johnson's. Afterward, Todd acquired a pair of miniature turtles in a small plastic box that had a pool in the center, surrounded by moss. By the time they returned it was early evening. Mrs. Haines had left and Faye was already dressed for the Curries. Todd's supper was waiting for him.

"He'll eat too fast because he's tired," she said, joining Anson on the terrace; "but at least he'll go off to sleep early. The man is coming on Monday to do the glass in the gables Mrs. Haines can't reach. She gets the higher points outside with the hose, but getting them clean inside's a production. With next week's brushup, we should be all set for the party."

"Good," Anson said.

"Well. How was he?"

"Fine. He always is, on outings. I may have let him eat something you won't approve of—one of those banana things with several kinds of ice cream and sauces."

"As long as he brushes his teeth. How were the questions?"

"He didn't ask any, at least not the kind you mean. I never saw him happier."

"Because you were with him. One day I didn't have to rack *my* brains," Faye said.

The day was not yet over. Todd came out, having dutifully brushed his teeth and followed with the Water Pik. He was carrying the turtles carefully, having filled with water the depression in the plastic box that was the lake. He placed it next to his glass jar.

"Who's sitting?" Anson asked, when Todd was at the end of the terrace, out of hearing.

"I told you this morning. Libby Draper."

"Couldn't you have found someone else, after that Kathy business?"

"Anson, you know what hell it is to get anyone, especially holidays. I couldn't ask 'Gertrude' and 'Alice' again. He won't scratch Libby, if that's what you're afraid of. I couldn't cancel; this is the night we're going to discuss Todd."

"Well I remember."

Todd stood, holding his glass jar. The jar had a film of moisture inside it, and when he lifted the lid, he cried out "Daddy!"

"What's the matter?" Anson asked.

"My salamander's dead!"

"Let's see. Bring it here."

"Don't call it *it*," he said to his father. "It's a him."

"Say 'a male salamander,'" Faye corrected.

Todd, bringing the jar to Anson for verification, ignored her. Anson looked inside and saw a dried, reddish translucence that had been the salamander, flattened in one corner. "Why did you keep the lid on the jar? You didn't give him air to breathe."

"I was afraid he'd get away," Todd said. He began to whimper. "I think the snail's dead, too."

The snail could have been alive or dead; it clung to the underside of the lid, motionless. "Well, salamanders die sooner or later, like everything else," Anson told him. "Find yourself another one. There are lots down by the stream."

"But not *this* one. I loved him! Besides, he'd only die, too. Why does everything die? Am I going to die?"

"A long, long time from now. Don't worry about it tonight."

267

At this moment, Libby Draper arrived. She had walked across the meadow and had a notebook and three books under her arm. "I'm cramming for exams," she explained.

Todd regarded her expressionlessly, saying nothing.

"We won't be later than ten," Faye said to Libby. "And we'll be over at the Curries'. You know their number, if you need to call. But you won't. He's been out all day and is already sleepy."

"Okay," Libby said.

"The funeral's going to be tomorrow," Todd announced when Faye and Anson were in the doorway.

"The what?" Faye asked.

"The salamander's funeral. Or I may put him away till next week."

It would be Libby's choice whether to take this up or not. Once in the car, Faye said, "At least we know the salamander was male."

"If it matters."

"Probably it does."

Anson drove along the winding lane, through a stand of pines, toward the Currie house. "Did you and Velma discuss Todd the other night?"

"Not really, no. I thought you should be in on it."

"And for it? From your attitude, you seem to think everything's my fault."

"I don't think it's entirely mine. Anson, let's not wrangle."

"You mean, wait for Velma to wrangle with us?"

"Have it that way if you like."

Sam Currie was sitting on the screened porch having a beer. His normally rather florid face was even pinker than usual from working in the garden. "Hi!" he greeted them. "The good woman's got her bust over the stove, but she'll be out in a minute. How was London, Anson? Get to any of the tit clubs?"

"Matter of fact, yes, I did," Anson replied. "Won thirty quid and lost it all back in two minutes flat."

"Looking at the bunnies, who are *not* flat," Faye said. "You didn't tell me you'd gambled."

"I didn't, really. It was part of lunching with Colin Vaughan."

"Who's he?" Sam asked.

"David Steen's London agent."

"Oh. What'll you drink?"

"Gin and tonic. Long on the tonic, please, Sam," said Faye.

"Something deadening for me," Anson said. "Martini?"

"Coming up," Sam said, going out.

The Currie house was a monument to permissive child rearing. Daylight revealed no square inch of wall, woodwork or furniture that had not been battered and scarred. Stray baseballs and bats and toys were always to be found in doorways and on stair landings, and bookshelves had been built high against the depredation of toddlers. Sam Currie seemed to regard his children as providential weeds; none was really good-looking, though showing marked resemblances to their parents, but all were strong and had survived the crises of childhood and those growing into their teens were responsible and adult for their ages.

"Oh, *shit!*" Sam said, almost slipping on a skate that had been left in the doorway. He handed Faye and Anson their drinks, half spilled, and Velma followed.

"I've asked you not to use that word," Velma said. "Hello, you two."

"Well, *merde,* then, or *merde alors!* if you prefer. Or *kuso*—I think that's it in Japanese."

"Dinner's on the back of the stove," Velma said. "I thought we'd have our drinks and relax while the house quiets down."

It was cool, as usual, on the porch, but inside the house was vibrant with sound and movement. There were clatterings in the kitchen, and somewhere a door opened and over the gush of a flushing toilet came the voices of the teenage

269

children cajoling the younger ones into bed. Bedsprings creaked, pillows flew, bare feet stamped.

Dinner *chez* Currie was always somewhat sketchy. There really were two dinners, the one the kids had, at six, and the one Faye and Anson had been asked for. It was always good, solid food, but smacked of warming over. The roast beef was overdone, the glazed potatoes waterlogged, the carrots pulpy. The salads were better, because Sam hid them from the kids and made the dressing fresh. Anson had a long drink with dinner to gird himself for what he knew was coming. The conversation was desultory; Faye's Tuesday night talk with Velma had laid down a coating of complicity which Sam's joviality could not quite penetrate. The underlay of what Velma had said about "The Assortment" seeped through the generalities twice, once when Faye forgot and made a reference to Sherm Draper's joblessness (usually never mentioned to the Curries), again when Velma made a crack about Martha Lavrorsen's drinking.

"But I'd no idea you knew Martha well enough to know that about her," Anson said.

"Velma and Sam knew them long before we did," Faye had to say. "Evidently Martha's always been a lush."

"And Stig's the biggest phallic narcissist I know," added Velma; having let the cat out of the bag, she proceeded to twist its tail. "Doesn't everybody know about Stig? Women do. I was telling Faye the other night, most Ridge wives have had a run-in with Stig. I had mine."

"What do you mean, a run-in?" Anson wanted to know.

"Shall we tell him, Faye? Faye knows about Stig, too."

"Knows what?" Anson persisted.

"Stig likes to show it to the girls."

" 'It' being?"

"Oh, Anson, really! You see Stig Lavrorsen five days a week on the 'Bug.' You're not that innocent." Velma laughed.

"So that's what you girls talked about the other night."

270

"You men go over us just as finely," Velma answered him. "I've heard more than one discussion not intended for women."

"We do, sometimes, talk about you," Anson admitted, "but not in the same way. No husband *I* know would label any wife of a friend—what was it you called Stig, Velma?"

"A phallic narcissist. Don't pretend, Anson. You know what one is."

"Why would I know?"

"Well, you know Stig."

"Can't we get off this?" Faye asked.

"But I'm interested in how Faye knows about Stig," Anson said. "Velma said you did, Faye."

"Do. It's general knowledge and perfectly useless. All right, you asked me, Anse." She gave the briefest account possible of her experience with Stig Lavrorsen in the bathroom, adding that it was long ago.

"I wish you'd told me at the time," Anson said. "I'd have punched his face in. I may still punch it in."

"Don't get hot about it, Anson," said Sam. "Nothing happens with Stig. That's the whole thing about it."

"Evidently Velma told you about *her* run-in."

"Velma tells me everything," said Sam. "Yeah?"

"Yeah. You *think*," said Velma. "I may be the mother of your children, but I still have a few scales I don't choose to run with you."

"Boasting?" Sam countered.

"No, just holding on to what little privacy I have left."

"Don't you two start," Faye pleaded. "Velma, I thought we were going to talk about Todd."

Velma waited, then said, "I think, to put it in the simplest way, that you and Anson know—instinctually—why Toddy's been doing the things he does."

"Define 'instinctually'—in relation to us," said Anson.

"Yes, do," Faye seconded.

"Radcliffe grad, Harvard grad asking to have 'instinctually' defined? Shame on you both! Anson, Faye must have told you about what happened at the group."

"She told me. *I* think you should have given him a couple; he might not have shat his britches the way he did."

"We don't punish children," answered Velma, "except creatively. Anson, you're hostile. We can't discuss hostility—"

"What hostility would we discuss, besides mine?" Anson flung back.

"To discuss yours is putting off discussing Todd's."

"I wish you'd tell me whatever you know about him that Faye and I don't—if you know," said Anson seriously. "For example, this salamander thing." He related the episode on the terrace.

"It's very complex," Velma said. "What you're both seeing in Todd is the love and affection of a five-and-a-half-year-old going through his Oedipal conflict. He's been scarred and hurt by something. He's trying to defend himself."

"From what, or whom?" asked Anson. "Faye and me?"

"It's not something that's affecting him from without," Velma explained; "it's something inside *him.*"

"Your coding is blind to me," said Anson. "Surely, if you know what's bugging Todd, we're good enough friends to be told what it is."

"I simply don't know how to handle his hostility toward me," Faye said. "I can't help being impatient with him sometimes."

"But don't you see, the child doesn't understand his own feelings?" Velma spoke very earnestly. "Surely, you understand that."

"Yes, I understand just about that much," said Faye. "And that he goes on beating himself down with this death thing."

"What should we do, Velma?" Anson asked.

"Well," Velma answered him pointedly, "you *have* been away, Anson. Probably, now you're back, the matter will clear of itself."

There was a silence, just long enough for Sam to ask if anyone wanted a drink. No one did.

Anson said, "Well, Velma, you've tried. But, to be honest, I don't think I've learned a thing I didn't know before."

"Anson," said Faye.

"I think Faye's much more worried and concerned than you are," Velma told Anson.

"I'm as concerned but not as worried as Faye," said Anson.

"And why aren't you as worried?" asked Faye.

"Because I love Todd. He knows I love him. I love him almost more than I love Faye, if that were possible. In another way, I'm trying to say."

Faye and Velma pointedly did not exchange glances. To no one's surprise, Faye said nothing, but neither did Velma, to the surprise even of Anson. He said, "That stymies you, doesn't it, Velma?"

Velma sat up stiffly. "Stymies me? No. You simply put me in a position where I can't say anything more."

"Love's not the solution, I take it," Anson challenged her.

"Well, I will say one thing more," Velma decided. "Love's fine, wonderful, perhaps even the solution—if Toddy *feels* he's loved. But from his actions, it seems clear he has doubts."

"This is getting nowhere," said Faye. "Velma, I know you've tried to be helpful—"

"Yes, Faye, I tried. You both bring to mind that old Spanish proverb: 'Do good, offer prayers afterward.' "

"Anson, you look tired," Faye said.

"Meaning that you're tired yourself?" Anson asked her.

"Well, it is late. I think we should be getting back. Libby

Draper said she's in exams, and she probably needs her sleep. And there's the driving her home."

Anson stood up and stretched. "I hope Faye's asked you for our party?"

"Yes, she's invited us, and we'll be glad to come as usual," Velma assured him. "I suppose it's for David Steen?"

"No, just for everybody," replied Anson; "the Steens will be there, of course."

"His book's sure hitting it," Sam said. "What's it called? *Time—for Something—*"

"Good Time Coming."

"I could use a good time coming myself."

"Do shut up, Sam," Velma said.

"Well, I got the idea, evidently," Sam told her. "Is the book as wild as they say? Sex, violence?"

"The book is about temptation," Anson answered. "Temptation on a pretty normal level. It's about sex in daily life, not aberrant sex, but sex as it happens to people like us. As for the violence, Steen's not in love with it, only trying to show it."

"Love of violence is the same as the death wish," Velma put in. "Violence is the box-office draw in America, and don't try to kid me."

"Maybe," said Anson. "But don't forget that violence in life goes before its depiction in the arts. If you're looking for something kicky, you can have a go at Galey Birnham's new one. Faye's reading it in manuscript now. She hasn't said how she likes it."

"Ask me that one when we get home, Anson. Birnham will be at the party, too. But we'll see you before then."

"I hope so," said Velma.

Sam walked out to the car with Faye, and for a moment Velma and Anson were alone. "Anson," she said, laying a hand on his arm. "Don't."

274

"Don't what, Velma?"

"You know what I'm referring to. Don't do what you're doing."

"Whatever you mean by that. I've talked all I'm going to, for now."

"I don't mean about Todd. I mean about Faye."

"Velma," Anson told her with irritation, "you are *not* God, nor are you Faye's analyst or mine."

Velma kept her temper. "No, only a friend, Anson. You can't stop me from offering up those Spanish prayers. Don't go to Borobudur."

"You girls seem to have dished up a storm the other night."

"We talked. Why not?"

"Good night," Anson said. He said nothing during the drive to the house, where Faye got out and Libby Draper got in.

"Everything went all right with Todd," he said when he had got back from the Draper house and Faye and he were undressing.

"Yes, evidently."

"Well, I learned one thing tonight."

"I'm glad someone did. I didn't."

"How much women talk."

"Well, it's all a disappointing salad," Faye said.

"What's a salad? Don't be deep. I'm ready to drop, but what's disappointing?"

"Marriage."

"Velma's recipe, no doubt. That *sage-femme!*" Anson got into bed. "What *did* you talk about with Velma the other night?"

"We tossed the salad. Back and forth."

"Adding Borobudur sauce."

"It's called being bitches together."

"I'm not going to argue that one," Anson said.

"Nor am I," answered Faye, switching out the light.

"Good night," Anson said to the darkness.

🌷 🌷 🌷 "ANSON."

"Mm?" He sat at the breakfast table, staring into his empty coffee cup.

"You're running late; you'll miss the 'Bug' if you don't hurry."

"Another half cup, please."

Faye poured it.

"What's today?" he asked between sips.

"Friday. All day."

"I know it's Friday. What's the date?"

"May thirty-first."

"Somehow I thought it was the first of June."

" 'Thirty days hath September, April, June, and November. All the rest have thirty-one, save February, which has twenty-eight, but in leap year has twenty-nine.' "

"What's leap year, Mommy?" Todd asked through his cereal.

"Don't talk with your mouth full," Faye said, letting the leap-year question go.

"Doesn't June ever have thirty-one days, Mommy?"

"No, never."

Todd finished his breakfast and asked permission to leave the table, got it, and, followed by Netcher, went out to the terrace to his glass jar and his turtles. Netcher was perfectly trained; she first sat, then lay down, her eyes on Todd, alertly watching. Faye always felt perfectly safe and relaxed when

276

Netcher was with Todd; if he strayed too far toward the road, the Doberman rose and quickly followed, walking close beside him, stopping when he stopped, never letting him out of sight, even following him to the stream.

Up to now, the conversation had been strictly for Todd. Now Anson, routinely getting up, asked, "Mrs. Haines staying with Todd while you're in town today?"

"I won't be going into town today."

"But it's Friday. Your day."

"I know."

"I heard you making arrangements the other night with Martha Lavrorsen to drive in with her as usual."

"That was day before yesterday. I've changed my mind."

Anson lifted his jacket from the back of the chair. "I thought we could meet at the apartment, have dinner, and take in a show. Nina can always wangle tickets for anything you'd like to see."

"Too hot."

"It's not hot." Anson lighted his first cigarette of the day.

"It will be," Faye said. She was quiet and abstracted. "Maybe the new plan to have all Memorial Days fall on Mondays will make for better Memorial Days."

"Except for the Velma stretch, I didn't think it a bad day."

"Maybe it wasn't, for you. I hated it, salamander and all. Velma just might have told us more if you hadn't been so resistive."

"She said enough. Todd's going through his Oedipal conflict. So?"

"*And* she said he was scarred."

"I said what I thought, what I feel. Everyone has Oedipal conflicts. Everything can't be explained by Freud. After all, there were fathers and sons before him."

"You're not making sense about the problem."

"Oh, come on, darling, change your mind about town. It'll be good for us to be together for a little, away from here."

"Togetherness is pretty much the same everywhere, I find," she answered him coolly. "I've no plans to go into town at the moment."

Anson, watching her, drew on his cigarette, exhaled. "I'm probably already late, but do you want to lay it on the line? What you're thinking but not saying?"

She began to clear the table, carrying the dishes to the shelf next to the sink, placing them in the dishwasher. She didn't look at him. "Anse, I'm frightened this time. There've been the other times, the other ones, but not like this one, this time. I suppose I must have accepted the others, but this time I can't seem to."

"I'd hoped we were through with the talk about Jeannette. Let up! You know what Fridays are like for me, the week's windup, my lame ducks."

"It's Friday for me too."

"You don't have lame ducks."

"Only a dead salamander." She turned, facing him. "The funeral's today, or maybe Todd'll cremate him. *I* don't know."

"Well, I have perennial Joanna Summers and God knows what others."

"Cheer up. Maybe one duck will have red hair."

He stood a last moment, checking car keys and money, picked up his attaché case, making the movements automatically while seeing her eyes, quietly and intensely blue, her dark hair tied with a matching ribbon, her body soft and relaxed with morning beneath the blue peignoir she wore.

"You don't answer that," she said.

He was desperately late now, but he went to her. "You didn't kiss me good night. You didn't even *say* good night. Kiss me goodby now." He kissed her ardently, receiving only indifference in return. "All right," he said, "have it your own way."

She held him with her eyes. "It's you who are having your

way, Anson Parris." Her lip trembled. "I'm surprised you know what day it is. You didn't know the date. For all I know, you're hoping it's the thirty-*second* of June, no date at all. I don't know how to say it. I feel you're getting into *some*thing I can't know about. That it's not good."

"If I do, I'll keep you out of it."

"Ah! There *is* something!"

"Truthfully, Faye—"

"Oh, yes, Anse, be truthful!"

"Will you let me call it—Borobudur?"

"Since you can't seem to call it anything else."

He was miserable and looked it. "If ever *you* have a Borobudur, I'll stick with you."

"Meaning what?"

"God, Faye—it's all so dull! 'The Assortment,' Velma, Sam."

"Well, you seem to have your own List. Capped, no quotes."

"Try to understand."

"You're trying to say if there's a man, *you'll* understand?"

"Can't you think of it in any other way? You looked up Borobudur. I know, because you left the encyclopedia open at the page."

"Yes, I guess I did."

"You must have understood my use of it—it just came out. An abstraction for something I couldn't put into words."

"Impatience with the marital grind. I got it."

"With Velma's help, it sounds like."

"No, I got it all by myself."

"You know I love you. But I do have an identity of my own."

"If you haven't lost it."

"Maybe I'm trying to find it."

She looked away. "I wish there were an emotional yardstick by which I could measure what's happening to us."

"More Velma."

"Do go now, before you miss the train."

Anson made the "Bug," but only because Ray Doyle and Chet Burgess had prevailed on the conductor to hold it for two strategic minutes.

"Car trouble?" Ray asked when Anson took the seat next to him, the only one not occupied.

"Call it that," Anson replied, getting rid of it. "So you're going to be a 'Bug' regular again?"

"Yep, I'll be off to the TV wars daily from now on," Ray said. He had a writing pad on his knee on which he was scribbling notes for the day's taping of "Love Me Today." "Irma—she's our long-suffering heroine—Irma's in jail, about to have Steve's baby. Out of wedlock, of course. Don't ask why she's in jail, the other writer got her there somehow. Anyway, Irma wants not to have the baby, but the big jail-dike matron is determined she shall have it, because she wants to move in on Irma and become, so to speak, the baby's 'father.' We don't develop the dikiness too much, don't have to; it's amazing what the American moms can figure out these days."

"Mighty soapy," agreed Anson. "How are Alma and the kids?"

"Kids fine, but Alma's bridling about my going back to do 'Love Me Today.' She'll have to chauffeur now, do the marketing and cook."

Anson opened his *Times* and folded it to the book section.

"Soap opera's all about off-stage screwing, illegitimacy, adoption and murder. You see, Irma's best friend, whom she met in the hospital while she was having *Jasper's* baby, was having a baby too. They have babies all the time; they've never heard of the pill; if they had, we'd have no show. I sympathize, because I know that if I'd been a girl, I'd have been knocked up all the time. Well, this best friend was pushed downstairs and killed by the librarian, who went white overnight. She looks younger in the puss now, natch, but she can't *remember*. It's even more complicated than 'As the Soup Tureens,' our major competition."

"Is it really called that?"

"No, that's camp, but you know the one. Both the mother and the daughter in *that* one are murderesses, one acquitted, the other unable to remember—*of course*—and *terribly* worried about whether the new man in her life loves her for herself or her money. We *have* to have murderesses. The moms dig them big, but you have to get them acquitted. When we're really stuck for a line, we just have someone ask, 'Would you like a cup of coffee?' And then go to black."

"You're wearing me out," Anson said.

"Now you may guess why I don't finish my book. Jesus God! *Moms!* If it gets any more female, someday I'm going to take a great big crap right in the middle of all the coffee cups, and on camera too. Don't worry, Anson. We tape."

"We'll all have to get together soon."

"Faye's called, asking us to your spring party. We're coming, of course. June eighth, isn't it?"

"Saturday week."

Amenities over, Ray went back to Irma's dialogue and Anson retreated behind his paper. Between pages he turned his mind to Joanna Summers, his ten-thirty appointment, the first of his lame ducks, formulating a casual, friendly questioning, hopefully designed to induce her to do most of the talking, so he could close in and try to get a promise of a delivery date on *Time and Place*, her long 1920's memoir, on which she had been working for the past six years. Lameduck days were difficult. He felt like the end of the week.

🌷 🌷 🌷 "Well, i see that you have remembered to wear your red-and-white yarn bracelet this morning," Dr. Cimino said, placing his small chime watch on the desk before him; the bracelet the taxi driver had given Jeannette had figured prominently in recent sessions; sometimes she wore it, other times forgot.

The hour had just begun. Jeannette, still a little breathless from the hurry of getting to Dr. Cimino's office on time, lay in her usual supine position on the couch, staring at the Jasper Johns painting of a bull's-eye target with its vivid, circular colors.

"Yes, this morning I remembered not to forget it," she answered.

"Or did you forget and go back to get it?"

"No, I remembered not to forget."

"One must remember not to forget, I suppose." Dr. Cimino chuckled in approval. He noted that Jeannette's hands were clasped together beneath her chin in an attitude suggestive of prayer. *Saint's hands,* he thought, then reprimanded himself for permitting such an irrelevance to intrude.

Good girl! Jeannette said to herself. *He likes me today!*

"Now," Dr. Cimino resumed, "I should like to go back a little to something you said during an earlier hour." He leafed through his notebook. "Ah, yes. Anson Parris' penis. You described how he wears no underclothing and mentioned how excited you were by that. You also expressed a fear that something might 'happen' to his penis."

"Did I?"

282

"I am reading from my notes exactly."

"Oh. Well, I've no recollection of having said that. *If* I did—"

"You did. If—what? What was it you feared might happen to it?"

"I honestly don't know."

"Very well, we may come back to that later, when memory may be clearer to you. And there is something else, your dream you had about riding on an elephant, in a howdah. You felt that the howdah really was a penis about to ejaculate. You found it different from an actual penis—"

Jeannette repressed a giggle, said, "Yes, I remember now that you tell me. There was an opening on the end of it, with fur around it."

"Do you care to associate?"

"I suppose the opening was me, my opening."

"Mm-hm," said Dr. Cimino. "And?"

"And—that's all. I always wanted a penis. I'll never get one, so I suppose I'll have to dream about having one. I haven't had any dreams since that dream."

"You mean to say, none that you recall."

"Yes, none I recall," Jeannette amended; she knew better, of course. One dreamed, whether the dream could be recalled or not.

"But penises do not have fur surrounding their openings," prompted Dr. Cimino.

"Of course not. I suppose once more we go back to that thing that happened to me when I was six. Or was it seven? I had been sent to the doctor to be examined for new eyeglasses. In those days, where I lived, the family doctor did everything, including glasses. . . ."

Dr. Cimino closed his eyes. He had heard the story often, had listened to it many times, never interrupting because he always hoped it might be just a little different; but it never was. He knew Jeannette's childhood conflicts as well as a

283

candidate for a doctorate, tabulating ablative endings in Chaucer, knows *The Canterbury Tales*. The family doctor had put belladonna in Jeannette's eyes, but had neglected, when the examination was over, to follow with drops to aid her pupils to retract. She had wandered all over the small Western town, where she had grown up, unable to see her way clearly. At some street intersection she could never remember, a man had approached her and she had panicked. "Though he was all hazy, I remember him as clearly as though it were yesterday. He was a beggar. 'Show me your little pussy,' he had said. 'If you will, I'll show you my pecker.' " The man had groveled under her skirt and handled her, and had unbuttoned his trousers and forced her to put her hand on his penis. Jeannette still remembered that his penis had seemed like a dog to her—"Not a real dog but a little one, with teeth. I was terrified it might bite me—"

Dr. Cimino, though listening, nodding as each point of reference in Jeannette's long journey from the doctor's office to her home was reached, was aware that he was not attending, was having attention lapses. He would hear one of her intense sentences, register it, and then find his attention switching to his own life situation. He was having severe troubles, not only with his wife, a manic-depressive, but also with his professional beliefs. He was becoming (and he so thought of it guiltily) an apostate of Freud. The master's once so lucid abstractions were now, no matter how he tried to think otherwise, somewhat shaky; no scientific proof whatever existed to support the effectiveness of psychoanalysis; the "reality" therapy he had instituted with Jeannette had gotten her nowhere she had not been at first. And (worse!) *his* therapy, or its patent unworkability, had helped turn him into a doubter. Had psychoanalysis ever truly been the frontier? Had he, actually, once conducted sessions with his chosen analysands with conviction? Yes, he had; he had been as intense and involved as a messiah, probing the long-

284

hidden mazes of his patients' childhoods, reproducing their problems as difficulties between himself and them with fervor, experiencing purest joy when the transference neurosis was effected. As with Freud himself, several patients had risen from the couch and embraced him, as proof of his dedication. But, especially since Jeannette had entered into this last year with him, all had come to seem so much moribund dogma. Dogma by the yard.

"—and it *was* a dog he had between his legs," Jeannette was saying.

Stop that! You, yourself, are relating! Dr. Cimino scolded himself, continuing to listen patiently, but his patience was wearing thin. It was all as unfirm as a mound of gelatine, ignoring the contours of its mold. Perhaps the master had been the ironical man he was because he knew this could happen. There were no ways to measure impulses, conflicts, fears; all that was known about them was that they existed, and were endless, like Jeannette's long, long childhood. This morning, Dr. Cimino felt worn down to a nub, deplored the very society that once had enabled him to *believe*. It was most depressing.

"Yes, yes," he interpolated, hoping to head Jeannette off before she reached the great *scena* of violation he knew by heart. "I remember."

She stopped, then said, "You know, that little dog, the one between his legs, makes me think of a dog David and I had when we were staying on Lindos."

"The Greek island?"

"Yes."

"You are full of serendipity this morning." Indeed, Dr. Cimino did feel rather like one of the heroes in Walpole's *The Three Princes of Serendip*, always making discoveries by accident of things they were not looking for. *I never seem to get to places like Lindos,* he thought. His wife detested travel; his Mexican trips had been made alone. *I seem to sit here with my low-back syndrome, listening to monsters talk about themselves. Herself.* His back was killing him this week and sitting had become very difficult, except for short periods. What would happen, he wondered, if *he* took the couch and reclined, put Jeannette in the Thonet rocker? He stood up, brushing his pad from the desk. It fell to the floor.

Jeannette stopped her reminiscence about Lindos. "What was that?"

"Merely my notebook. I dropped it accidentally."

"I thought there were no accidents, that everything is intentional."

Painfully stooping, Dr. Cimino retrieved the notebook. "I would like to suggest that we could better employ our time than in the way you are now employing it," he said, punishing her gently.

"Well," Jeannette conceded, "I guess I *am* blocking."

"Use simple ways of saying things. They're much better."

"Talking around it, then."

"Mm."

"David and I've gotten back to bed."

Dr. Cimino jotted *gotten back.* "To bed or to make love?" he asked, to see what he would get.

"To bed. It was love, too, I suppose; the kind of love we have. But nothing happened to *me. I* didn't feel anything."

"You did not experience orgasm?"

"That's what I meant."

"No pleasure of any kind?"

"Well, as I've told you before, I got used to it all long ago. With him. He kisses me, twice, usually, and I go in and have my bath while he waits for me on his bed. *And writes!*" She stopped again.

"Writes, yes," Dr. Cimino cued.

"I hate that."

"Why? If he did not write, you would not be rich, and being rich is what you like, isn't it?"

286

"I couldn't stand to be any other way, now. No, what I mean is, I hate all those jottings."

"But why?"

"I guess it's because I think he's only a journalist, not a real writer. It seems to me real writers must simply sit down at their desks and let a book grow—without all those notes."

"Have you ever tried writing anything?"

"I can't even make out a laundry list."

"Perhaps you are not in a position to know, then, how writers work." It was time to punish her, Dr. Cimino decided; and he was fortified by the memory of what efforts his few papers for *The Psychoanalytic Quarterly* had cost him; he was an inveterate jotter himself. "But you got off."

"Yes, well, I get myself all greased up for him, and then he goes all over me with his tongue—as though I hadn't bathed."

"A tongue bath, perhaps?" Dr. Cimino knew that was not *echt* Freud, but this was new material, and he could not resist it.

"Kind of. And everything is, I don't know, as though caresses come in matched pairs."

"Like the French furniture you so admire and collect? Pairs are very desirable, are they not?" Dr. Cimino asked, thinking how inconceivable other people's sex was.

"What?"

"You have put it vividly. But back to the pleasure. You experience it with other men, if not actual orgasm, pleasure?"

"Oh, yes; I go wild." Her voice changed. "If only I could *come!*"

"There has, perhaps—" Dr. Cimino stopped, rephrased, unweighting the question. "Have you been with someone since the time with your husband? The last time with him?"

"No, but I've thought of being."

"Did you fantasy anyone specific?"

"Yes. My taximan. I think of him all the time. I was even

trying to fantasy him when I was with David, but it didn't work. David's wrists are hairy."

"So we are back again at wrists, are we?" Dr. Cimino sighed. "Did the taxi driver bring you here this morning?"

"Yes."

"Happened to, or did you arrange it?"

"He kind of waits for me. He knows I come out of the building the same time every day I come to you, and he was just there."

Dr. Cimino noted *come to you*. "So you took his cab?"

"I told you I did. It was first in line. You take the first one, don't you? I do. And it was his cab. Fate."

"Will he be waiting for you when you leave here?"

"Sometimes he's here when I leave you, yes."

"And he'll drive you home then?"

"If I go home."

"You are evading. What do you and this taximan speak of?"

"Nothing, when he's driving me from home here. You've told me not to talk before my hour, said it makes the dream material fresher."

"Suggested," said Dr. Cimino. "Now. When you were in bed with David, did he experience orgasm?"

"Oh, yes; David always does—he's like a great, hot machine."

Dr. Cimino made a note but ignored it for the time being. "You were fantasying the taxi driver during your intercourse with your husband. It would help, I think, if you could remember *in what way* you were fantasying him."

"I tried to remember his white wrists."

Jeannette could hear Dr. Cimino's sound of impatience. "Backs of heads, wrists! Do you never think of a *whole* man?"

"Of course, sometimes. But you asked me what I was fantasying about the taximan, and I did succeed—a little—in seeing you."

288

A short silence developed, during which Dr. Cimino felt a chill. "You are aware of what you just said, I hope?"

"I think so."

"You said it was I you succeeded in fantasying. Partly."

"Did I? I meant the taximan, of course."

"I wonder."

"There are no mistakes. No forgetting. No not remembering? But I did. Really. Really I did, *Dottore!*"

"I think perhaps you don't know what you fantasy. One thing I do sense—you are hostile to me today."

"A little, maybe."

"And why?"

Jeannette concentrated on the bull's-eye. "You remember last week I told you I had figured up—or my unconscious figured it up for me," she said, and heard that small sound Dr. Cimino made, and which she so liked, indicating approval for her having said *unconscious* instead of *subconscious*. "You know, I mean that I could have had so many more Fabergé things, good French pieces, if I hadn't spent so much with you."

"I remember. Pieces, pieces."

"No, it's nothing to do with sex."

"Then why do you say that it does not?"

"No, I meant that figuring up, *Dottore*. And I got to thinking if I used the money I—David, actually—will pay you in the next years, I could buy myself a real folly and be happy."

"Folly?" Dr. Cimino bristled. "One does not seek to buy folly, as one does not seek to borrow trouble."

"No, I've found a real folly and I want it."

"Don't you mean you want the taximan?"

"Him, of course! But no, no! A folly's not a man, it's a house. A pavilion. *Pavillon.*" Her voice caressed the French. *"Pavillon."*

Dr. Cimino's education, like that of many analysts, had been somewhat specialized, and his general reference frames happened not to include knowledge of follies, or pavilions. "A folly is a house?" he asked, playing along.

"Oui, une folie, dans la Rue Saint James."

"We long ago agreed on not using French, except for concepts which cannot be otherwise expressed," he reminded.

"You are standing up," said Jeannette.

"I have been standing some minutes. Why do you interrupt the train of thought? I frequently stand."

"While I lie."

"It is impossible for me not to wonder if what you are saying may not be a lie."

"Lie, lay, lain. No, it's nothing to do with prevarication."

"Watch those *No's.*"

"It's true. I've found this folly, this pavilion, in Paris. It's for sale and is the perfect setting for David and me. It was a *maison de rendez-vous.* Purest 1760, by Chevotet. A low building with a central hall and branching wings. *Chinoiserie* by Pillement." Her voice grew ecstatic. "It has a temple of love in the gardens."

"A temple of love—for you?"

"Better than love itself."

Dr. Cimino was bewildered. He said, "I suggest that if you imagine—still imagine, after all our—your—years of therapy—that this house, this folly, whatever, is all you need to put your life in order, we can discontinue our sessions."

"Wasn't it rather *my* idea?" Jeannette asked, her eyes straying to the corner of the Jasper Johns painting where the chip of paint was missing.

"Do you put that as a question?"

"Obviously it's a question."

"It seemed to me that you put it as a statement of fact."

"Well, maybe."

"I must observe that you have often put questions as statements." His voice betrayed irritation. "What, may I ask, are you doing with your hand? Your *right* hand? Have you dropped something?"

"It's a thing I do sometimes," Jeannette said; "this couch is rather low, and I find my hand exploring beneath it."

Dr. Cimino let *rather low* go. "Exploring? For what?"

"It's just a nervous thing."

"Perhaps you imagine that the floor underneath the couch is not clean? Is that it?"

"Sometimes it's not."

Dr. Cimino was controlling. "In what way is it not clean?"

"Sometimes there are—we used to call them dust bunnies. On the floor. Where the maid has missed."

"Why do you call them, uh, dust bunnies?"

"That's what they are."

"To me it seems you may unconsciously be referring to those women at topless clubs, who are nude to the waist. You have several times mentioned them."

"But not today. I'm sick of this!"

"You are sick."

This time the silence was longer. It was Jeannette who broke it. "Did you ever really think you could help me?"

"We have been over that. Any help must come from yourself."

"And I can't *bear* to go over it one more time!"

Dr. Cimino, despite the grave turn matters were taking, automatically was exercising his last three vertebrae, lengthening and strengthening. "I will tell you the usual facts—we have been over them before, too. You always provoke one of these—so to speak—quarrels with me just before going into one of your fugue states, which are occurring with increasing frequency. You continually develop and redevelop almost identical ideas of reference. Now it is a house that is a folly, in which you tell yourself you and David will be happy. You want to discontinue therapy, obviously."

"Yes, I do."

291

"Such a shame. I had hoped, after what you told me earlier today about having resumed relations with your husband, that an improvement might confidently be expected."

"But I told you what a frost it was. I still can't have orgasm. Didn't. I'm tired of saying orgasm. Come."

"And you will continue to pursue—these persons you pursue. Like the taxi driver. Seeking the orgasm you so desire."

"Coming. Really coming a ball!"

"We will ignore your extension of that."

Jeannette laughed. "That's good—extension. If you'd like me to associate 'coming a ball' I can. I'd rather have two balls than one."

"You are no longer a serious patient," Dr. Cimino said sadly.

"Because I say what I mean—think? I used to come. I want to come again. I'm not going to add, as I used to, that I expect you to understand."

"No, do not add anything. What do you propose to do now?"

"Find someone who can make me come. You can't, that's sure."

"I meant when we have discontinued these sessions."

Jeannette had been opening and closing her right hand, having found something on the floor beneath the couch. It was vaguely triangular in shape, substantial but brittle. She brought it up to where she could look at it and immediately saw what it was: the triangular chip of paint missing from the bull's-eye painting.

"What have you there?" Dr. Cimino asked.

Without replying to his question, Jeannette got up from the couch, went to the painting, and held the piece up to it. It fitted the corner exactly. "There," she said. "You see?"

"It does seem to be the missing fragment," conceded Dr. Cimino, looking over his eyeglasses; to be absolutely sure, he would have had to go over to the painting, dismiss the difference between himself and—he reminded himself—a probably *former* patient. Unthinkable. It was bad enough that he was standing. He sank down in the Thonet rocker and concealed his feet beneath his desk. "Perhaps a symbolization," he said, "but rather too obvious a one."

Jeannette, the chip still in her hand, approached the desk. "I am not coming back," she told him.

Dr. Cimino raised and lowered his shoulders and spread his hands in the classic gesture of refusing further responsibility. "As I have always told you, that is the decision you must make by yourself. You are, of course, reacting defensively and negatively."

"Why shouldn't I? You haven't helped me, only led me back, farther back all the time. Never forward. And I'm always *just the same!*"

"I agree that your underlying difficulties are, in the main, untouched." Dr. Cimino looked at her steadily. "We are, in a manner of speaking, rather old friends, so I can confess to you that I look forward to discontinuing treatment with little feeling."

"You shit! And all that money you've made on me!"

"You are money-oriented, though money is the least of your troubles," said Dr. Cimino with patience. "You have no goals except physical end-gaining and the bored survival it brings. It is not the first time you have called me a shit. If you remember, during your first two years you called me almost nothing else."

"You sound so moral."

"There is only one morality that matters: that whose definition depends upon doing harm to others. This morning you remembered to wear that bracelet—"

"As you would say, we've been over that."

"Do you understand what your remembering instead of forgetting implies?" He stopped; he had spoken automatically. His professional fervor was fading, and he reminded himself that she was now an ex-patient. Her hour was about to run through; his next appointment was waiting and would hold it against him if the important Freudian protocol of promptness was not observed. This afternoon, when he did his correspondence, he would write a letter of quittance to David Steen, absolving himself of all responsibility.

They had been together for so long, Jeannette also was still in the pattern. "I remember the taxi driver's wrists."

Dr. Cimino did not, this time, remind her of her repetition troubles, instead impatiently said, "Yes-yes-yes," and gave her the look an orchestra conductor beams at a flutist who has bled three notes beyond the score. They confronted each other, each wondering what the last word would be, and which would have it. Dr. Cimino had an impulse to go back into an older analytic form of reprimand, such as his own analyst (still his invisible control, though long dead) might have used: *Madame, you have told me of penises and backs of heads and wrists* ad nauseam. *I am weary of them. Go to your taxi driver, pursue your elusive orgasm!* But he controlled himself and said nothing.

"I feel wonderful!" Jeannette said.

"Good, good."

"You don't care."

"Goodby, Mrs. Steen."

Hesitantly, Jeannette took the hand Dr. Cimino offered. "Goodby, then, Dr. Cimino." They had called each other by name at last. "And I'm going out and do everything I want to do," she added. "I'm going to be *myself!*"

Dr. Cimino's expression indicated he had said his last word. Jeannette laid the bull's-eye chip on the desk before him, and precisely as though it had been a check, Dr. Cimino refrained from looking at it. Then she went quickly to the door and opened it.

"When I think what you've learned from me!" she flung at

him. "It's *you* who should buy me my *folie,* not David. *Fuck Freud!*"

Dr. Cimino was not without humor. Of course there was no question even of admitting such vulgarity; she was gone anyway, gone in all senses; but he could not but reflect what an ill-matched pair Jeannette and Freud would have been. Freud had given up sex at forty.

❧ ❧ ❧ JOANNA SUMMERS was prompt. Anson greeted her with the special respect reserved for lame ducks of importance. Joanna Summers was seventy-five and admitted to it. She had retained a flavor of the Kansas prairies, from which she had fled to Paris almost half a century ago. Her face was innocent of make-up, her iron-gray hair brushed severely back into a scrubwoman's knot. She wore a prim gray suit and a homemade blouse with old-fashioned rickrack trimming. Despite the motherly exterior she presented, she was rumored to be warmly attached to Aroon Rigo, the poetess. Nina, when alluding to them, called them "the *poētae.*" It was difficult to know what their relationship involved; both Joanna Summers and Rigo had been married, both showed a tiredness and relief about men, relief at being no longer sexually approachable by them. Once, when he had been a junior editor, learning who the K and K authors were, Anson had attended a party given by Joanna Summers and Miss Rigo at the latter's apartment on Morton Street; punch, made of tea and cheap white wine, with fruits added, had been served, and he had drawn a strawberry; he had never forgotten holding this terrible mixture and not drinking it, watching the strawberry gather a whitish accretion, like mold, in the glass. He had never forgotten, either, a long story Joanna Summers had told about Edna Millay's honeymoon, which had an immediacy of presentation and believability wholly lacking in her long, "socially committed" novels. Lady-lover Joanna Summers might or might not be, but she smiled at Anson with *Pique Dame* coquetry, showing well-preserved teeth with gold at the back.

"Well, Joanna," he said, sitting down at his desk opposite her, "it's been a long time since we've heard from you." Nina had placed the Summers folder on his blotter, opened to a carbon of the firm's last renegotiation of her contract. Though she had been with K and K many years, there were few letters; she preferred the phone call and following descent. She had received several sizable advances, but also had a long history of sojourns at the MacDowell Colony and Yaddo, and had been the recipient of two Guggenheims, and, as Claxon Kennerly had complained at Wednesday conference, was always interrupting work on *Time and Place* to write criticism and serve as judge on book-award panels. "Do I dare ask how the book's coming along?"

"Of course you dare ask," she replied in her flat Kansas voice. "It's a long job and still in work. I don't want to let it go until I'm satisfied with it. I'm sure you understand that?"

"Yes, we understand that."

"I've just flown in from Chicago, where I've been reading at the Newberry Library. They have rich material on the period, you know."

"So do you, Joanna." Joanna Summers was known to have kept every scrap of paper, every letter, that had come her way; her files were bulging with ana about most of the important twenties figures.

"Oh, yes," she admitted, "I've always been a pack rat, still am. I've not entirely decided how much of my own material I wish to use. Both Yale and Texas have made me splendid offers." Which was a long way of saying that she held the aces to K and K's queens and knaves. "I'm not old enough, really, to have an archive; I can't let my things go quite yet."

Anson smiled briefly and waited. Born in 1935, he had no very strong impressions of the 1920's. Whenever he had to bring that time into focus, he found himself stuck with the recall of bits of imagist poetry, read in a course at Harvard, the many-times-told anecdotes about Pound, Joyce and Stein, and vaguely remembered TV retrospectives. The Place de l'Opéra, outmoded taxis moving jerkily across it, the camera panning to the terrace of the Café de la Paix, where women in cloche hats and men in absurd caps or bowlers waved frantically. Janet Flanner's warm, rich voice on the sound track, observing of Scott Fitzgerald: *He was not always as entertaining as he might have been.* And something else: *There was a gilt on the cage of life in those days that was entrancing.* . . .

The cage of life, he thought, Neile's green eyes swimming before him, then brought his attention back to Joanna Summers.

"The book is proving immensely difficult," she was saying, "because, of course, the period steadily loses clarity as it recedes in time. Holding on to the concept alone has been a big job."

"Which is why we're rather anxious to have you finish it."

Joanna Summers looked out of the window. Perhaps, Anson thought, she was remembering Margaret and Jane, Man Ray and Kiki, Zelda and Scott, Peggy and Kay and Djuna—and Carl Kastner, who also had been an expatriate, and had given Joanna Summers her generous contract. She had known everybody, had attended all those now legendary performances, from the premiere of the Sitwell *Façade* to *Ballet Mécanique.* She had dined with Picasso at Lipp's, knew things Cowley and Mabel Dodge and Harold Loeb and Hemingway hadn't written about, perhaps because they hadn't known about them. Carl Kastner thought of her in much the same way other publishers did of ex-Hemingway wives: *Would they tell before it became too late?* Joanna Summers' just might be the great, corrective memoir that would slow up those jerky old films, obliterate their scratches, which looked like perpetual rain, bring all into focus, convey the period to accurate perspective.

He said, when Joanna Summers had been silent for some moments, "Perhaps you'd let us have a look at what you've done thus far?"

She bridled. "Oh, no! I *never* show unfinished work."

"Well, possibly we could do the book a little good, during this period, by working out some advance publicity in the papers."

"Papers? There's only one newspaper that matters now," she said, "and it's trying to be everything to everybody. Though one observes that while they have pages of space for wives of industrialists, who serve teas in amusing old mills in the country, they have precious little for writers and writing. It's the period of monstrous nobodies, to quote James. I'd have to get into something from Rudi Gernreich and be photographed doing paella to get a line of notice. Not that *that* one—*that* one who wears a hat like a gondola—doesn't get columns for doing absolutely nothing." Her voice became bitter. "That *word saver!*"

Anson laughed. "Possibly it's because she likes the Dodgers."

"It's because I've always spoken my mind, was on those lists." She sighed. It was true, she had never concealed her political views and dislikes, and they had cost her dear. "Where is one to go? America's impossible now, unbearable. It takes courage to walk down Fifth Avenue at night, much less through the Village in daytime. When I returned to

America with the other exiles in the thirties, it was still wonderful to be an American. People were not terrified, as they are now; though it was the Depression, we were proud. Now I spend my time apologizing for being American; all one does is defend our attacking others—protecting ourselves from them, it's called. No one is happy now except the young, and even they suspect what awaits them."

"I was in Vietnam," Anson told her. "I know."

"The more fool you. But not being a Dodger fan will do as a way of saying I must get away from those murderers down in Washington. I shall try Denmark."

"And will you finish *Time and Place* there?"

"I shall hope to."

"And give us a fairly firm delivery date?"

"Is there some question of the further advance I asked for?"

"Not at all, Joanna; we simply want to schedule the book, bring it out in the season best for it. Fall, would be my guess. How about the fall after this?"

"I'll do my best."

"Where in Denmark will you be?"

"Aroon Rigo and I have taken a house at Vedsø for the summer." She was palming her aces, having showed them; there was nothing to do but throw down queens and knaves, give her the money—and hope she would deliver.

"Well," said Anson, "I hope you and Miss Rigo won't be leaving before a party my wife and I are giving June eighth. We'd love to have you come."

"We'll both be delighted," Joanna Summers said, from which Anson guessed Denmark arrangements were waiting on the K and K advance.

"Would you like the check now?"

"Why, yes; that would be most convenient."

Anson dictated to Nina a one-sentence amendment to the Summers publishing agreement, called bookkeeping for the check, and filled in the time it took to clear the comptroller by presenting Joanna Summers with copies of several recent K and K books, *Good Time Coming* among them.

"That execrable David Steen!" she said, tossing the book aside. "I certainly won't read that."

"Why not give him a try?" Anson persuaded. "Parts are very good. It's going to be at the top of the *Times* list all summer."

Joanna Summers turned over the copy of *Good Time Coming* she had thrown aside and looked without expression at David Steen's smiling face. "Well, best sellers make best sellers." Her voice showed how sour the grapes were. "*I* wrote about sex in my novels, too, but in a creative way, not this bludgeoning kind of pornography being done today. No one's cared to reprint *me* in paperback; but then, I was always too *sterling* to write for a market."

The check arrived and Nina and Anson saw Joanna Summers out. It was a mark of the respect in which she was held by the firm, lame duck or not, that as she was passing Carl Kastner's *gare centrale,* he came out to speak to her.

"You know," said Nina, as they watched Joanna Summers and Carl Kastner exchange formal kisses on both cheeks, "I've read all those novels she wrote, and all I can remember about them is that they always took place in the kitchen, around the stove."

"I remember that too."

"I hear they were lovers, those long, long years ago."

"Who cares?"

"Poor old girl. She has ankylosis."

"What's that?"

Nina was married to a Bellevue intern and knew medical terms. "It means stiffness or fusion of joint surfaces. See her feet? Do you think she'll ever finish *Time and Place?*"

"She fucking well better had," said Anson. "What a work-out! And she'd better put Carl Kastner into it. That's why he

300

gave her the contract—hunger for immortality, however small. Forget I said that."

"I knew it anyway," Nina said. "Carl asked what happened to you Wednesday. If I were you, I'd go to see him after Summers leaves."

Joanna Summers was already at the turning of the corridor that led to the reception room, and Anson, when she was out of sight, walked to the door of Kastner's office. Kastner looked up silently.

"Sorry about Wednesday," Anson began. "I—"

"Never explain," Carl Kastner answered. "It was only this." He reached into a drawer, brought out an envelope, handed it to Anson. "A little block of K and K preferred. Our thanks for the seven figures on Steen. This has nothing to do with bonuses, needless to say."

Anson was touched. "Thanks, Carl."

Kastner's old Lock hat lay on a corner of his desk and he was dressed in an old-fashioned, much-tubbed seersucker suit and madras bow tie, by which signs Anson knew he was getting ready to leave the office for the country before lunch.

"Stella and I are weekending with Claxon and Mary," Kastner said.

"How is Stella?" asked Anson.

"Never better. And how's Faye? We're all looking forward to the party." Kastner was putting a sheaf of papers into the battered briefcase he always carried. "The Birnham film sale going to mature?"

"It's cooking."

"Good." Kastner waited. "Anson, is everything all right?"

"Of course, Carl. Why?"

Would he, Anson wondered, answer without phrasing a question?

It was as a question. "Haven't you been a bit abstracted lately?"

"I didn't know it showed."

"It shows. None of my business, of course, but you're my head boy, and I can't help wondering." Kastner continued to busy himself with his briefcase, averting his eyes. "What is it. The Great Within? Matters of the self to be explained?"

Anson stood silent, feeling the guilt of a small boy.

"You gave Joanna her advance?"

"We're in so deep, I thought a little deeper wouldn't matter."

"Oh, she'll deliver—if she lives. We'll all deliver if we live. I used to know her in those gilded twenties."

"I gathered you did."

"In Europe. Berlin, to be exact. She was considerably older than I, which made it all just right. She had a wonderful way of seizing life as it went past—I'll never forget some of the things we did. I'd never have the guts now. But I'm breaking a rule. One of the axioms of growing old is not to talk about it. I could bore you during a four-hour lunch, but in the end you'd still have to learn all about it for yourself."

"I wouldn't be bored," Anson assured him.

"But I would bore myself." Kastner looked him full in the eyes. "I was born a long time ago, Anson. I recognize the signs. It happens at your time of life. I remember when it happened to me. It's rather like a journey you feel compelled to take, though you don't, sometimes, really want to. I elected to take it." He stood up, snapped his briefcase shut, and picked up his hat. "I've just finished looking over proof for our Fall Catalogue. If I do say so myself, it's a beauty." Giving Anson a friendly punch on the bicep, he went past him into the hall. "Well, see you next week."

Anson returned to his office, preoccupied, and with relieved familiarity threw himself into the rest of the morning. He took on the lame ducks in the waiting room one by one. Not all those under contract to K and K had the staying power of David Steen. There was the thirty-six-year-old editor of a ladies' slick, who had had a phenomenal best seller five years ago, but couldn't get his next novel out (though he had, meanwhile, written two Broadway plays, both flops) to whom Anson gave reassurances of his ability to come on twice, which he, Anson, did not truly feel. A rather sad, sixtyish man, whose *New Yorker* short stories had enjoyed a *succès de circonstance* in the magazine but had sold only five hundred and twelve copies in the handsome collection K and K had brought out two years ago, had to be told that a second collection would not be undertaken. How vigorously the paperback tail was wagging the dog of hard-cover publishing was again demonstrated when explorative calls began to come in from editors of reprint houses, who had been briefed by the bird about Birnham's *Little Marka*.

"So?" asked Anson. "You want it? You haven't even read it."

"Twenty-five blind."

"You can start by coming around to my hundred thousand ear," Anson said. Birnham's last paper sale had been twenty-seven five, and it had been like pulling hens' teeth to get that. "We're not even talking about it until next week. It's a bombshell, you're right, and whoever reprints will have to sit on the fuse with us."

Anson ordered ten more Xerox copies of the Birnham manuscript and prepared to shop it. Between interviews and calls he was experiencing the same obsessive fantasies and images about Neile that had plagued him all week, only now they were fortified by the afternoon he had played truant. It didn't matter how disciplined a method he used in an effort to exorcise them, or where he began or ended; they remained the same hypnotic itch, with or without variation or sense, folding in and in again on itself. As morning wore on, old memories arose from his memory bank of women, only to transform themselves into fresh hungers for Neile. It was not unlike a radio, playing from far away, tuned to multiple stations. The bird was talking; the Birnham fever was steadily rising. Ethan Fleming, fresh in from London, telephoned for Birnham's private phone number. Nina supplied it. Almost at once he rang back to say the number was D.A. By then it was a quarter past noon; Nina had gone to lunch and Anson almost did not take the call, fearing it might be Hanson or Stein, or both, nailing him for a husband lunch.

"Hello," he said guardedly.

"Fleming."

"Hi. Good trip?"

"Well, over the waves, yes. But we deviated. It took us three hours to come in at JFK, the sky was full of private planes." He told him about Birnham's D.A. "Boyo, is this town electric! How stands your disposition toward a tit lunch?" Fleming had a flair for Elizabethan rhetoric laced with both sides of the Atlantic mod.

Anson hesitated. His telescoping need for Neile was plaguing him, and he was hoping for the miracle of guilt that would return him to Faye and the Ridge and Todd and the salamander. He had last lunched with Fleming in London, at one of the topless clubs, moving up from floor to floor until the afternoon became a kaleidoscopic newsreel of a dozen different girls wearing *cache-sexes* and high heels, pouring Jack Daniel's in liberal streams into the biggest beakers he could remember. And whipped-cream breasts with peach centers, cherry centers. . . .

"Unless you're booked for lunch?" Fleming added during the silence. "But if you're not, my philosophy is that the proper study of mankind is bunnies. If you're not a tit-club member, I am."

"I'm a member," said Anson.

"Good standing?"

"Standing up."

"And you're free?"

"As can be."

"Well, then, since Birnham's in the cards, I'm not booked.

I'd like to kick the film thing around with you before I talk to him. And we can tuck into something substantial."

"Twelve-forty-five?" Anson suggested, making sure Fleming had the club's address. "I'll get us a table."

"Make it one—I'm having my bath."

"Done."

As he phoned for the reservation, washed hands, and took off for the club, he knew what he was in for, and what Fleming meant by *substantial*. He was one of the switched-on, with-it young Londoners in the forefront of the New Boy Network who had made it, broken through big enough to enjoy the Full Life. The day they had lunched he had shown Anson not only Tiles Street, W. 1, and the swinging noon underground, but after the bunnies they had taken a taxi to a subterranean afternoon club, The Jakes, where both had gotten rid of their crotch problems brought on by the long lunch with the untouchable bunnies. Anson remembered vividly the young girl who had been his—no more than sixteen—with a face painted in three colors, a seven-inch skirt over flaring, bell-bottomed trousers. The rest was a cartoon of frenetic jerking and bucking pelvises, *mons Veneris* minis and codpiece pants. It hadn't been a gang-shag, but it hadn't exactly been private screwing, either. Anson knew a lot about Ethan Fleming.

Fleming was already seated at the table when Anson arrived, a Saxon giant with flaming red hair and a spade beard. His bottle-green jacket—lapels precisely but flamboyantly cut, pockets lengthily flapped, a variation of the mod style but executed by Conduit Street tailors—symbolized his echelon: a top boy among top boys in the British film avant-garde. He was talking to three bunnies at once. Fleming was a connoisseur. What he dreamed of, he had confided to Anson in London, was 44-22-46; it was an improbable proportion, even among the most succulent bunnies, existed, perhaps, only among put-together girls, who had had injections of the silicone emulsion. Meantime, less impressive measurements did very well—40-23-44, 41-20-40, even 38-22-45. Anson was a quick estimator too.

"I see you're already in control," he said, sliding in beside Fleming. They shook hands warmly.

"Boyo! And now, bring on the Ameddican martinis. I haven't had a proper one since Edward's, at the jolly old London Ritz. The *downstairs* bar. Unless you'd prefer Jack Daniel's instead?"

"Too hot for Jack. A brace of your whitest, standing up," Anson said to the head bunny, as the two others haunched off with her.

Fleming had charisma. He talked and talked well. They sat watching the straight mumsy-dads in summer worsteds, with their scared hair plastered to their skulls, who were staring at the mammillary beauties dangling above their soup as though they'd never seen a set before; one was nipple-crimson with embarrassment, almost apoplectic. After answering a few questions about Colin Vaughan (he was planning to invest in the film of *Little Marka*, as he had in *Dimple*, was a man with fingers in many pies), Fleming came right on with his enthusiasm for Galey Birnham's book. "When Vaughan showed me the fax you'd sent over, I couldn't believe what I read. I've already got the father and brother parts signed up, and I'd not be here if I could find my Little Marka. She's got to be perfect."

"Wait, not so fast," Anson said as the brace of martinis arrived; "we hadn't even titled the book when I talked with you and Vaughan."

"It's implicit and inevitable. Besides, the bird flies far."

"So I gather. Birnham and I decided on the title only this week."

"Perfect for the film, too. I want to do it outrageously, nastily, almost entirely with hand cameras, the way I did *Dimple*. I've already got video tapes of children in breaking-out situations, reacting instinctually to erotic stimuli without adult restraint. There won't be any trouble. After all, my *Dimple, 491, I Am Curious (Yellow)*. Little Marka is everybody's childhood, with britches and panties down. Aphoristically, the story's full of hidden wish-dreams. I hope to do a film that will cause behavioral changes, the kind of changes that can't happen without first being indicated in literature, then on film. In short, I think Birnham has hit upon the *process* of the sexual breakdown implicit in what's happening both sides of the drink. London's a little ahead of New York, I think, and San Francisco's ahead of both."

"New York tries," Anson said. He ordered a second round.

"The film—if only I can get the right girl; she doesn't have to be a kid—I've *got* the kid ampexes—but she has to be a bit scruffy, not quite dry behind little shell ears—the film will invade the entire nervous system of everybody that sees it, wake up all those dead areas of sexual guesswork Freud never even got near."

"Where will you film?"

"London. Where else?"

"Well, you said you're on your way to the Coast."

Fleming pulled his beard. "I'm in the film racket, but primarily I'm in the skin trade—for myself. I fancy skin, if you remember our romp and tickle at The Jakes. I've about twenty-four hours of tactility waiting for me there. Then I'll fly back."

"Forty-four, twenty-two, forty-six?"

"Well . . . forty-*three*. Worth the flight. By 'the Coast' I mean Frisco, not Hollywood. Damme, Anson, that graveyard's had it. They've lost the whole damned audience over twenty-five. What's going on there now is an *entr'acte,* and there's no third act. They've learned little since Griffith. It was a good method for its time because everybody could get a hard on seeing Betty Bronson expelled from boarding school for having written a mash note to an actor. Now it's Brabra, or whatever-her-name is, heaving it around in those draggy tea gowns Alice Terry rejected for *The Four Horsemen of the Apocalypse*. Christ! The kosher Fannie Brice, yet. And all those superannuated cakes of beef carrying on the cowboy saga. That's all they can play. The hat and neckerchief and sideburns conceal the bald pate, the turkey neck, and they can pad in the side of the shirt to hide the pneumonectomy cavity. Faugh! How are you feeling, boyo?"

"Beautiful. Let's have another," Anson said and ordered it.

"Now," said Fleming with gravity, "for the brutalities. How much do you want for *Little Marka?*"

"We haven't talked about that, though we're handling film rights for Birnham. He has a hate thing for agents."

"As do I. Fifty?"

Anson carefully set down his glass near the table's edge. "We're starting the reprint talk at twice that figure. There'll be the paper tie-in with the film, don't forget."

"I'm not, but fifty is more than I paid for *Dimple*."

"*Dimple* was *Dimple*, *Little Marka's* got all the crevices, fore, aft and elsewhere."

"Heh. True. Sixty?"

"We've an idea what you're going to clear on *Dimple* before it's through," said Anson. "It's an influence on our thinking, natch."

"But taxes, man!"

"Even after, you'll keep a hundred thousand pounds."

"I wish to Christ that bird would shut up!"

"So I think you might offer Birnham six figures."

"Absolutely can't do."

"Eighty—and five per cent of the gross."

Fleming made his hurt face, but Anson could hear the relief under his breathing. "Possible. After we tuck in, can't we see Birnham and get on to a contract?"

"He wants script approval."

308

"They all do, though they don't want to write the script."

"He doesn't want the coronary yet."

"Figures. Birnham—is he difficult?"

"You read the book."

"Doesn't answer his telephone."

"Doesn't do lots of things. Does others."

"Come clean."

"He's mad, bad. Dangerous."

"Like *really* bad?"

"You read the book," Anson repeated.

"Sounds like we might get along," said Fleming. Anson suspected, after their time at The Jakes, that Fleming might fancy threesomes. He was priapic, without doubt.

"Birnham hates the female tit."

"All the more for me then," Fleming said cheerfully. "Boys?"

"Yes, boys. This, that. I don't know what else."

"Sounds as though one could go."

"Maybe you can. I'll try him now." Anson asked for a telephone and, when it was brought, leafed through his M & M address book for Birnham's number and dialed it.

This time, the receiver was lifted, cautiously as usual.

"Galey," Anson said.

"Where are you, man?"

Anson told him. "I'm with Fleming and he's ready to talk. How about meeting us in my office in, say, an hour?"

"Look," said Galey, who had a low laughter in his voice, "it's Friday, and I've got a little thing going here. I'm sitting here in my boho pants and nothing else with my feet up. Neile's here. Why don't you both come on down?— If this Fleming cat swings."

"He swings."

"Well, come on!"

"Shall I bring anything?"

"It's all here, mano."

"We'll take a cab to Birnham's place after we eat," Anson told Fleming, who was mulling over whether to have the *truite saumonée* or *truites en papillotes*.

"Easy as that."

"Be prepared," said Anson.

"One tries to be," Fleming answered casually. "I'd not in the least mind being planked, after all these yeasty chicks."

Fleming took food seriously, and as they ate, Anson had time and to spare to feel the net tightening around him. No guilty miracle was happening that would assure his making the train, returning to the salamander world today—this afternoon; it was already late for lunch. He was experiencing a curious relaxation, almost peaceful, as though he had been hanging on, just barely, to a spinning disc that was revolving faster and faster. Now he felt closer to the almost motionless center of the disc, quiet, empty of morning guilt, ready for anything. After a hassle over the check (Fleming insisted on paying) Anson left to wash his hands. He elected to call Faye from the booth there rather than from the phone at the table.

"Fleming's just in from London," he explained, "and I have to stay on this Birnham deal until we close."

"Meaning you'll be staying at the apartment," Faye guessed.

"I hadn't thought that far. If this thing with Fleming runs late, yes, I'll be staying in town."

"You already sound late."

"Frankly, it *may* run late with Fleming. How—how are salamander matters?"

"He seems to be still unburied. I think Todd's waiting for you."

"Darling, I'll be back tonight if I can possibly make it."

Faye said nothing.

"Faye—you still on?"

She still said nothing, though Anson could hear her breath in the transmitter.

"Baby, I can't work against this punishing silence," Anson said.

"I don't work well against punishment either," answered Faye, and said no more. She let him do the hanging up.

Anson and Fleming said elaborate goodbys to the bunnies, walked out to the street and hailed a taxi. The inside of the taxi reeked of stale cigarettes and other people's warmth. Rolling down the window on his side, Anson gave the driver the Mott Street address.

The driver seemed of two minds. "*Chinky*town?" Then, evaluating his probable tip, did them the favor. "But I won't say how far we'll have to detour to get there at this hour."

"Take any route you like," said Anson.

It was stifling in the streets, the city projecting its pulsing intensity, livid with afternoon sunshine, against a sky darkening into rain. It was the hour of the Friday rush, everybody trying to make it first, imprisoned in their private hurries, faces staring, bodies stopping short, colliding, fighting for space to turn around in, breathe, get out. The summer fumes of asphalt, grime, sweat, motor exhaust, the numberless effluvia of humanity, poured through the cab windows. A glass partition separating them from the driver, with a small aperture through which to pay fares, smudged with handprints, dimmed the forward view.

"New," Anson said of this. "New York drivers are afraid of their passengers."

Fleming nodded but said nothing. They sat in their post-lunch lethargy while the driver cut in and out of lanes, drove half a block, suddenly braked. This procedure was repeated many times. At 42nd and Seventh Avenue the clogged traffic halted them. The driver lighted a cigarette and beat a nervous tattoo on the wheel. All three watched a pantomime in the car ahead, a puffily outmoded and paint-flaked Ford,

311

from which sweating, onyx faces stared back at them. In the Ford's rear window dangled a doll with arms and legs made of springs and a death's-head, the malevolence of the world seen face to face. The driver, impatient, searched for a space, backed into it, cut around the Ford. They got onto Seventh and cooked through the garment district, passed Penn Station, after which the cab cut west and going was easier. They went by blocks of moldering tenements about to collapse, fenced-in lots where tenements already had been torn down. The lots were piled with discarded furniture and rubbish and garbage, steaming and fetid from the rain which was beginning. The indescribable detritus of Manhattan.

"Like London during the blitz," observed Fleming. "I was a mere kid during the buzz-bomb phase of the war. My family hung on in a house in Eaton Square. I used to get away afternoons and walk through the rubble, playing a hit-or-miss game with myself. I'd think myself capable of bravado if I did such a thing now; it wasn't that, simply contempt for the world I'd been born into. Once I came upon a corpse—one of the flying darlings had landed a half hour before—a young woman. She was just dead, her eyes were still open and she seemed to be smiling, though as I looked at her I realized it must have been a last grimace of terror. I remember her teeth, white, like porcelain, and the dust all over her lips. That was when I grew up."

The cabdriver's face was visible through the glass partition. He was attending to traffic while listening to what Fleming had said through the two-way mike somewhere up front.

"*That* war!" his contemptuous voice filtered back to them. "You boys should have been at Dienbienphu, when the angels came." He told a brief, chilling story of carrying a wounded comrade whose intestines he had had to hold in. "That's when *I* grew up. I made up my mind about one thing.

312

I see something I want, I take it; I don't wait for nothin'—including the wife." Then he was silent.

"I don't know how you live here," said Fleming to Anson.

"New York's all right as long as you never leave the mile-and-a-half radius of where we've come from," Anson said. "Beyond that all kinds of unpleasantnesses begin. Your balls sweat, your eyes smart, you cough, you begin to feel the deep resentment everywhere. You feel *I've got to get out!* I make it from Grand Central to the office and back, and to my health club and a handful of restaurants within a kite's fly, and that's it, usually." He remembered that Friday was one of his days at "53," and that he hadn't called Nina to say he probably wouldn't be back at the office.

Above the taxi's momentarily occupied rectangle of asphalt the sky was blackening. A spread of thunder followed a blinding flash of lightning and now the rain pelted down heavily.

"Consequently you live in the country," Fleming said.

"In a part of what's left of it, yes."

"Children?"

"A boy, going on six. You?"

"One of each. My girl's four, my boy two and a half. They're with their grandmother, in Kent."

"And your wife—did you bring her with you?"

"Never do," Fleming said. "Never works. She's doing a film in Rome."

Fleming's tone did not invite further inquiry. Enclosed in the cab, windows tightly rolled up against the rain, Anson felt a last ambivalence about traveling into the protected sink of Birnham's neighborhood, pinched off from the greater sink that was New York. He had waited for the random incident that would return him to where Neile was, now felt a numbed slipping, welcomed with alcoholic, afternoon melancholy the dip beneath the rim of day's reality.

"My wife is very jealous," Fleming said.

313

"So is mine," confided Anson.

"And are you jealous of her?"

"Very, though there's never been the need for my jealousy to become active. I *think*. What about you?"

"I once was jealous, but no more. If you have it between you, you have it, and other people really make very little difference, whether slept with or not," Fleming said. "I find it necessary sometimes to get away from the jealousies of women, be alone with myself—myself among others, if you understand that."

Anson nodded.

"Some of us have got to say yes to ourselves, offset those worthy citizens who deliver the napalm and peddle mail-order guns. Any day's good for cutting away from now. Now is eternal anyway. Spit into life's face before it spits into yours. Now will become past tense almost immediately, of course; now piles up from day to day, like accretions in a coral reef. Why wait for today's oblivion? There's always the eternal *but* to be taken into consideration, naturally, the *but* which has replaced Kipling's *if*."

"You speak as though you feel the sand shifting," Anson said.

"Yes, I feel it. I sense there's a star I should follow, too, my very own star, but I don't know its name. Put another way, the walls are encroaching on all of us, and soon the lintels will be off plumb and we won't be able to shut the doors, much less pass through them. Meanwhile, dreams tell us how to live."

The cab turned, squealing, into Mott Street, and Anson leaned forward to tell the driver where to stop, wiping away the moisture that had filmed over the window. They slowly passed the row of buildings being demolished, piles of rubble eroding in the downpour, plaster segments with black hairs sticking out of them, and the big yellow bulldozer, weekend quiet and glistening in the rain. Anson paid and they got out, a few houses beyond the one he had indicated. There was a shout and then a small avalanche of garbage hurtled down from a window above.

"Manhattan air mail," said Anson.

"I know," replied Fleming, ducking it.

iv

❦ ❦ ❦

Self-Light

❧ ❧ ❧ ANSON AND Fleming ran from the taxi into the entresol and pushed into the hallway beyond, the rain in their eyes. From somewhere above, a twang of electric guitar drifted down. On the Neile afternoon there had been a spidery glow from a skylight over the stairs, but the thunderstorm had blacked that out. An ammoniacal memory of the armpit soup hung in the air and Fleming, finding himself in darkness, hesitated.

"I say, boyo, are you certain one can go? Is this the place?"

"This is it," Anson assured him and shouted, "Galey? Galey?"

On a landing above, a door opened and a jerking beam of flashlight appeared, playing through the spokes of the sagging stair rail. The light beamed downward. Anson looked up, again calling. Then Galey held the beam steady above the stair well so it lighted the landings.

"Watch that turn there," he cautioned as the two climbed up. "Not much to hold on to."

Anson and Fleming used the walls for guide and support, avoiding the banisters, velvet with dust. Galey stood waiting for them, barefooted, torso gleaming above jeans rolled down to his navel and up to his knees. He greeted them soberly, wearing his straight mask until he evaluated Fleming.

"Ethan—Galey," Anson introduced.

Galey's mask at once dropped. Anson sensed that rapport would not be difficult, had, probably, already been established. It was stifling and hot, only a little less humid than outside; the thunderstorm seemed to have boxed in the heat. After the landing door had been bolted, they passed through a cubicle with sleeping bags stretched out on the floor, then went into the large room at the apartment's rear. Anson at once oriented; except for what was in it, and the taller windows overlooking the garden and the heaven tree, it was identical in layout to the one Neile occupied above.

When Galey had said Neile was there he had told only part of the story. Anson's impression was of a conglomeration of isolations, of gazes turned inward; the isolations were people sitting or standing apart in spaces they had staked out for themselves. The room was bare except for a bed in the center, two mattresses in the far corners and a low, makeshift table between. A single bulb depended from the ceiling, its wattage dimmed by a strip of varicolored paper wrapped around it. The air hung thick with smoke at eye level in the funky half-light. It smelled, Anson recognized, like his apartment the night Neile and he had gotten stoned. The guitar player, absorbed, sitting cross-legged in one corner, strummed softly; he did not look up as they entered, lost in a world of his own. There were two kittens moving through the haze, one with straight blond hair, almost white, hanging to her waist, the other a tall, slender black girl with a fuzzy top cut like a golliwogg's around her face; the black girl wore a miniskirt and white lace stockings. They were moving in a slow, kinetic dance with a stocky boy in codpiece corduroys. Their dance had nothing to do with the music, and the *wheak-*

wheak of the corduroys, slipped so far down that the boy's Batman jock showed, was the only other sound in the room. An emaciated boy in a G-string occupied a narrow space of floor between the mattresses; he was seated in full lotus posture, feet turned flatly upward; an eye was painted on each sole, and on his forehead a luminous fingerprint was emblazoned.

"He asylumed out of the Peace Corps," Galey said. "He's made the whole trek, Vietnam, Sweden, Crete."

The lotus boy was soberly shredding a *kif* wafer with a small file onto a cigarette paper laid out before him. *"La ilaha illa'llah muhammadun rasulu'llah,"* he intoned, staring up at them.

Beyond was a girl stretched out in sleep, stiffly, like an effigy. "We call her Hopeless," explained Galey, passing on. "And she's right. It is hopeless."

From out of the haze a hand reached up an end of a joint toward Anson. He shook his head. Fleming took it instead and blasted with flair, dragging hard, holding in the smoke until his face turned brick red, then exhaled in a cough, laughing.

"Ah!" he exclaimed when he could speak. *"Top* hash!"

"Maroc's best," said Galey. "Get rid of that roach, mano. Everybody gets his own thing here. That what you want, pot? We have the rest, too. Name it."

Fleming shook his head. "Grass is far as I'll go tonight. I've got to be in your Frisco Monday. And we've got *Little Marka* to settle." He looked around with approval. "Definitely one could come. One could get somewhat more comfortable perhaps, too?"

"Yes, shed that Madisonav drag," Galey said. "Take off as much as you please. No left or right dress here, all center flop." He laughed. "What about you, Anson?"

"I'm passing for the moment."

Galey shrugged. "I'll come back to you." And went off to get what Fleming asked for.

"Yes, yes in*deed!*" Fleming said. "One up on The Jakes, eh, boyo?"

Anson agreed. He was sweltering in the clothes he had put on that morning, and damp from the rain. He saw that Fleming had shed tie, shirt and shoes and was rolling his Conduit Street kaks down and up in the manner of Galey.

"Deference to our host," he said.

Anson's eyes had been trying to pick Neile out of the haze ever since they came in. He followed Fleming's example, gauging his mood of growing with-it by the careless way in which he tossed his own shirt and tie onto the pile of sleeping bags. The two kittens who were dancing raised their heads, not stopping their movement, but stacking him up. The saucer eyes of the black girl dug him. The others quickly judged Fleming and himself with the laconic friendliness that seemed to prevail, glad of the flesh they were and glad they had brought it. There were no conversations or arguments in progress, and the figures, each in a separate pool of space, were curiously varied in their degrees of verbal expression and reality. Some spoke without having been spoken to; others answered with detachment or were silent.

Standing beside Fleming, Anson began to absorb, connect. All were cynical beyond frankness; cynicism was their life. They had decided long ago that everything was on the way out, down, had been since the F_3 generation and way before that. They cared less than less. Man, if you could buy it, go ahead, but it's all so much shit and squat, that stuff splatters! *La ilaha illa'llah muhammadun rasulu'llah.* Shit. Pot. Stick me, mano.

Galey returned. Neile was not anywhere and Anson asked where she was.

"She's had her second quarter gram of mesc and was nauseated," explained Galey with a jerk of his head, indicating the door leading into the bath. Anson remembered Neile's bath, directly above, his making do and packing his jock. "She'll be out in a minute for her third quarter. I'll stop her there. Want to change *your* mind?"

"About the pot? No," Anson answered.

"Probably wise, best to stagger. I meant mesc. I've got the best—purest mesc sulfate, clinic-fresh. If you'd like to start. You want to go over, mano, and Neile's already primed. It's easy. Half a glass of water that tastes salty and you're on your way."

"Then what?"

"The nausea, perhaps. You may not have it. You'd begin to go up in half, three quarters of an hour. Then your second glass—I'd give you a half, then, because of your weight. It's perfectly safe—I've taken up to a gram. But don't worry," he added, reading Anson's expression; "I'm on straight black coffee tonight. My party. I'll watch out for both of you."

Before Anson could reply, the door of the bath opened and Neile came out. She floated toward Galey. "Head Cactus," she said, then saw Anson and stopped. "I hoped you'd come," she said. "Why didn't you come sooner? Why were you so long?"

"Odds and ends," said Anson.

"Like wives and children?"

"Not plural," Anson said. Neile turned and took the glass Galey held for her, drank it, then put her arms around Anson and kissed him.

Fleming had been staring at Neile from the instant he saw her and came up. "My God, Anson! Is this chick yours? Did you set this up, or is it a send-up?" He continued to stare at Neile.

"Neither," Anson said. "She wants a star. Vega," he added, remembering the night they met on the boat.

"Any *whirly* star will do," said Neile; she ran her hand over Fleming's face, then pulled his beard. She was laughing and floated away, flinging herself onto the mattress next to the lotus boy.

"Well, I see no reason she shouldn't have anything she wants," Fleming said seriously. "Including stars." He was blasting heavily, was halfway through his second joint. His eyes narrowed as he continued to watch Neile, and he squared his hands in the way cameramen do when visualizing a scene. "Yes," he said. "Ah, yes. *R*ather far along at the moment, isn't she, boyo? A tripper."

Neile's eyes were all for Anson. Still laughing, she said, "I'm going to go over this time, Anson. Coming with me? Anson!"

Anson was sweating and falling down from the martini lunch. His head buzzed from the waves of *kif*. It couldn't stay the way it was: he either had to go forward or go back.

"Fighting it, aren't you?" Galey, glass in hand, watched him. "Why?"

"I mean," Fleming was saying, "one knows, one knows absolutely." He stared at Neile through his hand square, watching every move she made. "She's Little Marka to the life!" he declared, grasping Galey's arm. "Do you see it? I came here to talk with you. We've got to talk."

"A minute," Galey answered, and turned to Anson. "Any time, mano." He held the ready glass in his hand. "This is for you. Why wait?"

Anson still hesitated, feeling a rising tension, rising excitement.

"I know—you can't afford to take chances."

"You're right. I can't."

"But you're here. You want to reach. Begin. Or is it the memory of that wind?"

"It's not that."

"Because, if it is, you'll be ten times higher than that on mesc. You don't have to go on after the first quarter gram unless you like. You can turn back before you take the half.

324

Think of those selves of yourself, Anson. Those flowering orgasms."

"Borobudur."

"I don't read you, mano."

"Nothing."

"I've seen Borobudur," the lotus boy said, looking up. "Don't hesitate, man—it's the correction of life."

Anson remembered the diapason, then looked at Neile and last doubts slipped away. Taking the glass from Galey's hand, he drank it down. It tasted precisely as Galey said it would. Fleming was now holding Galey by both arms, talking to him face to face. Anson turned and went over to Neile, stretching out beside her on the mattress.

"*La ilaha illa'llah muhammadun rasulu'llah,*" the lotus boy murmured, and Neile kissed Anson long and ardently; the kiss was acrid, like the taste in his throat.

"This week," she said, "do you know what I did? I took the phone out of the suitcase and kept it out. Didn't work. And you didn't call."

"I'm here now," Anson said.

"I did something else, when I got the rag off. One afternoon I made love to myself in the mirror. I thought of you as I did it. It's been a long time since I've done that. It wasn't any good. I wanted you."

"It's never any good by yourself."

"I heard what the beard said."

"Fleming?"

"He said something about Little Marka. That's the girl in Galey's book."

"He's the man who made *Dimple.* He's filming *Little Marka.*"

Fleming was talking to Galey; they were getting on like a double house, Fleming on fire, Galey cool and watchful. Fleming was telling about the footage he already had of children and how he didn't want the usual shit with all those

325

titles that make the audience get up and leave before the picture comes on. He wanted, he said, a cold beginning, showing Little Marka in her bassinet. "Catch their attention quick, don't you see, right off. Oh, God! She's three and already getting it from her daddy, the come-on, and the complete inspection of her little snatch by her brother—the section that forms so important a part in the beginning of the book."

Galey nodded, listening; but he was keeping an eye on everything.

"Gide, getting hip to his little cousin's genitals under the table cover would be, don't you see, too late for Little Marka. She's the infantilism of the age. She'll be up to full seduction at three and at four will be teaching both her daddy and brother kinks they never heard of. *All* hand cameras, closed sets and *no studio shit!* I don't want a director's picture, I want a *story* picture."

"And the penis bank—how will you do that?" Galey asked.

"By a little indirection. What you don't really show them, they incline to believe. We haven't talked about the money. . . ."

Anson, head on Neile's shoulder, slowly became aware of a billowing out of surfaces, some advancing, some receding. Fleming, with a fresh stick, was foremost. Then he was beside Neile, bigger than life, the red of his beard aflame, blue eyes two points of light. His eyes were only for Neile.

"I want a girl who can be a child while being adult and perverse," he said to her. "That's what the public wants too. Turn your face, lower your chin—*there.*"

Neile turned to Fleming, buying every word, caressing his beard.

"Excellent," said Fleming. "One can see it at once. Now, think only child thoughts. You are going on three. Smile—in wonder at the world around you. The whole world of

326

warmth is above, other people. You've not yet learned the hell other people are. Still better. I'm looking for a child who'll look *my* way into the lens."

Neile had deserted Anson completely and was crouched before Fleming in rapture. Fleming was making his two-handed square and squinting up at her. "Now, look into my eyes, pretend I'm the lens of the camera. . . ."

Anson experienced a blanking jar, his past, his nature, breaking away; alienation. It became everything to sink into the scene. Connections were beginning to work, to flow, the synchronization with the room enclosing him began. Galey was inscrutable, watchful, the stability that clung to the world while others went on to where they were going. He was the one who made it all go from moment to moment, made it seem the only thing, now, flowing, going up and not stopping on the way. *Explore,* his expression said, *and be patient. There's down and up. Accept both.* At some moment Galey handed him his second glass, thirstier, saltier than the first. It was going big now. Then there was a loud knocking on the landing door and all became silence.

The corduroy boy broke it. "Hell*shit*," he said, still and waiting, "there are four—no, eight—six*teen* walls, walls within walls between us and *them*. No fuzz can break this up."

The bulb wrapped in the varicolored paper went out then, and there was only moonlight. Through its shimmer Anson could hear the leaves of the heaven tree shedding rain, reminding him of the afternoon with Neile. She seemed so much cardboard, as real as the Peace Corps boy, whose *La ilaha illa'llah* threaded through the silence. The knock on the door had been a latecomer, a massive spade, already high, whose laughter filled the corners of the room, echoing, echoing, echo. The bulb winked on again.

"I'm going to clean out my mind," the Peace Corps boy said between his chant. "America used to be my country.

Now this is my country." He sucked on his *kif*. "It's a police state now. I'd rather be me." He spoke slowly, as though painfully recalling a language he had almost forgotten.

"That's it, man!" came response from somewhere across the room.

The guitar's strumming seemed to drop the heaven tree, like shreds of talk, down into the room.

"Go?"

"That Christ character never walked on water. He was just full of flight marks, man!"

"Here, there, it's the same. Trapped."

*"Un*trap, man, that's the thing of it."

Anson could feel his blood shuttling through his veins. The beautiful time began when the corduroy boy resumed his dance with the black girl. The blond kitten had dropped out, gone somewhere. Everywhere there was someone going somewhere, returning or not returning. The black girl moved in a slow rhythm all her own, sinuously approaching the corduroy boy but never touching him, then retreating kinetically, going into his rhythm while near him, lapsing into her own when by herself. The spade came into the circle of the dance. The black girl had brought her own style of life with her, a kind of old-timey camp on an old-time stripper. She began taking it off, a little at a time, and between shreds would drift to the wall and beat on it for applause before taking off the next thing. At last she stood before them all, mauve-black and glistening, her small breasts trembling. The spade stud was laughing and screaming in a strangled, screaming way. He went into a slow, dragging blues song about skin, short stanzas, long stanzas, mad material like *In a madhouse of wild quail, bay-beh, the wail is ail and ail is frail, bay-beh, and what-the-shit, it's tail.* The black girl rose high on her delicate feet, crying the song along with him, so gone with it, throwing her ass out flying, haunching, pumping, diving. The corduroy boy stripped to his Batman jock, then kicked that off too, jiggling priapically. Neile and Fleming got up to get into the dance.

At this moment Anson knew he was going to be sick; the salty taste rose like a gorge in his throat and he felt queasy and trembling. He stretched out a hand—he was steady as ever. Two things were forward now: the way he felt, the way he was happening to himself. There was something he must do. He saw himself over his shoulder and made a crawling, rising half-run for the bath and closed himself in. Everything flew at him with Kodachrome clarity. The bath was almost a replica of Neile's upstairs, the same long, blue urinal trough, low-set hand basin, retriculating toilet with high, oaken flush box. There were evidences of adaptation to masculine height —a square of mirror set into the kind of medicine cabinet bought at poor hardware stores had been attached to the wall, high over the basin. He stared at himself steadily in the mirror, trying to be sick, but nothing would come up. Thirstily, he drank from the tap, then opened the cabinet to see what was inside, his mind making a careful inventory, as though the nausea, which, as quickly as it had struck, was leaving him, had equipped him for special scrutiny of the exterior world. He counted four small glass ampoules filled with colorless liquid, a bundle of disposable plastic syringes, brown drugstore bottles from which the labels had been removed. Then, gratefully, he went to the long, blue trough to urinate, exotic as *toilettes* in the *Messieurs* of provincial France, depressed its flushing mechanism with childlike glee. The assemblage he had left in the half-dark room to perhaps vomit (though he had not: the metallic glow had come over him at the exact moment he had closed the door) seemed the most natural consequence possible in life up to this hour, equally exact. A long moment. He had not hooked the door and when he raised his eyes saw the lovely black girl advancing, delicate on her slender ankles, smiling, eyelids half lowered, lashes fine and upcurving as carbon wire.

329

Unashamed and uninhibited she came close and a frantic hunger for her breasts seized him. They were taut and small, barely pendulous. She was exquisitely young. He said something to her, then winced, recognized his words as they banged against the walls, striking his head in shattering echo. She knew what was happening to him and placed one long, straight forefinger against his lips, instructing silence. Her breasts seemed ripe and full of nectar and, without preamble, he fell to his knees and drew her down, burrowing into her. His nostrils found the bone beneath her delicate cleavage and he breathed in her dark, musky odor until he suffocated. It was potent and piercing as ammonia and, still hungry for it, he drew back. Taking his head between her hands she guided his mouth to the tip of each breast in turn. He felt the round, hard forms beneath her nipples enter and slip from his mouth. Her smile, permissive and slumbrous, wordlessly understood. She was the first since the nausea left him and the honey of her body seemed godsent reward for those moments of guilt and fear.

"Let me do you here, like this," he carefully whispered, remembering his banging last words. She let him move as freely as he liked over her, sampling, gasping, then raised him up, a sovereign offering the hand, the door, the carriage, and he saw her lips mouth in answering whisper, "Later. There's more outside."

He stood before her, glorying in his engorged penis hanging from his fly before outside *angst* reminded him to make the ducking, automatic male setting of genitals, dressing. But his state of erection made the gesture laughable. They laughed together. He frowned: *had* he urinated? As in his dream, he *seemed* to remember that he had, yet felt his bladder bursting against his belly: Fleming's *dreams tell us how to live.* Now there was no shame, only amusement at his plight, and he returned to the blue trough, long as a mile now, bluer than indigo, and hung his stiff penis above it.

Nothing came out. He waited privately, left hand on hip, for sphincters to relax. The interval of waiting was either too short or too long. He felt the girl behind him, her left hand slipping between his left akimbo, pressing herself against him, her right hand reaching round to seize his penis at its base. She fluttered it and he let his own right hand drop as she waved him circularly, and straining from him at last, his urine flowed, splashing golden pinwheels against the brightness of blue. He sighed. His urethra flared with relief and pleasure and, finished, he let her squeeze him out, then turned and crushed her to him. She let him invade her mouth but reproached gently with her tongue, whispering, "Later. We mustn't hold this down, there are others."

He cared nothing whether or not anyone came in, forgot even to dress crotch and zip up, meekly following her into the room, his penis bobbing like a billy as he walked. A shout went up as, disappearing, the girl left him standing alone. Laughter of approval struck him, less deafening than the bathroom sounds; rather it was deafening but removed. Primally, a hand clutched him, as though his penis were a handle, leading him to the bed. Sentences were being addressed to him, but each continued beyond its end into the beginning of the next, without caesura. In much the same way, his movements no longer were segmented, as if he had entered into a continuous state of movement, being. Time flattened and shattered. He remembered enough of the Mary-Jane time with Neile to look for her, found her, waiting, conjoined with others, Fleming, the blond-white chick, the spade stud, the black girl. *Like* them, indistinguishable. There was, between this waiting coil of flesh, the cloud of himself, his wonder at what he would do next obstructing the next minute. Hands then took hold of him and a shivering shudder suffused him as he felt first trousers, then socks and shoes peeled from him; he could hear the soft clatter of them as, thrown, they landed.

Somewhere was now and he saw the coil encircling him with objective, unquestionable clarity, a submarine brightness with aquatic diffusions, the only certainty there was, the one thing that had ever happened to him. Surges of happiness entirely unidentifiable rolled in, lapping ever faster, and suddenly, in as short a time as it took to shift one position, he found himself in another, better. Top. Top man: he knew he was there. The space he occupied stretched and burst and was full, filling all. It was a totally globular enclosing, 3-D knowing and feeling. He no longer saw and felt breath and mouths and hands and orifices, saw only one, perfect, complete sexuality that was everything, entirely encompassed by itself, unneedful of space. His sperm rode within him, a mercurial river, moving as he moved, traveling, receding, unspent, spent, expendable. *Wait, wait! It's too soon!* lips told him, not speaking. He knew. The beauty of each skin pore and membrane was now so overwhelming that he was in a continuum of awe at the joy it gave him. Sometimes he was sure he heard himself speak, pedestrian words. *Yes, yes. No, not that. Now. Gone!* And cried and laughed all at once. But the words gave no warning of the lustrous happiness that poured over him, nacreous and nurse-warm. As he churned within the coil, the beauty began to fragment and increase: every sensation came to him in concentrated essence because it had passed through others on the way, interrelated, everywhere recurrent. He had the sensation of trying to verbalize for himself—and failed utterly. At some point, not in time, not in his body, which now seemed for the first time in his life truly alive, he knew a tremulous jarring and saw two words, flamed in his hearing: *Pring Priad,* and understood, with all the transcendence of revelation, of thunders, of light breaking through clouds of storm, that he was twain. The rose is both mother and father to itself, lover and beloved, capable of possessing, capable of being possessed. With this auditory unleashing, the crux of all experience cracked and he stared through. He had loved women (*All, all!*) and had been loved by some, one, two; but this was unlike loving or having been loved by women. Precisely and in reverse degree from passion, conjugal love, this was near-annihilation, transcending both. He comprehended with ease spinning, peripheral meanings that revolved, like moon dust, about planetary words, Unity, One, Soul, God. He began to trace the thread of himself, lost in the labyrinthine maze, and at last found it, a single, fragile strand, knit in ever-changing patterns: Show me myself.

❦ ❦ ❦ FAYE SAT, curled up in Anson's big chair beside the bookshelves, reading. Netcher was stretched out on the rug at her feet. Faye was well along in the manuscript of Galey's novel, having returned to it in spare moments since beginning it the Borobudur night. Her feelings about it were mixed. She was a careful reader and, from time to time, stopped and leafed back to make sure some spelling or reference was consistent; if it was not, she made a note of it on a pad, then continued. Her left hand rested lazily on Netcher's neck. Netcher carried the cues of the household in her head and her bright amber eyes had been as eloquent with questions as Todd's. The Doberman's eyes were closed now, except for an almost invisible slit of attention; she, as much as Todd, waited for the arrival of the Porsche, and when it did not come, lay on the hall rug, nose pointed toward the door, waiting.

Faye had not been upset by the long set piece at the center of the novel, celebrating body hair; though she had read every word of it with attention, she had not found it interesting. She could not help, sometimes, thinking of the strange man obsessed enough to write about what she had always accepted as commonplace, just as she visualized David Steen, when reading his books, and when she came to the end of Little Marka's interior monologue about her lovers' hair distributions, she turned the manuscript on its face and broke for a cigarette. It was characteristic of her that she never smoked while turning pages, only between stints.

The house literally glittered from Mrs. Haines's cleaning and polishing; both Mrs. Haines and Faye were believers in laying party pavement far ahead. Everything looked ready for the party and almost was. Because the Haineses had no catering to do before then, Mr. Haines already had transported glasses for drinks, the dishware for the buffet, table-cloths folded inside plastic covers, tables that would be set up in the garden, if the weather was fine, or inside the house, should Saturday be rainy. Cases of liquor had been stacked in the guest room: gin and vermouth for the martinis most would take, Scotch, bourbon or rum for those who insisted, the mineral waters. It was too early to guess what Saturday's weather would be. Just now, it was raining hard, as it had all weekend; if Faye thought anything about it, it was that perhaps this was a good sign, it would rain itself out and then would come the dry summer weather in which they had given the party other years.

The house was quiet. Todd had brought his glass jar and the plastic box in which the turtles lived into the house before the storm, and they were spending the night beside his bed. All doors were locked; the station wagon was in the garage. Stacks of unread manuscripts and proofs Anson had brought home were on the coffee table. Yesterday, while Todd attended Velma's group, Faye had driven over to see Grace Burgess, passing the Ditten's Ridge station on the way. She saw the Porsche, still parked where Anson had left it Friday morning, and had gotten out to make certain it was locked; it was, and the windows were lowered an inch on each side for ventilation. She wondered, now, if the slanting rain would drench the inside, rather wishing she had followed her impulse to ask Grace Burgess to drive to the station with her to pick it up. She had intended to do just that, but during the visit had forgotten. One of Chet Burgess' patients, who lived on the Cape, had sent two bushels of refrigerated lobsters, and Grace had been on the phone when Faye arrived, calling "Assortment" members to invite them for a cookout Sunday night.

"I called you first of all," Grace said, "but you were out."

"I was taking Todd to the group. And I stopped to talk to Velma Currie."

"Oh. Yes." Grace Burgess rarely acknowledged Velma's existence. "Well, you heard me asking Ray and Alma. They're coming, as are all the others except Amy and Herb. Herb can't eat lobster. I hope you and Anson will come. There are two dozen, some weigh as much as three pounds, so we can really have a blowout."

"I think we'd love to," Faye said provisionally; "Anson's in town on a deal."

"Surely he'll be back by tomorrow night? Sunday?"

"I'm not sure."

"Oh," Grace Burgess said in her "Oh" voice. "Well, even if Anson doesn't get back, you can come by yourself."

That had been yesterday. Now she was feeling the Porsche could rust and rot where it stood. Without Anson, the house was heavy with absence, the rain imprisoning. She had known, from his voice when he telephoned, that he would not be home Friday. Even if he had returned late, it would have meant her driving to Stamford to pick him up; the Friday "Bug" came in at 6:43 and stood on a side track until Monday. Of course, he might have taken a Stamford taxi to the Ridge station and collected the Porsche, or have had the Stamford taxi drive him straight to the house. Both things

335

had happened in the past. Or—he could have telephoned to tell her about Fleming and the sale. He hadn't, nor had she called the apartment. She *had* waited for Anson to call, until well past six o'clock, before ringing the Burgesses to say that, after all, she wouldn't be able to come. By then, the cookout had moved indoors and she had had to repeat her refusal to various "Assortment" members pressed to the phone by Grace, Martha Lavrorsen among them.

Martha was well into her third martini. "You're getting to be a stick-in-the-mud," she told Faye. "I missed you, driving in Friday. Here's Stig."

"Face it," Stig told Faye; "you're going to have to go somewhere without Anson *some*time. I'll drive over and get you."

"It's too late to get a sitter for Todd."

"Bring him along—he can sleep upstairs."

"We never do that."

"Were your ears burning?" asked Stig.

"No, why?"

"We were talking about *you.*" Stig came on strong. "Amorous, glamorous you. Come on, change your mind."

Faye had stuck to her guns and stayed home. But now her decision not to call Anson at the apartment, or at the K and K night number, was wavering. Not only was she curious, but she was angry, not only angry with him but also with herself for being angry. Putting out her cigarette, she went to the phone and dialed both numbers. Neither answered. As she lowered the receiver, she wished she hadn't changed her mind; at least there would have been doubt in her mind. Now there was more doubt. Returning to her chair and Netcher, she resumed the story of Little Marka, who, after many hesitations and indecisions, had gone to Copenhagen for the girl-into-boy switch.

The staff at the Köbenhavn Klinik had engaging, often titivating names. All, resident surgeons, gland specialists, plastic consultants, anesthesiologists, were almost absurdly handsome. There was Dr. Knud Gress, whose credentials for undertaking Little Marka's penis-scrotum transplant were impeccable, a commanding Viking father figure, proud of his lifetime of work liberating those dissatisfied with the sexual prisons into which they had been born. There were the round-the-clock nurses, Violet, Hyacinthe and Lily, feminine and flowerlike as their names. And there was Dr. Saxo Palle, who presided over the Klinik's extensive Parts Bank, for no vagina or penis was ever wasted; Dr. Palle, himself a man of parts, was young, many-faceted, cultivated as well as cultured.

Dr. Palle brought to his work not only expertise but accompanied his examinations and recommendations with fascinating digressions; if parts were his profession, he was, also, an etymologist. "It is so lovely, your name," he said to Little Marka during preliminaries. "The Anglo-Saxon *mearc,* I presume. In Old Saxon, *marka.* Nowadays, *mark* means 'a field, open country.' In my tongue, 'a forest.' My dear child, you are indeed densely wooded."

"Let up on that tongue jazz and get on with the bit of changing me from Marka to Mark," Dr. Palle's patient impatiently replied. "And don't jeopardize my dense wood during surgery. Everything's hair now. My pansy shape will be perfect for my new life. Just hack out the slit."

Marka was now in mid-transition, between her old Daddy-Brother obsessions and the fresh career she was mapping for herself. (Himself? Some days she-he felt deliciously both.) Once fitted with the penis of her choice, she would be invincible. She planned to lead a life of pursuit of those *comme ci, comme ça* beauties of the international jet set, who would fall easy prey to her new weapon. *I shall begin in Seville, at the Feria,* she mused during the long transition days between pelvic cleanup and transplant. *Soon I can forget dreams of El Cordobés and really concentrate on those yummy nomad heiresses. It'll be toreador britches for me, rose between the teeth and mantillas for them. No wife will be safe from* me! *But I shall have variety always. Afterwards, perhaps a cruise in the Greek Islands. Lesbos, with a pair of shipping magnates' wives.* "Little Marka-Mark on Lesbos," *score and libretto by Ned Rorem, composer of Ameri-*

ca's most beautiful music! The St. Moritz-Acapulco shuttle. (Lots of old dikes I can best in Acapulco!) . . . Jamaica . . . And, of course, Capri, where reside all those retired mother types I shall, at last, FIX!

The early surgeries had been breezes; Marka's hormonal balance was now almost perfect. Daily her voice lowered into a deeper baritone. Her breasts, those maternal love mounds men so hungered for, had been, at Dr. Palle's suggestion, retained. "One never, dear," he giggled, "knows when they may come in handy. And you can punish with them, that's the whole *thing!*" Marka at first had protested—"Off with the knockers. No more banging against goal posts during hockey."—but had bowed to Dr. Palle's persuasion. The merest shadow of down showed on her upper lip and on her cheeks, but that was all to the good. "Don't you fret one bit," said Dr. Palle. *"Moustache* is feminine, *très* Goya, sometimes the lagniappe that turns the trick." Now a *zoftik* Diana, with a hint of *gamine,* Marka found herself eager for the transplant soon to come.

The early procedures hadn't been all jam. Nature, Dr. Gress explained, died hard. Though bursting with super hormones, which should have resulted in her putting her hands up the skirts of the nurses, she was still experiencing *frissons* whenever Dr. Palle entered the room, and even paternal Dr. Gress was hardly safe some days. But he explained that these hangovers from her reluctant hetero life would disappear after the transplant. Radical changes were taking place in her speech and behavior, and among them was a sportive raucousness and inclination to pun.

"Where *is* my cock?" Marka would cry gaudily, and then crowed in a voice quite ballsy.

"Patience, little lady," Dr. Gress counseled. "Ven de hormonal build-up hass been established—"

"Don't you 'little lady' *me,* you old Daddy-type!" And Marka crowed again, as she had never crowed for her real Daddy.

"Perhaps I voss being a leetle forgetful of your history," apologized Dr. Gress. "I zink, perhaps, you may be ready—"

338

"You zink! Damn right! I want my cock. Or why do you think I had the snatch out?"

"No one is going to snatch anything," Dr. Gress assured.

"Gress," said Marka, giggling deeply. "Knud."

"You may call me by first name if you like," sighed Dr. Gress. These over-familiar Americans.

"I'll bet you're hung like WOW, Daddycakes!" Marka beamed an eye at the good doctor's crotch, disappointingly concealed by his white surgical coat.

"Pleasze?"

"Do you Gress right or Gress left?" Marka went on in her sportive baritone.

"Pleasze?" Dr. Gress asked again; though he tried hard to comprehend the often bewildering phases through which patients passed, he did not always succeed. "A colloquialism?"

"Gress left, Gress right, no matter. I'll soon be making my own decision about *that,*" said Marka. "Though you really could take it off still, Doc. I'd love to see you in the Knud."

Dr. Gress realized the moment for The Choosing had come, after which transplant would immediately follow. He at once sent Dr. Palle to escort Marka to the Parts Bank to make her selection. Placed in a wheelchair and wrapped heavily in blankets, for the Bank was deeply refrigerated, Marka at last felt she was on the journey to her new self.

"*Wheeeeee!*" she cried euphorically as Dr. Palle wheeled her along.

"I know, dear, what this moment means to you."

"You saxy thing!" punned Marka. "And remember, I want no *cockamehmeh* mistakes, nothing *verkockteh!*"

"You? A daughter of Israel?" asked Dr. Palle in astonishment. "I'd never have guessed."

"Of course not, but Yiddish is *in* now, *le plus chic.*"

The Parts Bank was in two sections, and it was necessary for them to pass through an antechamber where, as though standing in maternal guard, were the frozen, waiting vaginas of patients who had made decisions similar to Marka's.

Dr. Palle paused for a brief moment. "I call these *my girls,*" he confessed musingly. "I knew them all. There's dear Mona . . . lovely Pia . . . Mabel. Though still unchosen, they're all happier now they have what you're going to have too." He pointed. "That, up there, is *you*, Marka."

"That *was* me," Marka qualified, thumbing her nose. "Let's keep going, pal. *On l'envie!*"

Dr. Palle, at once recognizing this *recherché* gem, smiled. "The motto of Iris March. A great work, *The Green Hat.* I reread it yearly. But here we are."

With a flourish Dr. Palle swung the door of the penis chamber wide. If it had not been so cold, Marka would have flushed with joy. There they all were, row on serried row, each in its antiseptic box, numbered, catalogued, begging to be liberated. Some, shyly limp, seemed still to be suffering from rejection; others, clearly happy to be gone and away, held themselves challengingly erect; a few even seemed to be smiling; and one, Marka was positive, winked.

"Never in my wildest dreams dreamed I anything like this!" she breathed ecstatically, her words etching themselves onto the frozen air.

"Magnificent collection, is it not?" Dr. Palle agreed, "Unique. Anything and everything: white, pink, mauve, *café au lait, tête de nègre*—all colors. Caucasian, Chinese, African, Asian, even Polynesian."

"And small, medium, large and extra-large, I see," murmured Marka, delirious at the display.

"Now, here is your acceptive group. Shall we choose?"

"*I'd* like to do a little shopping around first," said Marka.

"Of course, take your time. Shop and reshop, I always think; then there's less likelihood of mistakes." He indicated a sign, conspicuously hung: ERRORS CANNOT BE RECTIFIED. ABSOLUTELY NO RETURNS OR EXCHANGES.

Dreamily, Marka let Dr. Palle wheel her from selection to selection in her graft-group. He was helpful, but very discreet, careful never to actively suggest, but was, at the same time, gently guiding, several times even discouraging: "Um—are you sure?

Look a little more. . . . Oh, I wouldn't think *that* one; *he* was a female impersonator."

"Well, I'm going to be a *male* impersonator, so thanks for the tip. None of *that* dreary business." She indicated another goody. "And—*him?*"

"Much too Moorish for you, dear, much."

"And—that one?"

"Well . . . pretty. But pretty is as pretty does, my dear. I daresay you know that."

Dr. Palle continued to wheel Marka along until they came to a vast bay of windows. Marka gasped all over again. Often, in the seemingly short moments they were before each case (it was, Marka realized from the chill seeping through her, more like half an hour), Dr. Palle consulted the catalogue and read out an individual *histoire*. "I think," he urged, "we must soon choose or freeze. In one of my former lives I was a *vendeuse,* and I learned that one can, sometimes, see too much and not be able to choose at all."

"You? A *vendeuse?*" Marka asked, briefly diverted. But then, nothing about Dr. Palle surprised her now; he was so complete.

"You, too, can have your new life if you can make up your mind."

Marka, now half-congealed, at last narrowed her problem to two specimens, but her eyes still wavered in indecision.

"Think of completeness," prompted Dr. Palle, shivering himself.

"I'm trying." On the one hand was a great staff, superbly contoured, beckoning, almost commanding. "That one, he's somehow so *reminiscent,*" Marka said faintly. "What's the catalogue notation?"

Dr. Palle found it, read it, for once gave a totally negative hint. "A patriarch. *Pas des Daddies pour vous, je crois.*"

Marka rested her eyes on the other, but words failed.

"Him," Dr. Palle agreed with warmth, the only warmth in the chamber now. *"He* came in only about an hour ago, minutes, actually. No notation; too recent. Still warm, you see, still tumescent." Tenderly, he placed the bright case before her. As Dr.

Palle had said, it was barely chilled, still pink with life, glistening in the chilly light.

"He almost . . . *speaks*," said Dr. Palle softly. "Do you not hear?"

"Hear?" cried Marka, her baritone descending. "Why, Doc, it's an absolute *roar!*" She hefted it. "Well, in for a penis, in for a pound. That's it! You can call me Mark, now."

Happily Dr. Palle hurried his charge off to surgery. . . .

The Doberman suddenly tensed and raised her head, growling, and at once Faye heard footsteps coming down the walk. Netcher sprang up and went to the door, running her nose along the sill. Then she made a whining noise, by which Faye knew whoever was coming was known to the dog, no stranger. She waited for the knock and, with guard chain across the door, opened it. It was Velma Currie.

"Come in!" Faye opened the door wide. "Why, you're drenched!"

"I was walking by and decided to knock. I'm surprised to find you here. I thought you'd be with your 'Assortment.' "

Faye took Velma's raincoat and hood. "No, I decided not to go to Grace's lobster 'do.' They had to have it inside anyway. Now I've an excuse to have a drink."

"Alone?"

"Anson's still in town. What'll you have?"

"A light Scotch, I guess."

Faye returned with the drinks. "Walking in the rain."

"Sometimes I like it." Velma took her glass, sipping. "God, I hate Sundays! Don't you?"

"Well, sometimes."

"*Our* Sundays. When I think how easy most families in the Ridge have it, packing kids off to Sunday school and church. Sam and I've always faced it. They have us instead of the people's opium. You don't mind my barging in?"

"A human face. Why would I?"

342

"Well, it is late." Velma saw the face-down manuscript by the chair. "I hope I didn't spoil anything."

"No. It's Galey Birnham's new one. I'm almost through it."

"Any good?"

"Filthy-clever. Some of it fun, some of it depressing." Faye sketched the scene she had just finished.

"I daresay they'll get around to that transplant yet. Hearts, livers, then *those*. It's the penis-envy century, all right. I'd like to read it."

"I think you can have this copy. I'll ask Anson."

Velma looked around. "You look ready for the party. How many are you having?"

"We've asked about sixty-five, maybe a few more. Anson's secretary does the town end, works out car pools for bringing the K and K staff, secretaries, stockroom boys, the art director. The Burgesses will bring house guests. New blood never hurts. You know, I think you must have been right about Alma Doyle's bass fiddler being a fantasy. I called her to ask if he might know someone who could do the party music and she talked all around it. I finally gave up and called a place in New York Anson's secretary knew. We got a man from Trinidad with an accordion."

"Mm." Velma nodded. "I haven't had a chance to talk to you about Toddy since yesterday's group ended. Actually, I did try to call you a while ago, but your line was busy."

"Well?"

"He seemed a little abstracted. But he apologized to Kathy for the scratching in a very nice-mannered way. Not an easy thing for him to do."

"How did Kathy react?"

"She simply looked at him. Probably an unforgiving child. But with parents like Rose and Sherman how could she be otherwise? I think it means Todd's beginning to find his place in the group. He's getting along better with my Roger now, too. Though I'm having my troubles with Roger. I do my very best to pretend I don't know, but of course I do because he's so secretive about it. *And* he's overdoing it."

"What?"

"Masturbating. Has Todd begun yet? He must have."

Faye rose and went to Todd's bedroom door, which had been ajar, and quietly closed it. "Best to be safe," she said, returning. "He'll probably sleep through us, but you never know. He's a listener. Sometimes, when Anson and I've been talking, oh, not about him, anything, we find him standing in the doorway, all eyes and ears. As for that—no, I don't think so. Todd's still terribly innocent."

"Less so than you imagine, possibly. I can't wait to hear about the salamander."

"Uh. The one he's going to bury or the new one?"

"Oh. Are there two now?"

"The new one's larger and very lively—hates the glass jar; but at least I've prevailed on him to put screening across the top so the things inside can breathe."

"And is the live salamander in along with the dead one?"

"No, the dead one's all wrapped up in kitchen foil in a box on the window sill. He seems to be waiting for Anson to come home before burying it."

"That's the whole story, isn't it? Anson."

Faye had finished her drink rather quickly. "Do you mind if I fix myself another? You don't seem ready. But I've had one of those days. Two, three of those days, really."

"Go ahead, unlax." Velma waited until Faye had her fresh drink. "Never mind," she said then; "next year he'll be in school."

"And then, something tells me, my troubles really *will* begin. This salamander thing!"

"All kids have anthropomorphic preoccupations. It goes on and on through life. Think of yourself and birds."

"Well, I *accept* birds," Faye said. "Watch them mostly because Anson bought those expensive field glasses."

344

"Birds mean something to you whether you know it or not."

"Yes, I had the usual robin thing as a kid, bringing it in with a broken wing and nursing it. But never this business about salamanders and snakes and snails. It's not only in his jar that he keeps them; I find all kinds of things in those plastic boxes Anson gets at the hardware store to keep nails and screws in."

Velma's face changed from that of casual caller to professional listener. "Boxes, yes. But too small for salamanders?"

"Oh, yes; Todd puts flies and bees in those. Once, last year, a cricket. It died, naturally. All his things do, and then I have to go through the questions: 'Why do they die? What's death?' "

"What bothers *you* most about it?"

"The questions. 'If I turn him upside down, why can't I tell if it's a boy or a girl salamander? If it's a boy won't something run out?' Of course, I always make the 'male-female' correction, but my answers evidently aren't right. He asked this morning if the salamander had a cock. He's not yet six—where did he get that?"

"From my Roger, probably. Let them say cock, you can't stop it."

"I get so tired of men, males, *kids* even, going on about it."

"They never get tired of letting you know they've got it," said Velma. "Todd's obsessed with Anson, trying to relate his own sexuality—as I've told you both."

"He shouldn't have any trouble. Anson and I've always made a point of not being prudish. When dressing and undressing at the beach. Here. He began asking Anson what it was when he was four. Anson's very good about that and explained every natural way he could. But now, when I supervise Toddy's bath, he asks why isn't his as big as Anson's and when will it be. Honestly, Velma, when *I* was his age—Adelaide, she was my nanny, she simply said,

'That's your place and don't you think any more about it.' And that was that."

"But, of course, you thought about it a great deal."

"Not actively. At Sacred Heart, those years, the girls all bathed one body part at a time, using a shift."

"Like nuns."

"I suppose so. I can't remember ever wanting a penis, all that suppressed envy girls are supposed to have."

"You simply repressed it," Velma said.

"Maybe so. But I always knew, by instinct, what my 'place' was. Anson never alludes to me—there—except in ways that are poetic."

"Lucky you. Sam had, still has, the most depressing catch phrases for intercourse. Getting your ashes hauled. Getting the oil changed. Knocking one off—"

"Anson uses that one, come to think of it. After quarrels."

"And dipping his wick," Velma remembered. "I think if I hadn't had my social-service training, I'd never have got used to all of them. Of course, as I've said before, Faye, this whole salamander thing, the scratching of Kathy, the losing bowel control that Saturday—all of it's to do with Anson. Primarily."

"Yes. I'm miserable about him."

"Gone since Friday."

"On the 'Bug.' "

"Do you know why?"

"He's on the film deal for Birnham's book. I know that's true. But that's not all."

"There's that something he wants that's more colorful than everyday."

"Call it redhead. If ever Anson becomes that age that's supposed to be so dangerous for men—when is it?"

"Some say forties, fifties. Others sixties. It can be anytime."

"Well, I'll not be able to stand it. I'll have had it."

"Have you thought of another child?"

346

"We're going to have another," Faye said. "I think both of us are waiting, really, for this restlessness of Anson's to blow over."

"You could simply go off the pill."

"He'd never forgive me. Then we *would* have a little monster in our midst, and he'd blame me. Oh, no."

"There's the woman thing, too."

"Yes. But I won't trap Anson. He's terrified of that. The *minute* I happen to pause in a doorway, he's on his feet. *Has* to go past."

"Mm. I've noticed, but many people have that. When I remember the struggles Sam and I had at your age! Talk about trapped! We went right on, had the kids, and I've never been sorry. I had the upbringing of them and Sam had his suffering about Brittany."

"You told me."

"You and Anson have enough money."

"I dread the very thought of money, sometimes."

"A luxury of the rich," said Velma.

"My mother had an axiom, 'Marry a man with money, but always have a little of your own.' That's what she *really* can't stand about Anson, not that his grandfather was a Jew, but that he didn't *have* money."

"Won't he inherit something?"

"I doubt it. His father's already retired. Fifty-four. As I said, I dread money talk."

"Your talk is full of dreads."

"Yes," Faye said miserably. "If only Anson would come home! At least we could have a battle royal."

"Honey, you're in a bad way," Velma said.

Faye replenished the drinks. "And it could be so different. I'm so tired of being alone, Velma."

"I'm almost *never* alone, by myself. Sometimes I simply have to be, like tonight. And here I am, not alone."

"I hate it," Faye said. "I'm getting so I can't stand it!"

"Well, two can play, as the toucan said."

"I know. The toucan's been whispering in my ear a lot lately."

"Faye, any woman with your looks—"

"Can have anything she wants."

"Just about."

"I still really want only Anson."

"So you sit here and suffer and wait."

"Wait for Anson to come back. For the next bang-up quarrel."

"And you wonder why Todd's imprisoning his salamanders!"

"I simply don't know what to do about any of it, Velma."

"Has it ever occurred to you to do something like Anson's doing to you? Let him suffer?"

"Yes . . . but he's monstrously jealous. You've seen him at parties. You heard how he was the other night when I had to tell about Stig Lavrorsen following me to the bath."

"Anson's a type," Velma said. "A quick one on the golf course and an equally quick return to the dance floor—to make sure *you're* not in the bushes."

"I'm pretty sure that has happened. Once, after a dance, he had poison ivy all over his balls."

Velma laughed. "What it's like to be married to a real cocksman! Sexual athletes, *blaw!*" She was enjoying her drinks. "Not that I know, really. Sam wasn't one, heaven knows. But I did find out, once."

"But I thought you never—"

"Oh, yes; I *did*. I know the other night I implied I'd dogged it out, been faithful to Sam always, but it's not true. Once I got so tired of Sam's being tired, of all the problems when the kids were young, of Sam's Brittany, *Brittany,* that I simply got myself somebody else. He was a cocksman, like your Anson. No revenge on Sam, but it helped me. I was royally, often and repeatedly, just plain, proper *laid*."

"Did Sam know?"

"I don't think so. I was careful, though during that time I was like a bitch in heat. He was—he was like this." Velma made a fist and grasped her right arm with her left hand. "About as big. I was out of my mind about the thing; I got so I knew it as well as I knew the face that went with it. You'd never guess who it was."

"Someone from around here?"

"Someone plunk in the middle of your 'Assortment,' he was. Still is."

"Tell me!"

"Chet Burgess."

"I can't believe it—of either of you."

"Why not? You know Sam, a darling, but there it was. And you know Grace. Old, anal-retentive Grace—she'd withhold an ice cube from your drink. She withheld herself from Chet once too often. And I came along. Chet was as fed up for the moment as I was. Funny, there's only one word to describe what it was for me. He *cherished* me."

"*Chet?*"

"You mean, now he's going off. He was younger then, true. But when a man has that quality, the ability to cherish, not just wick-dipping, hauling ashes, nothing else matters. During my analysis—but no, I'll not bore you with that."

"You really *wanted* Chet?"

"Wanted and had. I don't care if anyone knows now. Chet would never talk, of course, not even on the 'Bug.' I wouldn't care if he did. I see him very rarely, but do you know, he never bills us for doing Roger's sinuses? Since I do the checkbooks, Sam doesn't know even that."

"I—"

"What are you thinking? Shocked?"

"I'm wondering what Anson's doing."

"Stop wondering. If he's with someone else, there's nothing you can do. Don't think about it."

"But I do."

"Do you take a role in your thinking about it?"

"I see him the way he'd be with me."

"With someone else, of course, he'd be different."

"I know him, his ways. There's not that much variation in sex."

"Faye, you're letting this get you."

"Yes. But why wouldn't I?"

"I mean. Sunday *night*. You've been here alone days."

"Except for going over to the Burgesses' yesterday. And lunching last week with Mother."

"If there's one thing you *don't* need in this situation, it's a mother. You need to get away. You have Mrs. Haines. Wouldn't she sit?"

"When I ask her, she does. Even stays over, if I want that."

"And is good with Toddy?"

"Old-fashioned good. He's always the same after he's been with her."

"Grandmotherly. Won't hurt him."

"All this may be my fault. Anson wanted me to meet him in town on Friday, go to a show. I wouldn't. I was punishing him."

"Rarely works, except in reverse," said Velma.

"Yes, I'm feeling punished," Faye admitted. "Since the thing about Jeannette Steen— I mean, if I went into town now, who would I ring up? She was my town friend, you know. She was unpredictable, but I liked her."

"Jeannette Steen is a mess," stated Velma.

"I like her still, except for the thing with Anson."

Velma stood up and yawned. "This lovely house, you alone in it."

"And will be."

"You don't believe it, that Anson's on some film deal?"

"I believe that, yes. But I know what goes on around any deal."

"Well," Velma said, "if Anson were mine, if I were in your shoes, I wouldn't be suffering it out here. I'd go right after him. If you find him with—you said she was a redhead—face the situation down. That couldn't be worse than what you're putting yourself through here. You've got the town apartment. Why not go?"

"Anson's not at the apartment, or wasn't when I phoned a while ago. Besides, I couldn't call Mrs. Haines at this hour."

"I'll take Toddy."

"Velma, you're a darling. But you wouldn't want the salamanders and snakes and turtles. Anson bought him turtles—"

"Snakes, salamanders, turtles, I've been through them all. Why hesitate? All you have to do is drive to Stamford and catch the ten o'clock."

"*Would* you?"

"I will. And if you're not back tomorrow, you'll know Toddy's all right with me. Faye, tomorrow's Monday. All day. Just get me a change of clothes for Toddy and his brushes; we've got Broxodents and Water Piks. He can carry the menagerie."

"I'll drive you over on my way." Halfway to Todd's bedroom she stopped, turned. "Oh. I can't, after all. There's Netcher."

"I'll feed and walk Netcher, and Sam can spell me. Netcher's been all right before when Sam and I took care of her."

"Poor Netcher, I'd forgotten her."

"Which goes to show how much you need to do what you want to do. Get away for a little. Instinct is telling you: *Go!*"

Somewhat to Fay's surprise, Todd made fewer objections than Netcher. Assured he could take his jar and boxes, he put on his slippers and dressing gown, raincoat over them, almost as though he welcomed a change in routine. After she packed a few things for herself and made her off-off-off, lock-lock-lock checks, she drove Velma and half-asleep Todd to the Currie house. The feeling she experienced as she set out for the turnpike, deciding to drive the whole way into town, was one she recognized as guilt, lightly laced with caution. She drove with extra care on her Scotches, reminded of times she had fibbed to Madame Doheny at the convent about taking a late bus after a forbidden movie. *The toucan said* . . . But no! No doubt Anson, whatever the negotiations had required of him, would be at the apartment by the time she arrived. Asleep, probably, and she would surprise him. And there were, probably, the same plays to choose from on Monday that there had been on Friday, when he had suggested a play. Give or take a few.

❧ ❧ ❧ THE FRESH brightness of American morning, so unlike the mornings of Europe, was beginning to stain the day. David woke spontaneously. He had slept badly. He and Jeannette had quarreled bitterly the night before, Jeannette drinking down her blue pills with her vodka, while he had remained doggedly sober: a fatal combination. It had made him reflect that at four in the morning American wives and husbands cry their eyes out, whereas their European counterparts took earlier to bed, turned backs on each other and gave up.

The city's roar rose fully beneath the bedroom window. Already the transition between what he had written yesterday and would write today crowded his head. Opening his eyes, he waited for the sounds he was accustomed to at this hour: Jeannette quietly preparing to leave for her hour with Dr. Cimino. Then he remembered Dr. Cimino's letter. Jeannette would no longer be getting up and leaving—leaving him to himself, gratefully alone, seizing himself for those priceless minutes during which he found himself and wrote. Dr. Cimino's letter, which ended almost seven years of Freudian probing. He heard Jeannette's somewhat uneven breathing and wondered if she was dreaming. Yesterday morning, he had gotten up and tiptoed past her, still slippered and pajamaed, had made it to his workroom without his silence being broken. What his writing mornings were to become now that Jeannette would no longer leave the apartment at 7:40, he dreaded thinking about. The new book was off to a fast start, was writing itself, almost without his being aware of it as it passed from him—the beginning of the story of the husband excluded by his wife's analysis, of that wife as she was to husband and world in the hours between her return *from* the couch and her return *to* it. Intensity and firsthand suffering were informing each other: this book was beginning differently and better than any of his others.

Jeannette, hearing him, stirred. "Time is it?"

David frowned, remembering that last night she had not taken her usual dose of barbituates. He was halfway past her and tried to get out of the room, pretending he had not heard.

"Duvidl?" She opened her eyes. "I asked you the time."

David held up seven fingers. Day had returned her to him, and though he had not spoken, he felt his magical silence broken. He would have to beat a path back to himself now, try to trace the beginning cascades of words that had wakened him. In rage he went out of the bedroom, closing the door firmly after him.

It was gone. Coffee did not help. He sat before his blank yellow foolscap in anguish and wrote not one word, thinking of Jeannette, wondering what he would do now. It was her story he was writing and she was clogging its flow, making him feel dry and dead. He hated her. This had happened before. He had learned to waste not even the bad moments,

353

knew what was best to do with them, picked up a sharpened pencil and began to scrawl in his irregular Pitman the words flowing from his mood. There was that traumatic experience of Jeannette's childhood, when she had been sent to the family doctor to be fitted for eyeglasses—he had heard it often, knew almost to a breath and pause the way she invariably related it, began to write it out. Then his workroom door, which he had closed, as he always did when not alone, opened.

"Duvidl."

"Go back to bed."

"I can't sleep, and now it's too late to take anything."

"Anything else, don't you mean?" he asked, not turning, remembering last night's blue-pill intake.

"I thought maybe if I told you I'm sorry I *could* sleep."

"All right, you're sorry. You always are."

She waited a long minute, still in the doorway, half in and half out of the room, then said, "I don't know what I'm going to do now."

"I don't either. Whatever it is, do it. Leave me alone!"

"I wish we could go, now, to Paris." She was whimpering. "I think if I could put my mind on my *folie* I might be all right."

"All right," he said patiently, "you go on ahead. I can close the apartment and follow you."

"I can't go alone, I can't!"

David spoke with restraint, in his lowest key. "Nettie, I don't care where you go or when, or what you do, but leave me alone *now!*"

"You wouldn't show me *Dottore's* letter."

"No, and never will."

"Why? Am I that crazy, that hopeless, that I can't know what he wrote you? I've never known what he said about me. In all these years you've never told me anything about that."

354

"I've destroyed the letter." At once he realized his mistake: he had handed her the weapon she needed.

Jeannette's eyes widened. "It's because you want to destroy me. For all I know, you want to kill me."

"Would you go back to bed, please."

"I wouldn't sleep."

"Take something, even if it is late."

"What would I take?"

"You know your pills better than I do."

"The ones that are any good work slowly."

David put down his pencil. Even without looking at her, he could see the dreadful fantasy building in her eyes. He searched for a fresh attitude—to tell her what? That she was already in fugue, on the edge of crisis, that she was doomed? In the usual course of their talk about her difficulties, he had been accustomed to taking the lead, softly suggesting, directing her away from the path of quarrels, but she had intruded on his morning, unfocused him.

"Look, darling," he said, getting up and going to her. "I know the break with Cimino is hard, you're having a bad morning—"

"Morning!"

"Well, bad time." If he continued in this placating vein, he would only end by becoming the poor substitute for *Il Dottore,* a role he had played, though unwillingly, many times, and which led nowhere. He temporized. "As soon as it's a little later, I'll call *Dottore* to ask if he has a further suggestion."

"Oh. His letter made suggestions?"

"Not really—"

"He thinks I'm too far gone, that's what *he* thinks, the shit! I told him he was one, did you know that? He can't help me; no one can help me!"

"Nettie!" David said peremptorily, taking her arm. "Stop this. If you don't, it'll grow into what it did last night."

She shrugged away, her eyes bright. "Did you think I'd take any *more* of those pills? Oh, no! You *want* me to take too many, to kill me, get rid of me. You don't love me any more, never did love me."

"I've always loved you and still do," he said tiredly. "When we made love the other day—"

"Why do you remind me of that? I was no good for you. I've never been good for you. *I* can't feel anything, come. With you or without you—"

" 'Though for her delight she tried many,' " he quoted to her bitterly. "Not that you'd know the reference."

"No, and don't tell me. Don't pretend you haven't done the same!"

"Only because you did first. You were the one who did first!"

This was where it always ended, though classic, predictable downgrade fragments remained.

"I've always known about them," David said. "The *téléphonistes*. The delivery boys. Taxi drivers."

"Never a taxi driver!"

"Though you're working toward it, I daresay. Where's your yarn bracelet? But Anson! At least you could have left him alone!"

Jeannette said nothing, waiting for the *congé* she knew would come.

It came. "If I know Anson, it wasn't he who did the work."

She stood just outside the doorway now, her nightgown wrinkled, her yesterday's make-up unremoved, lips smudged from the pillow. "You can't leave me anything, can you? Not even that. But you're right—I did the work with Anson."

"You usually do, I've noticed."

"It's because no one loves me. *I want to be loved!*"

"I love you."

"I don't believe you."

356

"I'm not going to say it again."

"No, don't," she said, turning away. He could see the tears beginning. Her shoulders rose and trembled. The strain of controlling, so the quarrel, meaningless from repetition, would grow no longer, had tired them both. "If you'll just tell me what to do now, David."

"There's the day. All of it. Spend it."

"I've never known how to spend any day, really."

A shiver of pity went through him. Her defeatism was catching, a virus that would rapidly incubate in him, multiply, invade all hours of this day. This last thing she had said held the kernel of all that was wrong—she had never known what to do with her days. Simplest of diagnoses, most difficult of any to cure. David sank into his swivel chair, watching her, saying nothing. His silence at last seemed to return her to a semblance of composure.

"I've ruined your morning. I'm sorry, Duvidl."

"I doubt you're sorry."

She began to walk slowly to the kitchen.

"There's coffee," he called to her. Now he could wait only for tomorrow's silence, hope for it. Nothing mattered.

"You're sweet to have made it," she said.

She came back into the living room, sat down in front of the coffee table, sipping her coffee from her large *bleu-de-roi* Sèvres cup. "It's almost eight-thirty."

"You'd be halfway through your hour."

"Yes, I was thinking just that."

"Do you want me to ask him to reconsider?"

"No. I never *really* liked him, you know. He lost me long ago."

"In the beginning you liked him."

"He always avoided my eyes. That's part of it, I know, not looking at you, letting you look. But even when hours were over, he looked past me."

"Then why did you keep going?"

"Somewhere to go. While *you* work," she said accusingly.

"All you have to do is *not* to speak before I speak. *Not* to open my door when it's closed."

"Familiar instructions. There are times when I simply can't stand to be alone."

"As there are times when I must be. You know that."

"I know, but I can't help resenting. You don't close your door the days I go—went—to *Dottore*. Did you?"

"No. Because you weren't here."

"And you close it now because I am here."

"Nettie, I must work. I can only work one way. Alone. Can't you accept that?"

"You're very happy to have me in on deals."

"Yes, but what leads to the deals has to be only mine."

She finished her coffee, set down her cup. "I'll try to remember," she said meekly. "Go back to work. Close your door."

"I'll close it, but I won't be able to write. Only letters. Will you be all right now?"

"Yes, now that I know how it's going to be."

It was as good a place to leave it as any, and David left it. He was aware that Jeannette said something else through the closed door, but he neither heard what it was nor wanted to. When, an hour later, his secretary arrived, Jeannette had dressed and gone out. He worked doggedly until well after one o'clock, dictating letters, filing, tabulating. It helped him to forget Jeannette. When he had signed his letters and had dismissed his secretary for the day, he wandered listlessly around the apartment, feeling a light-boned tiredness, the consequence of his poor night and the continuation of the wrangle with Jeannette. The day maid had come and gone while he worked, had made beds, dusted, marketed; the rooms were, as at most times, waiting for Jeannette's return. He remembered, as he ate a cup of yoghurt topped with strawberry jam, that she had said a last thing he had not

358

understood—nothing he could do about it now. But he could, *must,* call Dr. Cimino; though she had disparaged him, that had been her anger at his rejection. Her somewhere to go must be re-established. It was a good moment, ten minutes before two; he got through to the doctor quickly.

"Yes?" Dr. Cimino's up-inflected voice. *Well? Reveal yourself!*

"David Steen."

"Ah, yes."

"I received your letter."

"I supposed you had. It was a final letter, Mr. Steen."

"Is there no question of my wife continuing with you?"

Dr. Cimino said nothing for a moment; an adjustment to his silences had always to be made. Then, crisply: "Your wife has been my patient almost seven years, years she deeply resents, may I add? She has always responded poorly to treatment, though, as I think you must agree, I have tried. She will never be any different. The only solution—and it is a partial one—is simple therapy."

"I wish you'd tell me what it is."

"Her therapy is you, Mr. Steen. And medications. I can only suggest that you continue with her as you have been doing."

"You mean—and hope for a change?"

"As I have said, there will be no change. Not for the better, certainly; if there is one, it will be for the worse."

David slowly replaced the receiver. Automatically, he had taken down the conversation in shorthand, as automatically tore off the sheet and balled it up. Sighing, he stretched out on his bed and closed his eyes. He felt like the man on Calvary with the vinegar: he had soaked the sponge, held it at the end of a pole, but had no idea what to do with it; he saw the wounds clearly enough, but stood by, helpless. And then a low cloud of daytime sleep pursued him and he dropped into a long dream. It was one he had once or twice a

359

year, almost unvarying in its steady predictability, moving from the left of his sleep to the right in relentless causality, its warp and weft twisting and crossing. In the dream he was Hitler, a new, later, more powerful and sensitive Hitler, sitting in judgment on the Jewish Establishment that had never reviewed him and never would. And before him passed droves of cauled and shadowy figures, on whom he pronounced horrible deaths. The most terrible thing was that he was not Hitler alive, but Hitler dead, hideously scorched, only half burned, in the bunker among the dead guards and dogs dug up in the ruined garden of the Reich Chancellery. Dead of cyanide and smelling of bitter almonds among the thundering guns and crashing bombs, a charred, skin-clothed skeleton with but one testicle. Even in sleep he was revolted by this detail, then always accepted it, remembering that it was true, had been discovered during the medical examination at the post-mortem. The cauled figures, pallbearers now, advanced, picked him up and stuffed him, head first, into a shell crater. The dream always ended with Jeannette's voice echoing above the falling ruins: "Comrade Lieutenant Colonel, there are legs here!" Ended, but only began again, repeating itself with ghastly Wagnerian grandeurs until something caused him to wake. Sometimes he could hear himself moaning, other times screaming voicelessly through taped lips. He was staggering once more to his place in the tribunal for pronouncement when, before he could again pass sentences, a bell sounded, a faraway tinkling beyond his sleep, magnified, growing louder. At last the bell rang loudly enough for him to come awake and, with an involuntary gesture, his hand reached for the telephone. Shuddering, opening his eyes, he lifted the receiver and spoke.

❦ ❦ ❦ ANSON MOVED a little and tried to raise his head, mouth puckered in a grimace of thirst, from sheets maculate and torn. The night had washed him toward many shores, toward strangers in the disguises of love, their bodies traceless, gone. He had been his own double and theirs: *Doppelgänger* to them all. He felt the tiredness of death, heavy as life, his blood screened thin, surfeit, like a ballast of sand, pinning his flanks to the bed. Like mists, the ghosts of the night hovered above his dream; each time he tried to lift his eyelids his eyes heavily drew them back. Fire had played with him, and ice, until, drained of all desire and hunger, he had been able to feel nothing. All the conquests he had longed for, a lifetime of thirst, had cooled in his body. He tried to rearrange the mirrors in his brain so they would tell him who he was. He failed. The image of Neile was behind the mirrors—even if he could have reached out a hand, he knew she was not beside him. He thought of the other whorers, pimping for self-vision, but the hands and bodies of that churning, warm coil derided him. The other selves he had found in the long dream retreated with each effort to open his eyes. Not an *other* self, but a muted compassion for the returning self he was, pleading for daylight. Time, an interval of no length, passed. He tried again and, this time, succeeded: a splinter of gray half-light presented itself, slowly spread and widened at the edges, became a rhomboid shape, then a rectangle. A door opening.

Mano? The soft, dark voice spoke through the rectangle's widening. The voice could move and see, moved across the room, looked down at him.

361

He was sure he said something in reply, but could not hear the words.

You were way up there, mano. You were up there a long time.

"I—I don't know." This time he heard his words. The diamond-bright light streaming through the doorway hurt his eyes. He was coming back now, but slowly; the colors were less luminous than they had been in the bright world that was slipping from him, were like the Mary-Jane colors the night with Neile. The voice had form, glowed with warmth. He squeezed his lids shut until the door closed. The voice, a presence, moved to the bed's edge, depressed it. Painted eyes looked at him.

Was it good going? Easy trip?

He stared at the ceiling, nodded.

Worth it?

Again he nodded.

That was major fucking, mano. Remember?

"It's not like remembering." He struggled, bringing forth a gnat. "It's like—like half-now, half-then."

You're not quite back. The warm presence on the bed's edge was Minotaur-shouldered, firmly fleshed. *But back enough to know—no remorse, no regrets?*

"None." Proudly he could say it.

Absolutely?

"None." Prouder still. "Neile—the others. Where are they?"

Soft laughter. *You're still up if you don't remember that. You don't care where they are, mano.*

No. Silent admission. He felt descendingly happy, the weight and warmth of the body beside his pleasured him. "Is it late—in the day?"

Not so late, mano.

His eyes closed themselves: simpler. That way he *knew* better, knew there would be fissures in the transformed world of spacefulness and lack of inhibition; knew, too, that the everyday world of himself and guilts was returning. Behind his eyelids the black light faded, produced a beatitude, one of many shortening nirvanas. Then his eyes were again open, saw the room, lighter in daylight, empty of the bodies that had warmed its night. A cigarette burned on the edge of a table—no, it *had* burned, was cold, dead ash still clinging. He identified the maculate sheet as a fold beneath his chin.

Mano? he heard again, as the sheet was grasped by a square, spatulate hand and ripped down. The painted eyes followed its descent. Easily, the body that was voice, warmth, air-displacing presence, Minotaur-form, spinning words, stretched out beside him, the one tactility beside himself in the room chill with excluded summer. He felt the hand touch his lips, then move down his body, come to rest on his belly. There was no doubting the actuality. Sinewy arms embraced him, drew him close. He tensed, like a wrestler holding for a referee's decision, then slackened. His tiredness was too much. He reached in his mind for the revulsion he was certain was there to feel, *if he could find it.* He could feel only the animal exudation of the body next to his and feel gratitude for it. The gratefulness grew; with helpless tolerance for himself, he conceded it was pleasant.

Mano.

"I've got to get up. And out—" The third pride.

Not yet, mano. Darkly, certainly, the voice continued. *Too soon, much too soon.*

The hand lowered to his buttocks, squeezed. He tried to draw away but the hand held him, and eyes stretching wider now, he knew there was no strength that could make him flee this bed, this mattress, reeking bitterly of night and sleep. And bodies. There had been many in the coil, he remembered that. Neile, fiery but without identity . . . the black girl with the delicate ankles and uptilting breasts, who had felt like milk and tasted of brine . . . the others, unnamed,

363

unidentified, but whose tastes and tactilities still were fresh in him. And, yes, Fleming . . . red fire: Prometheus copulating with a roar. And . . . ? *Himself:* in the churning coil. It had been the dream enclosed in the magical world, revolving jewels in crystalline, unending space. The dream was splintered, spent, desiccated into the daylight filtering into the room. If a part of the dream remained, it was the warmth beside him. This body, dark as his own was white, was, part by part, ligament by ligament, a dark mirror of himself. Male. *Mano* became a longer, caressing warmth, extending. He felt parted lips breathing lightly along his pectorals, descending, tonguing his navel: rotating softness enclosed by a circle of moving stubble. The voice now was all body, roused; the body rose, straddling him. There was another penis beside his own, clutched in the square hand.

Cock, mano. All for us, for nobody else.

The hand released him and for a time he lay still, the fatigue of sand in his loins weighting him. Then he felt his foreskin retract, the flick of tongue along his penis, sore and tired from the night. There were no words for this male colloquy. He grunted—reflexive, obeisant homage to Faye, whose memory now intruded. At which moment was it that he had turned from jackanapes to husband? He *had* changed —from the first night he had known her, a rose flung in a vetchy bed; had, overnight, abandoned male apartment-sharing, overnight chicks, the broads of afternoons. Faye had melted into him; they had dissolved into each other. As the mouth with its rim of roughened lip consumed him, he experienced a moment of pure detachment, an unchaining; the thirty-three years that had determined what he was and what he would become were as many links, temporarily severed. The mirrors of memory revolved, flashing, semaphore-bright. *Sex is both cheap and dear, like life, like love; like love it gives itself for nothing, like life it is beyond price.* He remembered his excitement when he learned what Faye had

364

learned from Baumgartner and brought to him: jealousy turned inside out. Her passivity, her uninhibited hunger for him. The memory faded. Still grunting, he pulled at resinous ears until the tongue was still. The head rose up and the broad warmth stretched atop him, lightly, massive pectorals brushing his own, resting an elbow in the *politesse* that he, himself, used with women. *A gentleman always rests his elbows.* The painted eyes blurred closely.

Blow me, *mano?*

Legs dragged over his chest, gripped his neck, visclike. Gagging, he felt his breath stopped, reflexively and viciously bit as air rushed into his lungs.

The voice cajoled. *Try, mano.*

He lay, breathing through clenched teeth. "Get off me!"

Why not? Last night you— But you don't remember last night. Legs untensed, released his throat, buttocks rested on his belly, moved down. Again the rest of an elbow. The face came closer, stubble of beard and softness of tongue descended, brushing his lips.

"Not on the mouth!" Begun as an angry shout, emerging as a whisper.

The mouth withdrew its breath. *Okay, mano. Or do you like it up? We'll take our time.*

There was too much time. None of it was his to control, and he had no strength. He strained against the weight above him, but with each effort weakened more. The dark breath in his ears brought to him his powerlessness either to refuse or to submit. The voice, the body, had waited, and now, unspent and untired, as he had been at the coil's beginning, could pin him down. It was, at the same time, fascinating and a fresh sensation, a double-gaited way of making love to oneself; no threesome woman lay to hand to connect this with the coil. Fingers laced through his—himself, consanguine, a brother possessed, his own now flexing stretch of muscle flattened against the dark belly, matching stretch of dark, flexing muscle alongside. A laggard backwash of the magical night flowed through him, defeating any last ambivalence. He began to writhe, felt desire. Any desire. For anyone. For this body's hirsute, dark hardness.

Now *you'll kiss me, mano.* The quickened breath on his, a kiss full on the mouth, rough as male blankets unsheeted. He felt himself return it with all the hunger of first perversity.

The mirrors spun in his head: it was a mirror world now. He saw and felt himself, both strange and familiar, exhausted and primed. And it was like the sigh of the heaven tree in the garden. They kissed roughly, abrasively. He dug his nails into the hard, tight buttocks. He tried to fantasy himself a woman—any woman, even Faye—mounted and quelled. And could not. All he could think of was his own body, its treason, what would happen next. He wondered what genes had been falsely strung in him, that drove him, maniacally, back and back to his own pleasure. How would they come? And would it then be over? This phantasma in which he was now participating was as far from anything between himself and a woman as anything could be. With a woman, he would by now have roused her to the moment when entering her would be accomplished and the delaying, delicious tantrum between them begun. Her flesh would have become part of his flesh, a responsibility and an ecstasy—the mystery for which he breathed, lived. There was no mystery in this sinewy dark body above him, writhing, tonguing, sucking. Dazzling insight seized him, transformed itself into premature forgiveness: this might be happening, *was happening*—he was aiding and passionately abetting its happening—but it could never transform him into anything but what he was. His next woman would be all the more passionately approached: he was a woman's man, no less. This, then, was what it was to be fag, gay, queer, sentenced to the same sex, *the self.* He cried out his gagging loathing for this massive, triumphant Minotaur, throat raw with a sweet revulsion.

366

And desire: alongside, like a third runner, raced his own physical crescendo, beyond any control or stopping, rising, receding, rising again, taunted, tantalizingly delayed by the double-headers, the multiple orgasms of the crystal dream. *Could* he come again? It seemed an impossibility. Over and over he strained, almost made it (*to have done, to sleep!*) only to be stranded and fall back. Now the hands grasped his ankles, hooking his legs over massive shoulders, and carried him back, pinned.

In, mano. Slow.

The nightmare of strain and sounds, of his own voice, hoarsely cursing, threatening futilely, began, a rite of masses black and violet, night and fires: flaming magic of the coil returned as pain. A stroke of lightning pierced his buttocks and he grasped the bed's edge, the spring cutting into his palms. The pain flashed everywhere. And then came a grateful easing; he sighed, as though a flagellant cringing thanks for surcease of the knout, the hair shirt. He felt himself a swimmer, lungs tired to bursting, lashing through breakers toward a shore he could not reach—himself, peeled, muscle-stripped, heart revealed in luminous beating, rhythmic, stitching *diastole, systole, diastole, systole,* his brain gray and corrugated above, detached. Then a rap to order against his ribs, systoles in clusters, the *Faschings* and flushings of the heart! His penis, painfully engorged, slapped like a reliquary against his chest. Pain had fled, and now waves of pleasure, exquisite as the pain itself had been, drowned him, and he dropped through silence down the blood-laden ladders of his veins, the blood climbing, falling, climbing to eddy back into his heart. Wife unto himself, passive husband to the world. The ultimate, physical journey into the self. He moaned, womanlike, and his thighs relaxed against the burning thrust, deeper, ever deeper, longer. The instant was near for both of them.

Mano, mano, We're going to make it together!

367

Gathering the rage in his mouth he spat full into the face above him as he felt the final thrusts, the flare of alien semen breaking inside him. At the same moment he ejaculated in his own painful flood, a fall that drenched his cheeks and chin. He tasted his own sperm, acrid, thick. Disgust rose in him. If he could have vanished he would have. But he was aching with withdrawal; the mirrors revolved, blinding his eyes. The untrue and the past. Day outside filtered through the jalousies like sleep. It was sleep, the answer, platinum-gray and precious, brushed with a last nirvana. Time returning, time teaching that legends are only partly true; though he had flown, soared, climbed, had been drained by an ecstasy more fiery than any his body had before experienced, there was a fragility in his bones, a warning of the middle of the journey, of tasting too deeply. He had descried an epiphany, wrongly dated (*the first of June!*), but the manifestation had been less than divine. Smelling, touching, tasting, hearing *in excelsis,* but no diapason! Shadows—no bell-ringing roses. Bodies learned as earnestly as his own face—faceless. And as he dreamed the parts of this legend that were untrue, the candle of his guilt, *tacenda* of the self, blew out. *Tacet.* Be silent.

It was silence that woke him, sphincters dully aching. Silence became a necessity to rise, lightly and easily, to stand and walk about. The catalogue of morning (body felt as body, head recognized as head) declared itself: crux of hair on chest a pulling shield of sweat and semen; bush at crotch a matted furze. Morning then connoted Faye, Todd, salamander. FAYE . . . TODD . . . SALAMANDER flashed, neonlike, behind his retinas. *Must telephone, connect, explain:* adultery's protocol. As though a magnet the phone leaped to his fingers. With precision he dialed 1, area code, his Ditten's Ridge number. *Your number, please?* Dropping his eyes automatically to the small circle surrounded by letters and numbers, he found a blank. Somewhere he had the number, but could not remember where. From this unnumbered nowhere no calls beyond city dialing could be made. He protested innocence, ignorance, pleaded urgency, was referred to a special operator, a larkish voice that could not put him through. It became an incident, involving insinuations, accusations, allusions to police and FBI. Defeated, he gave up. But he could call his town number: reassurance of a kind. He dialed it, visualizing the apartment's waiting emptiness. *There.* Waiting for ten rings before accepting silence.

The shuttered light carried him through the rooms, front to back, to the windows overlooking the garden. He could remember some things—the sleeping bags were gone, emptiness dissolved to dark corners. The window lattice, horizontal, showed a yellow dawn washing the leaves of the heaven tree with gold. If there was sound in the world outside, it had been stilled. Overhead, pigeons in silent cinematic flight flared from a rooftop, wheeled geometrically, returned. It was the split-second moment of Manhattan morning, before winds blew from the rivers and bedlam resumed. No bulldozer choked, no golden ball crashed through walls. Then a bell, small and churchlike, sweetly tolled, a tocsin pealing out of sixty-year-old forgotten time, when Chinatown was new. Christ tinkling to Gautama, interspacing moments of mindless happiness with a thin, white euphoria. The world of Neile and Fleming was nowhere; it was a room cut off from the world.

Then Galey's voice, Galey raw-slept, easily asking, "Are you back?"

"I don't know."

"Let me see your eyes." Proximity, gaze of pupillary inspection.

Anson obediently endured. Almost, but not quite, he began to bring memory out of abeyance.

"Back enough," Galey pronounced. "Do you want to know how it went?"

Confusion. Pulling words down, like a conjurer, out of the night. "What—went?"

"Little Marka." Galey recited figures, which Anson could count in digits, like fingers. "Big bread. Big for Neile, too. She and Fleming flew off to Frisco."

Anson nodded, acknowledging an announcement impersonal as a calling of trains. He was beginning to recall the head-battering conversation in the bath with the black girl, to uncoil the coil; but reaching to the ends of Galey's sentences was less easy.

"Above a certain figure I couldn't care less." The sentence and others like it, conversational, stretched, contracted, eluded. "I'm cutting out for Maroc next week, Paris on the way. You know Paris, Anson?"

Like a bad joke in a dream, no good. *Parris!*

"It's wonderful," Galey went on, "if you know the *Positifs.* But they cut, too. Ten days, two weeks anywhere—enough."

The voice, either before or after the words were spoken, retreated. It was like the effect of the bell cutting the yellow silence. Time was a mode of being, endless but measurable.

"You seemed to be having a fabulous trip," the voice returned. "Did you feel the wind, the jelly becoming a box?"

"No." But memory cuing. "A *sun*-wind."

"Did you hear the sound you told me of?"

"No." The diapason. Haunted by memory of the sound. Concord. Consonance. Compass. Open. Stopped. All stops pulled out from viola da gamba to chryseglott and drum. Again discontinuance. The voice, questioning.

Then: "You should have taken both trips at once."

"Mesc—and?"

"Acid. LSD. '25.' Sometimes the best trip. Now would be the time, when you're still on top of the mesa for the take-off."

Anson stood, eyes closed, saying nothing.

"You fear the Fall," Galey said. "Your guilt poisons

everything for you. '25' is the esthetic consequence of mesc, last night. Its paradise is artificial, but you need to get outside yourself altogether, surround yourself and come back."

Anson's body felt light as he listened.

" '25' is the step beyond. Amplification. Digression of the self. Those selves of yourself, Anson—you met them?"

"Yes." Eyes still closed, seeing Faye, Todd, salamander . . .

"But only some of them. Others await."

Anson breathed deep, a last resistance fighting within him. He saw rather than heard Galey's words. No such thing as cause and effect. He was attending to different thoughts but could find no absolutes, no points to cling to. Conscious mind seemed to be pleading with the unconscious. He heard his voice, detached, isolated, sighed as he saw the miniature vial between Galey's fingers, fragile, crystalline, its label a parabola turning. Delysid (Sandoz).

"Trade name," Galey said, breaking the vial.

A droplet, tiny mouthful. This time no taste of salt, taste of no taste, dropping night's beetles from his eyes. Hearing better now, still pursuing memory, listening to waterfalls of words. Night washed and dried, ironed flat. A pinwheel with a tail of pneumatic sexuality clinging. *There is something I have still to do.*

Once more he was lying on the bed. Full erection. He flexed, looking down at himself, constricted scrotum, waved his trinity to the four winds. None of the coil bodies excited him now; sleep's laggard censor had wiped them clean. But a smudge remained. This was a different sexuality, a new hardness unresolved. The smudge became a mechanical hum. He let his eyes find it: Galey, standing in the bath before the basin, shaving. The humming shaver's tiny blades were birds of light in his eardrums. The bronzed body was naked, like his own, bouncing on night-blackened heels, buttocks alternately tightening and relaxing as he shifted stance. The folds and texture of the skin were marvelous. Faye? (*But as himself; no, as all flesh.*) Impossible. But there. He could not take his eyes from the superb buttock skin, the taut roundness with a division, like the voluptuous depressions sometimes seen in spherical fruits, the massive shoulders, reduced and simplified, like backs in Picasso absinthe canvases. He seemed to have developed X-ray vision: could see the double-trunked tree inside the legs, veining its way upward, conjoining at plexus, bunching at heart, climbing into nacreous skull. His erection was desire to possess that body, part of the clarity that was returning him to reality. Without shame in this shadowed cubicle, he reached for the bottom of this luminous hell and found resolve, got up, walked deliberately to the bath.

Galey was razor-absorbed, intent. Then, seeing Anson's face in the mirror, his eyes refocused, watchful. " '25' is a private trip. You should be on that bed, mano."

The razor hummed. Anson studied the face in the mirror, then his own face, beard beginning redly in darker perspective. A hissing began at the back of his head and ended in a flash of blinding light in his eyes. Mano. *Mano. MANO!*

"It was *you* who fucked me, you filthy queer! Fucked *me!*"

Galey paused, left hand lifting a fold of cheek. The hum stopped. "We fucked, mano."

"You fucked *me!*"

Galey's face in the mirror had become a changing mask. Anson saw his own, distant, becoming fluid, then many faces all at once.

The hum began again as Galey resumed his shave. "What happens happens," he said. "All right, I fucked you. We related for a few minutes. We synched. That's rare, mano."

"No man fucks me. My ass is my own."

"That's the best thing about it, the one thing no woman can have." Galey unplugged the razor, wound the cord around it. "I did the party straight because I wanted to see if I could get you. And I did."

One half of Anson's body felt different from the other. Euphoric power, irrational, bursting, was flowing from extremities into the center of himself. Omnipotence. He could do anything, kill, conquer, but most of all conquer. "I'm going to fuck you back."

Galey, random and easy, was putting something on his face. It smelled like wild, violent gasoline. "Can't do, mano," he said. "I'm a one-timer."

"You think!" Blue. Red. *Hatred*.

Their eyes met again in the glass. "Once only, I said. You were the hardest John I ever made. It's a curious kind of climbing, involving the shedding of each impossibility once it has been negotiated."

"I can't forget that *you* fucked *me!*"

"Don't remember—it's retreating into the past. There's only a momentary present—already it's almost past. Only the future's worth bothering with. You freaked. Forget it."

Omnipotence rising. "You are going to be fucked by me."

A curious expression flushed over Galey's features. Anson felt a release of all the ergs of energy ever shed in gymnasiums, lightning strength, power spreading through his body like a tide. Knowledge from another time dimly reminded him that Galey was heavier, a belt man; but he would have tried a mountain. Playing an instant hunch, he locked an arm around Galey's throat.

Galey tensed. "Let go, mano," he warned.

Anson held him hard against the basin. Eyes unswerving in the mirror, the struggle began. Being a jump ahead of time, knowing the next move before it happened, helped.

"Even if you could cold-cock me, it wouldn't change anything. There's no revenge for what we had together, and being buggered is not my scene. I've a perfect record on that, mano."

"I'm going to break that record."

"If it's the mat you want, we can begin." With a wrenching twist, Galey shrugged free. Anson felt the doorway cleave his back. Momentarily breathless, he waited. "No mat," he persisted through his breath. "You know what I want."

"And aren't going to get." But the X ray showed Anson the excitement in Galey's eyes.

"I'm going to give it to you as you gave it to me."

Galey laughed silently, confident, making a random movement of tossing a towel onto the rack. Anson, moving into advantage, smashed his fist against Galey's jaw. It was a murderous blow, lightning-sent. Galey fell back against the basin, dazed, then half lunged, half staggered out of the bath, right hand stiffly rising for the down-chop to the neck. Anson ducked, this time striking Galey full in the sternum, the resiliency of bone softening against his knuckles. Galey pitched backward onto the bed; gasping, he lay limply, torso heaving, pushing breath back into his lungs, legs angling to the floor.

"Cunt man!" he rasped. "Woman fucker!" He sat up in the bed. "Quit, mano. Quit now. You're under the edge. I could kill you."

"I'm not under yet." Anson moved forward. The zenith was momentary and he recognized it: the horizon where two worlds met.

"Don't try that! No John buggers me!"

The wide eyes triggered whatever last ambivalence Anson had. He threw himself onto the dark, sinewy body, like a corporal in a whorehouse in the last five minutes of leave, mounting, restraining, pinning back legs, holding, securing. He felt the dark penis flex hard against his own, and now memory, full-flushed, goaded him on. Top: where he belonged. *Was.* Spreading the strained buttocks, remembering himself, he found the path.

Galey turned his head from side to side. "Don't do it to me, mano," he begged.

Anson, in blind, circular searching, located a softness,

374

began to probe, the going painful and hard and slow. The resistive sphincter roundly clawed his tender bulb. "Let me in!" he heard his own voice command. Parts of his body no longer belonged to him. "I'll break you if you don't!"

Teeth gritting, hips savagely writhing, Galey made a last, tensing resistance, then, bested, lay still. Anson now flattened the rib cage beneath him and began entry in earnest. One last surprise remained: Galey, almost ceremoniously, vanquished relinquishing sword to victor, adjusted position, complied.

"You're killing me, mano!" he cried; but beneath his pain was an ecstasy of relief. "*Sweet* Christ, mano. Slow! Christ. *Christ!*" The dark voice lost breath, regained it as a whine. "What are you going to do to me, mano?"

"*Fuck!*"

The voice, whispering now, cajoling, began to implore. "Ah, give it to me! All my life I've waited for a man *man* enough! Fuck me, mano! Break me, kill me, anything. But fuck me! Tear me to pieces!"

Anson, needing breath, wordless, heard the rush of words. Time lagged, then coalesced. He experienced a blending of exquisite torment and purest joy. No time now: time itself. Lightning traveled along his penis' flushing delicacy, plunging like flame into the sheath of Galey's groin, circularly searching, grinding ever upward, deeper. When climax, the hardest work of his life, came to him, he lowered his face and spoke words in satanic accolade, which he could not hear. He felt himself flood and fall downward into a night bright with darkness.

"Ah, thank you, mano, thank you! Stay with me. See me through!"

There was a dryness of moth against his lips, and in a brief reprieve from the world engulfing him, he heard the other, alien, heart pounding beneath his, straining until its own hot flow penciled his belly. The punishing sphincter unswallowed his tenderness, flayed. Withdrawing, he cried out in disgust and rage. Maddened by this pulsing, grateful flesh, he rose above it, clamping its jaw between his thighs, seizing himself, his own pain and fury still gushing, and cockwhipped the staring eyes and moth lips until he was limp. He heard himself say, *I have to be sick!* The blue trough, a veil of crystalline vomit hung over its edge, ran to him and away: no longer a urinal but a dazzlingly blue-and-white *arrondissement* marker: *Quartier Idem.* The arched street was a long corridor, the proscenium himself, the curtain deepest night. He went forward and lifted the darkness.

✿ ✿ ✿   GOING BACK to the apartment after an absence of two months only deepened Faye's depression. It seemed smaller than she had ever remembered it, as though it were a part of her life pinching itself off before dropping away entirely. There were her aunt's Dutch paintings, the matching sofas flanking the fireplace, the small bedroom in which she and Anson had slept the first year of their marriage, before she became pregnant. Rooms now impersonal as exhibits in a department store, waiting to be chosen or copied. She looked at once for signs of Anson, but if he had been there since the maid's last cleaning, he hadn't slept in the bed. She checked the phone to make sure it was on, looked into the miniature refrigerator in the kitchen unit, outmoded, needing defrosting, holding only orange juice and frozen stews kept for emergencies. No sign of Anson there, either; the ice trays were solidly frozen in. She wound and set the bedroom clock by her watch: twenty minutes past one in the morning. She had no idea what to do after that but wait. The Scotches she had drunk with Velma had worn off on the road. She poured herself another and sat down in the living room before the cold fireplace. Outside, on the avenue, passing cars dictated their rhythms to the darkness.

The rooms had the calm she remembered from the day she had first seen them, thick, brownstone walls, packed and insulated between later buildings, so quiet it was possible to lie in the bedroom and hear almost nothing. She finished the drink, rinsed the glass, and found two Amytals on the bath shelves and took them. She hesitated about locking the door from the inside, then decided to let Anson ring and wake her. If he came in.

He did not come. Between reading herself to sleep on the Amytals and waking at her usual Ridge time seemed only a black ten minutes. The old, familiar, gray New York light seeped down the areaway. Barbiturates always gave her a slight hangover, and she made herself extra-strong coffee. She heard the rising hum of the elevator and sounds of a bucket and mop being set down outside the door—the super, preparing to do the floors. As much to convince herself she was where she was as to re-establish lapsed rapport, she unlocked the door and looked out.

"Why, Mrs. Parris!" the super exclaimed. "Haven't seen you in a coon's age. Must be months."

"I drove in last night to get an early start on shopping," she explained, as though it were necessary.

"I thought that might be your station wagon outside."

"No tickets on it, I hope." She smiled as she closed the door.

The encounter, meaningless, had taught her nothing. If Anson had not come in by now, he would not be coming, would go straight to the office from where he was. Was. Of course he was, *is*. He's got to be somewhere. She waited until the super had finished the floor, then went out to the newsstand on Lex for a paper, bought cigarettes at the corner

377

drugstore, passed the time of day with the druggist, who hardly remembered her. She read the paper. That got her to ten o'clock, the earliest she could begin a series of telephone checks to find out what she could, without, she hoped, her anger and anxiety showing through. First she called K and K, asking for Nina Gerson.

"Faye, hello. I'm afraid Anson's still on his way in."

"I called you, really, to ask for Galey Birnham's number. Somehow we don't seem to have it out here." Implying she was calling from the Ridge. "And for the name of Fleming's hotel; I want to nab him for the party."

"He always stays at the Saint Regis. That's Plaza three-four-five-oh-oh. I'll look up Birnham."

Faye could hear Nina flipping through her book. She didn't write down the St. Regis number because she already knew it, as she did those of other mid-town hotels where she and Anson sometimes met. But she noted Birnham's because she knew it was unlisted, wondering if Nina saw through the ruse of her call.

"Shall I have Anson call you back?"

"Yes, do." Faye hung up. *Let him ring and ring and find me lost as he is lost to me.* It was still early for New York, but she dialed Birnham, receiving only silence. She then called Velma, who answered on the first ring.

"Todd's fine," Velma said. "Stop worrying. Sam's off today and he's taking Roger and Todd fishing. They couldn't care less whether you or I exist, any of them. Men and fish. How are you?"

"I'm glad I came in. I needed to get away."

"How's Anson?"

"As usual. I've just seen him off to work," Faye lied.

"Have yourself some fun before you come back."

Morning had hardly moved, and the skein of lies would grow; it was still not eleven. To make the clock turn faster, she called her mother in Greenwich, then regretted it. But

378

the conversation, almost entirely one-way, was long, a tale of Adelaide.

"You know how she's always been about going to doctors," Vera Williams said. "She's been having this feeling of fullness in her stomach for some time. I've urged her and urged her to go and see about it, but no. Sassafras tea. Milk of magnesia. Yesterday she was so poorly I called Dr. Copeland myself and *he* insists that she see some big stomach man in Danbury, of all places. I'm driving her up Friday. Would you believe it, that was the first time we could get? We'll stay overnight. I thought we'd stop by the Ridge on our way back Saturday."

"What if the stomach man puts her in a hospital?"

"Don't borrow trouble. I'm making a novena to Saint Jude."

"Saturday's our spring party."

"Oh. What time?"

"Five on."

"We'd have come and gone before then. I want to see Toddy before we sail. I've rebooked, and only hope Adelaide's going to be all right. I promise to stay only half an hour." Vera Williams then went through a lengthy discussion about Father Callahan, and seemed vague and abstracted as she, with characteristic abruptness, hung up.

Faye sat on the bed's edge, for the first time in her life feeling really alone. This was the way it was for countless women, older or younger than herself, well or badly off, alone for one or many countless reasons. She *could* not go on, saying things that were, however unimportant, lies, turning her into someone she was not. At last, after two more cigarettes, she left the apartment, not thinking of the station wagon at the curb, deciding to walk. She could, at least, shop; her cancellation of her Friday trip with Martha Lavrorsen had left her with a list in her bag. As she walked down Park she consulted it, then set her sights for Saks Fifth. She bought Morny soaps, a shipment of which had just come in from England, two pairs of slacks for herself, a sweater for Todd—and another pair of slacks, starched white lace, with a matching blouse, for the Saturday party. Though these purchases consumed time, they did not take her mind off Anson. When she came out onto Fifth, it was almost two o'clock. She looked up at the floors of the building where K and K had its offices, wondering if she could make herself go in. She couldn't. Even if she found Anson there, it would be stiff and wrong; if he weren't— But she chose not to think of that and walked on.

It was a bright, breezy day, with the banners of the city spanking in the wind and the hesitant fountains playing. She seemed unreal to herself, shunning strangers, losing herself in the crowds, fighting what she did not know. *If I can just get through the afternoon, the next few hours. . . .* Day would, probably, settle all, given its time. She would give day its time. She walked up to the Plaza and had a late lunch in the Palm Court, lonely among other women. Time dragged even more slowly as she dallied with her consommé madrilène and picked through her white-meat turkey sandwich. She was not really hungry. But she could pay the check and wash her hands, and did.

Ladies' rooms, she thought, as she touched up her lipstick and combed her hair, were the truly private female domain. There, with the maid-attendant shuttling with towels, needles with threads of different colors pinned to her black lapel, ready for runs and stitches, the masks worn for men were dropped. Two dowagers of the kind found only in turn-of-the-century hotels were snapping and scratching at each other, debating the amount to be left in the maid's saucer.

"But I tell you, Esther dear," the first said, "a dime's quite enough. Don't leave a *quarter!*"

"I always leave a quarter, even if I don't sit down," said the other.

"Now, be sensible. Leave the dime. And straighten your fur before you go out."

The maid, expressionless, seemed to pay no attention to this colloquy, but after the two women had gone out, she smiled at Faye. Asking sympathy? Faye smiled back. She had carefully washed hands, used several towels, so she left a dollar bill in the saucer; it was not her usual tip, but it somehow made her dislike the dowagers less. Nothing helped the sinking feeling in her stomach. She knew, now, that she would have to see someone, someone she could talk to, and who would—even more necessary—talk to her. Perhaps it was for times like this that Father Callahans and Madame Dohenys existed, though both, had she told them how she felt, would have reached for platitudes, final and neat as imprints in sealing wax, and as brittle. Knowing it was wrong, she found a booth, again called Anson's office, this time was transferred to some unknown young secretary who announced, with authority, that Mr. Parris had left for the day. True or false? Did she care? Desperately. Enough to make one last call—to David, David if he answered; if Jeannette picked up the phone, Faye decided, she would hang up without speaking. After five rings the receiver was lifted. David answered.

"David, it's Faye."

A long yawn, then, "Oh, Faye. A minute—"

"Were you asleep?"

"Sound asleep," David answered with his usual candor. "You in town?"

"Very much so."

"At the apartment?"

"Not at the moment."

"Faye, what's wrong?"

"I—I need to see you. Are you alone?"

"All by myself. Come on up."

"I'll catch a cab."

Faye felt a nakedness as she left the booth. *Her hands*— she had left behind in the Ladies all three rings she always wore. Luckily, she had made the discovery within minutes. She went quickly back. The maid, seeing her, smiled and nodded, almost happily, as though some small argument they had had between them had been decided in her favor.

"I remembered," she said, reaching in her pocket. "I was going to give them to the desk—"

"Oh, I can't thank you enough!" Faye exclaimed in relief, taking the three rings, slipping on, first, her wedding ring, then her engagement solitaire. She held the third ring in the palm of her hand as she found her wallet, extracted two twenties and a ten and gave them to the maid.

"Oh, it's too much, madam," the maid said.

"It's not nearly enough. You—you see, leaving the rings here told me—told me something I needed to know."

The maid murmured something as Faye went out, the third ring still clutched in her palm. Again in daylight, standing on the steps, she opened her hand. The ring, a spur-of-the-moment thing Anson had bought her in Paris, was a simple gold one, a wreath of *repoussé* leaves, inside which was engraved CAR VOIS-TU, CHAQUE JOUR JE T'AIME D'AVAN-TAGE, AUJOURD'HUI PLUS QU'HIER ET BIEN MOINS QUE DE-MAIN. How often she had redreamed the day the ring had become hers! *For, don't you see, each day I love you more and more, today more than yesterday and less than tomor-row*. Slowly, she dropped the ring into her purse and snapped it shut. *Avantage*. Advantage. *J'ai perdu, vous avez l'avan-tage*. I have lost, you have the better of the game. *Anson, my Anson*.

She looked up. An enormous delegation swarmed around her on the steps of the hotel, African potentates they seemed to be, huge, glistening men in bright-printed cottons, with anachronistic Persian-lamb hats shaped like overseas caps. Their wives, equally massive, Aunt Jemimas off a pancake box of childhood, milled between them. All were being fed, by twos and fours, into taxis by the doormen, who, with each slamming of cab doors, yelled, "United Nations!"

Taxis extending around the corner had been commandeered; it was hopeless. Faye walked to the east side of Fifth—all cabs full and fleeing downtown. She crossed to Madison, where, at least, traffic was proceeding in the direction she wanted to go, then gave up and walked the dozen blocks to the Steen apartment.

❧ ❧ ❧ DAVID OPENED the door. "Hi."

"Hello, David," Faye said.

"I thought perhaps you'd changed your mind about coming."

"No, just couldn't get a cab. I walked."

"Sit down. Move those papers if they're in the way. They're my first drafts for the new one. You look ravishing."

"I don't feel ravishing. I feel awful."

"Like a drink?"

"No, but you have one, if you're going to."

"I'm not going to, just yet."

Faye looked around the familiar room. It always surprised her how many new things Jeannette could assemble between visits; the apartment was always changing. "Jeannette's still not here?"

"No, and I've no idea where she is. Care to guess?"

"If you'll guess about Anson. I haven't had a word from him since last Friday. He said then he was with Fleming on the Birnham film sale. I've been out of my mind with worry. I came into town last night, thinking he might be staying at the apartment. He hasn't been. I called his office several times and got the run-around. I even called Fleming's hotel, but he's checked out."

"I tried to reach Anson today myself. Nina said he was in conference and couldn't be disturbed."

"Conferences at which he can't be disturbed are Wednesdays."

"I knew Nina was covering for him. He hasn't called back." He looked at Faye intently. "We're two of a kind, aren't we?"

Faye looked down at the table, stacked with books and manuscripts and piles of David's yellow foolscap sheets. It made her think of Anson's table.

"Why haven't we seen you, Faye?"

"Well, you were on the Coast. Jeannette was out at the Ridge one Sunday you were away."

"I know about that Sunday."

"Do you?"

"Yes. Not only did I lunch with Anson after the sale, but I picked up from him the story of that visit of Jeannette's. He didn't say anything, except that he'd driven her home, but I got it."

"I haven't seen Jeannette since."

"She's why you weren't at the boat party for *Good Time*."

"I know about that Sunday too, David. I wish they hadn't, don't you?"

"Surprising as it may seem to you, no, I don't care. I'm amazed it didn't happen sooner."

"I guess I've been dreading this moment," Faye said. "These are eggs, David, and we should tread carefully. I've suffered over Jeannette and Anson. I wish *I* didn't care! Anson and I quarreled bitterly about it. He stayed at the apartment almost a month afterward."

"But he's been home since. You've forgiven him."

"What an old-fashioned word! Yes, I forgave, for all the good it did. I feel so depressed. I've considered everything, but done almost nothing to find out where Anson is. Do you think I should notify the police?"

"For God's sake, don't do that! There are other ways of checking. Anson may have gone back to the Ridge, if you've been here since—Sunday, was it?"

"This morning early, really. He's not there. I left Todd with Velma Currie."

"You must have been worried to do that."

"I was and am. David, I must find Anson!"

"Or you could let him find you." David had been making marks on one of his pads. After a moment he put it down and said, "I saw the girl at the boat party."

"And I saw her in the papers." Faye felt cold as stone. The day had been one of anxiety and strain. "I think after all I'll take that drink you offered if you'll have one with me."

"What'll it be? A gimlet?"

"Anything else."

"I hate those damned things, as why wouldn't I? I've two bottles of champagne on chill. Pol Roger, '59. Bottled bliss."

"That sounds wonderful," Faye said. She watched David go out to the kitchen, heard him setting glasses on a tray. He brought the tray in and placed it between them, opening the wine expertly. When he handed her her glass their hands touched. She held her glass, brimming, waiting.

"Shall we drink to anything?" David asked.

"We can drink my good wishes for *Good Time,* since I wasn't at the party," Faye said.

They drank. The champagne was golden and full-bodied. "I haven't been very polite. Though we've talked about Jeannette, I haven't asked how she is."

"She's—the same. Which is to say, probably out buying something. It's the only thing that seems to ease her." David waved a hand. "Look at this place. You can hardly move for the detritus of old duchesses, old *faubourgs.* She's out of analysis."

"Oh, good."

385

"It's not good. Her analyst is through. He wrote me quite a letter to say so. I didn't let Jeannette see it. It had a remarkable phrase in it: 'Continuing fugue states and consequent compulsive behavior may confidently be expected.' It almost scans."

"I've never really gotten it through my head what a fugue state is."

"She becomes listless, forgets what's happened even an hour before, has an almost total abstraction about what she'll do next. Then she does what she does."

"Poor David!"

"I've lived with it for years. I love Jeannette, you see. What would I do without her? Sometimes she's herself for weeks—her old self. For example, she usually screens all the papers and mags that come into the house, makes sure I'll not see reviews or flak pieces. My secretary's been doing it lately, but she's less good at it than Jeannette. So I saw Isidor Cohen's scathing review of *Good Time*."

"I read it," Faye said. "Who *is* this Cohen?"

"A hatchet man. All papers have them. Not to drag out that old duck again, but he's a writer who can't write, so he reviews. His piece bugged me. It's revenge, of course, for my having refused to be interviewed by him after my last book. The *Times* review had been lethal, and K and K complained —in circles where it mattered. So they thought to offset the review by doing a Sunday piece. It was too late, not for the book—that book was going great guns and nothing could stop it—but too late for me. I'd had it up to here. Jeannette took the call. 'Duvidl, they want you.' I knew who they were. I simply told her to tell them to *gay cocken aufen yom.* Literally, go shit in the sea. That's what's eating Cohen."

"I thought his review unfair."

"Cohen wrote a long novel last year and couldn't unload it anywhere. I got hold of a copy—just to prove I'm the shit he always implies I am. It was unbelievable."

386

"I think Anson and I read it," Faye remembered. "It was submitted to K and K. I remember because Nina said it wasn't *quite* the worst, but almost."

"Cohen doesn't know it, but his bitch piece on *Good Time* was a selling review. He'll sell another seven to ten thousand copies for me. It never occurs to them that the ephemeral novel of today may well prove tomorrow's evidence of the way people lived in this year of ungrace. There are genuine critics, but very few, mostly in the Jewish Establishment. But they *really* hate me. When a Jew makes it as big as I have, he's running a *schlock* operation."

"I don't know what that means, David," Faye said, finishing her glass.

"If you don't sell, you've got a chance with them, you're *gehshtruft*—perhaps unlucky. If you sell two hundred thousand, they dismiss you as *schlock*. Think what they did to Mary McCarthy. But I got off. I'm not being very polite myself, going on like this, when you have your problem."

"I wish you would go on. I'm sick of my problem." Faye handed David her glass and he refilled it as well as his own. "I see you've got a fax of the new Birnham."

"And have read it. Have you?"

"Most of it. But I doubt I'll finish it."

"That's the worst thing you can say about a piece of writing."

"Why *is* it that, sometimes, you can be almost through a book and then not finish it?"

"Every writer faces the awful possibility that somewhere along the way he'll lose his reader. Most awful of all is to lose him after the last page."

Faye was beginning to relax, to feel glad to be where she was, with David, talking easily, in the way they had at the beginning of the friendship. She said, "Birnham's clever, and outrages me; but I don't know, I went with Little Marka through the banks, and that was it for me."

"All that queer stuff upset you?"

"No. I could write a passable homosexual novel myself, I think; I've read so much about it."

David laughed. "There's one side of the street and there's the other. But why won't you finish it?"

Faye slowly sipped her champagne. "Maybe it's my convent training. When I was at Sacred Heart, I took a short-story course. We read a story about a little boy and an orchard. There wasn't much to it; it was a little like Chekhov, no real beginning or end, only this little boy who would go out into the orchard and look up at the sky through the apple branches, watch the blossoms slowly ripen into fruit. That story sank itself into me indelibly. Sometimes, when I watch Todd play, I remember it, I hope he'll be like that boy in the story looking up at the sky. It's as though I flushed some of the beauty of that story into Todd when I was carrying him, because during my pregnancy, I thought about the little boy and the orchard almost every day. It wouldn't have mattered if Todd had been a girl, it was the orchard, the childhood. Do you know the story?"

"No. But I recognize a genuine writer behind it, making you understand the little boy by telling how the apples grew. How is Todd?"

"Let's just say almost six. I can't talk about him tonight. I'd rather you told me about Jim. How's he?"

"Let's say he's seventeen. And all right. It's because of Jim that I'm the kind of writer I am, Jim and Sarah, my first wife. But you don't want me to talk about that."

"I'd love it, David. Do you know, we haven't been really alone together since that time in France. Whenever I see you it's with Anson and Jeannette or with others. You talked to me in Cannes like this sometimes, remember?"

"I remember trying hard to talk you into sleeping with me."

"I meant other times."

"Though you remember that drive back from Grasse as well as I."

"Let's don't talk about that. Tell me about Jim and Sarah."

"You know, once I could tell about little boys in orchards. My early work had that quality. In my short story "A Hot Line to Heaven." The story of what Sarah and Jim and I went through in a depressing bungalow on Halldale Avenue in L.A. There was a 'peanut' stove in which we burned newspapers to keep warm. California's miserable during that rainy season no one discusses. I used to gather the abandoned newspapers on the Western Avenue bus and carry them home for fuel. Then Sarah got cancer. There was about sixty dollars in the sugar bowl, and that lasted about ten minutes at the clinic I took her to. In a week I owed hundreds. So I began to write anything and everything that would bring in a buck. Brochures for manufacturers. Speeches. Will-she-or-won't-she stories for the ladies' slicks. My *Satevepost* pieces. We had to eat so Sarah could die. The prognosis was negative from the beginning, and she knew. After I buried Sarah, I was blocked, I couldn't write a word. All I had to keep me sane was Jim. He was seven and utterly bewildered. I knew I had to get through to him. And I did."

"How?"

"I don't know how it came about, really, only remember how things were at the time. He hated the Halldale Avenue house and so did I. So I bought a cheap trailer and we set out, just wandering, stopping each night wherever we found ourselves. Nogales, Santa Fe, Denver, places in the Pennsylvania coal country, the South. I must have driven a hundred thousand miles. Thinking all of it. There comes a time, you know, when you're either going to be a good father or a bad one. I had to be Jim's mother, too, and that part worried me. I didn't want a *fehgeleh* for a son."

"That's what's worrying me about Toddy. I said I couldn't talk about him, but now I can. Sometimes I feel the way you

389

must have felt, as though I'm trying to be both mother and father. I—Anson and I've done something wrong, I don't know what. We've analyzed everything, and always seem to come up with no answer."

"Yes," David said, "I know. Or don't know anything." He stopped, watching her.

"Go on; I hadn't anything else to say."

"Well, in those wandering years with Jim, I succeeded in learning what it is most children spend their lives trying to forget—all that family overreaction supposed to mean love, but that's really the anxiety parents manufacture by not knowing what to do. Childhood's a primitive time. Jim had that animal thing, horned toads, even a Gila monster once. I'd not have been surprised if he'd decided to go and live with a nest of rattlesnakes. I let him alone. Then, one day, not unlike your boy in the orchard, he seemed to understand Sarah's death, to understand me, too. I saw he was ready to accept that I wanted to marry again. I had met Jeannette in the crazy way people do meet, in a trailer camp, and we thought we were perfect for each other. At first we were. And she was wonderful with Jim, she saved the both of us—from each other. I knew then Jim would be all right. I wrote my first really good book. It was well reviewed, but in a way that killed sales, and it didn't make much money. Then I wrote my second, which everybody decided wasn't up to scratch. It was better than many second novels."

"Yes, I know it's the second one that's hard."

"Hell, they're all hard, but the second one's not the charm, you're right, or hardly ever. But mine enabled me to put Jim into good schools and to give Jeannette what she'd always wanted, luxury. When Jim left us, I gave him only one piece of advice: Don't let the girl get pregnant, otherwise it's your world. Luckily, he wasn't around when Jeannette had her first big breakdown. She began her analysis, but we'd spend holidays with Jim anywhere I happened to be or it was convenient to meet. If I was doctoring a play in Chicago, it would be there; if I was abroad, I'd fly him over. I don't know why Jeannette went to pieces. It may have been the big money. Success is a bitch to handle, and I think I've handled it. Jeannette couldn't. When it came, she fell for all the *grande couture* and this *damned* auction-room kick. She's right at home with those old horrors, clutching purses stuffed with thousand-dollar bills, waiting to pounce on some old duchess' Fabergé egg that opens up into a sewing kit. And furniture made for the small people of the eighteenth century. That thing you're sitting on is called a *canapé à corbeille* and is signed Cressent. Do you care? I don't. But anything to help those fugue states!"

The small ormolu clock on the mantel chimed six. David waited until the last note had sounded. "I think I've got things fixed so that Jeannette will always be secure, though she can't get at the money in the Swiss banks, except for the interest at my death. I've entailed everything to Jim. Do you know what Jeannette wants now? A *folie*. Some dank old pavilion in the Rue Saint James built for somebody's screwing. By Chevotet, she says, though if I know my Paris—and I do—it's late Lopez Willshaw."

"Surely *you* don't want that!"

"No, but I'm Jeannette's victim: I do what she wants. My own idea is the *grand albergo*—let the *filet mignon bouquetière* be sent up and the serving table removed. This apartment was supposed to be home; at one point Jeannette's analyst said she needed this kind of security, so I bought it. Now it's a *pied à terre* in Paris. It won't amuse her long. There'll be the decorating and coverage in *Connaissance des Arts* and we'll give a few parties, and that'll be it. She can always sell things at a profit. She's a born trader. She's why I can make money. She'll sell the pavilion to one of those really rich Americans, you know, who seem to have two millions to spend after taxes. Inheritors, not earners like me."

"So you don't really get anything *you* want."

"Oh, yes; I've got the little place in Klosters. I had to have that to establish accounts in the right cantons. I'm Jeannette's victim, but she's mine, too, in another way. She's the heroine of the new one."

"But David, how can you?"

"Easily. It's a compulsion to use the suffering she's brought me. You see, Faye, once a situation has collected in me, it has to come out in my work."

"You work all the time, don't you?"

"I'm working now," he answered, watching her through the smoke of his cigarette.

"I think I'm a little afraid of you."

"Because you hope I'll some day write about you. I won't."

Faye laughed. "How can I be sure?"

"I'll tell you how you'd begin to know. My future characters—victims—can be foretold, because before I begin to use them, I lose interest in them as people. They've already become characters. As I told Anson the other day, I need a wife—not Jeannette, because the book's about her—but a wife into whom I can pour her."

"But—how can you make yourself do it?"

"Fitzgerald did it with Zelda, almost straight. Hemingway, too, though his concealments were at once simpler and more elaborate."

I don't understand that."

"Neither do I, completely. We're talking around something else."

"Yes," Faye said, "I'm aware of that."

"Let me fill your glass."

"No. Oh, all right. I don't seem to be getting tight, only less tense. David, you're helping me to live through this day."

"I've been very full of myself."

"No fuller than I am of myself."

David paused in the doorway, uncorking a fresh bottle.

The cork flew across the room. "We lock horns, in a manner of speaking, don't we?"

"I thought only men could wear them. But if any wife has a right to them, I'm the one. Do you *know* this Eythe girl?"

"The one Anson was with at the party?"

Faye took her glass from David and held it a moment before speaking. "Yes. My reward for punishing him about Jeannette. You see, I saw her when they ran the tape of the party on TV."

"The half-hour or the hour version?"

"The longer one. 'A fabulous affair never before duplicated in New York City,' I remember that was the lead-in."

"How marvelous! That's better than 'most unique' or 'best and only.' Jeannette watched, I didn't. Well, this girl. One has two choices, I've found. Either don't let your spouse out of your sight—which makes for suffocation of both parties—or love with your left hand."

"You mean, don't really love."

"Don't expect fidelity. I've come to the conclusion it's not possible."

"It's always been possible for me," Faye said.

"So far. I was faithful to Sarah and she was faithful to me. But I've often wondered if we'd have continued, had she lived. And I was faithful to Jeannette until she started having it off with everybody—including my editor, your Anson. But I know about you, Faye. You're an anomaly, a real one-man woman. Even if Anson should die, I think you'd never want another man. Isn't that true?"

"Less true than it was. But yes, I was that kind of woman, until lately."

"Don't tell me you're weakening?"

"It's not a question of weakening, it's more one of being broken down and eroded. I used never even to *think* of the possibility of sleeping with someone besides Anson. Now I think of it. He says his sleeping with other women doesn't have anything to do with *us*. I'm pretty sure if I slept with someone else it wouldn't mean anything to me, but at least I'd find out that he may be right. You know our 'Assortment' at the Ridge."

David nodded.

"It's become rather internecine. I now know, for example, that Velma had an affair with Chet, that Amy can't stand body hair and gives Herb the wax baths, that Alma's bass fiddler is fantasy, probably revenge on Ray for getting starry-eyed over husbands—who've quite possibly already slept with her. That Stig likes exhibiting his eight inches, or whatever he's got, though, according to his wife, he can't do anything with it, nor can she. I know how many customers the jersey-suit boys—our village queens—have on weekends; I've even had graphic descriptions of what they can be seen doing through peepholes in doors. The only thing I haven't heard discussed is what 'Gertrude' and 'Alice' do."

"I remember them. They may simply snuggle. Or use everything from bull dikers to merkins."

"I know what the first is, not the second."

"A merkin is a pubic hairpiece worn by strippers who have shaved down to the G-string. They wear it to excite *their* customers, who otherwise can't become erect. Lesbians use them, I'm told, for kicks. I'm a reader of dictionaries, you see."

"That's not in any dictionary."

"Yes, both Webster and the new Random House have 'merkin.' "

Faye set down her glass, thinking, *Madame Doheny never prepared me for this, nothing did or could.* "I must go, David."

"Where will you go?"

"I don't know."

"We could have dinner. I'm starved."

"Yes, I'm hungry too. No"—she put a hand over her glass

394

as David lifted the champagne—"no more. I want to keep this, the way I've felt being with you. You've made me forget."

While David made reservations, Faye repaired her face in Jeannette's bath, observing, as she had many times before, the luxe of gold-topped jars and bottles, the flacons of perfume. A Magritte hung on one wall, brightly painted fish finning against a cloud-filled sky. A lipstick lay, nakedly uncapped, on a shelf.

How comfortable it was to dine with David, who knew the rules of never too much, not less, not more. He ordered for both of them, sparsely and wisely, dictating that they would drink only a further glass before eating, a brandy afterward. Faye lingered over her fragrant, crystal balloon, her eyes pensive.

"And now," David said.

"Yes, I know. I suppose I'm waiting for you to ask me to go to bed with you." She couldn't believe what she had heard herself say; the words flew from her, consequential as the escape of a bird from a cage.

But she had said it, because he answered. "No problem. Let's do."

"There's the problem of Jeannette."

"We won't go back there."

"It would have to be now, though. If you still want to."

"I very much want to. There are hotels."

"A *hôtel de passe?* Oh, no, David, no!"

"They're not called that in New York."

"That leaves our—*my* apartment."

"Doesn't that raise the question of Anson?"

"The door bolts from inside. That's what bolts are for." I have achieved an ascendancy over myself, she thought. For what it's worth. It seemed the achievement of her life to have gotten through this day. Tipsily, they walked through the sultry evening, up Park, to where the station wagon stood, twice ticketed beneath the windshield wiper. Faye hardly noticed.

"It's so long since I've been here," David said when she had unlocked the door. "The wonderful times we all had here."

"It's been a while since I've been here myself," she answered him. "Yes. The four of us. Now it's two against two."

In the half-light filtering from the street he caught her up in his arms. "This was why you came to me today, so we could be together like this, wasn't it?"

"I came to you because I'd exhausted everything else, myself, as a matter of fact. By default."

"One gives thanks for certain defaults."

Faye drew away. David followed her into the bedroom. They undressed with separate modesties, each avoiding looking at the other.

She said, as she heard him put down his watch on the dressing table, "This is the moment I dread. After it I'll be all right, but be patient with me now." She turned and looked at him.

"You're more than ravishing," he assured her. "Yesterday you couldn't have been as lovely."

"And there's tomorrow," she said. "I feel it's the end of something for me, at last seeing you, all of you." Her eyes registered his familiar dark hairiness, his skin tanned darkly as she remembered. He was Anson-white where his shorts had covered him.

She extended herself luxuriously on the bed and waited for him, feeling relief that this at last was happening, realizing that it had been submerged beneath her dreams for a long time. As he knelt beside her, then covered her body with his, he said, "This could be a beginning for us. You could learn to love me, you know."

"But I won't," she said.

"Why not?"

396

"Because I can love only Anson. I'm sorry. Am I spoiling it for you?"

"You're making it better. I like taking what belongs to someone else, especially if it's someone I love as much as I do Anson."

"You're perverse."

"Yes, I am. You'll see."

"That makes Anson almost here," she said, then was silent.

He closed her parted lips with a kiss and at once she felt desire. At once he found her vulnerability, caressed it, dazzled her senses with what he seemed to know, instinctually, would excite and please her, and soon she was letting him do everything. She felt a marveling detachment; almost he brought her to the peace within herself she had lost. At some moments she remembered Baumgartner, her Jew of long ago, but this was a maturer and better man, dedicated, almost uxoriously, to extending what she was experiencing in herself, putting his own pleasure second. She reveled in his pneumatic heaviness, aware that this night would not afterward change the affection between them, but would be a bond cementing them differently. She was less pleased with him than with herself for letting her prove to herself that she could desire him. For the first time she was learning what it was to enter into an act of emotion without losing control of that emotion.

"Anson!" she breathed, once, and was lightly slapped, grateful to be. David's face above hers was a palimpsest, a face from which the features of Anson had been erased to make way for a composite of others. His dark warmth, the pattern of his breathing, seemed an intermittence of Anson's, as though as he drew in air, Anson exhaled and waited, holding his own breath, until David again breathed. She meant him to invade her, to unearth her secret, believe it, resolutely forgive her for it. She was brazen, wanton, sur-

397

prised by herself. His almost Persian delicacy lighted her from within—Marvell's golden lamps, rekindled and glowing. She felt haunted by her future. Behind the bolted door rose the scaling walls of her marriage, beneath her feet lay the rubble of quarrels not yet begun. She saw her life extend, a dream defeated, the slow, deep river quenched. That she had sought him out, removed her denial of herself to him, stated, repeated, half rescinded in a rising mistral of long ago; that she could find him one man, David and Anson and Baumgartner and all men; that she was for too long unslept with, was flowing toward him, an insurgent stream; that she could do with him things she had done with no one but Anson, and glory in the doing of them—beside these things her slow, sad yielding to him, her struggle with herself, were as nothing.

"Do I hurry you?"

"No, no. You're wonderful."

He prepared her, almost professionally, for his delicate eellike entry, surprised by the bright fleece of rapture that quickly burst within her. He paused, tense and waiting, as her contractions pinched him, slowed, almost but not quite subsided.

"God!" he said. "You're incredible! Do you always come like this, so quickly?"

She heard the sorrow in his voice. "No, not often. Only sometimes." She remembered the dry, windy afternoon on the road from Grasse to the sea, when he had roused her, when her quickness had surprised Anson. She was still just off the heights, gliding slowly down. She said, "You see, this began long ago with me, David."

"You remember. That's when it began for me too."

He had controlled, now quickly pursued his own pleasure, finding the shadow beyond which it lay, gasping as he came. But his caresses continued, until they were both replete, tired and searching sleep.

"Tell me," she said, as their bodies separated, as he rolled to the bed's far side, "do you satisfy Jeannette?"

"I once did. Almost never any more."

"You satisfy only yourself with her?"

"When I sleep with her. That's almost never, too. She's virtually impossible to satisfy."

"Perhaps that's why she is as she is."

"It's a convenient peg on which to hang it."

"I wonder if she came with Anson."

"No. I asked her. She didn't. Does that please you?"

"A little. Perhaps his one defeat."

"It pleased me more than a little. You see, I haven't the bunch of keys Anson has, so I am, as all men are about that, jealous."

"But how could you know *that* about Anson?"

"Everything's known, Faye. Including that."

"What happened between Jeannette and you?"

"I've thought about it for years. It was as though a pane of glass slowly formed itself between us, not rigid and cold, but some warm, malleable kind that fits us both, outlines our separateness. The death of one body for another. Hers finding mine dead. I'm beginning to find hers dead, too."

"David, I'll never forget this."

He smiled wryly. "Well, it wasn't straight fucking, as it started out to be, was it?"

"No, but nothing to do with love, either. It was"—she kissed him full on the lips—"it was help, help for a woman who's the kind I am. And I'm grateful."

"For proving to you you're capable of being unfaithful?"

"That, yes; and much else."

"Now it's begun for you, it won't stop with me, you know. There are bound to be others."

"I wonder. I don't feel at all the way I expected to."

"Which was guilty?"

"No, as though I've learned something. Nothing I wanted to learn, but I've learned it."

"How the links of love are severed?"

"Mm. And how they're forged as well. All I can think about is Anson, where he is, whether he's all right."

"I think you're going to find he's all right."

"After I found out I wasn't." She shivered. "You see, David, I was through with this before I started. I don't suppose you understand that."

"Yes, I understand it." He yawned. "I mustn't go to sleep."

"I wondered if we would."

"No, we must not. I have to get back."

"To Jeannette? But you don't know if she'll be there or not, do you?"

"No, but I'll go back just the same."

"And what will she have done today? You said you didn't know where she was."

"I didn't and don't. Whatever she does, she does." He got up and began to put on his clothes. "You see, Faye, I'm Jeannette's therapy, and in a way she's mine. I love her, though it's a drained-out kind of love now. I'll always stay with her and—I guess the word's endure."

"Endure. I know about that." She got out of bed and found a peignoir, walking slowly behind him to the door. "David," she said. "Poor David."

"Don't pity me; victims don't like pity. I could pity you, too. Poor Faye."

"Yes, I suppose I'm a victim, too."

"What will you do now?"

"Go back to the Ridge. Like you, go on enduring. Have you forgotten the story I told you about? The little boy in the orchard?"

"No, I haven't forgotten. Good night," he said.

"Good night, David."

v

The Thirty-Second of June

❦ ❦ ❦ THE DARKNESS was gossamer-light, easier to lift than day: he rose up with it as primal light broke in blinding splinters, flaring a peacock sky. In this dilated world, a channeled road beckoned through purple smoke to a palisaded memory of which he was the center: *as* child, *as* children, *as* self when young, *as* self now, loving, *loving* himself. *Anson! I am Anson. But what am I?* Laughter, lovely, polymorphous, exotic, superfetal. The world he dragged with him into this paradise of frozen self was self-explanatory, pinpoint accurate. The odors of the sky, self-perfumed, exalted, a million sperm whales deprived to convey this moment, breathful, extending. In the prenatal abyss below flowed a current, supporting a flaring pyramid, of which he was the apex: mother and father, grandmothers and grandfathers, great-grandmothers and great-grandfathers. The world before he *was:* faces immediately recognized, others strange, computer-multiplied. Voices heard and recognized, lips which spoke only silences in other languages. Drifting down into mist and myth, he examined them minutely: begetters. He viewed, then, himself, godlike, thrusting up through a Sargasso Sea, complacent, all phallus and rosy-gray scrotal sac emerging, triumphant, above the surface, the universe his toy. It was at this moment that the sound, eons old, phallus-tabulated, penetrated to him. He had only to choose a note, and at once, all diapasonal possibilities attended, orgasmic, played in him. As in his self-dream, sperm plumed from him, pale with promise, atomically occupied the skies as explosions of clouds, abalone-textured—the pyramid growing, rising ever higher out of the mist.

The water was deep around him: sound to be expelled from his lungs. Inhaling deeply, he blew it out as he rose, bright and flashing from the sea. The foam a color never seen or known, the island ahead jagged with light. He floated to it, clambered ashore, rested beneath a tree, flowered, porcelain-perfect, slept, a seed in a pod. He awoke, knowing fully he was the seed, bursting the pod into fresh life. The spreading sound and the pyramid (one, now) had never left his consciousness, had stretched through life, death, eternity, had lain within him in the pod, now burst with him, olfactorily gorgeous. Fire of life, fire of death. And the tugging world below once more cued: Rise. Listen. Fly. The wings beneath him, a thousand hummingbirds flown to his folded scapulars lifted him spreadingly. He soared upward, empyreanly, through a mobile and radiant medium: Time, the hummingbirds a deafening green-and-violet wind, lifting him up, up, forever. The sound toward which he was rising now spoke and directed, entered his heartbeat. *Rippling crescendo, heart of my self. Unimmortal lyre of my heart, strumming to minutes, sustain me now!* He could count in thousands his heartbeats of an hour: a smooth, complacent knowledge. He heard a single note: The One. Octave, second octave, third, fourth. And the secret: the major third, a major seventeenth above, multiplying, writing life, erasing sound, finding the life and sound beneath. Millionth root of infinity, instantly tabulated. A daylight beyond dreams blinded his eyes: Phaëthon, driving his chariot of flames across the sky. Rapturously frozen, he hung in air, hummingbirds sustaining, fluttering, holding. Wings he had won for himself. He wept blissfully, and in fervent love the wings released him and he soared, unaided, to the light unseen. *I am the root. I have died to live. You will rise, again, my dust, after a short rest.* He felt an unsheathing: incognito of the self disappeared. *I have found myself. At long last I know who I am.__ . . .*

A chest of throbbing viols played within his rib cage. For longer than he could remember, it was the same with his eyes closed as it was with them open. He opened and closed them and it was the same. Then, very rapidly, the batting of his eyes became an uneven repetition. What he saw then was like film: no two images were precisely identical, yet, if he thought of them all together, they were an unraveling continuity. Vision. He emerged from the darkroom like a blind man beating his way into daylight.

Then, instantaneously, *now,* he stood on a street corner. The excitingness of pure being flooded him, an extraphysical sense. There was no one with him. The reality of his aloneness struck him like the explosion of Chinese firecrackers. The sunlight on the gray pavements of summer burned his eyes. His breath was steady and even. He felt like dull lead, heated and unpoured, with no mold to go into. Ahead of him was a triumphal arch leading away from a square, Washington Square, and beyond stretched Fifth Avenue. As soon as he could move again he would walk through it and go—where? He became conscious of parts of his body, of burning hunger in his stomach, of the way he stood, grasshopper-light and empty, drained. Where was where and why was he hanging, thin and light and foul-smelling, in this thin air?

Memory circled his skull, a planet returning to orbit. *I am Anson Parris.* For the moment, he had no idea who Anson Parris was, but that would come to him, for had he not found himself? He would learn that the same way he would learn to walk toward the arch. If he moved from where he was, he would continue the reality that was holding him in place. A couple, gaily swinging hands, walked toward him, drifting in their own constriction of happiness, passed him, and he watched them as they disappeared into MacDougal Street. He was proud of himself for knowing that. Out of the blue, panic again struck. He knew he had abandoned something, someone, somewhere, in order to find something else, another someone, another place. And he had found everything he had set out to find; it had been laced into him, like another system of blood and arteries that would, to the end of his life, drain into him, infuse him, a second heart secretly beating in time with his own. He had penetrated beyond the nightmare borders, rediscovered the warmth of the womb, the secret memories that traveled the blood stream. Never, never, never, *never* again! With this promise to himself his heart raced more slowly, and he followed clues of reality back to everyday.

He began to walk through the Square, as he moved becoming more conscious of his hunger, the aching of his body. His knees, abraded, counted each step he took. He turned east, walked up University Place. There were great panes of glass, now, in which he could follow himself as he walked. He stopped, appalled he had not been apprehended, packed into a paddy wagon and dumped where people who looked as he looked were dumped. But no one really watched him. He walked on. A cafeteria's revolving doors brought smells of frying fats and steaming food and he went in. The cashier, eyes unseeing, indicated a machine proffering a check to be punched; it bonged as he plucked it; a tray, knife, fork and spoon wrapped in a napkin, slid into his hands. He ate monstrously, until he was almost sick, and that had been right; now he knew the next step—get up, pay, pass on. His wallet yielded bills, the bills brought bright gray change. He asked the cashier, still not noticing him, for cigarettes.

"Of please packs L and M Filters two."

She noticed him then, frowned slightly. He repeated what he had said, slowly and clearly, as though articulating for the deaf, to make her understand. On the third try, seeing her expression, he stopped, realizing he was in trouble, pointing, instead, to the cigarettes. He got them and lighted up.

"We get all kinds," he heard the cashier say as he went out.

Outside, in the street, trouble and confusion multiplied. He still held the wallet in his hand, flipped through its mixed informations. Credit cards, yes. Driver's license, yes. Indeed, he *was* Anson Warren, Anson W., A. W. Parris. Eyes blue, hair light auburn, height 5 feet, 9 inches, weight 180. DRIVER MUST WEAR EYEGLASSES AT ALL TIMES. His addresses were —the Park Avenue address, the Ditten's Ridge address. Of course. A cab cruised him, he got in, tossed the wallet to the driver.

"What's the idea, Mac?"

"Not Mac. Anson."

"Okay. Still don't get it."

"Figure it out."

"Man, are you sick? Figure it out yourself." He tossed the wallet back.

Miraculously, the mixed bag of things he already knew had not changed. The numbers conveyed most, were possible even to read and say. " '53,' " he tried it, not sure he was getting it in sequence, leaned forward and exhibited the plastic card to the driver.

"Oh, '53'!" He geared up and they were off. In the eyes watching him in the rearview mirror was an easily discerned laughter. "Man, you can *use* a bath. What's the story?"

Telling the story was fun, riotous, helped memory's feedback. He realized he would not be here at all if it had not been for the handful of blue sedatives forced into his mouth

407

—by whom? Memory refused, but he had slept, could now laugh, as the driver was laughing.

"I saw right off you had your ass in the air over something. Been over the falls. Making the MacDougal Street scene?"

"Another street."

"Man, that's Shit Street, wherever you make it. One thing —never let the fuzz see your flight marks. That what you had, A?"

Now it was clear and possible to say it straight. "No, mesc, then a flight on acid."

The driver slowed, obliquely glanced back, impressed. "All I ever had was half a fix and a sniff, and that put the bad mouth on it for me forever. Man! If shit was brass, you'd have enough for a whole band!" He drew up before the doorway of "53" with flourish; for a moment the morning lighted his mask of laughing complicity; then Anson paid.

He stood in the club's entresol. The place was Tuesday-morning empty. He asked the pool man, who admitted him, for Fowler. He had some difficulty making Fowler understand that he would have made his usual appointment had circumstances permitted. Fowler brushed this aside. As could be seen, it was early. "For you, Mr. Parris, anything."

"I'll need the works, as you can see."

Fowler smiled; the hangover he could not cure had yet to be invented. Anson still was experiencing flashes of the soaring world, golden in his eyes. He recognized his opening parley as hallucinatory reflection, asked for three of the sedatives he knew Mary Fowler kept in the club's pharmacopoeia, swallowed them.

"And I'll need to make some calls."

The phone was brought, plugged into his cubicle as he undressed, peeled away torn clothes he wanted never to see again, that seemed never to have been his. Astonished at his clarity, he dialed the Ridge, could not believe there was no answer, asked the operator to dial, finally accepted her assurance his number was D.A. The mandatory connection with Nina was immediate and easy: she would send over the extra suit in his office closet and a fresh shirt at once by Frank, the office boy.

"Want a fresh tie, too?"

"Yes, tie too."

"We hear the *Little Marka* deal went through with Fleming."

"With a bang."

"Yes, I guessed—you're the whimper. Faye called for Fleming's and Birnham's numbers. Wanted you to call her back. That was yesterday."

"I've just rung her."

"Well then."

Obviously it was the moment to say the word to Kastner. "Is Carl in today?"

"Just. I'll transfer you."

"You all right, Anson?" Kastner asked, asking everything.

"As rain. A little poky in getting in, as you may have gathered."

"Well, knowing Fleming, I imagined you might be. Why don't you rest up?"

"Thought I would."

Solitary, he sprawled in the sauna, before the bright fire. Sweat rained over the crystal labyrinths within his skull, biting his eyes. Remembrance turned, knifelike, in his groin, seeking guilt, waiting for it to shred and shatter him. His encounter with Galey had begun here, but as he searched his mind, he found only what he recognized as an entirely academic revulsion, if anything a resentful irresponsibility, admission and acceptance of his periodic need to make himself into a beast, descend to depths which were the springboard back to the life to which he always returned. The acceptance had about it the impersonal quality of chemical change; a catalyst had been involved, had entered into change and, itself unchanged, left no trace. The coagulate, moving corridors of light and time between the tasteless drops on his tongue and discovering himself in the street, had coalesced into a hard ball of shrinking dream. His rise from the sea. His island sleep. The bursting pod. The flight on wings of sound. Phaëthon's blinding progress of flame: *Le jour qui doit éclore, Phaon, luira pour toi.* From now on he would be different, but in his naked state he had no intimation of what his new self would be, understood only that it would be new. Whenever he had been away from Faye and Todd, the glass pyramids supporting his house, apprehension smote him, a still and quiet rage at what he was capable of. He stared into the fire, hearing Faye's voice, its Sacred Heart believingness, its sometimes shrill endurance rising to quarrels. Faith long rejected: but rejected faiths are perhaps stronger, more nagging. Todd's watchful, waiting eyes, demanding imponderables. His sad glass jar with its still-life waiting to be suffocated. The salamander, days dead now, awaiting burial. The death of any small animal loved, a mutation of self-love, the self's love for others. Death—lurking on every platform and roadway, supreme, confident, awaiting its inevitable moment of victory. Life—a rushing wind blinding the heart, stopping breath midway. Unanswered telephones ringing. The beloved's shadow copied obliquely on the blind. Nostalgia's nimbleness, memory's mysterious alchemy. . . .

Fowler's voice cut through his reverie: "You must have sweated it out by now."

He rose, slipped into the robe Fowler held for him, walked ahead to the massage table, stretched out, shriven. The sedatives and sauna had brought him down to where he could laugh at Fowler's humor, heavy as his hands were light. Both he and Mary Fowler were under the impression that some marital celebration-quarrel accounted for the tail-between-legs picture he had presented on arrival. Mary

410

Fowler had been fascinated by the TV run of the Steen party, in which she had seen Anson, finding him, evidently, more believable by tube than in life. Already history, a kinescope skin shed. Fowler sponged off the oily sweat, lightly rubbed, fingers avoiding sore muscles, tired ribs. He disinfected Anson's knees, suggested a shave was the final step to completeness, provided a buzzing razor and bay rum. Freshly shirted and suited, hair damply combed, Anson walked into the warm and windy noon, a triumph over the impossible: himself as he had been before. It seemed another long, light day before he reached the end of the thread back to Ridge reality, taking a taxi from Stamford, finding the Porsche in the station lot where he had left it, still damp inside from weekend rain.

🌷 🌷 🌷 JEANNETTE WALKED from her apartment house toward Madison, and the first thing she noticed was that her usual driver was not parked at the stand, waiting. But why would he be? Early morning was the time when he had, sometimes, waited. It was now almost noon, the time of day she dreaded. The sunlight lay pale and gold on the bright surfaces lining the avenue. She had worn a light summer dress and her hair, hatless, blew free in the beginning noon breeze. She had nowhere to go, except to escape from day and herself. At the entrance to Parke-Bernet Galleries she paused, seeing again the sign telling her that there would be no exhibitions or auctions until fall, then walked on. But there were her shops, and she began her round, contriving, unconsciously, to pass by the taxi stand. He still was not there. She knew now why she had worn her red-and-white-yarn bracelet. Pursuit had now begun, and she would walk and return to the stand until she found him waiting. Her last days had been white nightmares, all devils pursuing her, and nothing she had done had lessened the distance between herself—and herself; they were bursting within her, demanding to be let out. She tried all her old ploys, talking with her favorite shop people, toying long and anxiously over a tiny *optique* which charmed her for the time she spent in its purchase, asking that it be delivered, then forgetting it almost immediately. No matter what she did or where she wandered, her steps led her back to the cab stand.

She saw him before he saw her, not certain at first that it was he because she had never seen him outside his taxi, only sitting ahead of her, at the wheel. She now found him both somewhat disappointing and better than she had hoped for. There he stood, talking with other drivers in the sunlight, white shirt open at the throat and sleeves rolled up almost to his shoulders, cap pushed back on his head. She saw that his torso was long and his legs shorter than his white wrists and hands had promised; but he appeared freshly scrubbed and shaved, and as she came toward him, he took off his cap and smiled. The other drivers, seeing that she was a regular fare, walked away.

"Hello," he said. "I thought you must have gone away."

"No, no; I'm here," she said, going toward the taxi door. He opened it for her and she settled inside, seeing that his thick black hair lay far down on his forehead.

He took his place at the wheel and looked back at her. "Where to? The place I usually take you to?"

"No. I'm not going there any more. Just drive me anywhere."

"You mean, like, ride around until you make up your mind?"

"Yes."

He drew into traffic and turned uptown. She examined

him more carefully. He was somewhere in his thirties, she guessed, and she remembered his muscular stockiness and light gray eyes.

"Say," he said, "what kind of a place was that I used to take you?"

"Why?"

"Well, you were always like half asleep when you went in, and when you came out you looked, I don't know, like you'd been up to something, kind of."

"Up to what?"

They were moving in and out of the traffic lanes now, easily; he made decisions without asking her, turned left into the park. "If I didn't know who you are—"

"But you don't know who I am. Not my name."

"Not your name, no; but I know you're that writer's wife."

"And don't know his name either."

"I know him when I see him. I know the kind of cars you have."

"Go on with what you were going to say," she said.

"You won't get sore if I say it?"

"Of course not."

"Well, I—and not only me, the other guys at the stand, too, they kind of wondered about you too. We got other women we take to certain addresses, certain times of day or week. Regulars, we call them. At first we figured you might be one of them. What we couldn't figure was why you always went in the early morning. With the others, it's always late afternoon, or night, when the men they go to have finished work."

"You thought I was a call girl?"

"Not that, no. I told you, I didn't want you to get sore."

"But you did think that."

He shook his head. "Some of those mornings I collected you, you looked like you'd been through, I don't know, something."

"I had."

"You can kill me if I'm wrong," he said, and looked back again to check her expression. What he saw evidently reassured him. He said, "All kinds of people live in this town. I don't draw beads on people."

"Neither do I," Jeannette said.

He had braked for a stop light. "So where are we going?"

"Just drive."

"But I've got to have an address to put down on my schedule."

"Write 'Madison and Seventy-third,' the way you did the day you waited for me while I shopped."

"Not that again," he said, coasting slowly. "I was three hours with you and nearly went nuts with the double-parking. The pounds I made waiting weren't worth it."

"Pounds?"

"In this racket we say pounds instead of dollars. So tell me, where shall I go?"

"You're wearing your bracelet," she said.

"Yeah. My grandmother knits them all the time. Look, there's nothing hard about this. What you want. I know what you want. I want it too. The question's where. You got a place?"

"Can't we get away from this part of town? And you could just—pull up."

"I thought the idea was pull down."

"I meant park somewhere."

"Parking anywhere's tough. That's the dangerous way. Wait. I know a place. It's way to hell and gone, down by the docks. It is a dock."

"Why not?"

Now he had a destination, he relaxed, taking off his cap and placing it beside him on the seat. Jeannette lay back, gazing abstractedly out of the windows. The taxi smells reminded her of the first time he had driven her—a time he had had to recall to her. Was it the day he had given her the bracelet? The ashtrays on the armrests were full of cigarette ends, smelling acridly. She wondered if the rest of him was as white and hairless as his wrists. The world through which they were passing now was as removed from where they had started as Timbuktu—traffic-clogged streets lined with small stores, some long gone out of business, their windows either dusty or broken or both . . . poured-concrete motels . . . white-tile eateries . . . hot-plate, fly-by-night, crumbling hotels . . . bus stations with blacks and Puerto Ricans loading into twodeckers for Philadelphia and the South. He spoke very little, occasionally snarling at an unmoving truck ahead, or throwing back a terse commentary on a place they were leaving behind.

"Spades," he said. "Spics and spades. Everywhere. You dig spades?" And, not waiting for an answer, "All the same to me, as long as they go just so far and no farther."

With the sight of the river came smells of briny spray. Old, discontinued ferryboats floated in rotted slips; their names, once proud, declared the end of an era—*Mary McGuire . . . Flora Hobson . . . Jersey Queen.* They passed painted and cracking metal fronts being demolished, with new brickwork rising alongside. The dark overhead ramp above West Street shadowed them and, at last, he turned the cab onto a deserted pier.

"This is it," he said. It was a long, ramshackle grayness, gray as the river, scheduled for demolition and fill-in. He stopped at the cluster of pilings at the far end. "Out in the open, that's safest. We can see anybody coming." He got out, opened the back door, climbed in beside her, his eyes traveling over her in frank appraisal. Placing a hand on her knee, he rubbed it back and forth. "I guess you don't get what you gotta have, if you cruise guys like me. What's the trouble? Ain't that writer your husband?"

"No, he's not. I lied to you about that. My husband's an invalid."

"You mean, like, in a wheelchair?"

"Paralyzed from the waist down. Korea." His eyes showed a fleeting sympathy. He believed it. So, for the moment, did she. "But the daylight," she said.

"I told you, that's safest."

He gathered courage and embraced her, kissing her hard on the mouth. He tasted of cigars and beer, but she liked everything about him now. She let him put his hand up her skirt. He explored her brassière.

"Wait," she said. Panic and despair struck her. "I can't. I mean, I can't here, in this place."

"What d'ya mean, this place? We're here, right? There's nobody else here, right? You got me hard and going for you. It won't take long."

"Maybe not for you. But I—women are different."

"You're telling me they're different! I oughta known you'd get my balls in an uproar and back out. Cockteaser."

"No, no," she protested. "I'm not like that. I want to do it." She sought to enter into his idiom. "I'm in an uproar too. That's why I want it not to be so fast."

"So how do you want it?"

"Isn't there *some*where we can go?"

"I've got a wife and three kids," he said with irony. "They might get a charge out of it."

"Those motels."

"A cabby cruising into a motel with a dame? 'Gimme a double and a pair of towels for a couple of hours? Get the cop on the beat to park my cab while I screw'?"

"Say that again?"

"What?"

"Screw."

"Screw. Come on, let's."

"No," she said. The daylight, at first exciting, was beginning to terrify her. She needed one of her red pills to go through with this, but couldn't take it in front of him. She knew she looked well, but he was years younger; he might

416

think her old, older than she was. "It's only that it's too light."

"Another one who can't do it unless it's dark!"

"I mean, a place with a roof. Walls."

He moved away from her. She had put him out of sorts. He stared at her gloomily. "Look what you've done to me," he said. "I know your kind. Feel me," he commanded. She felt him. "You going to call it off now?" He looked around. The pier was deserted.

"If we went someplace where there's a bed, I could undress for you," she argued, stringing him.

His eyes were fixed on her breasts. "You could take them out for me right here. Take that thing off that holds them up. I've been thinking about them, guessing. I'll bet I can almost tell you what they're like. Bigger than they look under that bra. Right? You got those dark rings. Right?"

It would be a contest between crotch and brassière. Breasts were his obsession, clearly. How often *Il Dottore* had commented on the mammillary fixations of American men: their mothers had nursed them too long, or had not nursed them, she couldn't remember which it was. She said, "I'll pay for a place."

"And take all day? I gotta check in at three."

"You mean you'll lose money."

"Well, yes."

"I'll give you whatever it is," she promised. Anything to get off this lonely outpost of nowhere with gray, lapping waves around it. She had a momentary sensation of being at sea, of the piles swaying beneath in the river mud. "Just tell me how much."

This seemed to interest him. His pale eyes regarded her with a shifting interest. A fool, a soft one. He could touch her for anything, take her rings and bracelets, ransack her purse. *Find out who she was.* "Aw, shit," he said, laughing. "The time we've been here already it could have been over. It

417

wouldn't have cost you a cent. I used to have a girl—Polack —we never did it *any*place but in a car, and front seat at that. She wouldn't let me get into her. I mean, all she would let me do was—" He stopped.

"What? What did you do to her?"

In reply, his hand moved up her skirt. He spread his fingers and tugged at the lace of her panties. "She was just like you—held herself tight together like you're doing. It was hell to get her to unloosen, but when she did!"

"What was it you did to her?"

"What d'ya think I did? I got into her *that* way and she kept a lookout. Like you could do now."

"And she did nothing for you?"

"She pulled me off after, in whatever there was."

"What was—whatever there was?"

"Handkerchief, Kleenex. Once she used a piece of waste that had oil on it. My dong was sore for a week."

"Waste!"

"Stuff to clean motors off with."

"Oh, yes."

"You know? How?"

"I know lots of things." She pushed his hands away. "You still didn't tell me what you did to her."

He flushed, then with effort said, "I muffed her." Whatever this admission had cost him, she saw he would do anything she said now. But she waited, and as she waited, he said it. "All right, your deal. The roof over your head, not so light. But I'm not a real diver. Only to warm up. I like it front and center."

"Yes," she said. "Yes."

"No motel, I said." He thought. "We could go to the shed."

"What shed?"

"Where the company's cabs are serviced. Okay?"

"Up to you."

He got out, returned to the wheel, carefully backed and

turned around, and once more they were beneath the shading highway ramp. There were the banana boats between piers, being unloaded, and oil tankers, empty and high in the water, riding the river swell. After what seemed to Jeannette miles, they came to a sharp turnoff and entered a winding path of dust between construction sidings.

"They're still servicing us here," he explained as they came out into an abandoned customs wharf, immensely high, with a vaulted glass ceiling. "Next week, next month, they'll kick us the hell out. New York. One day one place, tomorrow another."

The place was so big it echoed and re-echoed from the laughter and talk of four workmen in white overalls gathered around a dozen taxis in various states of repair at the far end. She recognized the trademark device on the cab doors, tense now, worried by the reverberating, overhead sounds.

"Don't you worry," he reassured her, driving slowly past the cabs, waving at the mechanics. "They all know me here." He circled to the other end of the shed, into a space surrounded by shiny black oildrums stacked on their sides in rows, four or five above the cab's roof. It was not quite a cul-de-sac: at the farthest end of the drums was a row of high-set windows, looking toward the Jersey shore. Beneath the windows, burlap-wrapped bales rose almost to the level of the sills, and on the cement floor beneath were empty crushed beer cans and butts of cigarettes. "Some of the guys sleep here between shifts." He got out and opened her door.

Her hesitation was genuine, fearful. "Are you sure it'll be all right?"

"Sure. Nobody'll bother us. Even if they had any ideas about us, they'd leave us alone." He took her arm, leading her across the expanse of oil-spotted cement to the bales, then lifted her up, pushed her down, lay down beside her. Delay had sharpened his desire. "We can do anything here."

"Do what you like."

He went for her breasts, unzipping her dress halfway, at

once finding the fastening of her brassière, undoing it. "All yours," he said. "I knew they would be. Christ!" He attended to each, taking her dark, ovoid areolae into his mouth. "Lady," he said, between breaths, "if I hadn't seen for myself, I'd never believed. They're gorgeous."

She thanked him, putting her hands at the nape of his neck, stroking his black hair, holding him. His tongue lulled her into a soft, breathing silence. She could hear each breath as she drew it in, as she could hear, still, the shouts and laughter of the workmen. Then his mouth began to tire her. She said, "But this isn't all you want?"

"What's the hurry? Come up for *air!*" His face was without expression, cheeks slightly reddened in the gray daylight filtering from the expanse of dome above. He undressed to his socks and shoes and she saw he was beautifully made; he helped her with care and politeness to shed her dress, pleased by the lace, then, as part of the same movement, his tongue moved lower, began to probe. She felt herself a spectator, watching with the abstracted attention of school days, when she did not know the answer and was afraid of being called on. She was fully enjoying her fear. The rough, abrading voices around her, the oily stench, seemed invested with a sexuality she had never surmised. A drumbeat was beginning, and beyond it were the voices, hollow, still laughing. Somewhere something was dropped, its clatter on the floor an explosion of shattering sound. As long as she could watch his dark, thrusting head, feel his tongue, outstretched and phallically hard, she felt safe and invulnerable to the world of outside danger. At first she closed her eyes, avoided looking up at the dusty ceiling panes, at the row of windows, fascinated by the thrilling fear that was blossoming in her. As long as he did not stop, she could lie as she was forever. But then she sensed he was tiring, felt him bring his hands into play. With every movement and sound he was conveying to her his effort, imploring her to find her climax and finish. She saw his yarn bracelet, flattened and damp on his wrist against her thigh. The laughter of the workmen had stopped. She looked, then, at the line of river windows, saw the faces, almost silhouettes against the river light, watching. Three were gray and shadowy, the fourth featurelessly black, faces of strangers, but clearer and somehow more familiar than any faces she knew, existing in a condensed clarity. These men, overalled and grease-smeared, now seemed the very arbitrators of her life. She began to breathe heavily, turning her head toward them, as if inviting them to share the ecstasy slowly climbing in her. Suddenly the ecstasy stopped.

"Oh, don't!" she implored. "Don't stop!"

"You're holding out on me. Why?"

"I'm not, I'm not!" she cried. "I was almost there!"

He wiped his mouth with a forearm. "You're freaky," he told her. "Now it's going to be all for me." He was ready, she saw; she had been conscious that, as his tongue plunged into her, he had been preparing himself, rubbing against her legs. Disappointed, she tolerated his entry, his quick consummation, his snapping withdrawal and the silence of his disgust.

He looked around, saw the watching faces, laughed, made a wide, curving gesture of come-on. "One of *them'll* have to finish you," he said, and walked to where he had thrown his clothes, falling on them, panting, angry, through.

She was only dimly conscious of the others who followed, heard, rather than felt, as they swarmed into the passage of oil drums, mounted her, took turns, finished; it was all a listening within herself. Her dress lay beneath her, an opened sheath. Sometimes two or three were on her at once, between her thighs, straddling her face in the grudging daylight from the windows, while semen and sweat and oil from their hands smeared her belly. She cried and moaned, and whenever she could see beyond herself, had an image of men, naked or with coveralls undone, penises dangling in varying states of erection, leering, laughing, gulping beer from cans, cheering each other on. She lost all sense of time or sequence. Minutes lengthened, multiplied, became one long, remembering chain of hours in the vault above. She realized, then, that there was one more, the black, unzipping his coverall and shedding it.

"Low man on the pole," the others taunted him.

He was laughing. "What you mean, man, *low* man? Sloppy fourths sometimes is best," he said, grinning into her face. "All right, Baby, let's get with it. Don't fight it, let it come."

"I'm trying . . ."

"Keep on trying." His breath was velvet-soft and black. "That's it, Baby. Heist it. There. A little. Go with the flow."

"You're marvelous," she gasped. Her choking, panting breath became a roar in her ears, dropping from the fading daylight overhead. "Better—better than all the others—"

"—put together," he finished for her, his breath flowing and easy. "Ride it, Pinky. This is a rev-up."

She rode it, listening to his riff of instructions, answered him, her responses prayers for herself.

"Split, Baby. Like run now."

"I'm running. . . ."

"Right up there. On it. Wanna stay on it." His face became suddenly clear to her, and his soft, coaxing voice, even when she could not understand his words, assumed a paralyzing warmth. His assumption of absolute power over her deprived her entirely of identity: she could remember nothing, now hear nothing, see nothing but him. She began to know where it was, began to find it, went wild and screaming beneath him.

"Let's go!" she cried. "I'm going to make it!"

"Go!" he said, and then they made it to the cheers of the others, their laughter dying in the vault above. It spread over her like soft drums thrumming, rising from a low beat to a tattoo so fast it was like one single, thrumming beat and then, gently, slowly, the rhythm tapped back. And stopped.

422

The excitement that had begun with her walking round and round the block had come full circle. It had been all hers. She had drawn the world into her and made it her own, had been held in thrall longer than she had dreamed possible: the great enough, at last. She went, limp, into a blackness, strangely calm and unafraid.

She had a last, diminishing memory of the place, and a long hour during which she had trouble crossing in front of trucks speeding downtown, at last getting across. The terrain of skyscrapers hedged by low, old houses was unfamiliar to her. She found a corner tavern, an antiquated pub with swinging doors and opaque, frosted windows etched in elaborate designs. It was night—the bar clock had stopped, dead, at some day hour, but she knew anyway. She ordered a double vodka, drank it neat, then went into the washroom, found pills she had needed earlier, tripled them, swallowed them dry. She washed and restored herself to a semblance of recognition. The pills began to pick her up because she had chewed them. Again at the bar, she drank other doubles, to wash the chewed, dusty taste from her throat. The bartender was kind, saw and understood her shattered state, helped her get under way when she could. It was past four in the morning when she found a taxi, reached the apartment.

She staggered in. "David? Duvidl! Where are you, Duvidl? *Answer me!*"

The rooms were empty. There was a half-emptied bottle of champagne on the table. She drank that, though it was flat, though she did not want it, drank it because she must. Then she saw that there were two glasses, that one stood in a wet ring. Sweepingly, she picked up the tray and dropped it to the floor, flung the offending glass out the window. It was easy, then, to go into David's room, the sanctum she hated. *His privacy!* Which was the reason for the way she had killed her day, her night. She opened desk drawers and files, pulling out their contents and hurling them at the walls. With effort

423

she lifted the old Remington, neatly covered, and crashed it down beside the desk. By the time she had finished, the place was a shambles, and that was the way she wanted it. Two, she exulted, could be punished as well as one. That was when the tears came, and with them, the slow opening of the door.

"Nettie! My God! What's happened? Where have you been?" David raised her up from where she had fallen, holding her to him.

"Oh, Duvidl." She wept. "Duvidl. What's going to happen to us?"

"Why did you do this?" His voice was tired.

"I saw the two glasses. Someone was here. You had someone here!"

"Yes. Faye was here."

"And you slept with her."

"Yes, I slept with her."

"Here? In my bed?"

"No, not here."

She began to tremble, her teeth chattering. "That's the way it goes, I suppose."

"Yes, that's the way it goes."

"I hate you and I love you."

"Yes. You'd better get to bed now."

"Yes. Help me."

He supported her to the bedroom, undressed her as though she were a child. "You're bruised—you've been beaten!"

She sat on the bed, arms crossed over her breasts, staring at the floor. "Don't look at me. Get me something to sleep. The yellow ones, in the cabinet."

He found the bottle, handed it to her.

"Only four," she said. "I wish the bottle were full."

He brought her the water she needed to swallow. "You'll be all right now," he said soothingly, drawing back the sheet, lifting her feet onto the bed, tenderly, lightly, laying the sheet over her.

424

"I won't be all right, ever. You know it. I know it."

"Sleep," he said, "soon you'll sleep."

"*Sleep?*" she repeated after him. "What's sleep? I haven't really slept in years." She coughed.

"Shall I get a doctor?"

"No, I'm my own doctor. I . . . I . . . I . . . I— There were so many of them, I—"

"Don't talk," he said. "Don't tell me. You don't have to tell me anything."

"But I—I *must* tell. I *want* to tell. If only I couldn't remember. I . . . I . . . I . . ."

"You'll forget," he said, going to his own bed.

She began to babble, but between her coughing and repeating there were long, lucid, terrible phrases, and reaching for his bedside pad, he mechanically took down every syllable she uttered. There were pages and pages. Then the babbling increased and overtook her muttered coherences and he knew that she was about to go under the heavy medication she had taken. He continued to write for a long time, until he had exhausted the pages on the pad, but what he wrote was not at all like what he had begun; it was new, neither about Jeannette nor Faye, but the woman he knew would wake him in the morning and goad him, relentlessly, past the sleeping figure beside him and to the center of his secret world, his desk. A persona, a character: his book.

❦ ❦ ❦ THE STAMFORD taximan had driven Anson before, and if he wondered today why he had not waited for the "Bug" connection, but had chosen to be hurried to the parking lot, he made no comment and Anson made none, riding the entire distance in silence. The Porsche's motor was wet and took a moment to start. He was glad he had taken the train that left an hour before his usual one, had saved the hour he would have spent waiting for the "Bug"; he was in no mood to see or talk to the Ridge regulars. He needed to see Faye and Todd; their lovely, familiar names, soft on his tongue, guided him to the image of himself: home, love, continuity. He was fairly sure he knew what lay ahead, when he would walk into the house, and wanted to face it quietly and freshly, in his own way.

The glare of sun was in his eyes and he put on his dark glasses. He seemed to see everything with new clarity, felt a strong awareness of the zones through which he had to drive before reaching his house. He knew each of the houses in a sloping curve of the Ridge, below the road, though he didn't know the people living in them. There was the train crossing, with its old-fashioned, swinging warning bell, which Martha Lavrorsen had been agitating for years to get rid of and replace with an underpass. There was the fine, old salt-box, the oldest house in the village, spoiled by gray asbestos shingling and aluminum storm windows, hermetically sealed winter and summer. And the road stand that sold gas and, in summer, vegetables and flowers; its stand was loaded with red and white peonies in bunches; the fat woman who ran it was at the pumps as he passed, jamming the gas hose into a tank. The metamorphosis from country split-levels to the rigidly zoned section where he and the Curries and "The Assortment" lived came suddenly, after the second turn beyond the road stand. Then the three shining pyramids of his house rose into view. He noticed at once that the mobile on the tallest gable stood motionless in evening quiet—there was no wind, not a sign of breeze—and that the doors of the garage were closed.

He drew into the drive and got out. The front door was open, and through the screen he heard a voice, at once

426

recognizing it as Velma's. She was talking to Netcher in a cajoling, impatient way, the way people alone with a dog talk to it, posing questions and then answering them.

"Come, now, Netcher," she coaxed. "Time now to go out. You want to go out, don't you? Of course you do. Oh, why won't you go? You *need* to go—you haven't been out since morning! No out-and-in, no din-din." *Out-and-in, din-din,* Faye's shorthand for the dog; it sounded odd transposed into Velma's voice. Hearing him, she stopped talking, saw Anson open the screen.

"Anson!"

"Hello, Velma." He walked into the hallway, sensing at once the absence of warmth of the presences he had hurried to return to. "Where's Faye?"

"Isn't she with you?"

"Would I ask if she were?"

As though not believing him, Velma went past him and looked out. Netcher was trembling and making a noise of squealing desperation. She came to Anson and nuzzled his hand and barked.

"Anson, I'm so relieved you're back. Not that Sam and I've *minded* looking after Netcher, but don't tell me dogs aren't as neurotic as people. She'll hardly leave the house, in fact, I wouldn't be surprised if she'd contained the whole time. And she's not touched her food, though I gave her what she always has. I can tell you one thing, you'll never have to worry about this house being burgled—whenever I come up the walk she barks the place down. I have to ease in slowly, until she's sure it's me. Now you're here, she'll go right away."

Anson swung the screen open. Netcher, still trembling, lowered her haunches in the path; her need had been desperate, evidently; she was perfectly trained and normally waited until she crossed to the field.

"Dogs," said Velma. "Worse than children."

427

"Velma, where *is* Faye?" He spoke quietly, aware he was a man found wanting in her Freudian eyes, remembering what she had said to him when last they were alone.

"But weren't you together in town? The one time Faye called me, she said—no, she did not *say*—" Velma, ever truthful, reducing truth to minimum content, revised as she talked. "She did not *say* she was with you, but implied it."

"I'm alone," Anson said. He began to walk through the empty rooms, seeing Todd's rumpled bed, Faye's bed unslept in, his own made up with spread and bolsters days ago. "When did she go?"

Velma told him. "When she telephoned, well, as I said, the implication was she was with you. I never thought to worry."

"And now you are worried?"

"Well, aren't you? Anson, I can't—*we* can't go on pretending. She went into the city to find you. I've been keeping Todd, and Sam and I have come over three times a day to let Netcher in and out and feed her. *I* don't know what this is. Unless you'd care to tell me?"

"I don't know either, really."

"You don't know anything, do you?"

Anson said nothing.

"I always think you do or you don't, Anson."

Netcher was back and scratched at the screen. Absently, Velma let her in, then looked at her watch. "I walked over. My exercise for the day. Quite a day it was, too. Perhaps you'll drive me home?"

"Of course. Todd all right?"

She sighed. "All right-confused, as why wouldn't he be? Children have intense emotions, you know. He wonders what's the matter as much as I do. He asked about you only once, after Faye's call. I told him you were on a deal in New York. He just looked at me with those eyes."

"And?"

"I'll tell you the rest in the car." She went out and climbed into the Porsche, Anson following.

428

"I can guess from your face there was trouble," he said as they got under way.

"Anson, you've got to do something about that child," said Velma, looking straight ahead. "I know how little you relish being told how to bring up your son, but this time I won't mince words. He needs you. You to talk to. You to talk to him. Needs to be touched and loved. You ask me if there was *trouble?*"

"What was it this time, the same as before?"

"No, everything seems all right in that department. Touch wood. This was much more serious. You should be told. You know about the two salamanders?"

Anson nodded, eyes on the road.

"There was the dead one in foil, and the live one in the glass jar. Todd brought his entire menagerie with him. The dead salamander began to stink, and I thought, Let him bury it, it might be some symbolic realization he was trying to work out. He and Roger did bury it. That was normal enough, kids love burying animals. But it was this other thing, with the second salamander, the replacement salamander, so to call it. It was in the jar, very lively, but wanted to get away. I suggested mildly that Todd let it go, but he said it would dry up and die if he let it loose. He kept the glass jar on the porch."

"The lid on it?"

"I think so. Or on and off. I'd had a busy day, I'd delegated responsibility to Roger— they're getting along better than they used to, thank goodness—and perhaps wasn't paying too much attention. Then Roger came in without Todd. He looked white around the gills. I asked what on earth was the matter. At first all he would say was that he'd seen blood and felt sick. It took me a while to get the story from both of them, but I got it—saw it, too, which was horrible. Todd had taken the live salamander to the back fence—you know, the split-rail we put up last year—and while Roger held it, Todd pounded a nail through it so it

429

couldn't get away. Todd then proceeded to cut it up with a razor blade. Part by part, and enjoying every minute of it, according to my Roger. He laughed while he was doing it, Roger says, and then he brought the whole mess inside in his hands, to show me. The salamander's head was still living, the way they do, apparently. But its little feet and tail! I tried, without scolding, to explain to them what they did. Roger cried and said he was sorry, but Todd said nothing, only looked at me with those eyes of his. Those eloquent eyes. You know them."

"Yes, I know them."

"Well, that was this morning."

"And that's all of it?"

"How much more do you want? This is bad, Anson."

"Yes, I know it is. I never suspected Todd of cruelty; Faye and I have always been so careful that he should learn kindness. What I can't understand is, what does his doing that mean?"

"It means he loves you as a prisoner loves his jailer. He's a child, loving more intensely than he ever will again. He wants to get *out*."

"Out of the chrysalis of childhood, yes; you've told us that."

"But you're giving him nowhere to go, Anson. Here we are. From now on, it's your problem. I never had such difficulties with Roger. Todd maneuvered him into this thing, and I can tell you I didn't like it one bit."

"But you said Roger held the salamander."

"Todd's influence, that's very clear."

Roger and Todd were on the porch.

"Daddy!" Todd cried, running forward. "Daddy, Daddy, Daddy!"

Anson lifted him up and kissed him, almost asking if he'd been good, then remembering.

"Get your pajamas and toothbrushes," Velma cued.

"Roger, you go with Todd and make sure he doesn't forget anything."

"We found a new salamander down by Todd's stream," Roger said. "A great big one, this time."

Velma shuddered. When they were alone again, she said, "If Faye doesn't come back tonight, what will you do, Anson? Of course, I'll take Toddy again tomorrow—"

"I'm taking tomorrow off. You won't have to worry."

"But *you* worry, Anson. Todd *needs* to be with you. Perhaps it's a good thing you'll have him to yourself for a little. During the time he was here, he kept gravitating to Sam, when Sam was home. Sam's good with kids, but of course then Roger became jealous. I had that too."

"Velma, I appreciate everything you've done."

"Todd's had his supper."

"Thanks for that as well."

"Let me know about everything." Velma put a hand on his arm. He saw how much the incident had upset her. "Don't hold it against me, what I said to you the other night about Borobudur."

"I did go."

This seemed to upset her even more. "Well, other people's lives. I said my Spanish prayers for you and Faye, Anson, because Sam and I love you, you know. Love you all three."

Todd and Roger came out of the house, Todd with his pajama bundle under one arm, glass jar under the other. Roger carried the turtles.

"Thank for your visit," Anson prompted.

Todd nicely thanked and got into the car, setting his jar carefully down on the floor between his feet. Anson saw that, as Roger had said, there was a new salamander, larger, livelier than the others. Velma had a last word with Anson.

"Todd will be staying with Roger during your Saturday party. Roger's a little old to be sat, but not quite old enough to sit Todd. So I'll have Libby Draper if my own girls have dates."

"Yah, Libby Draper!" said Todd and Roger. "Do we hate *her!*"

"Why didn't Mommy come to get me?" Todd at once demanded when they had left.

"Because she hasn't come back yet."

"From where? Town?"

"Yes, town."

"Why?"

"I suppose she took a late train."

"Why?"

"I don't know. We'll ask when she gets here."

"Why didn't she come back with you?"

"Probably she had last-minute things to do."

For the moment Todd seemed satisfied, and as soon as they were back in the house, Anson put his mind to the problem. Todd was functioning like clockwork—that was what was so terrifying—placing his Broxodent brushes in the rack, using his Water Pik without being reminded, transporting his glass jar to the terrace, lifting the lid to one side, securing a screening to its neck with a string for ventilation.

"We're going to have a talk," Anson said, sitting down in one of the terrace chairs. He drew Todd to him, putting his arms around him.

"What about?"

"You."

"She told you. Mrs. Currie."

"Told me something, yes."

"It was supposed to be secret."

"What was?"

"What we did."

"You and Roger?"

"It really wasn't Roger. I did it all by myself. *He* only helped."

"How did he help?"

Todd evaded this. "He chickened and went and told."

"Maybe you'd better tell me what happened yourself."

"I just killed it," he said, eyes lowered. "He was going to die anyway."

"Why did you think he was going to die?"

Todd considered. "Well, they always do die. Anything I find and want to keep dies."

"Perhaps if you didn't keep them in the jar they'd live."

"But if I didn't keep them in the jar they'd get away."

"It might be best to let them go free. Haven't you ever thought of that?"

"No," Todd answered without hesitation. "Why would I catch them and want to keep them if I wanted to let them go?"

"You killed the salamander because you thought that was a way of keeping him."

Todd nodded. "Roger held him while I nailed him down and then I cut him into pieces."

"That was cruel. I thought you liked the salamander."

"I did, but I liked cutting him up better. He bled. Not like people bleed, different. His blood was watery, shiny, sort of. You know, like his color. You could see through it. It was thin."

"And you weren't sorry?"

"I—I don't know."

"Why did you take it into the house and show it to Mrs. Currie?"

Todd blocked on this.

"Because you wanted to scare her?" Anson prompted.

"No. Because she hates me and I hate her."

"She doesn't hate you. You're not supposed to hate."

Todd's lower lip protruded. "I hate her because—that day—when I had to go to the bathroom she followed me and undressed me and made me get under the shower."

"Well, in the circumstances, that was necessary, don't you agree?"

"I hate her. She treated me like a girl."

Something had uncovered itself, Anson sensed: Todd, relaxed now, in the crook of his arm, leaned against him. He waited a moment before he said, "Look. We can't do anything about the dead salamander, *salamanders,* the ones that are dead. But I want you to come with me. Get your glass jar and we'll go down to the stream where you found the new one and we'll put him back."

"I don't remember the exact place."

"But near enough. Come on."

"Why?"

"Because then he won't die like the others."

"You mean," answered Todd with insight, "that then I won't kill him and cut him up."

"Yes, I mean that."

Todd said, "Daddy, where's Mommy?"

"I told you, in town."

"Why do you go away so much? Don't you love her?"

"I love her more than anything in the world."

"More than you love me?"

"I love you both the same. We were talking about the salamander. Mommy'll probably be back by the time we've set him free. Let's go down to the stream while there's still light."

Todd hesitated a last moment, then fetched the glass jar. Together they walked along the road to the fence where a path led to the stream on the protective acres Anson had bought.

"I found him about here," Todd said.

"Take him out of the jar."

Todd removed the screen, reached in and brought out the salamander, vigorously wiggling, redly translucent in the last sunlight.

"He was here, in the mud."

434

"Put him back in the mud," Anson said.

Todd dug a shallow trench with his free hand and laid the salamander in it. The salamander immediately burrowed down and disappeared. "I'll miss him," he said.

"Yes. Give me your hand."

"It's muddy."

"It doesn't matter." Anson reached down and grasped Todd's hand. "Aren't you glad you let him go?"

"Yes. No. I don't know. Maybe."

"You won't have to worry about his dying now."

They retraced their steps on the path and reached the house just as dark was falling.

"Bed, now," Anson said. "Did you have your bath at the Curries'?"

"Yes, before supper. Shall I put on clean piggies?"

"Yes, better had." Anson remade Todd's bed. The night was hot and he folded the single blanket at the bottom, smoothed the sheet beneath Todd's chin.

Todd yawned, exhausted by his day. "Daddy," he said, "I'm glad you're home. I miss you so when you're gone."

Anson kissed him, seeing again the wide, questioning eyes as he drew back. "Sleep tight, be my good little boy."

"I hurt," Todd said, his voice already blurred with sleep. "Hurt? Where?"

"Here." He touched himself between his heart and stomach. "It aches and I can feel it."

Nothing he knew instructed Anson in what to do. He reached out a hand and stroked the soft blond head, so like his own. "You're growing," he said.

"But I can feel it."

"It will go away." Todd, already asleep, half smiled. Anson turned out the light, leaving the bedroom door slightly ajar. The salamander burned behind his retinas, a double, taunting mystery. I wonder, he thought, if I did that right.

This time it was he who consulted the reference shelf.

Taking down *The Shorter Oxford English Dictionary,* which had never yet failed him, he found out a great deal he did not know about "Salamander ME. [a. F. *salamandre,* ad. L. *salamandra,* a. Gr. σαλαμάνδρα.] . . . **c.** S. (*Her.*), an emblem of constancy, is represented in flames . . ."

The night crept quietly across the lawns, drawing in from under the trees, snuffed out and took away the colors of day, slowly stole silver from the pebbles of the drive. The garden stood dark, despoiled with emptiness. Lest the shadows steal him too, he broke ice from trays, stirred himself his dusty martini, passing the vermouth ritually above the pitcher, chilling the glass, and sat down to think where he might be, track back to the world he had left only long hours, short days ago. He had lost this world, found another, lost that, returned. He was on his second drink when he heard the station-wagon tires on the gravel, heard the garage door electronically fly up and the wagon move inside and stop. There was a silence then, as though Faye had seen the Porsche and was hesitating about coming into the house. Then the door opened. He sat, watching her over his glass, seeing her new and fresh, her dark hair a little rumpled, her face quiet and unsmiling.

She looked at him a long time before she spoke. She spoke bitterly. "A long way to go—to find you here."

"Darling," Anson said.

She ignored his reaching hands, walked past him to Todd's room, went inside, came back, closing the door behind her. "You have your nerve," she said. "Don't 'darling' me!"

"All right, I won't 'darling' you. Aren't you going to ask where I've been?"

"I'm not going to ask you anything. I'm tired."

"Tired? But you're never tired!"

"I am tonight." She went into the bedroom. He could hear her as she took things from her bag, went into the bath, showered. He wasn't hungry and saw no reason not to have

436

another while he waited for her to come back. When she came, her hair was tied up in the ribbon she always wore to bed.

"I said I wasn't going to ask you anything—but one question: How was Toddy when you went to get him?"

"Himself."

"Meaning?"

"There was what Velma calls trouble. You don't want to hear it."

"I asked how he was."

"All right." He told her the story as he had had it from Velma, as he had further clarified it with Todd afterward. He told her, with his usual, sharpened, martini exactness of words, of returning the new salamander to the stream.

"My God!" she said. "Salamanders!"

"I think I did it right, Faye."

"What makes you think so?"

He shrugged, watching her. "I simply have the feeling I did it right. That's all."

She sat down slowly. "That's not a suit you've worn this summer."

"I changed at the office. At '53,' rather."

"After you went to Borobudur?"

He waited before he answered. "I have been," he said.

"And were gone long enough, God knows!"

"Yes."

She waited. "Are you going to tell me about it?"

"No. Or not tonight." He watched her face intently. "No post-mortems. Capsules only."

"You think if you don't tell me now it'll be different when you do?"

"No," he said again, "it'll not be different. And I'll tell you another time, as much of it as you want to hear. But I can give you the capsule version now: I found the center of my myth."

"What?"

"I played my own game within myself. I can't tell you anything more tonight."

"What's different about tonight?"

"I'm tired too."

"You don't look it."

"But I am. I'm dead on my feet. I only held up until you got back."

"What made you so sure I'd come back?"

"The thing that made you know I would, I suppose."

"Whatever that might be," she said.

"I'm going to have one more. Want one?"

"No. I've had dinner."

"I haven't and don't want any."

"Then why drink any more?"

"Now I know I'm home. I'm going to drink my next."

She got up. "Well, *I'm* not going to sit here and watch you get plastered!"

"I won't get plastered."

"Just stinking. You haven't asked one single word about me."

"All right, one word. You're okay?"

"That's two words, which seem hardly enough."

"You look fine, wonderful! I've never seen you look so wonderful!"

"I'm not wonderful. Are you? After that salamander story?"

"I think we've had the end of that."

"You think. It may well only be the beginning."

"Of what?"

"Of what you've done to him. All that horrible cruelty is because of you, Anson. Your work, not mine."

"Now, wait a minute! He's with you far more than he is with me."

"He'd be with you more if you'd come home as any father should!"

438

"I told you on the phone, I was on a deal."

"Selling Buddhas in Borobudur? Or buying them? That call was Friday, before you left me sitting here for days, imagining I don't know what!"

"And then *you* left him—to Velma. That's where it happened."

"I'd never have gone if you'd been here. You don't ask about me because you think you know."

"I don't think I know. I want to know, but not tonight."

"What is there about *tonight?*"

"I came back to you. You came back to me."

"You think it's as easy as that!"

"It's not easy at all. But we're together. Here."

"The *here's* right, not the *together*. If this is a prelude—"

"We could stop this and go to bed."

"And take it from there? *Oh,* no!" She laughed. "You're not going to lay a hand on *me!*"

"All right, I won't. I won't touch you."

"You're right about that!"

"There's tomorrow. I'm going to be home all day."

"I suppose I'm to be grateful for that."

"I'm grateful for it—and for you."

"I think I'll just plain go to bed," she said.

"You couldn't wait for me?"

"Why should I?"

"You could kiss me good night."

She stood in front of him, eyes blazing, watching his face. She laughed again, unpleasantly, a sound unlike her usual laughter, as though laughing privately, for herself. "It may be too late for that, Anson. *You!* Asking *me* to kiss *you* good night! After where you've been!"

"How do you know where I've been? Just kiss me. Please?"

She saw the pleading in his eyes and pity for what he was feeling, however little she understood it, flooded through her, but she stood where she was, unmoving.

"It would mean everything to me," he said.

"I can't. I'm not sure what you're trying to say to me, or what this is, but no."

He stared into her eyes. "I know what it is. My fox lily. You've foxed me!"

"Yes," she said.

"You've been with someone else!"

"Yes."

He turned his face away, suddenly blank and sad. "And I thought you'd saved me."

"You're drunk."

"Not very."

"Drink some milk and go to bed."

"Too much effort, the milk. But I'll go to bed. Now. Before I drop." He walked to the bedroom, straight and careful and light on his feet, and she followed, turning out the lights. She watched him undress with his usual precision and care, hanging up his shirt, folding his trousers over the back of this chair, putting his signet ring and watch noiselessly down on the bedside table.

"Your knees!" she said, seeing the abrasions, reddish pink, beginning to scab, the yellow bruise beneath the caps. "Did you fall?"

"La Chute," he said, and laughed.

"It's not funny."

"Don't worry, Fowler fixed them."

"Fowler?"

"Fowler at '53.' "

"Oh, yes."

That was his good night. He fell forward, face down. He had not lied, he was beyond tired, asleep even before his head touched the pillow. And he had not lied about something else: he had held up until she returned—for whatever it was worth. She looked at his smooth, broad back, abstractly relaxed, and clean, and wondered what squalors Fowler had massaged away, along with his attention to knees. Always he returned to her, clean and groomed like this, and for that she was grateful. Leaning down, she kissed the nape of his neck, then went to her own bed.

Now she was alone. She lay awake a long time in the darkness, listening to Todd's light breathing, laced with Anson's heavier breath, but her time alone was not having its customary relaxing effect, for it was during this time that she usually prepared herself for acceptance of anything Anson had done, and forgiving him for it. Almost she had forgiven him, as she had already forgiven herself, realized she had looked forward to the moment of forgiveness. But something had restrained her from doing as he had asked. Forgiveness, she reflected, is not unlike an act of contrition; there are limits to the number of times it can be invoked; like a drug too often administered, tolerance to it becomes established, its efficacy lost. Then she thought how it would have been if she had come into the house and found it empty, and was grateful, no matter where Anson had been, or why, no matter what he had done, was, simply, grateful that he was beside her. Perhaps, she mused, as she dropped into sleep, forgiveness is a coin: two-sided; or, better, like the inconstant moon, one side bright, the other dark. . . .

🌼 🌼 🌼 ANSON SLEPT with the complacence of the dead while Faye got up and opened the house, let Netcher in and out, began the day. He had not snored, even once; she thought he would at least wake partly or turn over when Todd came into the room, but he slept blissfully on. She gave herself entirely to Todd during his breakfast in the kitchen. Anson's recounting of the salamander story had horrified her; she had a gnawing curiosity to know more about it, yet dreaded knowing; but she dreaded even more not being able to discuss the incident if Velma brought it up, and Faye knew she would. Todd seemed unusually relaxed, seemed to have taken his stay at the Curries' as par for the course.

"What did you do in town, Mommy?"

"Shopped. I bought you a sweater."

"A sweater! But it's too hot."

"You'll need it in the cooler weather. You're outgrowing all your others."

"Why did you go away at night?"

"It seemed easier to drive in than take the morning train."

Todd accepted this, with reservation. "What else did you buy?"

"Something new to wear at Saturday's party."

"Oh." Disinterest. He ate his cereal and drank his milk without urging, but he was watching her every move. "I have to go back and stay with Roger while you give the party. I heard his mother say so."

"You've stayed with Roger during parties before."

Pause.

"Was Daddy with you in town?"

"Of course."

"Then why didn't you come back together?"

"He had to pick up the Porsche and I drove back in the wagon."

The documentation of the two cars, their reunion in the garage, seemed to satisfy him. It came out about the salamander, then, without Faye's having to probe. "Did Daddy tell you what I did?"

"Yes. And I'm ashamed for you."

"Why? Daddy and I let the big salamander go, down by the stream."

"I mean the one you killed. Aren't you the least bit sorry?"

442

"He—" Todd considered. *"Now* I am, a little. But not while I cut him up. I did it all by myself."

"It was nothing to be proud of."

"But *I* did it, *not* Roger." He looked at her with the somewhat sly satisfaction of one who still keeps a secret. He went out on the terrace to play. Faye, after rinsing dishes, poured herself a second cup of coffee and returned to bed to savor it.

She thought of the sex she had had with David. Sex was, after all, evidently, one of the few things not guessable about anybody. She experienced a shudder of pleasure as she remembered how warmly he had dedicated himself to her need and fulfillment; he had rekindled in her the first excitement of Baumgartner, though he was older than anyone she had ever slept with. She went round and round the mulberry bush of the hours she had spent with him, listening, with new placidity, to Anson's deep, steady breathing.

It would have seemed more normal to be in an emotional turmoil about it, feel guilty; but she could find no guilt to summon up. Perhaps, she thought, this was the way Anson felt after he had slept with someone else. Nothing, no guilt, simplest of remembrances; perhaps, in his headlong rush to devour life and the next thing, not even that. But whatever he felt or failed to feel she could never really know. Not knowing about him seemed to cancel out his knowing about her. But not his *caring.* He had picked it up right away: *My fox lily. You've foxed me.* And she had confirmed it. *Yes.* Fox lily, feathery and bright. Foxglove. Fox-fire. *Go ye, and tell that fox, Behold, I cast out devils.* Luke, chapter and verse unremembered. Madame Doheny, explaining Herod, an authority on Herod, but never explaining *my place down there.* Anson knew about her in the way she always knew about him. She addressed herself, now, in the tone she had learned from Madame Doheny at the convent, Jesuitical, strict, the method by which, in adolescence, when she was a believer, she prepared the words she would recite in the confessional, rigidly edited for truth, to save the Father's time. And no sooner had she relived the time with David than she felt purged, but reminded herself that she must maintain the experience as a collateral against Anson.

The telephone rang. She picked it up quickly, in the middle of the first ring, answering almost in a whisper. It was Martha Lavrorsen.

"Well, I guess you've heard?" Martha demanded somewhat loudly.

"Heard what?"

"They've killed Bobby Kennedy. Right after midnight."

"Oh, no!"

"Oh, yes!"

"But why? Where?"

"Don't ask me why. At some Christ-awful hotel called the Ambassador in Los Angeles." Martha had no patience with any place west of the Eastern Shore. "Stig was staying in town at the club and he called me right after the news came through. I was dead asleep. 'Well, they got him,' he said. 'Got who?' I thought maybe he meant the President. This is such a country for assassinations. But it was only Bobby Kennedy."

"What do you mean, *only?*"

"Well, it's not as bad as the President, I suppose, though God knows, if they could get *him,* Fairfield would be the happiest county in the nation."

Faye felt her hand cold on the phone. "But it's horrible! *I loved* Bobby Kennedy!"

"Well, they got him."

"Is he really dead?"

"Not yet, but he soon will be. The newscasters are preparing us for a big rehash of 1963, you know, the way they weight everything. One bullet grazed the forehead, but another they've just taken from his cerebellum. Cerebellum, *get that!* Even if he should live, he'd be an idiot."

"Oh, Martha!"

444

"The Kennedys were never my dish of tea, as you know. They're such micks! And he did rather ask for it, the way Martin Luther King did. Shaking all those hands. I simply *had* to have a drink after Stig told me. But it wasn't Scotch, you can bet, because they say the Kennedys get a dollar on every bottle comes into the country. Vodka. No wonder they're rich. The old man *bought* JFK those marginal hundred and nineteen thousand votes, just as he bought the ambassadorship to London. Was *that* a tacky bit! I was there. I *know*. Read Chips Channon on it. You know, Faye, there are times like this I *love* the American people. In the end, they can't be bought—not with Kennedy Scotch dollars—"

"Martha," Faye interrupted, "do they know who did it?"

"Some Arab kid."

"An *Arab?*"

"Sirhan something. I watched and listened all night."

"And went on with the vodka."

"And dozed. It's all on TV right now, the re-run of films on it."

"You mean there are *films* of it?"

"They did less well with this than with Oswald. Not the actual shooting, no, but everything else. Sometimes America disappoints me. The land of the painfully rehearsed happening, represented as quote live unquote, cut and edited for public consumption. And then they fall down on the *real* live part like this, the shooting itself!"

"Martha, how can you?"

"I wish you'd come on over. Bring Todd. We can watch together."

"I'm going to keep as much of this away from Todd as I can," Faye said, remembering the grim, seemingly endless TV coverage on JFK in 1963. "Besides, Anson's home today."

"Oh, well. I wish I had someone who'd lay *me*. I called you on Sunday. No, Monday—or maybe it was yesterday."

445

"Anson and I were both in town."

"But you canceled with me Friday!"

"Later I decided to go."

"*Hm,*" said Martha. Faye could hear the ice clinking in the glass at the other end of the wire.

"Martha, I'm still in bed, and Anson's sleeping."

"We'll talk again." Martha hung up with a bang.

Anson had slept, undisturbed, through the conversation. Faye at first thought of waking him, then decided against it; the mood he had gone to bed in precluded anything but letting him sleep himself out. She got up, drew the curtains, and switched off the bell of the phone before she closed the door of the bedroom after her. This was as well, because the phone rang again almost immediately. Faye took it on the kitchen extension.

"Faye, it's Rose. Isn't it awful?"

"Yes, it's awful."

"What are you going to do?"

"What can anyone do?"

"I'm simply going out of my mind with the kids. Libby studied late and turned on her radio and heard it before she went to bed. She woke Sherm and me to tell us. The others are all soaking it up on TV. They look a while and then come and ask me to explain how it could happen. How does one explain?"

"I haven't had to talk to Todd about it. He doesn't know yet."

"Know what?" Todd asked, suddenly appearing in the doorway.

"It's going to be a nice day," Rose Draper said, "hot but nice, and I'd planned to pack a lunch and drive us all somewhere for a picnic. I'm still going to, to get away from this until it's over."

"You mean, until he dies?"

"I suppose I mean that. Anyway, would you like to come?

That way, you could keep Todd away from it, for a while, anyway."

Faye looked at Todd. There was no keeping him from it, eventually, but it would be good if he could be away from the house for other reasons too. "I think it's a fine idea," she said; "if you'll take Todd without me. Anson's home."

"What's one more to me?" Rose agreed.

"I'll make his sandwiches and get him ready. In an hour? Good."

"Get me ready for what?" Todd asked when Faye had hung up. "Who's going to die?"

Faye wanted to do it right, but found herself speaking in her mother's voice. "Someone shot Mr. Kennedy. They're afraid he's going to die."

"The President?"

"Mr. Kennedy's not the President. Mr. Johnson's the President."

"I thought Mr. Kennedy was the President they shot. Roger says they shot him in Texas and he died. How could he die again?"

She remembered her mother trying to explain to her about her father's going away to war, and what war is, her total incomprehension. "The Mr. Kennedy who was shot today is the brother of President Kennedy."

Todd's forehead was furrowed. "Is he different from the colored man they shot, Mr. King?"

"Yes. But we don't say 'colored,' we say 'black.' " It seemed wisest to let comprehension take a slow course. "Mrs. Draper's having a picnic, and I said you'd like to go. You would, wouldn't you?"

"If old *Libby* isn't going," Todd qualified.

"Libby's in school. What have you got against Libby?"

"I'd like to cut her into pieces," Todd said.

"Hush!" Faye scolded him as the phone rang; it was easier to forget what he had said, answer before he could say more.

447

Hugging the phone to her ear with her left shoulder, she said into the transmitter, "Yes, Grace, I know."

"Know?" Grace Burgess' voice seemed surprised. "Oh, about Kennedy. Yes, frightful, isn't it?" She hadn't called about that, but to ask if she and Chet could bring their weekend guests along to the Saturday party. "They're people we met at a medical convention Chet and I attended, and I'm afraid they're rather crosses. Say no if you like."

"Of course, bring them," Faye answered, her thoughts going back to what Velma had told her about herself and Chet Burgess. Perhaps Grace was as dry and acerbic as she was because of that affair, perhaps because of others as well.

"As for the Kennedy thing," said Grace, "America's always had carpetbaggers in one form or another. When Chet heard about it at breakfast, all he said was, 'Well, three down and one to go.' He never lets anything upset him the days he operates."

"I'm making the kind of sandwiches you like," Faye told Todd at the end of Grace Burgess' call. "Peanut butter and jelly. Now go and put on your white shirt and shorts. And try to be quiet." He went out as the phone rang again. It was Amy Nowells, this time, wondering if Faye and Anson planned to go ahead with the party in view of the tragedy.

"I hadn't thought not to," Faye answered. "It's a tragedy, Amy, but he hasn't died yet. He just may live."

"Herb says it's a million to one against it. Herb's glued to the set. Well, we do always seem to shoot the wrong man."

Faye was glad that Rose Draper arrived a little early, her old, creaking station wagon crammed with kids. "They're already playing 'Shoot Kennedy,' " she reported; "I guess it's as good a way as any for them to realize it, don't you?" Her lined face looked tired. "I'm afraid he's about done for. Have you heard the latest?"

"I haven't been watching," Faye said.

"Even if he dies, that'll not be the end of it. You know

448

America, you know the Kennedys. It'll be a bigger show than last time."

The ringing phone spaced out the morning. Faye thought how wonderful it would be to be able to anesthetize oneself at such times, until they were over. She slowly walked to the television: there was no escaping. She switched from station to station. The news was the same, careful bulletins, which all meant there was little hope. The set had developed a low, almost inaudible hum, as it did on hot, sunny days, and now the sun outside and the hum seemed one hypnotic blur. Cutting off the set, she went out to the terrace.

It was strangely silent, so still she could hear the mobile twittering on the gable. There was never much traffic on the road, but now it seemed to have stopped entirely. She thought of Ethel Kennedy, pregnant with her eleventh child, of the other Kennedy children, being apprised, again, of tragedy. She thought of poor Martha Lavrorsen, still alone, probably, drunk and disorderly by herself, pouring out her glasses of hatred. She thought of how Bobby Kennedy must look now, in Good Samaritan Hospital, operating surgeons and phalanxes of nurses around him, all unexpectedly touching this precariously poised life that had reached out to touch theirs. The suffocating protocols of public death, already being set in motion. One still photograph, repeatedly shown on the screen, Kennedy sprawled on the hotel kitchen floor, arms and legs extended, his face whitened by the halation of flashbulbs—half a crucifixion. That he had asked them not to move him was, to her, the most poignant thing; despite her almost inflexible resistance to her mother, she felt an impulse to pray, tell beads in the way she had been taught, though rosaries had disappeared from her life long ago. For a moment she implored a spurious comfort, thinking of the saints to whom once she would have appealed, the wealth of comfort the Church deployed. Her eyes filled with tears. The television, which she had turned off in revulsion, now again

449

beckoned, a blasphemous altar before which she seemed compelled to sit. She went back into the house, again watched the widening images of confusion and repetition, only dimly aware that the phone was persistently ringing. 'Gertrude' or 'Alice'? Velma? Twice she let it ring itself out, then heard the opening of the bedroom door and Anson's voice.

"What's happened?" he asked, coming into the living room. "I've been aware as I woke up there's something going on. I answered the phone, but whoever it was had hung up."

"Yes, it's been ringing all morning," she said, and told him what had happened. "Martha, Rose, Amy, they've all called to tell us. And Grace, who couldn't care less."

"Don't tell me about her. Tell me about Bobby Kennedy!"

She repeated, patiently, what she knew. "That's all there is."

"But why didn't you wake me?"

"It wouldn't have made any difference. Todd's with Rose Draper and the kids. On a picnic, to keep them away from TV."

Anson stared at the screen, rubbed his eyes, then sat down beside her. "Poor bastard!" He had put on clean pajamas, having slept in nothing, creases still sharp, smelling freshly of sun. He leaned toward her. "Kennedy notwithstanding, can I kiss you good morning?"

"No, let's not." She turned her face away.

"All right," he said, hurt. "But I think the no post-mortem last night was right, don't you? I gave you the capsule."

"If you remember it," she said, not looking at him. "Do you?"

"Of course. I remember everything."

"You slept the clock around."

"I needed to, as you saw. I'm starving."

She got up dutifully. "I'll make anything you like."

450

"Coffee first, then the works."

She brought his first cup, black and scalding, as he liked it, then made two shirred eggs, four rashers of bacon and whole-wheat toast spread with marmalade, the breakfast he ate on mornings he slept late. She set the tray down on the coffee table in front of him.

"It looks to me as though Kennedy's had it," he said. "Did you hear?"

"I was out of the room." She sat down in the chair opposite.

He began to eat hungrily, still watching the screen. "Sometimes I think David's right. Get out of this *fucking* country full of murder!"

"That's what you said last time, about King."

"Did I?"

"You did." She lighted a cigarette, watching him as he finished.

"It's a natural enough reaction. Many people must have it. I wish you hadn't let Todd go on that picnic."

"I thought it would be better for him than watching *that*." She blew a smoke ring. "For one reason."

"For another?"

"Us. Last night you said it wasn't the time. We've got to make time," she said slowly. "To talk about us, Anson. Anson?"

He was staring at the screen. Her repetition of his name seemed to rouse him. "Shut that damn thing off! We probably know all there is to know."

She switched off the set. The brighter-than-daylight image quickly telescoped from a smiling close-up of Kennedy to a pinpoint of light, then blackness.

"Begin," she said.

"I wasn't lying to you when I phoned you Friday," he said. "I *was* with Ethan Fleming."

"I believed you."

"You didn't sound it. I remember telling you I can't work against your punishing silences."

"And I said I can't work against your punishment. Where did you have lunch?"

"The tit club. It was Fleming's choice."

"I imagine you didn't exactly mind."

"I've never seen a pair there I couldn't look at twice."

"I'm beginning to see it all," she said.

"No, you're not. You don't know Fleming."

"Why would I, since I've never met him?"

"I've only seen him abroad before, never here. He showed me London when I was there."

"Swinging London, I'll bet."

"Yes. It was you who threw me out after the Jeannette thing. What did you expect me to do, go into the bathroom and beat it?"

"A few more notches."

"You assume. I was under an obligation to show Fleming some kind of time here in return. In addition to firming up the Birnham deal. Fleming's bursting with life. A see-through man, always trying to squeeze another one in, and succeeding. You know, everything from whistle bait to 'Oh, sorry, I thought this was *my* cabin.' His etchings are always out being framed, but the girls don't care."

"I get it. You must have been a pair. Doing swinging New York."

"Skip that, if you want me to tell you. We went on to Birnham's place then, and did the deal. That's the way it went. Fleming's going to do the film of *Little Marka*. Bassinet through penis bank to the switch pay-off."

"I quit after the penis bank."

"You didn't finish the manuscript?"

"No, and don't expect to."

"But why not?"

"David asked me that, too. He finished it."

"Ah," he said. "I guessed that's where you were."

"I guessed last night that you guessed. Go on."

"What *about* David?"

"We'll come back to that. You finish first."

"That was it. It was a fantastic party, way *way* out. I stayed until the end, a little beyond the end, as a matter of fact."

"Then where did you go? The Saint Regis? That's where Fleming was staying, Nina said."

"You checked on me?"

"Why wouldn't I? I didn't let any cats out of bags. I asked her on the pretext of inviting Fleming to the party. I left a message."

"We stayed at Birnham's."

"On Mott Street!"

"Yes."

"Where the redhead lives."

"She lives in an apartment at the same address, yes."

She looked at him steadily. "I'm good at guessing, too. Speaking of who's punishing whom—was there any reason you couldn't have called me?"

"I did try to call you. Several times."

"When? When did you try to call me?"

"I—I think it was early Sunday."

"Leaving Friday night, Saturday in between. I was here."

"Galey's phone has a blank in the center of the dial, where his number should be. So, after I'd dialed you and the operator asked for the number I was calling from, I couldn't give it."

"But you have his number in your address book."

"I didn't have the book on me at the moment."

"I see the kind of party it was."

"I always have to look up his number. I rarely use it, Nina usually places the call. Well, even the special operator wouldn't put me through. Finally I gave up. I tried the apartment, too, but you weren't there."

"I went into town that night."

"Why did you?"

"Why *did* I? I was worried sick about you, that's why! You left me here, beached, no explanations, nothing. I was ready to go out of my mind. When Velma offered to take Todd, I couldn't wait to go."

"And then you started checking."

"And got nowhere, though I called all *around* you."

"But I did think of you."

"You, and the ladies of the telephone, who did not."

"It's true, and I tried to reach you from '53,' when I got back from Birnham's place."

"It must have been quite a party."

"It was. Really—*whirly.*" Neile's adjective, the first thing she had said that had made him really notice her, came to him, tardily but accurately. "The deal, the party, I went to '53,' and now I'm here."

"Quite a condensation," she said. "Back from Borobudur."

"If you insist on putting it that way."

"Meaning, you did things you can't do here, with me. Those farther horizons? Your moon without orbit?" she cried angrily.

"Yes, all that."

"You took a trip!"

"I wanted to, *had* to, to prove to myself something about myself. It took me a while to break down and do it. I kept thinking of you and Todd. And that *damned* salamander!"

Her eyes widened. "What did you take? Marijuana or what? I keep reading all these things about barbiturates, amphetamines—"

"Who wants amphetamines? There were no barbiturates involved, except at the end, when I was coming out of it."

"*What* did you take?"

"You want me to tell you? When Fleming and I got to Birnham's, the place was already flipping. The party'd been under way for hours. Fleming digs the Full Life, as I said.

454

Galey brings his *kif* from Morocco, but he has everything else, apparently, too. Fleming was flying to the Coast next day and didn't want more than the *kif*—"

"So *you* flew."

"Yes. On mescaline, then LSD."

She looked at him a long time before she spoke. "And you expect to come home and pick up again, with me, as though nothing happened!"

"Don't take it so hard. It's part of the time we live in; it's always been part of other times, too, if you think of it. The stuff called to me like those sirens in poems. I sensed that a part of me was dark, unrealized—corners never lighted by anything I knew or could find out about by learning. I had to do it. For myself. Try to understand. It was a one shot. Neither drug's addicting."

"From what I hear, there are no one shots."

"Oh, yes. There are people who stop with one, others who go on and take forty, even fifty trips. Some are terrified when they go into the experience, wish they'd never begun. Have bad trips. I wasn't terrified—I knew right from the beginning it was going to be good. I never want to go back, do it again, because I found out what I wanted to know."

"Which was?"

"I told you last night—the myth of myself."

"Meaning what?"

"The real me. The real Anson Parris. The end of all those shadow patterns moving in darkness, those cues to the identity of myself I couldn't pick up, even with prompting, those loose ends I've been unable to tie up. I had a moment of real panic, at the end, when I was afraid I wouldn't get back, but I slipped back into myself like a hand in a glove. I can't talk about it any more, except this—you were so worried about the redhead."

"More sick of what she represents. The one more you can't pass up."

"Well, relax. Fleming lifted her from me without my knowing or caring. He can't believe I didn't lead him to her. She's going to be his Marka."

"I thought she was writing a novel."

"She thinks—thought she was doing many things. Anything to get into the whirl. *Whirly* was her word."

"I didn't suppose it was yours."

"Faye, bear with me."

"I'm bearing."

"What it comes down to is something you must always have known about me. I've always wanted something, that something I couldn't put a name to—*avoir besoin de quelquechose.* I don't know who it was who said *'Que j'ai besoin de m'encanailler un peu.'* But that's it."

"You've been at my *Petit Larousse.*"

"I could say it better in French than English."

"Not that it isn't perfectly translatable—you have a need to make a beast of yourself. Yes, I know. And you did?"

"I did. And that's the part I can't tell you about."

"You've been doing pretty well," she said. "All about you. Nothing about me."

"Well, since this is turning into such a confessional, tell me."

"Please don't use that word."

"I think I know."

"How would you?"

"You said we'd come back to it. David."

She reached for a cigarette and lighted it. "You guessed."

"But tell me. I told you."

"I was miserable, lonely. The salamander thing was going on. It rained and rained. Todd was here, but lost in whatever that thing is he's lost in. I needed to be not alone. David was wonderful to me, talked to me—"

"Talked?"

"Yes, the talk was part of it. And I did what I think I've

wanted to do for a long time. Pay you back in your own coin."

"Punish me."

"As you've punished me. It was punishment for something I've never done." She spoke slowly, choosing words carefully. "You don't realize that you can't just go off and leave me, then come back and expect me to be the same. Assume that the marriage we have won't change, will weather it. You've never been able to be faithful to me. No, don't interrupt, please. The first time it happened, I thought it was once. I forgave. The second and third times, too; I thought they might be all. Then I began to realize it will always happen. Jeannette, redheads. I have more to say." Her voice became brittle. "*And*, as I tell you, please remember your inevitable insistences to me that your infidelities had nothing to do with *us*—"

He interrupted. "Faye, they haven't! I *swear* they haven't!"

"Swear. It's more than I'm prepared to do. I slept with David. I liked it. He knew why I slept with him, but he was as wonderful with me as though he didn't know."

"The shit!"

"David's not a shit. He's a man like you, in a way understands more, that to take is sometimes a way of giving, too."

"How mysterious!"

"Who's full of his own mysteries, if not you?"

"You mean, he's better in bed than I am?"

"He's nothing like you at all. He's simply—different. Oh, David knows about you, Anson."

"What does he know?"

"What everybody does. That you're supposed to be such a cocksman."

"Are you implying I'm not?"

"No. Only saying that people aren't fools; they know, from the way you present yourself, what you think you are."

"I think I'm myself."

457

"You're aware of the impact you have on people. You preen."

"Did David put this into your head?"

"Of course not. But he knows you well. Isn't that your big role? *Jeune premier,* in his thirty-fourth year of performance?"

"I'll kill him for this!"

"Oh, I don't think you will. You know what David's like, too. Those shoulders. He may be older, but I can tell you, he'd be no pushover for you."

"You're really telling me, aren't you?"

"Why not? After what you've been telling me? I'll tell you something else, too—the important part, to me. I found out that, though I love you, I can enjoy sleeping with other men, as you sleep with other women. And I found out that you may be right—my going to bed with David doesn't, really, have much to do with my sleeping with you."

"I'll make a deal with you—"

"If I'll be faithful? No, it's too late for that. I'll do as I please about that. As you've done."

"And you think that'll *work?*"

"I've stayed with you, haven't I? I came back to you last night, didn't I? As you always come back to me?"

"That's supposed to be irrefutable?"

"Can you refute it?"

The telephones jangled; they sounded louder in the living room, where all extensions could be heard at once.

"Are you going to answer that, or shall I?" Anson asked.

"I'm not going to answer. You answer if you like."

"I want to finish this."

"If it can be finished."

They waited for the ringing to stop. Then Faye said, "Whatever else convent training didn't do for me, it did teach me to know what I think. I told you, you wouldn't like it."

"No, I don't."

458

"There it is. I'm not quite the same as when you left."

"Don't do this to me! I love you!"

"You forget. I have done it, as you've done it to me."

"You make it sound so final. Don't shut me out like this. Faye, dearest, let me get *to* you!"

"Where do you want to get? We're where we are. If you think this can be settled by tears and daytime bed, as it used to be, you're wrong. I haven't any tears. I still remember David. I've no idea what you remember, but it's not going to be that easy."

"Oh. How hard is it going to be?"

"I simply have to get over it, that's all. Until I decide what I'm going to do."

"Do?"

"Mother's suggested a separation, even a divorce. I've thought about it. She even wants me to come with her to Europe this summer, to think about it."

"Faye, you can't mean this! Think of Todd!"

"Think of him yourself. I do nothing else, almost."

"I've just noticed," he said, "you're not wearing the ring I bought you in Paris."

"No. It's in my purse, along with the rest of the day I spent in town, wondering where you were. I had lunch alone at the Plaza, and when I went to wash my hands, left my rings on the edge of the basin. I went back for them, of course, and I realized that by forgetting them I'd made a decision about myself."

"You could put it back on."

"I can't. I remember what's engraved inside. Do you?"

"By heart."

"It's a sentiment for long living together, days taken together as well as separate days. I don't want to talk about this any more. Speaking of separate days, we've a party to give. Amy Nowells wondered if we were going to give it, in view of what's happened to Kennedy."

"I think we have to give it. It's all set up. Nina's worked out the car pools and everything. I've asked lots of extra people."

"If David and Jeannette come, there'll be that."

"They'll come," Anson said. "I know how I'll feel about Jeannette, if not David."

"I intend to give a first-rate reading of the part of Mrs. Anson Warren Parris, and Jeannette can make what she likes of it," said Faye.

"You wear your horns and I'll wear mine."

"And they can wear theirs."

There was a knock on the door.

"This is one interruption I welcome," Faye said, going to open it. It was Velma and Sam.

"Oh, you're *here,* Faye," Velma said, relief in her voice.

"I came back last night."

"We both were worried. I phoned several times, and always got a busy signal, and then when I called other times, the phone rang and rang and there was no answer. We didn't know what to think."

"Have you been watching Kennedy?" Sam asked.

"Off and on."

"We've been watching since morning. We can't stop," Velma said. "I said to Sam, 'Let's go over and see Faye and Anson, at least we'll be away from it that long.' But of course we talked about it all the way."

"How's it going?" Anson asked Sam.

"Oh, Kennedy's going to die."

Anson turned the set on and in silent agreement the four sat down before it.

"If it's going to be this depressing, I'm going to have a drink," Anson said. "How about the rest of you?"

All agreed, and Anson went to get ice.

"It's awful," Velma said. "I feel really guilty, as though we were celebrating."

"Martha Lavrorsen's celebrating," Faye said, telling them of Martha's call. "Rose is upset, but coping enough to take the kids on a picnic. Grace Burgess couldn't care less, nor Chet."

"And you," asked Velma, when Sam had gone to the drink tray to help Anson, "how are you?"

"Anson and I are locking horns."

"I guess we shouldn't have come."

"Please stay. Unless you have to get back?"

"We don't have to get anywhere. Sam's knocked off for the day, as I gather Anson has. Oh, yes, he told me he'd be home. The kids are all out and I've nothing to do till dinnertime."

Between making drinks, Anson dressed, and the day wore on. Kennedy might be dying, but nothing could stop the paperback bidding for Galcy Birnham's novel. The phones rang all afternoon, Anson taking calls relayed by K and K in the bedroom. Often he was out of the room for a half hour or more, and then Sam made drinks.

"Anson told me about Todd's cutting up the salamander," Faye said, during one of the times she and Velma were alone.

Velma shuddered. "I hated to tell Anson, but I had to."

"But Todd seems very much himself today, now Anson's back."

"That's the key."

"I wish you'd tell me what his killing the salamander that way means."

"Anson asked me that too, and I'm not sure I told him the right thing. Todd has—he has a memory of some kind, it's called a screen memory, meaning that it partly hides and partly reveals some earlier and deeper memory. I don't know what that early memory is, nor do you. The sight of sadism, that nerve of evil that runs through us all, is never pretty to see."

"And what shall we do now?"

"Stay with him, make him feel wanted and important—keep him from knowing about those locking horns. I gather you took the toucan's advice in New York?"

"I did."

"And?"

"You were right about punishment, what you said about it. It works in reverse. I thought I was punishing Anson, but I still feel the one punished. And I still want only him. Though this time I've not told him that."

"And don't," Velma said as Sam came back with fresh drinks. "Not this time or any other."

❦ ❦ ❦ THE DAY on which the quarrel, the worst of their marriage, had relentlessly hardened, deepened and made more despairing by the Kennedy killing, had come and gone. Faye and Anson remembered the November days of 1963, when JFK had been murdered, days they had assumed had fallen into time and were at least partly forgotten. But the death of Bobby Kennedy requickened these old memories; there was something about this span of days so bad that there was no name for what they felt, either about Bobby Kennedy or themselves. The news, bright, documentary, live enough even for Martha Lavrorsen, dragged on. Todd had accepted the assassination, had forgotten about his glass jar and the turtles, and could now not be coaxed away from the television.

"Best to let him feel it fully," Velma counseled, the day after Kennedy died. "I think he's going to be all right. Faye, it's yourself you should think of. You look miserable."

"I am miserable," Faye admitted.

Her words had a deafening echo; they were the ones Anson had used to her that morning, when, before thinking, she had asked how he felt. Any morning's question. "Did you sleep well?"

"I slept wretchedly. I'm miserable, if you care."

"Will you call me from the office?"

"Yes, I'll call you, if there's anything to call about."

She said nothing, to make up for having asked.

"You don't care," he said, and went out to make his solitary breakfast, while she detained Todd in the bedroom.

Both knew about quarreling days, days when she did not get up to make his breakfast, or ordinary days, when, for one reason or another (a very late party, or the last days of her pregnancy, when she had been ill), she stayed in bed, but these days were different. Now she got up as soon as he had left the house, finding evidences of the second, hurried cup on the sink board, spilled Nescafé, the squeeze bottle of saccharin lying sideways beside it. Breakfast of anger.

Secretly, she admired the serious, determined way he had talked the night of her return, the intuition with which he had surmised her activities while away; and though she could not understand why he had done what he had, his very being there when she walked in had renewed her dependence on him. She had put her *plaque* on fidelity and lost. She had put her *plaque* on infidelity, winning once. Or had she lost? As in a game of roulette when playing for too-high stakes, one was supposed to ignore the ball until it settled, show indifference if one lost, casually slap down the next counter. She felt cheated of the edge she supposed her night with David had given her. Though Anson had been truly hurt, she could see that he did not feel threatened by her retaliation. On the surface, he seemed his usual, assuming self: the principle by which she lived. It was into his eyes she had looked, searched for and found herself each day. Now she hardly looked at him and found nothing but misery. That had been the thing about David: she had not been able to see herself; each hour the memory of him became more blank. Without Anson she was nothing to herself, and knew it. And suspected that he knew that she knew it.

She was grateful for Mrs. Haines's presence; she could hardly show what she was feeling in front of her. Both worked steadily, getting the house into its last party order. When Anson came home, on schedule, Mrs. Haines was leaving, and he went directly to shower. Faye met him in the hallway, on the way to the living room. The encounter had about it a faintly military air, as though they were officers under orders to be civil until the end of an armistice.

He asked, "How are you?"

"Oh, I'm hanging in there," she answered, going past him with an armful of freshly ironed clothes; party or no, relentless household chores went on.

They had stopped smiling at each other and become grave, even in the presence of Todd, before whom always before they had kept up the best of fronts during disagreements. Long ago, Todd had learned the difference between a quiet quarrel and an open one. Sometimes he had said, "You're not talking to each other. Why don't you talk?" And so, this time, by unspoken agreement, they talked, even talked about the assassination.

"I remember *my* moment of deepest feeling when JFK was killed," Anson said. "It was when Jackie—Jackie Kennedy, told that there was blood on her stockings after Dallas, said, 'Let them see it. I want them to see it.' "

"Mine, this time, was when Bobby Kennedy asked them please not to move him," responded Faye.

"Did he really say please?" Todd put in disconcertingly.

"It would have been so like him. That was when I really felt what had happened."

"Did you cry?" Todd asked her.

464

"Yes, I cried."

"So did Mrs. Draper. We all cried."

To an eye less sensitized than Faye's to his moods, Anson appeared more preoccupied than miserable, no matter what he had said. She was aware that he was quite probably suffering in the situation as she herself had, on learning of his first fall from fidelity, during her pregnancy. She found no comfort in this. It was like suffering from a virus of similar but not identical strain; she understood its course, how it felt in herself, but this helped not at all, if anything, added to her despondency by proving once more that the interior facts of a marriage, shared by both, have different consequences when separately considered. She knew that Velma knew, intuitively, of Anson's trip, Borobudur, supposing it to be the beginning of an ebb tide in her marriage that would, in time, remove Anson from her, while she, as his wife, following instinct, was sure that what he had told her about its being once was, probably, true.

Anson was preoccupied. He had known from the beginning of his talk with Galey Birnham in the sauna that he would do what he had done, and no guilt about it entered his mind at any time. It had been so completely what it was, an insightful debasing of the self while tasting knowledge as dangerous as it was sublime. It was past, and in a curious way—the way in which he resolutely resisted introspection—it was, also, untrue, peripheral experience beyond the limits of belief and reason. But he understood, now, how men with the destinies of loved ones in their hands could jeopardize themselves and those loved ones for a taste of the forbidden, even the forbidden which had in his case been of positive, almost therapeutic value. The chambered pistol held to the temple, with one chamber loaded, or all loaded but one— depending on the Russians you knew. Never again would he lack comprehension for the Birnhams of this world, having himself trespassed onto that dark, unhappy territory, having fled from it into forgetfulness. All that was forgettable, already forgotten, a lie in the way in which intelligent lies are nearer to truth than half-truths. The memory he had brought back from his experience was his enduring passion for Faye and his love for that mysterious, extended part of himself, Todd. The conversation that was strictly for Todd's benefit continued:

"Is the *Little Marka* paper deal maturing?"

"It's going to be bigger than any of us expected, evidently."

"Who's on top now?"

"Quantum's bid's the last one in. They're hot for it."

"Not Everest this time."

"I think Jim Brown shot their wad on *Good Time Coming*. Of course, we're trying to keep Birnham out of it until we close. Not at all the way we work when it's David—" He stopped.

She looked up at him as though to say, *Go on, use David's name, why not?*

"I mean, Birnham has no Jeannette at his elbow."

That distilled a silence, too, and they were grateful when Todd was put to bed and went to sleep, so they could continue their double silences together. Faye's performance had been as promised. She defied him to find the question or the look in his eyes that would break her down. She remembered their tabling of it:

You wear your horns and I'll wear mine.

And they can wear theirs.

She had an absurd dream in which she and Anson, with cuckold antlers sprouting from their foreheads, locked with David and Jeannette, similarly equipped.

The night before the party, they sat over their coffee in the living room, which was polished and plumped to the nines, the trick fireplace banked with ferns from the garden and the lavish flowers which the Kastners and Kennerlys always sent

466

ahead before parties. They had been silent a long time, and Faye was reminded of stories of *gemütlich* evenings of royalties, each spouse chosen from portrait likenesses sent back and forth between kingdoms by couriers and matchmakers—*they* must have spent evenings like this, getting through formalities, civil, not touching, surface-calm, protocol-courteous. Again she dreaded and hated the need she had of him. She was angered anew by his attitude of waiting for the usual forgiveness. For what, this time, and why? So he could punish her? He sat, legs crossed, reading, a disturbing, phallic force, impersonal, abstract, yet the most personal force she had known in her life, sure of himself, of winning—whatever winning now entailed. He had the dedicated courtesy to her of young priests she remembered, when first her religious doubts began, certain of all doubts passing, or, at least, the end of her flight from belief and certain reconversion.

She said, "I think I'll turn in early, in view of tomorrow."

"All right," he said. "Good night."

"I dread the party, don't you?"

"Yes, I dread it." He obediently got up and carried their coffee cups to the kitchen; she could hear him rinsing them and placing them in the drain rack.

"I've looked at the list again and again," she said when he came back, "and I don't for the life of me know whether to be grateful for our 'Assortment' or sorry we asked them."

"Well, our 'Assortment' is our 'Assortment.'"

He was giving a performance at least as good as her own. It suddenly stultified her that they both were incapable of reopening the discussion that had brought them this far. As he waited for her to precede him to the nightly check of Todd's room and then to their bedroom, she almost turned to him in tears.

As they undressed, shuttling in and out of the bath in ritualistic order, he told her more about the bidding on *Little*

467

Marka, and she listened, nodding, with a comfortable sense of his ability to shift and control the weight and power of others, tip it to his ultimate victory. It might have been easiest to let go with him now, but she saw he was working out something for himself. Everything they said to each other seemed to cancel out, like a scene in a play. She got into bed and turned off the light as a way of telling Anson, once more, that it would not be easy. If he had known, she thought, how frail were the bonds of her resistance, he would have been beside her in a moment. But he went silently to his own bed.

SATURDAY DAWNED humid and hot. Already, at seven-thirty, when Todd became too impatient to stay longer in bed, the cicadas could be heard beginning to weave their blanket of overhead sound in the trees. Todd, now it had been decided to let him experience fully the end of the Kennedy obsequies, turned on the television immediately after his breakfast, and by shortly before ten, the grim recounting of Masses to be said, the route of the funeral train and the stops it would make along the way to Arlington, last kisses and fingertips laid on the now familiar coffin, intensified. The TV screen seemed to ooze the already sweltering gray heat of the city. Faye stopped to watch from time to time; somehow the despair she felt about Anson and herself seemed linked to the many wives and husbands, moving across the streets, entering the cathedral. To get away from it, she had a late-morning cup of coffee on the terrace, while Anson slept to his customary Saturday hour; his Friday at K and K had been a heavy one, evidently. She closed her eyes at the thought of the long hours before the party would begin, and helplessly watched Todd's growing apathy, almost a sullenness, as he silently stared at the screen. And there was, more depressing than anything, Anson's continuing determination to be as ungiving as she. Later, she was able to place exactly the moment when everything about the day began to go wrong—when Mrs. Haines, sounding not at all her capable self, called to say that Mr. Haines was down with an intestinal virus and she'd have to do the party without him.

"Oh, dear!" said Faye, after listening to how Mrs. Haines had been up most of the night with her husband. "But can you? I'll help, of course, but we've asked a lot of people."

"Oh, yes; I've handled parties singlehanded," Mrs. Haines assured. "I'll have my usual woman in the kitchen and everything's ready, except for last things. The aspics and the salads. And, if it's all right with you, I'll ask my sister's boy to tend bar. He usually asks ten dollars. He's nineteen and very good at it. His name's Gurdon—you must remember him, from Mrs. Lavrorsen's Christmas?"

"I remember," said Faye, giving thanks for the Mrs. Haineses and Gurdons of this world. She recalled the party, even Gurdon, a tall young man with a great deal of blond hair and steel-rimmed eyeglasses.

"So we'll be there around lunchtime," Mrs. Haines said, "and we'll have everything in apple-pie order long before four. Not to worry."

"I wish it were over."

"Oh, they'll have all come and gone before you know it," said Mrs. Haines, and hung up.

The telephone woke Anson. The bidding for *Little Marka* was continuing, despite the business week's having ended, and by noon Faye had delegated answering the phone to Anson, since all calls were for him. She listened absently to his clipped but jovial responses to what was being said to him. He heated his own coffee and went back to bed, receiving and making calls from there. Once he came out to say, "That was Ethan Fleming. He's back from the Coast and is coming out with Galey and the girl I told you about. Neile Eythe, who's going to play Marka."

Faye looked at him but said nothing.

"Well, you did call Fleming's hotel and leave a message asking him to the party. It's only natural he should be coming with Birnham and the girl."

"I'll wear my gloves," she said.

Lunch was a pickup affair of sandwiches on the terrace, and since the *Little Marka* bidding had recessed until Monday, Faye persuaded Anson to take Todd swimming at the Drapers'. Todd was to have no nap, so that he would be healthily tired by the time Anson dropped him at the Curries', to be sat, along with Roger, by Libby Draper. Faye had hoped for a nap for herself, but had completely forgotten her conversation with her mother earlier in the week. She had just lain down when she heard the sound of a car pulling into the drive. Looking out, she saw that it was her mother and Adelaide. They looked hot and tired from their drive from Danbury.

"But you're not watching the funeral!" Vera Williams said the moment they were inside. "Adelaide and I've been listening on the car radio, but that's not the same as seeing it."

"Adelaide, how are you?" Faye asked, kissing her fondly.

"Don't you know about doctors?" Adelaide asked in return. "They don't tell you anything."

"Now, don't you worry, Adelaide," Vera Williams said; "you're going to be fine, just fine."

Adelaide didn't look as though she believed this. "Sure, and I can read *your* mind, after all these years," she said. She looked small and shrunken and refused her usual tea. She, too, wanted more than anything to pick up the progress of the Kennedy train. Faye turned on the set, hardly cold from Todd's watching.

"And where *is* Toddy?" demanded Vera, after she had looked at the screen for a moment.

"Mother, I'm afraid I forgot. Anson's taken him swimming, to get him out of the way of the party."

"I should have thought you'd have canceled. Respect for the dead."

"We talked it over and decided to go ahead."

"Well." Vera Williams stood up. "We won't keep you." She had, she explained, spent the night at the hospital, in the room next to Adelaide's, and would be glad to get back to her own bath. *"I've* heard you *catch* things in hospitals, that staph, whatever it is. And there's Father Callahan's Mass; we mustn't be late for that." As Adelaide got into the car, her mother drew Faye aside. "Of course, I think they're simply not telling her. I think it's you-know. What's worse, she suspects. It's a terrible world."

By the time Faye had seen them off, it was after three and she went to bathe and dress. She was ready in half an hour, wearing the white-lace slacks and blouse, which Saks had delivered specially to Anson's office, and which he had brought out on the "Bug" the day before. It was a little hot for it, but she wore it anyway, glad that it was cotton.

"You look smashing," Anson told her, smiling for the first time since their quarrel.

Faye did not smile back. "I feel smashed. Mother and Adelaide were here, it seemed hours. Adelaide's been in the hospital for tests. They insisted on watching TV. I think you should unplug the set for the party."

"I agree," Anson said, and did it. "What's wrong with Adelaide? The Irish Rebellion of 1916?"

"Don't be horrid. You'd better dress."

"I feel like staying in swimming trunks. It must be ninety-five."

"It's over ninety."

There had been someone waiting in the kitchen all during the visit of Faye's mother and Adelaide—the accordionist

471

Faye had engaged by phone from the agency in New York. It was not clear why he had arrived so early and Mrs. Haines and the woman in the kitchen found him in the way. It turned out he had taken a train an hour too soon and had been delivered by the Stamford taxi. A flashy, tall Trinidadian with pretensions to romantic looks, he seemed almost an incarnation of Alma Doyle's fantasied blackamoor. He carried a small suitcase.

"I do not know de kind of affair it is, Mistress," he explained, in a heavy West Indian accent, "but I have brought my tux and my Spanish suit."

"No tux," Faye told him. "It'll be daylight during most of the party." The Spanish suit, into which he changed in the powder room off the downstairs hall, turned out to be red gaucho pants, black boots and a white ruffled shirt. There was nothing for him to do, since Mrs. Haines didn't want him around, but to walk up and down the white gravel square, where guests were to park, chain-smoking.

Anson decided a seersucker suit, with shirt open at the neck, was formal enough, and said he intended to take the coat off if it got any hotter. He and Faye made their usual dollar bet as to who the first guest would be, a pleasantry more for the morale of Mrs. Haines and Gurdon than for themselves. Anson guessed turnpike traffic would be light, because so many people were watching TV, and that Carl Kastner, always an early arriver anyway, would be first. Faye thought Velma and Sam might walk over early.

Both were wrong. First to appear was Miss Grumbacher, followed by Miss Taylor at a few paces. They had chosen to walk from their farm in the valley, and as they came up the walk Faye wondered if either woman was aware of the resemblance they bore to the famous pair of the Rue de Fleurus, or whether, unconsciously, they imitated them. "Gertrude" was wearing an ecru linen suit with a mid-calf, accordion-pleated skirt, "Alice" a silk print dress and what was once called a cocktail hat. Both had the look of being aware they had come too soon and wishing they could leave secretly and make a second entrance.

"The boys offered to drive us, but we know they have a houseful this week and so decided on shanks' mare," Miss Grumbacher explained. "Besides, I enjoy walking, heat or no heat."

"It's terribly hot," said Miss Taylor. "I don't suppose I may ask for iced tea?"

Iced tea was no problem to Gurdon, and he brought two glasses. Faye asked how many were in the boys' houseful, not too pleased, remembering she had used all the tact she had to suggest that the terrace was small and the party had no need of extra men.

"Five, I think," answered Miss Grumbacher. "They simply can't wait to meet this Galey Birnham, or whatever his name is."

"He'll be here somewhat later," Anson said.

"It's been Galey Birnham this and Galey Birnham that all week long," Miss Taylor reported. "I've never read any of his books; I think neither of us has."

"I doubt they'd be for you," said Faye.

"But I have read that terrible thing you've just published," Miss Grumbacher said. "The one somebody paid a million dollars for. Doesn't Kastner and Kennerly have any sense of responsibility to the public?"

"Publishers like to make money sometimes," replied Anson. "So do writers. David Steen will be here, of course, but he's not our only pride. Joanna Summers is coming, too, as is Aroon Rigo."

Miss Grumbacher turned and looked at Miss Taylor. "Don't we remember them, ducks?"

Miss Taylor remembered perfectly. "Joanna Summers was everybody's mistress in the twenties, including Carl Kastner's. Of Miss Rigo I have nothing to say."

473

This colloquy was cut short by the simultaneous arrival of three cars, two of which Faye and Anson recognized—the Kastners', bringing the design people, whom they always picked up because they lived near them, and the Kennerlys', who had in tow Jeannette and David. Anson had supposed David would drive up in the Lamborghini, then remembered that he and Jeannette were spending the weekend with Mary and Claxon Kennerly. The third car, a spanking-new white-and-black Rolls, held the couple Grace and Chet Burgess had met at a convention, pleasant-appearing people in their sixties, and the Burgesses themselves.

Carl Kastner said, "Anson, Claxon's been filling me in on the way the Birnham paper sale is building. If you pull off another seven figures, we'll have no choice but make you president of the firm."

Anson laughed. "It won't be seven. We're shooting for around three. Three and maybe ten, fifteen above."

"That's what we thought during negotiations for *Good Time.*"

"Relax," said Anson; *"Little Marka's* appeal is limited."

"It was certainly limited with *me,*" Mary Kennerly said. "But Claxon says I'm prudish, that everything's about homosexuality now. I kept wondering why Marka didn't get a nose job while she was about it."

A loud, rippling cadenza from the accordionist and laughter at Mary Kennerly's comment seemed to cancel the rather strange beginning made by "Gertrude" and "Alice" and started the party on its way. The Trinidadian, smokily handsome in his costume, seemed to have taken inspiration from the white-and-black Rolls, adding, to a somewhat remarkable agility of execution, all kinds of graces and embellishments. Faye and Anson led everybody out to the terrace, made introductions and Gurdon took the drink orders. Suddenly there were many more people—a phalanx of "The Assortment," which tended to arrive and depart in groups, the Doyles, the

474

Drapers, sponsoring the young Carlsons, their new tenants, Amy and Herb Nowells. Carlson was an engineer for Eastern Airlines, and young Mrs. Carlson, pretty and blond, was pregnant.

"How far along is the train?" Mrs. Carlson at once asked Faye.

"Train?"

"Kennedy's. We thought it was the *most* awful thing, those deaths of innocent people along the way." No one within earshot had heard of these deaths, so both Carlsons, who had been watching up to the time they left for the party, gave a very thorough briefing of it.

"We've watched, of course," Faye said, in light reprimand, "but I hope people will manage to forget what's happened and enjoy themselves." Perhaps meeting the lion would get the Carlsons off the funeral train. "Come," she said, "I know you'd like to meet Jeannette and David Steen." She wanted to get the first minutes of the confrontation over with, and the Carlsons seemed a good buffer.

Jeannette and David were standing a little apart, near the transplanted holly, David with his cigarette in its long holder, held before him, almost, Faye thought, like a weapon. He was talking to Jeannette in a low voice. Jeannette was simply and perfectly dressed in a heliotrope color. It was the moment Faye had dreaded.

"Darling," she said, and closed her eyes as she brushed Jeannette on both cheeks. "Darling Jeannette, how are you?"

Jeannette said, ducking the question, "Dearest Faye, how lovely your garden is! June flowers!" What her outpatient eyes said was quite different; Faye felt her greeting, conventional as it was, had been wrong. Jeannette was so relaxed that Faye guessed David had seen to it that her medications were a little more than adequate.

"And—David," she said. She had seen Anson's and Jeannette's casual kiss when the Steens came in. Smiling, she

475

kissed him lightly on the lips, then introduced the young Carlsons. "I'm so happy about *Good Time,*" she said, for Jeannette's benefit.

Jeannette seemed to be underreacting, behaving, almost, as though she were deaf. "You must be new blood, you two," she said to the Carlsons.

"Yes, I'm afraid we are," Mrs. Carlson said. "We've just moved to the Ridge."

"Ah," said Jeannette. "Well." And said no more.

The young Carlsons looked embarrassed, and Faye was glad that Ray Doyle had followed her across the lawn, so she could leave. Ray and David had met before. Ray warmly congratulated him on *Good Time Coming* and its phenomenal success. "How does it feel to really make it?"

David shrugged.

"Oh, come," Ray pursued it. "When those big checks come rolling in, you must feel something."

"Checks don't roll, they flutter," David answered.

Ray turned to Jeannette. He had a way of overcomplimenting wives of men he considered as successful as David Steen. He admired her dress, then said, "I've found, in my own case, anyway, that it's the wife who spends the money. What are you going to do with one million dollars?"

Jeannette stared at him. "I've bought myself a *folie.*"

Ray didn't seem to know what a *folie* was, and David, who seemed anxious to keep Jeannette from saying too much, briefly explained. "Personally, I hate the damned thing," he added. "We'll probably put in central heat and then get rid of it."

"At a profit," Ray guessed.

"I try to make a little something," said David.

"I've heard," said Ray.

"I could have predicted you'd say that," Jeannette told David.

Ray then told them about his return to writing for soap

opera, a recital the Steens listened to in silence. Finally, Ray gave up and left.

Faye congratulated herself she had gotten through the meeting with Jeannette well, but wifely curiosity compelled her to keep an eye on Anson, who was now coping with the arrival of Joanna Summers and Aroon Rigo, who were in the first of the car pools set up by Nina Gerson. Nina, as efficient at gatherings as she was in Anson's office, at once saw to it that the secretaries and stockroom boys got drinks and were introduced. They were led up to the Kastners and the Kennerlys for jovial greetings, then paired off with two lameduck novelists, who, in her opinion, had their nerve to come, since their last books had been published many years ago and their new ones, if new ones there were, far from submission. The Hansons and the Steins, who had transported other K and K staff, also helped.

Not only young Mrs. Carlson was agitated about the progress of the Kennedy funeral train (explaining, rather once too often, Faye thought, that she was in exactly the same month as Ethel Kennedy and feared for her and her child), but Joanna Summers, too, asked how the train was progressing. Indeed, she seemed almost in tears over the assassination, and after she had accepted from Anson a martini over the rocks, launched into a discourse on the killing's political aspects. Her resonant voice could be heard all over the garden, and soon she and Aroon Rigo had gathered a group of listeners around them. Amy Nowells, the only woman besides Miss Taylor in a hat, and wearing short white gloves, was fascinated by women writers. She seemed intent on securing from Joanna Summers her views as to whether or not the assassination was part of a larger conspiracy.

"Well, it was not a political accident," Joanna Summers said to the group around her. "It did happen in California instead of Texas."

"And what's wrong with California?" asked a belligerent voice. It was the wife of the doctor who had come with the Burgesses. *"I'm* from California."

"Look at what you elect," countered Aroon Rigo.

"I know what you mean about Texas," Amy Nowells said. "I've always hoped it would secede. I was there, once. Horrible place, with all those millionaires lying around in piles, like snakes. And no man—no man *I* met, anyway, ever *heard* of deodorants."

"Here we go," Alma Doyle, who had heard this, quipped.

"Well, Texas is only about twice the size of Germany," Amy went on. "And who'd miss it?"

"As long as LBJ is there when it secedes," put in Martha Lavrorsen, who had just arrived with Stig, who was in tennis flannels. Velma and Sam Currie had preceded them. "You know," Martha announced with full alcoholic authority, "they killed JFK because he was about to cut those millions Texas oil people get each year for keeping their wells capped. Twenty-five million they get. *Each.* And tax-free, probably. JFK wanted to cut it to twelve and a half million."

Aroon Rigo, who was drinking ginger ale, listened to this with disdain. "Oh, I'm *so* glad they didn't cut them," she said. "Poor Texans! However would they be able to afford Neiman-Marcus and those His-Her jets?"

This did not please Martha Lavrorsen nor the wife of the Rolls-Royce doctor. "I was quite serious in what I said," Martha told Aroon Rigo.

"So was I," Aroon Rigo answered, laughing. "I worry about people with twenty-five millions."

"All right, you worry," Martha flung at her, leaving the group.

"I think you're all perfectly ridiculous," the Rolls-Royce wife said, but she stayed.

Joanna Summers was being more serious. "American politics will never be the same after this, never."

478

"Oh, I doubt they'll be very different," Stig Lavrorsen said; he had listened to the exchange between his wife and Aroon Rigo. "JFK's murder didn't change anything, and Bobby's won't either. Nor Martin Luther King's."

"The man who conducted my 1966 audit was the spitting image of that Martin Luther King," said the Rolls-Royce doctor. "You can imagine his attitudes. He questioned my having taken sixteen hundred for my transport. I said to him, 'Let up, boy, let up. If you don't, I'm going to hire myself a Caddy *with* a driver and you'll be sorry you ever questioned my sixteen hundred!' That did it."

Joanna Summers gave him a look but went on. "No one knows anything about how history happens," she said. "Bobby Kennedy may be far more effective *as a force* dead than he might have been as President. As in the case of Che Guevara, too."

"That henchman of Castro!" said the Rolls-Royce doctor, with a curl of his lip.

Joanna Summers grimaced. "Che Guevara's murder by the CIA has done more to underline American imperialism than any other one thing."

"You mean, any other one American murder," put in Alma Doyle. She was standing as close to the accordionist as she could get. The accordionist knew his business, and with a rippling swell of chords obliterated Aroon Rigo's answer to this.

This blast of sound served also as fanfare for the arrival of the jersey-suit boys and their guests, several of whom looked as though they had been horizontal since the weekend began. There were seven in all, and when Faye saw them, she wished they'd worn a little more than they were wearing. All were in briefest swimming trunks, either barefoot or wearing sandals, and two of the more athletic ones sported dangling gold necklaces.

"We came as we were," the first boy said to Faye, intro-

479

ducing the five she didn't know. "I hope you don't mind. I love what you're wearing." He had rather pleasant manners.

"Of course I don't mind," she said. "I rather wish I were in a bikini myself."

"Well, let's not *stay* as we were," said one of the boys, whose manners were less good. "Where's the bar? I'm bone-dry."

"Have your drinks," Faye said, leading them in a troupe to the table where Gurdon was dispensing drinks, "and then I'll introduce you."

"Oh, we'll just introduce ourselves," another of the boys said. "You've got a swingo going here, did you know? We could hear it all the way down the hill."

The boys, with their drinks, moved to the edge of the Summers-Rigo group.

The Rolls-Royce wife was talking loudly. "The CIA, the CIA!" she cried. "I've never really known what CIA stands for. Is it a branch of the FBI?"

"The CIA sucks," one of the boys with a necklace said.

"The Central Intelligence Agency," explained Joanna Summers, "is our Ogpu. You remember Ogpu?"

"Never heard of it."

"Well, you're old enough to have heard of it!" Aroon Rigo said.

"I still say the CIA sucks," said the boy.

"The CIA kills," Joanna Summers corrected him.

"If you'll permit me a word," said the Rolls-Royce doctor, "you are misinformed. Now, I can tell you. We're from Bucks County, and I'd be the first to admit that we have resident CIA agents down there—"

"And are grateful to have them!" his wife put in.

"What do you mean, *resident* agents?" Alma Doyle wanted to know, though her question was academic; her eyes were glued to the Trinidad accordionist.

"The ones that simply squat and keep an eye on people in

480

strategic communities," Stig Lavrorsen said. "We've got them in this county, too. They always seem to live near bridges. You know, a couple, no visible means of support, but two cars? The wife usually mousy, rarely goes out, but he tries to be one of the boys?"

"I think you're terrible, talking about America like this!" The Rolls-Royce wife was almost in tears. "Why, where would we *be* if we didn't have people to watch out for all the hidden Communists? We've got them down in Bucks, I can tell you! Of *course* there are people living next to bridges! Bridges are very important when trouble comes."

"How about bridges in Vietnam?" the necklace boy asked her.

The Rolls-Royce wife looked him up and down. "You *would* ask a question like that. *Since* you ask, we believe, with Bill Buckley, that we should bring that war to an honorable conclusion."

"The war we've lost," said Joanna Summers.

"You talk like a Communist!" the Rolls doctor shouted at her.

"Lady, why don't you get yourself a green beret?" the necklace boy inquired of the Rolls wife.

"Why, I never wear berets—"

"You should get one," Joanna Summers finished for him. "You could wear it in Bolivia."

"Where the CIA still sucks."

"Will you please stop saying that?"

"No, I'll say it sucks as long as it sucks. I could say worse—I could say the CIA's the Black Kiss."

It was clear things were going to get rough. Making their way to Grace and Chet Burgess, who were in a group talking with Faye and Anson, the Rolls-Royce couple made no bones. "I think, Grace," the wife said, "we'd best be on our way. You remember, we wanted to get a good start on traffic anyway. I simply can't understand meeting people like—

481

like"—and, forgetting her manners, she pointed—"those men and women over there. Meeting them in a home like this, I mean to say. Why, even down in Bucks, we don't have freaks like that."

"I'm sorry you've not been having a good time," Anson said. "Let me introduce you to someone else. Do you know David Steen?"

The Rolls-Royce wife put up her hand. "No, we don't care to meet David Steen. I've read some of his books. Sorry. But thank you for having us."

Grace and Chet Burgess looked of two minds whether to go or stay. David, who had overheard, came up.

"Perhaps I'm the fly in the ointment," he said to Anson.

"No, stallion, stay," replied Anson. "Without you my stable wouldn't be what it is."

"Are we going to choose seconds?" David asked.

"Do you want to?"

"No," David answered, lighting a cigarette. "I think we should all be little birds in our nests and agree to forget it."

"I confess I see no other way," Anson said.

"What is this?" Faye asked, as the two shook hands.

"It's called the double swap," said Jeannette. "They're bastards. And we're the bitches."

"I warned you what crosses they were, Faye," Grace Burgess said. "Chet and I are relieved to see the end of them. We want to stay."

"And do," Faye urged. "Anson and I've got to do something about breaking up this political rally, or whatever it is." As was her custom, she had kept an eye on the table on which hors d'oeuvres were set out, as Anson had kept his on the bar, making sure everyone got what they wanted and the way they wanted it. After the Burgesses had burrowed into one of the "Assortment" groups, she drew Anson aside.

"I can't understand it," she said. "No one's touched the

cocktail food Mrs. Haines went to such trouble to prepare. Not a shrimp, not even an olive."

"They've been drinking enough."

"Maybe Gurdon's making the drinks too strong. Something's the matter. All stacks seem ready to blow."

"I'll speak to Gurdon," Anson said.

Gurdon was mixing a shaker of martinis, which seemed to be what most were drinking, talking, meanwhile, to one of the boys with the necklaces. He smiled at Anson through his steel rims.

"I think it might be a good thing if we can slow drinks up a little," Anson said to him quietly.

Gurdon stopped stirring. "You mean make them weaker? Water them?"

"No, simply slow them up."

"But I thought the idea was for everybody to get high," Gurdon said, obviously feeling his efficiencies had been questioned. "They all looked like dead when it started out, so I've tried to make it jump a bit."

"What do you mean, jump?"

"Oh, I distributed a few bennies and millies where I thought the dead spots were."

"What dead spots?"

Gurdon looked from Anson to the groups standing about and back, then shrugged.

"You've been passing out pills?"

"No, just dissolved them in the drinks. I thought it would help."

"Where did you get this idea? Not from Mrs. Haines, surely?"

"It's something people do at parties. Mrs. Lavrorsen always told me to watch for the dead spots, the older ones. First give them a miltini—Miltown instead of that lemon-peel jazz they all make such a fuss about—and the next one

483

with a benny in it. I haven't overdone it, Mr. Parris. I keep close track. I have a good memory."

This explained a good deal about Martha Lavrorsen's parties as well as the general high pitch of contentious conversation which the accordionist's efforts could not conceal.

"No more of that," said Anson. "Do you understand?"

"You're giving the orders, Mr. Parris."

Anson turned away, hearing a snatch of seriously whispered conversation between the necklace boys that was not intended for him.

"Lay off him," the first necklace boy was saying. "He's local, and that woman who's bringing out the dishes is his aunt or mother, I don't know which."

"I was only talking to him."

"Talk to some of these old bags instead. Besides, he's not of legal age."

"Then what's he doing feeding people bennies?"

"Call them aspirins, dear."

Between the necklace boys and Faye, Anson was briefly detained by Alma Doyle.

"Wherever did you find that divine accordionist?" she asked.

"I think Faye called some agency in New York."

"He's simply rocking me," Alma confessed, moving dreamily away.

"Well?" Faye asked when Anson got back to her.

"Gurdon's been loading the drinks."

"Loading?"

"Making miltinis and benninis, I guess you call them."

"I should have guessed from my first drink."

"What was it?"

"My usual martini to get started, then my long ones, so I can coast."

"Well, he probably loaded those too. I've told him to lay

484

off. Forget it," Anson said. "It'll all go better now those cubes who came with the Burgesses have gone."

"*Do* you have a television, Mrs. Parris?" inquired a voice at Faye's elbow. It was young Mrs. Carlson. From her expression, Faye, who at first did not hear her because of the talk, growing louder by the minute, imagined she was asking where the second bath was.

"We do, of course, but we've unplugged it for the party."

"Oh! Couldn't we turn it on? We're simply dying to know where the train is. Others want to find out too."

The Carlsons, cold sober, were not being an asset to the party, and Faye suggested to Anson it might be as well to let those who wanted to watch have their way. He went inside, followed by the Carlsons and a troupe of K and K secretaries and stockroom boys, who clearly considered viewing the Kennedy progress a far better show than the party, and Anson's hooking up the set the nicest thing he could do for them. The Carlsons sat down on the floor, the others draping themselves on chairs and sofas, and once more the gray, slowly moving cortege appeared. Anson returned to the terrace.

Above the swells of the accordion and the increasing clamor of voices, a clattering putt-putting could be heard. It was a helicopter, flying barely a hundred feet overhead, and in its plastic cabin could be seen Ethan Fleming, his beard redder than ever, with Galey Birnham and Neile. Fleming circled briefly and then brought the copter down neatly in the field separating the Parris and Currie houses. All the guests, excitedly exclaiming, made a rush through the house and went out to the drive to watch.

"You didn't tell me it was going to be such a production," said Faye to Anson.

"I had no idea myself," Anson told her with honesty. They stood a little behind the others, watching, as first Birnham, then Fleming, climbed down, and, last, Neile Eythe.

485

"So that's your redhead," Faye said. "Cradle snatcher! Excuse me, I've got to go inside and speak to Mrs. Haines. And get my gloves."

Joanna Summers had seen helicopters before, her expression conveyed, and after the first excitement was over returned to her soapbox, Aroon Rigo still beside her. The group to whom they were talking had changed slightly, but not the subject.

"*Warren* Report?" Aroon Rigo was saying as Faye passed them. "Why, nobody believes that lousy detective story. Or only in America."

"Where else do you want them to believe it?" asked Stig Lavrorsen, bronzed and handsome in his tennis flannels; he had persuaded Miss Rigo to give up her ginger ale for one of Gurdon's martinis.

"Europe has always disbelieved it," Joanna Summers said. "It was a put-up job from beginning to end. From the Ruby thing to all the people who just up and died so conveniently. Like the people being killed right now in the path of the Kennedy train."

When Faye returned from the kitchen, everyone was back on the terrace, except the group huddled around the television, and since Fleming had taken the attention from Joanna Summers, she wanted to make doubly sure that her Hyde Park tactics would not resume.

"Miss Summers," she said, including Miss Rigo in her smile, "do you and David Steen know each other? I know you're both in Anson's stable—"

"No, I don't know him. I'd like to meet him. I've a few things I'd relish telling him, and Aroon has, too, I think."

Later, Faye wished she'd left the whole thing as it was and let them find their own rope. She led the two women through the groups forming around Fielding and Birnham, taking a long look at Neile Eythe on the way, to where the Steens were talking with "Gertrude" and "Alice."

486

One group had hung back at the bar—Martha Lavrorsen and the jersey-suit boys, who looked nakeder than ever. Martha was being her usual caustic self, perhaps made a bit more concise by Gurdon's step-ups. The boys, evidently, were being amused, and, Faye thought, after the Summers debates, no wonder. She wished the subject had changed. It had not.

"Oh, I think the Kennedy girls *have* their mourning veils, don't you?" Martha asked.

"All but one," replied the taller of the necklace boys. "Mrs. *Rose* went *in person,* I hear, to choose hers only yesterday. At Bergdorf's."

"I think you're all being ghoulish," Faye stopped to say, giving Martha an imploring look. "Can't anyone talk about anything else?"

"What else is there to talk about?" one of the boys asked innocently, and Faye went on, though she could still hear them talking.

"And to think," Martha sighed, "there's still one left!" She had found her sets of ears and was going to blow the works of her Kennedy hatreds.

"Yes, we'll probably have to go through it all again," the necklace boy conceded. "Which one was your favorite?"

"Well, if you can accept the wigs. I've always felt the Kennedys were personally responsible for hair—"

"And *Hair,* too."

"My dear, you're divine!" several of the boys told her in chorus.

"Of course! They *must* have been wigs!"

"But I think you must be a witch, to know that," said the necklace boy.

Martha loved it. "As long as you don't spell it with a 'b.' Yes," she warmed to it, accepting another drink from Gurdon, "I am a witch. How did you guess?"

"You have the evil eye."

Martha closed one eye and stretched the other wide, ogling each of the boys in turn. "Yes, I do. Who do you *think* brought on the plane crashes? The parents', the brothers'? *Little old me!* I tried to get Edward, too, when he was flying to that convention, but the best I could manage was a broken back." She stopped. "But you're not *listening!*"

Not only were her ears not listening, they had begun to leave her midway, during what she considered the best part. "Hey, *you!*" she shouted after them. "Come back here a minute!"

It was a loud shout and three of the boys turned.

"I think you're all cute as can be," she said. "I know about you. But I've always wanted to ask one thing. What do you do for sex?"

"If you know about us, you should know that," one of the boys told her.

"No. I mean, what do you *do?*" Martha persisted.

"We do what the CIA does, maybe," one boy said slyly.

"Well, *I* don't!" another huffily stated. "Who in hell *is* this character, anyway? Asking *us?*"

"Yes, why do you want to know?" asked the sly boy. "Are you a queen's moll or what? Haven't you got a husband?"

"I've got the best-hung husband here," declared Martha, louder than ever. "Not that it's ever done *me* any good. Or him either!" She was weeping, close to hysteria.

"Oh. Which one is he?"

"That's him, over there."

The last boy left was polite enough to look. "He sure as hell does wear a big belt and buckle," he conceded. "But that's not everything."

"You're telling *me?*" Martha cried, and sank down in front of the bar table.

It took Gurdon and Stig Lavrorsen to get her on her feet. She didn't want to go home, she said, wanted only to lie down. Stig held her up. "Give me a couple of her usual," he said to Gurdon, who produced two white pills. "And with water, not vodka." Faye, who had been watching, led the way to the spare bedroom.

"What the bloody fucking hell is *wrong* tonight?" Stig asked when they had settled Martha and were on their way back to the terrace.

"Gurdon's been putting pills into the drinks."

"We always do that. It's not that."

"Whatever it is, I wish everybody'd eat and go home."

"Before they do, you'd better cast an eye on Alma. All hell's going to break loose if you don't. She's openly cruising the accordion man, and Ray, not to be outdone, is behaving shamefully with the jersey-suit boys."

"*Chacun à son goût.*"

"Yes, but each of them seems to want the other to know. They meet, as though on schedule, to glare at each other. From the last glare, I expected she was going to scratch his eyes out."

"*Chacun veut être heureux,* then, I don't care," Faye said. "I may do a little scratching myself before the night's over."

"Faye," said Stig in the hallway.

"Yes, Stig?" Faye paused.

"What about you and me? You know I've always had a big thing for you. Come outside with me now. I parked beyond the drive. Who'd notice?"

"Have another drink. I've a party on my hands."

"And I have a hard on. I've a need to be laid."

"It won't be me. I hated that time you followed me into the bath, Stig. Try it on someone else. Like your wife."

"Martha's out cold." He smiled at her with his eyes, again trying. "Martha's simply no good for me, you know that."

"I hear it's the other way around, Stig." Faye shrugged away from him and they passed through the living room.

"My God!" said Stig. "The Catholic Hour!"

There were many more gathered in front of the set than

before, all absorbed, intently watching. Mrs. Haines and the woman who had been in the kitchen were now behind the tables, setting down stacks of plates, beginning to serve; but only a few seemed interested in eating, and Gurdon was filling fresh rounds of drink orders. Ethan Fleming had asked for wine, evidently, and a bottle of Nuits-St.-Georges was being uncorked for him. He and Birnham and Neile were in the center of the group that had formed around them, the boys in swim trunks, all of whom wanted to meet Galey, standing nearest him. Fleming was talking to Anson.

"You see?" he said, making a descriptive, head-to-foot gesture toward Neile. "Already the necessary *mystique* is forming. She has star quality. People want to *eat* her, tear her clothes off. Rare, rare."

Neile did appear changed, a happy Trilby looking to Fleming for her cues. Though her red cowlicks were the same (they were, explained Fleming, to be clipped even shorter for *Marka*), her green eyes and pale, aqueous skin were radiant. She wore a skintight suit of bright orange kid, britches, boots, and pull-over with a V so deep the moons of her small, round breasts showed.

"No, no." Fleming pushed aside a drink Gurdon had brought. "Coke for her; the eyes must be clear for tomorrow. She's had the week of her life. All producers want her, now she's been found. Monday she has picture sessions with *Look* and *Avant-Garde* and six others. *Avant's* cover will be a vag-shot in full color, no retouching. Tuesday we're all off for London."

Neile smiled at Anson. "I can't quite believe it comes like this, so fast. I'll always remember it was you who put me on the whirl."

"Whirl Girl," said Galey.

"Is it really whirly enough?" Anson asked her.

Neile made a small, shuddering gesture of delight, casting up her eyes and clenching her teeth in a wide smile. "The whirliest. I'm going to make it. Glad for me?"

490

Before Anson could reply, Fleming again took over. "Stop that. I've told you—no overuse of the face. Save that for the cameras. We only came for a few minutes," he added, turning to Anson, looking at his watch. "Boyo, we certainly *went,* what?"

Some kind of communication was taking place between Galey Birnham and the boys in swim trunks, a kind of staccato radar, all begun sentences, unfinished phrases, double takes: homosexual freemasonry's language. As Anson had before observed about Birnham, his eyes constantly searched outside the group around him, checking to the farthest perimeter of the terrace. Quickly he considered, evaluated, dismissed.

"Come on, my people," said Fleming. "Up we go." He made a point of searching out Faye, thanking her for having asked him, regretting his stay was so brief. Neile stood next to Galey, watched by the other women, saying nothing, herself watching Fleming. When Fleming gave the come-on sign, a wide, upcurving arc of his right arm, she went up to Anson, standing very close.

"One for the whirl?" she asked, looking into his eyes.

Anson kissed her lightly. "Good luck." He turned, watching her skip across the terrace after Fleming.

"Well, Anson," said Galey.

"Goodby. Stranger. I'll cable you the final paper figure."

Galey shrugged. "I'll be with Fleming on *Marka,* then Maroc."

Anson and the three walked around the side of the house to the field where the helicopter waited.

"Stand back!" Fleming cried, revving up the motor. The copter seemed to waddle, tip forward and back, then whirled upward, soon becoming two winking lights in the sky. The sky was beginning to darken when Anson returned to the terrace. From inside the house, the television screen cast flipping black and gray images through the glass of the gables. Though the accordionist, now openly pursued by

Alma, who was, in turn, stalked by Ray and the taller of the necklace boys, had resumed with a bravura flourish, the party had died with the helicopter's leaving.

Faye was standing alone, looking around her. When she saw Anson, she said, "I wish you'd tell me what to do about everybody. At least your friends from Venus were quick to come and go."

"This isn't a party, it's a wake," he agreed.

"Yes, and it's becoming a tribunal."

"Darling, thanks for not taking off your gloves. You saw how it was, didn't you?"

"Yes. If only you knew, I'd never put them on. *That?* Competition for *me?*" And she left him.

Couples of "The Assortment" were now gathered near the bar, discussing the descent and departure of the helicopter and its occupants.

"She was sweating under that thing she wore. Can you imagine? Leather, in this heat!"

"Who was the beaver?"

"The *Dimple* man."

"And the other man?"

"Galey Birnham."

"So that's him! He doesn't *look* as though he writes dirty books."

"*I* thought at first she was a boy, too. I've been reading about how the sexes are not only beginning to dress and look alike, but *be* alike. How soon nobody will be able to tell which is which."

"I'll always be able to tell," Chet Burgess said. "Come on, Grace, let's eat and go. I'm worn out."

"*You're* worn out," said Grace. "Chet Burgess, when we pick up with another convention couple, you'll read about it."

"I rather liked her," Chet Burgess said.

"I pray I may grow no older if you liked *her.*"

Nina Gerson, who had done the best she could to keep the groups in her car pools circulating, now had her mind on the time it was going to take to drive back to town. Going from one to another, she suggested they begin to eat. Mrs. Haines dished up the food, now helped by Gurdon, who supposed his bar duties finished. They were not. The swimsuit boys were now pouring their own drinks, and the one to whom Martha Lavrorsen had confided her marital secret was helping Stig to get as drunk as possible. Stig had become sullen.

"Oh, she said that, did she?" he questioned the swimsuit boy. "Yeah, that was my wife, all right. So what's it to you, you big fairy?"

"I'm not a fairy," came the answer. "I'll bet you play a good game of tennis."

"Fair, but as I said, what's it to you, you—"

"Don't say it again. You look as though you need to pop them."

"I always need to pop them. So?"

"I'll pop them for you."

Stig was weaving. "Yeah? Like how?"

"Guess." The swimsuit boy laughed. "I guess you've never heard of *I Am Curious (Yellow)*."

"Curious *what?* Boy, you are drunk!"

"It's a film. Swedish. I saw it in Stockholm this spring. Everybody flies over from London just to see it, that one film. Blow jobs, muff diving, right on the screen."

"Swedish, huh?"

"You know about Swedes?"

"I should," Stig said. "My folks were Norwegians."

The last Faye heard of this conversation was the swimsuit boy's "You said you're parked outside, right?"

"Right!"

"And your wife's passed out, right?"

"Right!"

"Well, come on! What are we waiting for?"

At least most of "The Assortment" were now eating.

"No, no," Rose Draper was explaining to the young Carlsons, who had been inveigled away from the television long enough to be served. "You wrap up your meat, bird, whatever, in heavy foil and do it in a three-hundred-and-twenty-five-degree oven. When it begins to make sounds, you take it out from time to time and baste off the fats and stock. Then freeze what you baste off and throw the fat away. That way, you don't use too much current *and* keep the essences."

"If you put a pot roast into the oven in foil and sprinkle dehydrated onion soup over it, it's simply heavenly."

"Yes," Rose agreed, "but *that* you keep at a hundred and twenty-five degrees for at least *eight* hours."

"Yes, yes; I do it eight hours. Sometimes even nine," Mrs. Carlson said.

Amy and Herb Nowells were being served by Mrs. Haines.

"Is your pill still working?" Amy asked him, whispering.

"Fine. Haven't peed once."

"Herb, please. Not so loud. I think just some of the aspic for him, Mrs. Haines."

"I don't want the aspic," Herb said. "I want the cold beef and mustard."

"You know you shouldn't," Amy argued. "You'll wake up your gout and will you be sorry!"

"All right, I'll wake it up. I'm sick of diets. I went onto Butazolidin yesterday so I *could* eat Mrs. Haines's cold beef."

Herb got his cold beef.

Not all were going to eat, however. The Hansons and the Steins, who had deserted the terrace to join the television group, came out of the house, shaking their heads.

"They're never going to get him in the ground tonight," Mrs. Stein said. "This strain must be awful for the family." Then she saw Faye. "Faye," she said, "I'm afraid we're all rather feeling the heat. I simply couldn't eat a thing. I hope you won't mind."

494

"We'd no idea it had gotten so late," added Mrs. Hanson. "But all the *staff* we brought have eaten. Thanks to Nina. So we'll say good night and thanks for such a lovely party."

"Good night," Faye said.

"I don't see Anson, so give our goodbys to him, too, won't you?"

"I will," she assured them, watching them go.

"I hear you and Anson are having a battle royal," Grace Burgess said to Faye as she came up to thank her for the evening.

"I'm sorry it shows."

"I've had them with Chet myself. Don't think you can keep things from friends like us. Who is it? That girl wearing all that hot leather? She looks like somebody getting ready to fly from Earth and be devoured by androids."

"You've been reading space fiction, Grace."

"Did you see that business between Stig and one of those jersey-suit boys? Though now I'll have to call them beach boys or something."

"Yes, I saw it."

"Poor Martha!"

"Or poor Stig. Who's to say which it is?"

"Faye, you look *so* unhappy. Listen, dear, it's going to happen to you the way it happened to me. And get used to it. My advice is, *let* her leave Earth in all her leather. The androids will eat her. Hold on to Anson."

"What are you two jawing about?" Chet asked, coming up.

"Men," said Grace. "If you knew how transparent you are!"

"What have I done now?" he asked Grace as they left.

The departure of the Hanson and Stein contingents had left a gap in the TV watchers, and presently the Kastners, who had eaten quietly with the design people they had brought and Velma and Sam Currie, also left. Nina was seeing to it that no one was missing from any of the car pools. Her plate of aspic in her hand, she came up to Faye,

495

followed by the Drapers, the Curries, and the young Carlsons, whose goodbys were in keeping with the way they had behaved throughout the evening.

"*I* think they're going to have to bury him tomorrow," Mrs. Carlson said to Faye. "You were sweet to let us look. And I'm sorry I'm not a drinker and neither is my husband. But we simply *loved* meeting all the famous writers and everybody."

"Faye, it's been lovely," Rose Draper said. "But we've got to go. With Libby sitting Toddy and Roger, I don't like to stay away from my little nest too long. You will see that Libby gets home?"

"Of course, Rose," Faye promised.

The Drapers had offered to drive the Curries home, and waited until Velma had said, "I don't know where or why everything got off, but we'll hash it over later. Funeral-baked meats!" She shook her head. "Those Kennedys may be the death of us all yet."

Nina finished her aspic and set down her plate. "I've got most of the brood on the way. But I can't leave until whatever's going on over there breaks up." She indicated the group near the holly, where Anson was talking with the Steens, Joanna Summers, Aroon Rigo, and "Gertrude" and "Alice." Whatever it was looked like a pantomime seen through glass. Joanna Summers would say something, gesticulating elaborately, and Aroon Rigo would second her with vigorous nods of the head. Then David would reply. He looked furious and hardly able to contain himself, and Jeannette seemed galvanized into resentful silence, though she was following everything he said with dogged attention. "Gertrude" and "Alice" were obviously amused.

"I'll see what I can do, Nina. I've been watching, and evidently Anson's been unable to halt the flow of Miss Summers' verbiage." They went to join the group by the holly.

496

"Mary and Claxon Kennerly want to leave, but they can't until the Steens are ready," added Nina. "Meanwhile, they're watching TV."

David, whatever had been said to him, was angry but holding his temper; he had, clearly, been Joanna Summers' and Aroon Rigo's target for some time.

". . . the ability of the novelist to order experience and imagination into an illusion of ordered reality and truth that will hold the reader," Joanna Summers was saying.

"If you know so much about it, why don't you write a novel that's readable?" David asked her. "Your last was thirty years ago. Why pick on me? You daughters of foundation charity should earn that charity."

"I'd like to see *you* get a grant. Of any sort," Aroon Rigo spat at him.

"What is so terrible about you, Steen," Joanna Summers continued, "is that you have a talent, a very small one, and you have the ear of the world. But you pour poison into it with your slick assumptions that people behave the way you say they do. Moreover—wait, wait!—I *insist* on saying it, Anson. Moreover, you use this narrative ability on the behalf of evil against good!"

"You're just peeved because you can't get it out," countered David, calmly lighting a cigarette and placing his long holder in his mouth. "*I* have read you— one of your few readers—you see, I know your sales figures—"

"How? How would you know my sales figures?"

"I know everybody's sales figures. I find your writing, such as I've been able to find, dreary, dull and boring. You may have solved *your* personal problems in your fiction, but none for your readers."

"I've not written fiction in years, it's true," Joanna Summers answered. "Fiction's dead. Through." She made a slicing gesture with her hand. "Kaput!"

"Look," Anson tried to put in, "I think if you'd both—"

497

"I said, Anson, I insist, and I do. When I wrote fiction—"

"You ordered experience and imagination into an illusion of ordered reality," David put in. "I heard you. But you never held your readers. Your novels were dull."

"I return the compliment!" Joanna Summers said hotly. It was the adjective critics had beaten her with all her life.

"You see," said Jeannette, "my husband is *read*." She gave Joanna Summers and Aroon Rigo a baleful look. "Why don't you go *back* to the Rue du Bac, where you lived in the twenties, along with all the other numerical lesbians? Number One sleeping with Number Three, Number Five with Number Eight? I think you're both *sickening!*"

"Jeannette," said David, taking her arm.

"No, I'll not apologize," Jeannette said. "And *you* two," she flung at Miss Grumbacher and Miss Taylor, who obviously had been enjoying themselves simply by listening. "Bull dikes! Or one's the plain one. Who's bull would be hard to say. Maybe *you!*" She pointed at Miss Taylor. "The ones in frumpy frills are quite often the bulls, I've been told!"

Joanna Summers and Aroon Rigo turned, as one, and walked away. Nina waited, then said, "Good night, Anson. Good night, Faye. I'll see that they get home safely. And that'll be the end of my day." She left.

At some point during the altercation the accordionist had stopped playing, and Jeannette's words echoed across the terrace. Mary and Claxon Kennerly heard them through the walls of the house and over the television and came running.

"What on earth's happening?" Mary Kennerly asked.

"Miss Summers was looking for a ritual sacrifice to assuage her jealousy," David explained, "and I refused to be that sacrifice."

"Well, I think we'd all best be going," Claxon Kennerly said. "Everyone else is gone, almost—except those boys in swimming gear."

Jeannette turned to Faye and Anson. The party had been hard for her, she appeared exhausted. "We both love you,

you know," she said to them. "I hope we're not going to quarrel. If we do, we'll only find ourselves with—with what's just been here. Like those people David and I know abroad. You remember them, Faye."

"I remember, Jeannette," Faye answered. "And thanks for trying to say it."

"I can't help the way I am. God, Faye, how I wish I were you!"

"This sounds like home," said David, whose composure had returned completely. "Before we go away, will you come to us for a night on the town?"

"We'll come," Anson promised.

Mary Kennerly kissed Faye. "You win a few and you lose a few," she said. "Forget it is my advice. Oh. The casket's reached Arlington. It's not clear whether they're going to have commitment tonight or not."

Miss Grumbacher and Miss Taylor had stood by silently. Then Miss Grumbacher said, "I've found it all very interesting. I'm so glad I only read and don't write. Faye, I wonder if your friends would be kind enough to drop us at the farm?"

"We'd be more than pleased," Claxon Kennerly assured the two ladies. They all trooped out to the Kennerly car and drove away. None of them saw what was happening in the black Cadillac that belonged to Amy and Herb Nowells.

Whatever Ray Doyle had had in mind as he had followed and joked with the necklace boy had, evidently, not been very clear to either. He seemed unable to catch up with Alma and the accordionist, who had kept moving just ahead, weaving in and out of the groups of guests. He had had a few too many of Gurdon's drinks, and the necklace boy, when he heard about the novel Ray would never get to write and next week's taping sessions of "Love Me Today," lost interest. He kept returning to the bar, giving Ray so many brush-offs that, at last, Ray said, "Aw, all *you* guys care about is each other!"

"Of course!" answered the necklace boy, who was wondering where his necklace friend might be. "That's the whole *thing! What's* the name of your soap opera? 'Vale of Tears'? You look as though you're trying to play all parts at once."

Ray did look sad, and when Amy and Herb Nowells, soberest of all, except the young Carlsons, left the house they found Ray inside their Cad.

"Why, Ray!" Amy exclaimed. She was as fastidious about her car seats as she was about everything else, and she saw that Ray had been sick. "Wake up!" she said, shaking him. "You're in the wrong car."

"Don't want to wake up," Ray answered, looking at her blearily. "Sorry. Alma locked our car—sorry, I mean *her* car— and I'd walk home rather than ask her for the keys. She's the wife with the keys."

"We'll take you home," Herb Nowells said.

"It's all shit," said Ray. "Shit the whole way. I thought the party was shit and I hated the people. David Steen is a shit. *I* could write that shit he writes by the yard, if only . . ." He trailed off.

"Let's get him home as soon as we can," Amy Nowells directed. Ray had started talking again. "I always hated that word, and it seems to be the only one he knows."

They did their duty and got him to his doorstep and made sure he had his key.

"This is all shit, too," Ray announced. "I had a barn once, a barn where I could burn—I mean write—"

"Yes, we know," both Nowells said. "Good night."

The pills Gurdon had given Stig Lavrorsen to calm Martha had done their work, and she and Alma Doyle emerged from the bedroom just as the Kennerly group left. The accordionist had gone to change back into the clothes in which he had arrived.

"Where's Ray?" Faye asked Alma.

"Don't know, don't care," answered Alma. "Stinking, when I last saw him. Probably crying into his barn by now.

500

Oh, *sorry!* He *has* no barn to cry into. You won't have to worry about getting Cuffy back to Stamford. I'm driving him." She dangled her keys.

"Cuffy?"

"Didn't you know his name? He played dreamily, I thought."

"Yes. I noticed you thought that."

"I think he's just waiting for you to pay him," Alma said coolly.

Faye went into the house and gave Cuffy the fee they had agreed on, plus a liberal tip. He had played well, had been the only thing about the party that had been right. He and Alma left.

The swimsuit boys were sticking like barnacles to the bar. Martha, making up her face, sat a little beyond them. No one was talking, and Mrs. Haines and Gurdon were clearing the tables.

"Why don't they go?" Faye asked Anson. "They can't drink much more and drive."

"How about another drink all around?" Anson said to them.

"No more for me," Martha Lavrorsen spoke up. "Faye, I apologize for being such a mess. I *am* a mess."

Nobody contradicted her.

The swimsuit and necklace boys had gotten the idea, refusing more drinks. "We can't go," one of them explained, "until Harris comes back."

"Who's Harris?"

"He went out to find a gold brick or something."

"I know the one," Martha said.

The front door opened and the boy named Harris and Stig Lavrorsen came in.

"Oh, there you are, Harris!" the shorter of the necklace boys said in a fake cockney voice. "Well, time to shove off, chaps."

"You!" said Martha to Stig. *"You!"*

"Now, Martha, don't jump to conclusions—"

"I'll jump to anything I like," Martha snapped. She turned to Harris. "Don't worry, pretty boy, I'm not going to scratch your eyes out."

Harris regarded her calmly. "I'd only have to jump back into the bramble bush if you did," he told her. "You were right about your husband. He may be hung like you said, but he hasn't got the ass to swing it."

"You bastard!" Martha said to Stig.

"Come on, let's go home," Stig said. "Before you start making trouble."

"Home is where it *isn't,*" Martha said, getting up. "Why not? I'm going to make trouble for you *you'll* never forget, Stig Lavrorsen!"

They didn't even say good night, though the swimsuit and necklace boys did, elaborately and politely, and when they were gone, Faye and Anson were alone on the empty terrace.

"You'd better get Todd from the Curries'," Faye said, as though it were any other party they'd given. "I promised Rose you would, so Libby can get home."

"If you're sure everybody's gone."

"They're gone. I'll take care of the extra woman and Gurdon."

"You can give him a Mickey for me," said Anson as Faye went past him into the kitchen.

"We're pretty well cleaned up," Mrs. Haines announced. "But what a shame! All this lovely food. Why, you'll be eating it for days."

"I wish you'd all divide it up and take it with you."

"But Mrs. Parris—"

"Please take it," Faye said. "Take it all. It's a night I want to forget."

"Well, in a way I see what you mean," sighed Mrs. Haines as she took off her apron.

The house was empty and Faye was going through her off-off, lock-lock routine when Anson carried Todd, sound asleep, into his room. Together they covered him, turned out his light and closed his door.

"Did everything go all right?" Faye asked then. "Did Libby say?"

"She didn't say anything, so I suppose it went all right."

"Cross your fingers."

"Want a drink?"

"Yes. Slug me."

"I'll slug us both."

She went into the living room. The television was still on. Kennedy's casket stood lonely and unlowered in a half-light, through which blurred figures moved in the background.

Anson brought in their drinks. "Have you had it?" he asked.

"Yes, turn it off," she said.

❧ ❧ ❧ HE SAT down opposite her and for some moments they were silent.

"Our little celebration was rather poor sport," he said.

"Yes, for us. Not for Alma."

"Or Stig."

"Don't forget the jersey suits in swimsuits."

"Let's not talk about them. Let's say to hell with them."

"Yes, let's."

"Shall we talk about us?"

"Well, Anse, if there's going to be a post-mortem, it had better be soon," she said.

"I love you."

"I know. I love you too. We can't make a post-mortem out of that."

"Just so you believe it."

"I believe it."

"Even during our bad times?"

"Yes, even then. Are you tight?"

"No. A party's always a job. I faked a few."

"So did I."

"Were you upset when you saw her?"

"The redhead?"

"Who else?"

"Well, I had to cross my bridge to Jeannette."

"And I had David, remember."

"I saw your handshake."

"What else could I do? It wasn't *droit du seigneur*, he's my friend. You can't go back and undo anything."

"I thought that about Jeannette, too. I'm devoted to her. When I saw all the others, I remembered all the friendship we've had between us, the good times. I know she's sick, but I can't help loving her. She's—they're both caviar when stacked up against the fresh-baked bread of Sam and Velma. Our 'Assortment.' "

"I thought we weren't going to talk about them."

"All right." She finished her drink. "Make me another? Please?"

"The same?"

"One more slug should do it."

He made it and another for himself. "Of course," he said as he handed her the glass, "we'll talk about them. Can't help it. Those Carlsons! He looked as though a little more calcium as a child would have done wonders."

"And she's so Avon Representative Calling."

"You're in good form. You haven't answered about the redhead."

"Must I? I was disappointed in you, if you really want to know."

"She was your fault, really. I'd never have gotten mixed up with her at all if you hadn't frozen me out that month. If I hadn't had to go to David's party by myself."

"I can't talk about that month, Anson."

"Don't. But it's true. That kind of freaking kid could happen to any husband with balls. Especially over thirty."

"Is that the age when jailbait begins to appeal? Are they going to get younger as you grow older?"

"What about you and David? He's no father figure, but he's no boy either."

"David was *your* fault, if we're going to go on faulting each other."

"Do you want to?"

"Not especially."

"Neither do I."

"The redhead—is she in your bones?"

"I thought for a little she was, but no. When I took the trip I lost her. No loss. I think she was trying to build me up into something too. What she wanted, really, was a toe in. She's got it with Fleming."

"Evidently."

"If you knew how glad I was to get back to you! Shall I tell you?"

"If it's about me and not her."

"It's about you. During the LSD—not the mescaline, that was different—"

"Oh? How?"

"Don't open that box. I'll never open that one."

"I hardly could."

He went back. "During the acid thing, I felt something about you I've never felt all the time we've been together.

There was a place inside me I'd never been able to get to. Well, I got to it."

"Buddha's third eye?"

"Rather. The eye was only for you. I felt that the more I live with you, the more I'll love you, because with you I have the only harmony and proportion between myself and life. There was that part, about time, when there was no time, when I had yet to happen to myself. For the first time in my life, I had—I don't know how to put it—" He stopped.

"You're doing all right," she said. "If Borobudur's all that wonderful, I want to go too."

"Don't joke. I told you, I'd never do it again."

"But maybe I'd like to. For myself."

"I don't want you to," he said.

"Why not?"

"I don't know. It's like jealousy, all right when I do it, but I can't stand it when you do."

"I wonder if we'll ever outgrow our jealousy?"

"I don't think I ever shall. I'm still burning about you and David, no matter how I try to forget it."

"I'm still burning, too," she said. "But you were telling me. For the first time in your life—what?"

He thought. "Maybe Rimbaud came closest. *'Je est un autre':* 'I is someone else.' I found that out."

"Don't be silly. You're you, always will be."

"Yes, I am what I am, of course; but what Rimbaud said of himself is true of me, too. And you're part of that me. That part that is you I can never betray. I may have betrayed myself many times; I may betray myself many times more, but never that part which is you. It's love."

She leaned forward and put down her glass. "Oh, Anson," she said. "I'm so suddenly tight. Nicely. All the time you were away, all during our times apart, our bad times, I thought that perhaps what we've had between us had gone. Burst. But it hasn't. The bubbles are still there."

"Do you want another drink?"

"No, I'm too happy simply to be here with you to want anything else."

"I don't want another either."

"I'm so tight and happy you can do anything with me you want."

"And I'm going to. But first we'll come to that part where you ask me to promise you again. You ask it, you always do."

"I won't any more. No promises. And you'll not ask me."

"Meaning that you'll sometimes go back to David? Someone else?"

"You see, promises are no good if they need to be asked for, need to be given."

"You're right," he said. He got up and walked to where she sat on the sofa beneath the books. "I want you. Now. Have you any idea how much I want you?"

"I've an idea. I want you too. The same way."

"Without promises."

She fell against him as he sat down beside her, burying her face in his shoulder. "Well, perhaps one."

"Ask it."

"If you go back to Borobudur—"

"I won't, not ever."

"But if you do. Don't go without me."

"I promise," he said as he kissed her.

❦ ❦ ❦   ABOUT THE AUTHOR

In addition to *Good Time Coming,* Edmund Schiddel has written
A Bucks County Trilogy: The Devil in Bucks County (1959),
Scandal's Child (1963) and *The Good and Bad Weather* (1965),
as well as six other novels, which have been translated and pub-
lished in many countries. In 1966 he was awarded the ribbon of
Chevalier du Mérite Culturel Français.